I AM
AYAH
THE WAY HOME

ALSO BY DONNA HILL

I AM AYAH

AYAH

THE WAY HOME

NATIONAL BESTSELLING AUTHOR

DONNA HILL

Entangled Publishing, LLC
644 Shrewsbury Commons Ave., STE 181
Shrewsbury, PA 17361
rights@entangledpublishing.com

Sideways is an imprint of Entangled Publishing, LLC.

Visit our website at www.entangledpublishing.com.

Edited by Stacy Abrams and Viveca Shearin
Cover design by Bree Archer
Cover images by Cincinart/Depositphotos, and
Pobytov/gettyimages
Interior design by Toni Kerr

ISBN TP 978-1-64937-146-1
HC ISBN 978-1-64937-145-4
Ebook ISBN 978-1-64937-168-3

Manufactured in the United States of America

First Edition May 2023

10 9 8 7 6 5 4 3 2 1

ꙍIDEWAYS

To my mom, Dorothy Hill, my nana Clotilda Braithwaite,
my gramma Mary Hill. I am because you were,
and I thank you.

At Entangled, we want our readers to be well-informed. If you would like to know if this book contains any elements that might be of concern for you, please check the back of the book for details.

AUTHOR'S NOTE

To my readers,

I Am Ayah is a product of love and nearly two years of writing, researching, and rewriting. While I took a bit of creative license, the tale remains rooted in history.

In the end, I was in a way reborn, more aware of the importance of who we are—the culmination of all those who came before and embedded in us the memories, the myths, the legends, the truths.

The stories of our ancestors flow through our veins, as my character Alessandra discovers. She reminds us that we are all in search of where we belong in the world, searching for a place called home.

We are our ancestors' wildest dreams.

Say their names.

Donna Hill

I wish to tell you a story. My story.

The story of how I come to be here in this foreign land. Sometimes what I tell you will make no sense. Sometimes it will sound absurd. But in between those moments of doubts and dismissal, you may come to believe it possible that within each of us lives the essence of our existence—beginnings, middles, and endings—the paths that those before us took to bring us here.

Some of you will close these pages, toss them aside. But there will be those of you who will embark on a journey of discovery word by word, image by image, memory by memory, from the beginning until now—with me and for you. I speak to you now through the voices and struggles of those who came before and after me—so that you would know.

My journey to here began on the beaches of Mendeland.

. . .

It was 1839. I was in my fifteenth year, happy, looking forward to my marriage to my beloved in six months' time, on my sixteenth birthday.

Oh, how I loved him. I would make an excellent wife and mother, I knew. My babu had taught me to hunt, to kill with my bare hands if no weapon was handy, to protect myself against man or beast. My mama taught me to cook, to mend, to keep house, to take care of my six sisters and brothers, to heal wounds with herbs, to honor my elders.

None of that was to be, though. None of it.

You may have heard or read of the revolt of captive Africans on a ship called La Amistad. You may have heard that an enslaved man, Sengbe Pieh, led the revolt, or you may know him as Joseph Cinque. That is all true. But there is little more than folklore known about the young girl who helped him, who found the fabled loose nail that unlocked his shackles and those of the others. She was among the hundreds of Africans, along with Cinque, captured on the shores of Mendeland.

The first half of our torturous journey was aboard the ship Tecora. Below deck, they separated the men and women in holds not big enough for a small child. For days, hours, weeks, unimaginable horrors of darkness, the roiling of the ship, stench, sickness, humiliation, torture, and madness rampaged through the infested hull.

Disease and lack of food and clean water plagued the deadly journey. By the time of transfer to La Amistad in Cuba, they had reduced the enslaved numbers to little more than half. The crew had thrown fifty dead and diseased captives overboard. Those who survived were put on board La Amistad for the second half of the journey to Port Principe, Cuba, but within days, the revolt led by Cinque ensued. The men forced the remaining crew to head back to Mendeland—to home.

During the days, the crew seemed to head back to Africa, but at night the devils turned the ship around toward Cuba. Back and forth, east, west for two months until La Amistad grounded near a place named Montauk Point, Long Island.

Safe, finally free! But the United States government took the ship, the captives were thrown in chains, taken to Connecticut and imprisoned, deemed "property" and therefore part of the ship's cargo.

The ship's manifest read fifty-three. But when my brothers and sisters were sent to the Connecticut prison to await the trial that would alter the course of slave trading, there were only fifty-two.

I had escaped.

Say my name.

CHAPTER ONE

New York City, West Village, Winter—Present Day

"I understand. I'll be there as soon as possible. Yes. Thank you." Alessandra Fleming squeezed her eyes shut and slowly placed her iPhone facedown on the metal work table in the studio. She dragged in a shaky breath and willed herself not to cry. Blinked. *No. Don't you dare.*

The time for crying was long gone. Wouldn't matter anyway—her father didn't need her tears.

She and her father, Jeremiah Fleming—Jerry to his friends—had a strained or, if she was being honest, nonexistent relationship. They'd barely spoken in more than two years. The last place she wanted to be was back home.

She flipped her phone over and checked the time. It was barely nine. She'd arrived at the studio two hours earlier to get a head start on her work, but so much for that.

Alessandra collected her heavy down coat and leather tote bag from the hook on the wall, then scanned the table that was covered with her photographs: majestic images of modern cityscapes, dark caves, the aftermath of earthquakes and floods, weddings and births.

She'd traveled extensively around the country and to the Caribbean photographing the best and the worst of humankind. Clearly, she had enough material to mount her show; the problem was finding the thread that held an idea or theme together. She was lacking cohesiveness. The thing that defined her as an artist, that gave her work meaning.

Her signature.

She gave the images another look, sighed, turned off the lights, and hurried down the narrow gray hallway to the flight of stairs that led from the work rooms up to the main level of the art gallery.

The heavy glass double doors opened onto a maze of stark white walls that guided the art lover to move in and out of the space, unable to bypass any part of an exhibit. Strategically placed illumination targeted the framed images and sculptures and projected just enough light to draw the observer closer to experience every detail.

"Hey, Leslie." Alessandra stopped at reception.

Leslie had just arrived and was settling behind her desk. She slipped off her glasses and turned away from her computer screen, casting startling sea-blue eyes on Alessandra. "Hey. Finished already?" she asked.

"No, not exactly. Listen, I have to go home."

"Sure." Leslie frowned. "See you tomorrow."

"No, I mean *home,* home. Back to Sag Harbor." Just letting the two words slip across her lips made her skin hot and her stomach churn. She cleared her throat. "My...father had an accident. Broke his hip."

"Oh no! I'm so sorry." She reached out and briefly covered Alessandra's copper-toned hand with her own white one.

"Thanks." Alessandra pressed her palms against the

lip of the desk. "I actually don't know how long I'll be out. Hopefully only a few days."

Leslie nodded. "Tough time for this to happen with your show coming up. I mean… It's awful about your dad—" she added clumsily.

Alessandra offered a small smile. "I know what you mean about the show." She slowly shook her head, sighed. "It'll be fine." She glanced over her shoulder. "Is Steven here?"

Steven James was the gallery owner and curator. He'd opened this West Village location about fifteen years ago, and during that time he'd steadily built a reputation for finding and showcasing some of the most talented up-and-coming artists and sculptors in the country.

Alessandra had met Steven by chance shortly after she'd graduated, when she was photographing the opening of the memorial at the World Trade Center. A man had come up to her and made some suggestions about lighting and angles and said he liked her style. He'd given her his card, and it took all of her self-restraint not to gush. This was *the* Steven James.

She'd taken him up on his kindness and stopped by his gallery. He'd offered her a job curating exhibits *if* she promised to hone her own skills. She did, and her reward was a coveted show at the Steven James Gallery. It had taken her five years and hard work, but here she was with her dream coming true: her own show coming up in barely two months.

"Just missed him," Leslie was saying. "Said he'll be back in a couple of hours."

Alessandra's stomach fluttered. The last thing she wanted to do was blow things with Steven. Not now. "I'll give him a call and let him know what's going on. And I'll have my cell if anything should come up while I'm out of town."

"No problem. Take care. And a speedy recovery for your dad," she called out.

The waiting list to get a show with Steven was well over a year, which was why Alessandra had to do whatever she needed to in Sag Harbor and get back immediately. She still had so much more work to do. This was not an opportunity that came often—or ever, for so many aspiring photographers—and she Could. Not. Blow. It.

Not after all this time. And certainly not after what she'd turned her back on to get here.

As an icy wind whipped a swirl of snow around the corner of Fourteenth Street and sought refuge down the back of her neck, she was reminded of who she was and why she was here. *Her father*. Manhattan was a way to escape him and everything he reminded her of. Behind her camera lens, she could create her own reality, see what she needed or wanted to see—not what whirled in her head and made her soul ache.

As she hustled down the narrow, crowded streets, passing bistros, bars, smoke shops, sex shops wrapped around old brownstones and newly arrived condos, she took a moment to relish the vibrancy of the part of the city she'd come to call home. The West Village was the hub of the nouveau and old guard, an eclectic blend of tastes, races, gender-bending definitions, social classes, and financial fluidity.

A place for those who sought to create their own normal.

Her one-bedroom apartment was within walking distance of the studio, both a blessing and a curse. A blessing because she didn't have to rely on public transportation or drive through the teeming streets of Manhattan; a curse because she often found herself still working into the early hours of the morning, knowing that home and her queen-sized bed were only fifteen minutes away.

She opened the waist-high iron gate and inched up the concrete stoop, mindful of the snow that had begun to cover the steps. As she turned her key in the lock of the heavy wood-and-glass door and stepped into the narrow vestibule, she was again grateful for her apartment on the second floor of the six-floor walkup, right above Ms. Edith, one of her favorite people in the world.

She climbed the steps, the polished wood creaking beneath her feet. When she opened the door to her space, a sudden flash of seeing herself stepping into a dim, lantern-lit room that smelled of damp wood, sea moss, and dirt floors leaped in front of her. The surreal moment seized her breath. She gripped the doorframe, shook her head, and the image scattered like startled birds.

But, for a moment, the scent of damp wood hung in her nostrils.

Alessandra blinked rapidly, dragged in a shaky breath, and the aroma of the fresh flowers that sat in a vase on the hall table replaced the scent of dampness. She frowned, then closed the door behind her. That—whatever that was—had happened before.

At first, she'd thought the images might be remnants of photos that she'd taken at some point and forgotten. But then they seeped into her dreams and she'd awaken, unnerved and melancholy. And nothing could account for the scents.

Whatever it was, it was starting to rattle her.

Alessandra dropped her purse on the hall table next to the vase of flowers, slipped out of her coat and scarf, and hung them on the rack. She toed out of her Uggs and walked down the hall to her bedroom.

On either side of the hall, she'd hung framed black-and-white photos of Manhattan. She'd taken the shots over the years, replacing them periodically with new versions and visions of New York. The one closest to her bedroom was the only one that she had of home: the dock at Sag Harbor, lined with boats of varying sizes—white with red stripes, blue stripes, names of the owner's heart's desire emblazoned on their sides—their sails flapping in a summer breeze. Her mother, dressed all in white, her dark hair gleaming against her sand-toned skin, had finally given in to her daughter's pleading and posed for the camera.

She'd taken it when she was about fifteen, before everything went wrong in her world. Her mother had fussed with her about "taking that camera everywhere," but it was the last photo she'd taken with her mother in it, and no matter how painful images of home were, this was one photo she would not part with. Ever.

She opened her bedroom door and had an overwhelming urge to simply flop down on her unmade bed and sleep for hours, but knew that was not an option. She took a suitcase from her closet and began to pack what she thought she'd need for the next week or so, being sure to include heavy sweaters, wool socks, and her one pair of flannel pajamas. Being near the water in the middle of winter was a recipe for icy days and chilly nights.

She added her sneakers, slippers, and a pair of dress shoes. She tossed her toiletries into a smaller bag, checked her laptop case for her power cords and chargers, and added her Nikon camera, flash drives, film, and batteries to her oversize tote.

As she scanned the array of bags, the reason for them being there truly hit her.

She bit down on her lip as a tear dribbled along the curve of her cheek. It was those nurses who had wanted her to come—not her father, she was sure. He'd never ask for her, she knew, and her throat clenched. She swiped at her eyes.

He hated her. That was the truth of it. Blamed her, always had.

Her chest heaved. Alessandra walked to the window and lifted the white embroidered curtain aside. A siren cried in the distance in harmony with the rumble of delivery trucks and honking car horns. The humps of dirt-covered snow lined the avenue like bent old men, only to be dusted again with white powder, as if that would somehow obscure the truth of what lived beneath.

She snorted at her own analogy. How apropos. A testament to her life.

She turned away and let her eyes roam over the sun-drenched space. The carefully selected furnishings of Manhattan chic—on the low end—gave her a moderate sense of accomplishment. But the accessories of pottery, bold-colored throw pillows, and handwoven scatter rugs from the litany of boutique shops that peppered lower Manhattan were no more than a fancy coating over her own life.

Hmph. That was something for a grown-ass woman of almost thirty to have to admit. But things were changing. Everything she'd been working toward was finally in her grasp. All she had to do was go see about her father and then get right back home. To her real home.

To Manhattan.

CHAPTER TWO

The faint, mouthwatering aroma of sizzling bacon drifted beneath the space of her front door, pulling Alessandra away from the dusty corners of her mind. She half smiled, realizing it must be ten o'clock. Edith Samuels cooked bacon every single morning at ten like clockwork.

Mrs. Samuels, the one constant in my life. Mrs. Samuels looked out for her—not in an obvious or nosey way, but Alessandra knew that the invitations to dinner were Mrs. Samuels's way of making sure that Alessandra was "doing good."

And she could listen for hours to Mrs. Samuels's stories about coming "up North" during the Great Migration; how she'd fled Virginia in the dead of night with only a few crumpled dollars, a brown bag of fried chicken, a sack of clothes, and a will for something better. She'd run from a hard life of sharecropping, constant terror, and everything she'd ever known—good and bad.

Alessandra could not imagine going through all that. Moving away from her childhood home in Sag Harbor was about as difficult as her travels had ever been.

There was a featherlight knock on her door.

She frowned, went to the door, looked out the peephole, and smiled. "Ms. Edith. How you doing?" she greeted, pulling the door open wide.

Edith Samuels was barely five feet, with solid white hair and smooth-as-silk skin the color of a new penny that belied her eighty-plus years. But her diminutive appearance was a facade for the steel that ran down her spine and flowed through her veins.

"I'm blessed," she said in her usual greeting. She held out a sturdy paper plate covered in aluminum foil. "I don't know what got into me this morning. Started cooking and couldn't seem to stop. Heard you come in and thought you might be hungry. Grits, bacon, home fries, eggs." She laughed, and fine lines of joy teased her dark-brown eyes.

Alessandra took the proffered plate. "Oh, Ms. Edith," her voice cracked, "you didn't have to." Her stomach didn't agree. She'd run out at six thirty that morning with no more in her stomach than a half cup of coffee.

Edith patted Alessandra's shoulder. "No trouble. No way I could eat it all." She tipped her head to the side and studied Alessandra for a moment. "Sometimes you just have to let go and move on faith," she breathed. She stroked Alessandra's cheek with the pad of her thumb.

Alessandra blinked and blinked, but she couldn't stop the sudden surge of tears from falling.

"Oh, chile." Ms. Edith turned her around by the shoulder and walked her inside. She shut the door behind them, took the plate, and placed it on the circular table. "Come. Sit down."

Alessandra was on a full-blown crying jag—heaving shoulders, runny nose, and hiccup voice—as she attempted to tell Edith about the phone call, her dire straits, and her greatest fear: going home.

Edith listened, nodding and cooing, intermittently patting Alessandra's shuddering shoulders and wiping her eyes with a paper towel.

"I'm sorry," Alessandra said, sniffing back the last of her tears. She blew her nose with the remnants of the paper towel. "I didn't mean to dump that on you." She blinked and could feel the swelling of her lids.

"It's all right. Sometimes as much as we fight against it, destiny pulls us the way we need to go. You spent the better part of your life running away *from*; maybe it's time to run *to*."

"What are you saying?"

"Pretending that your past don't exist won't make it go away. Ignoring the call won't make it stop. When I left—from Virginia and that life, as much as it was all I knew and as much as I was unsure what the North would hold for me—I knew deep in my spirit that if I didn't try, I would never have no peace.

"And it was a hard journey. Many days I thought I should go back. But I didn't turn 'round. I made it. I made a life. My only regret is not getting to see my folks one last time, make peace, tell 'em how sorry I was for leaving them behind."

"I'm sorry," Alessandra said softly.

"Long time ago. I done forgiven myself." She waved her hand, then focused on Alessandra. "Things different now. You kin go back. Get answers to all the questions you been too scared to ask. Make peace with your father *and* yo'self."

"You really think so?" Alessandra's voice wobbled as her eyes searched Edith's for confirmation.

Edith smiled gently and pulled Alessandra to her flattened bosom. "I know so," she whispered.

• • •

After Edith left, Alessandra reheated her breakfast and devoured her food as if she hadn't eaten in days. She mused over Edith's words of advice. It had been more than ten years since she'd been back home. Over two since she'd actually spoken to her father. The last time they talked, she'd asked for five hundred dollars to cover her rent, as she'd spent too much on a new camera and lighting equipment—a fact she didn't share with her father—and he went on a rant about how she was living; what was she ever going to do with her life; why couldn't she come home?

She'd railed right back about how it was her choice. She was grown. She had a life in New York as a photographer. Why couldn't he understand that and support her dreams?

"You'll never forgive me. Never. Never. Never. It wasn't my fault," she'd screamed before tossing the phone against the wall.

But the following day, when she'd gone to the bank instead of the ATM to save on fees and withdraw twenty of her last two hundred dollars, it stunned her to see that a balance of fifteen hundred had been wired into her account. She wanted to call and say thank-you, but thank-you would have meant admitting that her father was right, and if he was right, then she was wrong about everything. And if that were true, then her life made little sense.

So, as ashamed as she was to admit it now, one day turned into two, then a week, a month. The more time that passed, the harder it became to turn the page back to a simple thank-you. And that was two years ago.

Now her father needed her. Their roles were reversed. After all these years.

She could make up for the excuses, the not coming back because of the ghosts of guilt that still lived in that house and behind her father's eyes. As Ms. Edith said, maybe it was time to stop running *from* and run *to* instead.

· · ·

Alessandra boarded the Jitney at Fortieth Street and Lexington Avenue, hoisted her bags onto the overhead rack, and took a seat in the last row next to the window. She shoved her hands into the pockets of her down jacket and felt the cool metal of her ring of keys. She pulled them out.

The silver key stood out among the faded faux gold of the rest. She fingered it between her thumb and forefinger. It was the key to the front door of her father's house. Her stomach clenched as she squeezed her eyes shut, but she couldn't blot out the memories that bloomed to life behind her closed lids.

She'd left that home the week after her eighteenth birthday and hadn't been back since. First it was school and study and tests. Then she was invited to friends' for the holidays. Summer vacation, she wanted to hone her photography skills. Soon, her father stopped asking, and she stopped having to come up with excuses as the years rolled by.

But the distance never seemed to put enough space between her conscience and the past.

She leaned her head against the back of the seat, tucked her arms tightly around her body, and between the warmth of the Jitney and its steady movement she drifted into an uneasy sleep, plagued by images she couldn't understand.

Two hours later, the Jitney pulled into the last stop. The dozen or so passengers filed out, met by family and friends in big warm cars and SUVs. Alessandra sloshed down the narrow street to the cabstand, pulling her bags behind her, the plastic wheels banging and bumping across the snow-dusted cobblestones. After a brief wait, she piled everything into a green taxi. The closer she drew to her destination, the faster her heart raced.

When the driver pulled up in front of her childhood home, a modest, two-story, white-framed house with black trim, a simple front porch and a neat lawn all blanketed in snow, her pulse quickened and a flood of heat rolled through her limbs.

The driver got out and took her bags from the trunk, then set them on the curb. He gave her a quick nod, got back in the car, and pulled away. She froze, as stiff as the icy branches.

She stood there for a moment, staring at the house, the darkened windows, the short lane to the front door covered in snow. This was a terrible mistake. What had she been thinking, coming here?

She had to get back to the city where she belonged. She stumbled toward the curb, hoping to wave down the cab driver. Too late—the taillights were disappearing into the twilight. Her heart thumped as she turned back toward the house, dragged in an open-mouthed breath of bitter cold air—then finally draped her tote and laptop bag over her shoulder, propped her carryall atop her suitcase, and released the handle. She trudged to the front door, stopped at the first step of the porch, and fished for the key.

"Hey, excuse me. Can I help you?"

Her body went on alert. She glanced over her shoulder, drawn by a voice that flowed like a lazy river with the intention of dragging you away from shore. The porch lights cast a shadow across a tall, bulky physique. Lovely. The last thing she needed on top of everything else was to be a victim in a *Lifetime* movie.

"Help me?" she asked, a lift of indignation in her voice.

"Into my own house? No, I don't think so. I'm fine, thanks."

He held up his gloved hands in surrender. "My bad. Sometimes I forget myself with the whole woman-independence thing. You got this." He bit back a grin.

She rolled her eyes and muttered under her breath, then grabbed the handle of the suitcase. But no sooner did she take a step than the suitcase got stuck in the drift. Great. Now she *was* the *Lifetime* movie, *and* she looked like a fool.

"You must be Jerry's daughter."

She tossed the guy a look. He was just standing there with his arms folded, watching her.

She tugged, and the carryall perched on top tumbled onto the snow. She bent down and spewed a curse. And when she glanced up, and his face became illuminated by the one lamp on the short street, she nearly tumbled backward. The air stuck for an instant in her chest, and she coughed as a blink of recognition came and disappeared.

"Whoa." The man helped her to her feet. His fingers clutched her upper arm, and the contact appeared to shock them both. He cleared his throat and took a step back.

Alessandra came eye to chin with the body and the voice. Her gaze drifted up. Her eyes snapped like the lens of her camera, capturing the half smile that was a mixture of sexy and "I told you so," the dark eyes, sleek lashes, smooth skin. Oddly familiar. But that wasn't possible.

"Thanks," she managed.

This time, he didn't bother to ask. He reached for her bags, lifted the suitcase, and carried it under his arm as if it were no more significant than an empty backpack, carrying the smaller one in his other hand. "Alessandra Fleming, right?" They inched up the three steps to the porch landing.

She adjusted her tote and computer bag on her shoulder. "Are we supposed to know each other?" she asked, feeling anxious and perturbed by whoever this guy was.

He chuckled. "Not directly."

"Meaning?"

"I try to check in on your father when I'm in town to see my grandmother. Been more often the past six months or so. Jerry talks about you all the time."

Her stomach tumbled.

"I… I was the one who found him."

She stopped. She could kick herself for being so bitchy now that she knew that this guy had been there for her father instead of his own daughter. Her lips parted, but no words came out at first. She swallowed. "Thank you."

"He's a good man. Just hope he's gonna be okay."

"Yeah," she muttered. "Me too."

They reached the front door, and she dug in her pocket for the key she'd been playing with earlier. "Hope it still works," she said over a sputtered laugh.

"If not, I have one."

She looked at him and frowned. "What?"

"Your dad gave me a key." He offered a slight shrug. "In case something happened. Good thing he did, I guess."

She stared at this man for a moment. Dozens of thoughts raced through her head, but one realization was clear; her father had to rely on a stranger to look in on him because she couldn't—or wouldn't.

What did that make her?

The key fit, turned with ease in the lock, and she felt irrationally vindicated.

She crossed the threshold, then slid her hand along the wall by the door and flipped on the light. When she turned, he was standing in the doorway. Her pulse thumped in her throat.

His eyes were dark as midnight but kind, and he had a

rich umber complexion so smooth he could do one of those skin-care commercials. A dark-gray wool cap covered his head to his lashes, which were full and dark as his eyes. The small scar on the right side of his chin gave him just enough rugged to inch him from Boy Scout to Bad Boy. *A scar*. Her thoughts shuffled through hundreds of images, memories, things just out of reach. She blinked, blinked again, but the elusive image wouldn't come into focus.

He set the suitcases inside the door, then shoved his hands into the pockets of his thick tan-colored jacket. "All set," he said. "Have a good evening." He turned to leave.

"Thank you," she spouted.

He glanced over his shoulder and smirked, then raised his hand in acknowledgment. "Sure."

"I…it's been a long drive in from the city," she blurted. "I've forgotten my manners. Can I get you anything?"

"'Preciate the offer, but I'm fine," he said, tossing her own words back at her.

Inwardly, she winced.

He flashed a slight dimple right above that tiny scar. "You should probably check for any supplies you're missing," he said, lifting his chin toward the kitchen.

"Thanks."

He gave her a quick nod and started off again.

"I don't even know your name," she called out when he'd reached the bottom step.

He turned. "Zach Renard."

She smiled. "Then thanks again, Zach Renard."

CHAPTER THREE

Zach hunched his shoulders against the spinning wind and snow and made his way down the short street and diagonally across. He glanced back once at the closed door of the Fleming home.

She was nothing like what he expected, or what he'd heard from Jeremiah—a sweet girl who loved to take pictures and listen to jazz. Maybe it was because his work trained him to look beneath the surface, to see behind the invisible walls people erected around themselves as protection, that he could see that there was vulnerability beneath the big, hard, city shell Alessandra encased herself in.

He snorted a laugh as he put his key in the door of his grandmother's house. "More like an eggshell," he muttered at his assessment.

His training and his inquiring nature always gave him a need to dig, to peel away layers to see what he had to see. In his work, he found satisfaction. In relationships, he found them wanting. His liaisons, that spanned the globe, had always been more exploration than intention. Once he flipped through most pages of the women he met, he found that after the inciting moment, there was no reason to move to the next chapter—which, ultimately, was fine with him.

His wanderlust never kept him in one place long enough to set down roots—or anything else, for that matter.

The warmth and soft scents of cinnamon that settled in the spaces unseen embraced him as he entered the house. There was a comfort in this kind of familiar. This had been his safe place, his go-to from the time he could board a bus from his home to his Grandma O's kitchen.

He toed out of his Timberlands and left them in the shoe rack by the door, hung up his jacket, and walked down the short hall to the kitchen. The light over the stove was the only illumination, while a plate covered and sealed tightly in aluminum foil sat on the stove. He smiled, went to the sink, washed his hands, and unwrapped his meal. It had remained warm—as it always did. When he peeled back the foil, jollof rice and steamed fish were his reward.

He pulled his cell phone from his back pocket and placed it on the table, then dug in. He closed his eyes and hummed as the spices flavoring the fish popped and awakened his taste buds. Gram had not lost her magic touch. If anything, her cooking had gotten better and better over the years.

He savored every mouthful, even as his thoughts unwittingly shifted back to Alessandra Fleming. For some reason, he thought she'd be taller, thicker. *Silly.* She was tiny compared to him; even in her heavy coat, he could tell she was a lightweight underneath. And she barely reached his chin, which was probably why she tried to appear tough and in control with that flash in her eyes and the sardonic curve of those full lips.

It was more than that, though. In the instant when he reached for her suitcase and she looked into his eyes, he felt a jolt hit him dead center. He thought he might have groaned, but if he did, she didn't notice. He wanted to follow her inside when she'd invited him, but he knew better.

He chewed, savoring every morsel. Maybe it was her voice that stirred him. A jazz singer's voice, low and throaty, laced with riffs and scats, notes that slipped in and out to their own rhythm, a voice that caught you off guard with its inflection. He harrumphed at his poetic analogy and shook his head. He was a man of history—of facts, not poetry. But as new to him as Alessandra Fleming was, he couldn't shake the sensation that he'd always known her.

The sound of his grandmother's shuffling, slippered feet drew him back to the world in front of him. He glanced over his shoulder as his grandmother crossed the threshold. Instinctively he got up and went to her, leaned down, and kissed her cheek.

"Didn't mean to wake you, Gram."

She waved her slender hand. "Oh hush, you been waking me up from good sleep for long as I can recall," she lovingly teased. Grace Oweku's thick silver hair was plaited in a single braid that hung down to the middle of her back in sharp contrast against her cocoa-brown skin.

As usual, she was in her favorite blanket robe of brilliant red and gold with dancing horses, handed down from her great-grandmother who'd found safety, love, and marriage for many years among the Shinnecock people right outside Sag Harbor. The robe was worn at the elbows and frayed a bit at the wrists and hem, but Gram would never part with it. She was proud of the Native American blood that ran through her veins and manifested in the silken waves of her hair and the warmth of her skin, traits that she'd passed onto her daughter and grandson.

"Saw the lights on at Jerry's place." She ambled over to

the stove and put on a pot of water for tea.

Gram never missed a beat. He smiled. "Yes. His daughter is there."

"Ohhh. Met her, have you now?"

"She was struggling with her bags when I drove up. I helped her."

"All grown up, I expect." She took a mug from the overhead cabinet and placed it on the table. She sat opposite Zach and linked her long fingers together.

"I guess she has."

The teapot whistled. Zach jumped up from his seat and fixed the tea for his grandmother.

"Just one squeeze of lemon," she reminded him, as she did every time he fixed her a cup of tea.

Zach took the directive in stride. "Of course, Gram." He placed the tea in front of her.

"I'm going to take this upstairs." She slowly got to her feet. "Good night, sweet bird." She cooed the nickname she'd given him when he was ten years old, curled on her lap, having fled his home to hers, for the first time of what became many. She said she always knew he would fly from one place to the next until he found the right spot to build his own nest. "Don't stay up too late thinking about Alessandra Fleming."

She squeezed his shoulder and left him with his mouth wide open.

• • •

Alessandra shut and locked the door behind Zach, feeling unsettled by their meeting, by him. She wanted to attribute the off-balance sensation to being back home, but it was more than that.

She shook her head, dragged in a breath, and by degrees took in the space she'd once called home. A wave of nostalgia washed over her as she saw herself standing next to her mom in the kitchen, learning how to slice onions without crying, or curled next to her pouring her heart out about Gary Davis, her eighth-grade crush. Sometimes she wondered if she'd romanticized her mother simply because she was gone, or had things been as storybook as she remembered?

She went into the overcrowded living room that hadn't changed in decades. The brown leather recliner showed its age with its worn arms and headrest, its color faded from deep brown to dark tan after years of use. The overstuffed couch and matching chairs and love seat were in the same spot she remembered and the china cabinet still held the "good dishes" and crystal.

She walked over to the wall unit that contained the stereo system that commanded the corner. She lifted the smoke-colored lid and blinked in surprise. Sitting on the turntable was *Sarah Vaughn's Greatest Hits* album.

Well, I'll be damned.

She lifted Sarah to see what was beneath, and lo and behold, *The Essential Billie Holiday — Carnegie Hall Concert* was waiting its turn.

Alessandra hummed in appreciation. *Yes, yes, yes.* Classic, classic music for all time. She turned on the stereo, let the Billie Holiday album slide down the spindle, and placed the needle on the first groove of the album, just the way her father had showed her when she was about eight or nine.

For a moment, her lids lowered, and a smooth smile tilted her lips as the achingly beautiful intonations of "Lady Day's" rendition of "Body and Soul" filled the room. It was one of the few things they had in common — their passion for music — but like most things between them, they disagreed on what was better. Her father worshipped every note of the iconic musicians: Miles, Coltrane, Gillespie, Ellington, Monk, "Bird," while her affinity rested with the vocalists—Vaughn, Holiday, Wilson, Carter, Fitzgerald—who interpreted and brought the music to life.

Curious that Sarah and Billie were cued up to be listened to. Maybe after all these years, her father's tastes had changed.

Memories. So many memories flooded her consciousness. She lowered herself onto the club chair, leaned her head back, and closed her eyes. Billie's voice moved through her veins, a plaintive lullaby. She didn't realize she'd drifted into a light sleep until she jerked up at the sound of a ringing phone.

It took a moment to realize where she was. The remnants of her interrupted dream of a woman—in a small cabin, seated with a young girl between her knees, combing and braiding her hair to the firelight from the hearth—hovered for a moment like a morning mist, only to be replaced by the memory of Zach Renard's smile before both dissipated.

Her heart thumped. Blinking to clear her head, she dug in her back pocket and pulled out her phone.

"Hello?"

"Hey. Why didn't you call me, let me know what was going on?"

"Steven. I'm sorry. I should have—"

"I had to find out from Leslie when I got to the studio and asked where you were."

She pulled in a breath, still a bit shaken. Steven James was not only the owner of the gallery but her mentor and benefactor. It was Steven who was fronting the cost of mounting her show. She knew he'd wanted more—he'd made that clear—but he also made it clear that he respected her wishes not to cross that line.

"Steven, I'm sorry. Everything happened so fast. I'd

planned to call you." She checked her watch. It was after six. *Damn*. She hadn't even contacted the hospital yet.

She stood, rubbed her eyes, and tucked a stray loc of hair back into the topknot on her head.

"So…how is he?" His question sounded more like an accusation.

"I haven't gone to the hospital yet. I only arrived about an hour ago. I was… I'm leaving soon. They have visiting until eight."

"How long do you plan on staying out there?"

Her head jerked back from the phone. "I just got here. I haven't even seen my father yet."

"That's not what I meant. Came out all wrong."

"What did you mean?"

"You still have so much work to do for this show," he said, his tone suddenly all business. "You need to be ready."

"I will be," she said.

He paused. "I can come down for the weekend if that would help. We can go over some ideas…"

"Um…" An unwarranted image of Zach Renard sprang into her head. "I don't think that's necessary. There's going to be so much for me to do, I won't have time."

"Well, if you're gone more than a week, expect company," he said with a flat chuckle. "And you let me know if there's anything I can do."

"I'll keep you posted. I better get going. Thank you, Steven."

"Sure."

"Talk soon." She disconnected the call and frowned as she placed the phone back on the cradle, still feeling out of body. Dreaming about a strange woman and a girl and some man she'd just met… What was that about?

She expelled a breath and walked back out into the hall

to retrieve her bags. She took them upstairs to the spare bedroom, knowing that when she returned from the hospital, she'd have to find clean sheets and blankets to put on the bare mattress.

She sat on the edge of the bed, plucked her phone from her pocket, and scrolled to Traci Howard's number. She and Traci had become best friends in her freshman year at NYU when they'd met in an art history class. Traci was the yin to her yang, the friend who had no problem saying exactly what she meant, even when it made Alessandra cringe—which was what she loved about her bestie.

Traci answered on the second ring, and Alessandra told her what happened and apologized for not calling before she'd darted out of town.

"Girl. I would have come with you."

"I know. But it's cool."

"Look, sis, everything happens for a reason. I know things ain't been cool with you and your dad for a minute," she paused, "but maybe now is the time to cross some bridges."

Alessandra squeezed the phone in her palm and closed her eyes. Of course Traci was right, but Alessandra didn't know how or if she could cross that bridge. It had been so long.

"All you gotta do is say so. I can be there in a heartbeat," Traci said, making Alessandra smile.

"I will. Promise. Hey, T…"

"Yeah?"

"I, uh, met this guy."

"Say what? You just got there," she said with laughter in her voice. "I know I've been telling you all work and no play will have you growing cobwebs down there, but dang."

Alessandra burst into laughter. "Girl. Stop. It's not like that. He helped me with my luggage. Told me he's the one who'd been checking on my dad." She cleared her throat. "He was the one who found him."

"Wow," Traci said on a long breath, stretching out the word.

"Yeah. Exactly." Zach's smile, the curl of his lashes, the darkness of his eyes, and the smoothness of his warm brown skin materialized before her. The shells of her ears heated.

"So, does this knight in shining armor have a name?"

"Zach Renard."

"Hmm, sounds familiar."

"I know, right?" Her heart beat faster; maybe the guy was famous, and that's why he seemed so familiar to her, too? "Anyway, I gotta go. I'm heading over to the hospital. I'll call you."

"Love you, sis."

"Love you too."

Back downstairs, she got into her coat, took the car keys that her father kept in the wooden bowl in the hall, grabbed her bag, and headed out into a light snowfall. *Perfect.*

Her plan had been to drive her father's car, but she hadn't figured on having to dig it out first. Why they'd never got a garage built was always a mystery. For several moments, she just stood, unable to move or think, and then out of nowhere she felt the burn of tears sting her eyes and clench her throat.

Being back here. Her father. Her mother. The memories. The guilt.

She sucked in air, trying to stem the tears and clear her head.

"Hey! You okay?"

Her gaze whipped in the direction of the voice. Zach was

heading toward her. She wiped at her eyes.

"Saw you just standing here. We gotta stop meeting like this." His teasing grin faded and he paused, his head angled to the side, his voice lowered. "Everything cool?"

The depth and comforting undertone of his voice was almost her undoing. It took sheer force of will to keep her from pressing her head against his chest and pouring out her hurt and confusion and resentment.

She licked her lips instead, put on a smile—she hoped. "I was heading over to the hospital, but," she glanced at the car parked next to the house, "I'm so not up to digging out a car." She planted her hand on her hip and slowly shook her head, hoping she looked more annoyed than shaken.

Zach chuckled. "I know the feeling. Listen, I know you're all independent and whatnot, but I can take you to the hospital. All-wheel drive," he singsonged like an advertisement.

She grinned. "My independence means I'd happily choose to independently ask for your help when I needed it. Thank you."

"Come on." He returned her smile. "It's really starting to come down."

She looked up at him—at the sparkling flakes that clung to his thick curling lashes, dusted his broad shoulders—and hitched a short, silent breath. And when he placed his hand at the small of her back, then guided her across the street to where he'd parked his black SUV, the light pressure of his fingers short-circuited her thoughts.

The chirp of the car lock got her back to reset.

Zach held the door open and helped her in. When he slid behind the wheel, he said, "With any luck, we should be there in about twenty minutes. Roads are pretty slick."

"Sure." She made busy work of fastening her seat belt,

hoping to reclaim some sense of regularity to her pulse. That he smelled good enough to curl up next to on a winter night just like this one didn't make sitting mere inches away from him any easier.

Get. Yourself. Together. You're here to see your hurt father, not drool over some guy you barely know. She folded her gloved hands on her lap.

"Music?" he asked.

"Sure." Had she lost all ability to communicate beyond one word answers?

Zach pushed a button on the dash, and the cozy interior was bathed in the magic of Dianne Reeves's rendition of "Better Days."

She angled her head in his direction. "Dianne Reeves. I'm impressed."

Zach gave a short, rough-hewed laugh. "Really? Why is that? Small-town guy…?" He let the rest hang in the air.

"No, no, that's not what I meant—"

His amused side-eye cut her off.

Sheepishly, she bit down on her bottom lip. "Okay," she sighed, duly embarrassed by her elitist comment. "That is kinda what I thought. And I'm sorry," she added.

"Now you're supposed to say, 'No offense.' And I reply, 'No offense taken.'"

"Touché."

Zach laughed. "As quiet as it's kept, I read books, too." He winked.

"Ouch," she said with a half grin. She settled into the warm leather seat, and a sense of calm bloomed in her center for the first time in hours. They drove in silence for a good ten minutes, the music filling the space. "So, do you live out here?" she finally asked.

"I actually have a townhouse in DC. Moved back to the

States about two years ago."

"Oh. Back from where?"

"All over, really; Europe, the Caribbean. Mostly Africa for the past few years."

"Oh." Her brows rose. He was more interesting by the moment. "Work? Personal? If you don't mind me asking."

His mouth quirked into a half grin. "Combination. All my work is personal."

Zach turned his full attention on navigating through the snow, which had grown in intensity. He flipped a lever on the steering wheel, and the wipers picked up speed.

In the dim interior, she studied the lines of his profile, the strong jaw with a hint of a long day's shadow, the sleek nose with just a flare at the tip, the full lips that almost pouted, then on down to the long fingers that gripped the wheel. She wondered what he was getting at about his work, and why he didn't seem to want to elaborate.

"Hopefully this will let up," he murmured, leaning forward as if willing himself to see through the storm, and successfully derailing her visual stroll along his exterior.

She blinked, licked her bottom lip. "I remember my childhood winters here," she said wistfully. "Sledding and ice-skating."

"I'm still trying to get used to these winters."

"Humph, I can imagine." Her brows knitted. "You said 'moved *back.*' When did you live here? I grew up in Sag Harbor. Pretty small place. I don't remember you."

"You wouldn't."

She studied his profile. His jaw was set, his gaze focused.

She started to ask him what he meant, but he lifted his chin, peered closer at the windshield, and said, "We're here."

Zach pulled into the hospital parking lot, cut the engine, and hurried around to help her out. He grabbed an umbrella from the back seat, snapped it open, and held it over her head. He slid an arm around her waist, but before she could react, they were making their way gingerly across the snow-slicked asphalt.

The wind whipped the snow sideways, then snatched the umbrella and turned it inside out before hurling it into the night. They burst out laughing, even as pellets of snow stung their cheeks.

Zach pulled her close against him again, using his body to protect her from the elements, and for a minute it felt as though he were commanding her body to yield to his, as if this was what they were used to. Her mind swirled with the snow, but suddenly it wasn't snow; it was rushing, angry black waves tossing her about, slamming her body. Everything was moving, rocking. Voices screamed. Her heart thumped.

The bright lights of the hospital lobby momentarily stunned her. It took her a minute to realize where she was.

"Man," Zach said. "Worse than they forecasted." He stamped his feet, paused, looked at her with concern tightening his brow. "You okay?"

She swallowed, shook her body free of snow, and pulled her burnt-orange-and-gold wool hat from her head. Her hair sprung free from the loose topknot and tumbled down her back and across her shoulders. "Yes. Fine," she said on a breath of uncertainty. "Guess I wasn't ready for that onslaught." She forced a smile, the intensity of his stare making her look away. "Need to go see my father," she muttered, off-balance.

"He's on the third floor, but you'll need a pass from the front desk."

There it was again, that thin paintbrush of annoyance that stroked her surface realizing that this...*stranger*...knew more about her father than she did. Annoyance. Guilt. Whatever. He simply stroked—rubbed—her the wrong way.

She clutched her hat in her fist and strode off toward the information desk.

"Good evening. My name is Alessandra Fleming. They brought my father, Jeremiah Fleming, in yesterday."

The woman behind the desk lowered her glasses to the tip of her nose, focused on the computer screen, and began tapping on the keys. "Third floor. Pavilion B, room 1839." She hit another key, and the printer spat out a visitor's pass with Alessandra's father's room number. "Elevator to your right." She handed Alessandra the pass.

"Thank you." She turned. Her breath hitched. Zach was standing right behind her with a look in his eyes that she couldn't place. "Like you said, third floor." She ran her tongue along her bottom lip.

He nodded. "I'll wait for you down here. Actually, I'll be in the cafeteria. It's down that hall to the left. Food's quite good, and I'm hungry. Again." He chuckled.

Her stomach agreed about being hungry. "I can't ask you to wait for me. I don't know how long—"

"So, uh, how were you planning on getting back, then? Sled? A cab would be hard to come by in this weather." His mouth curled in amusement.

She twisted her lips to the side and laughed. "Got me there. Don't know how long I'll be, though."

He shrugged his broad shoulders. "No worries. Take as much time as you need." He pulled a worn paperback from his jacket pocket and held it up like a trophy. "Food, good reading." He gave a light chuckle. "I'll be just fine."

Before she could offer up another feeble protest, he was already on his way to the cafeteria.

Alessandra sucked in a long breath and walked to the elevator. The ride up three floors happened much too quickly. What she wanted to do was hit the down button, find Zach in the cafeteria, and ask him to take her back. A trickle of sweat slid down her spine.

What if he didn't want to see her? What if he told her to leave? What if they had nothing to say to each other? What if she started crying, like she felt she would do any second?

Oh God. She wasn't ready for this. Not for any of it.

CHAPTER FOUR

The musical ping of the elevator signaled her floor, and the doors swished open. Her heart thundered. She stepped off and walked across the walkway to the adjoining pavilion. Intensive Care to the right. Cardiac wing to the left. She walked toward the doors on her right and pressed the intercom. Moments later, a disembodied voice asked for the room number.

"1839."

A hydraulic hiss and the doors opened inward. She gripped the pass in her hand like a talisman and walked to the nurses' station.

"Hello," she whispered, library-soft. "I'm here to see my father, Jeremiah Fleming."

The nurse offered a bright smile. "Yes. He's a character, that one. Teasing and flirting with all the nurses, even in all that pain. But he barely complains," she assured her.

Alessandra tried to match up the man she knew with the one this nurse described, but she couldn't. "Hmm. Really?"

"He's three doors down on your right."

She nodded her thanks.

• • •

Alessandra stood at the threshold of her father's room, but she couldn't seem to put one foot in front of the other or open the door. Her feet felt stuck ankle-deep in thick, dark, wet mud. The space in front of her was blanketed in darkness, a darkness so black that she couldn't see her hand in front of her face. Her heart raced as terrifying sounds of howling dogs threatened to overtake her. Voices echoed; then, as suddenly as the vision had begun, it cleared, and she saw her father through the square pane of glass set into the heavy metal.

Her stomach clenched as her racing heart slowed to a knocking thump. She squeezed her eyes shut for a moment and fought to clear her thoughts. *What is happening? What is happening*?

When she opened them, her gaze rested on the figure that was slowly taking shape in front of her. This wasn't the strong, burly man she remembered. He looked small, fragile beneath the white sheets, and even from the other side of his door, she could hear the *beeps* of the machines and swore she heard the *drip*, *drip* of the fluids that hung from a pole next to his bed. That antiseptic smell filled her nostrils. The sight of her mother covered by a sheet hurtled her back fifteen years and rocked her on her feet.

"Can I help you?"

Alessandra startled, glanced over her shoulder. A nurse stood behind her.

"Oh, um, no thanks. I was going to go in and see my dad, but looks like he's sleeping."

The nurse smiled benevolently. "I have to give him his meds. Come in. I'm sure he'll be happy to see you."

The nurse stepped around Alessandra and pushed the

door open.

Alessandra looked down at her feet. *Boots, that's all.* Not shoeless feet encased in mud. She breathed deeply and walked behind the nurse as if using her body as a shield between her and her father.

"Mr. Fleming," the nurse said gently while she checked the drip on the bag of fluids. She made some notations on her iPad. "Mr. Fleming, time for your meds. And you have a visitor." She turned her smile on Alessandra.

Jeremiah moaned. His eyes opened, then closed, then opened again. "How's a man 'spose to get any rest round here with you pretty gals waking him up every minute?" He tried to laugh but coughed instead.

The nurse cradled the back of his head and brought a cup with a straw to his lips. "Here, sip this," she said softly. "Easy. That's it," she cooed as if talking to a child. "Your daughter is here." She lowered his head to the pillow. "I'm going to release the dose of pain meds into the IV, then I'll leave you with your daughter. Okay?"

She gently patted his shoulder, then pressed several buttons on the monitor next to his bed. She made more notes on her digital chart, then looked across at Alessandra. "All yours," she said before walking out.

Don't leave. Please don't leave me here. He doesn't want to see me. I can't do this. Not yet. I can't.

Jeremiah turned his head toward where Alessandra stood glued to the floor. His eyes squinted to bring her into focus. "Ali? That really you?" His rough voice held notes of incredulity.

Whatever had held her in place slowly released its grip. It had been so long since she'd heard the pet name come from her father's lips. Her throat clenched, and she realized just how much she'd missed it. Her eyes burned.

She dropped her purse on the chair that hugged the wall and tentatively walked over to the side of his bed. "It's me, Dad." She dared to take his hand, and when his long fingers wrapped around hers, her heart sang.

"Ali," he said like a prayer. "You came?"

She nodded. Her nostrils flared as she sucked in air while trying to halt the burn in her eyes. She blinked rapidly and drew closer to his bedside. "What happened, Dad?"

"Wish I could say. It was so fast. One minute I was at the top of the stairs…the next I was in an ambulance. Damnedest thing." He winced, gripped her hand. His eyes creased shut. "Thank goodness for that boy Zach." He puffed. "Could you fix this pillow behind my head?" Beads of perspiration dotted his forehead.

"Sure. You okay? You need me to get the nurse?"

He waved away her concern. "No, just takes a minute sometimes for the morphine to kick in," he said, halting between every other word.

Alessandra adjusted the pillows. "Better?"

His eyes drifted close. "Hmm," he hummed. "Thank ya."

As she stood there, looking down at her father with pins and rods in his hip, attached to tubes and machines, a man who flirted with nurses and was genuinely glad if not surprised to see her, she tried to remember why she'd left, why she'd stayed away. She'd needed something to point to, someone to blame.

She couldn't stop the tear that dripped onto the white sheet. She brushed her eyes with her fingertip and sniffed back the threat of more. For several moments, she watched the steady rise and fall of her father's chest as he seemed to settle back into sleep before she leaned over the bedrail and placed a gentle kiss on his forehead. "We can talk more later," she whispered.

"I'd like that a lot," he murmured, offering up a smile. His lids fluttered. "Things we need to talk about."

Her pulse quickened. "What things?" Even now, was she ready for a real conversation with her father? What did she have to say for *herself* was the real question.

The nurse pushed open the door. "I'm sorry," she said with soft authority, "but visiting hours are over." She nodded and let the door close.

Alessandra turned her attention back to her father. Was the nurse coming in at that exact moment a reprieve?

She leaned down and kissed his forehead. "Time for me to go, Dad. I'll see you tomorrow. Rest well, okay?"

He murmured something she couldn't make out.

Alessandra took one more look at her father, picked up her bag, and walked out. As she was leaving, the nurse at the front desk stopped her.

"Ms. Fleming."

"Yes?"

"Did you want to take your father's things?"

"His things?"

"Yes, his clothes, shoes… You can take them with you."

"Oh, okay. Sure," she replied, taking a minute to put together what the nurse was saying.

"I'll get them for you. They're in the closet in his room."

She came from behind the desk, went to Jeremiah's room, and returned a few minutes later with a large plastic bag. "Here you are." She handed over the bag.

Alessandra forced a smile. "Thank you." She looked at the contents protected by thick plastic and felt a wave of anxiety sweep through her. She started for the exit, then stopped and turned back.

"Excuse me. Sorry to bother you," Alessandra said to the nurse behind the desk. "Is the doctor around? I wanted to speak with someone about my dad."

"Let me page Dr. Clark for you, hon."

"Thank you. I'd appreciate that."

After pacing in front of the nurses' station for about ten minutes, Alessandra heard the doors leading into the ICU swish open. A woman, about her age, clad in the standard white coat approached. "You paged me, Gloria?"

"Yes, Dr. Clark. Ms. Fleming wanted to speak with you about her father, Jeremiah Fleming." She lifted her chin in Alessandra's direction.

Dr. Clark adjusted her black-framed glasses and studied Alessandra with blue eyes of concern. "How can I help you?"

"I wanted to get an update on my father's condition. His prognosis."

Dr. Clark slipped her hands into the wide pockets of her white coat. "Let's talk in the lounge." She led Alessandra down the corridor, past medical and food carts pushed by orderlies and dietary staff. "Right here," she said, and moved to open a glass-and-chrome door.

The small cozy space that could easily substitute as someone's living room was empty. Alessandra took a seat.

"When your father was brought in, beyond the seriousness of his injury, he was disoriented," the doctor started.

"I'm sure the fall had a lot to do with it."

"Partly. But the CAT scan indicates that your father has suffered a series of transient ischemic attacks, or TIAs."

"What? TIA?"

"I'm sorry. TIAs are mini-strokes."

"Mini-strokes!" Her crossed leg dropped to the floor. She gripped the arms of the chair.

"I take it you knew nothing about it."

"No, I didn't," she said.

"Did he ever mention weak limbs, confusion?"

Alessandra shifted in her seat. "I...my father and I..." She pressed her lips together for a moment. "We haven't been in touch."

Dr. Clarke nodded. "I see." She offered a placating smile. "Families can be our most difficult relationships."

Alessandra glanced away, then back at Dr. Clark. There was nothing she could do about the past. She was here now. She lifted her chin, ready for the next blow.

"Well, we believe that one of those mini-strokes caused him to fall."

Alessandra's chest tightened. "So... What does all of that mean?" Alarm lifted the pitch of her voice. "What are you saying—*exactly*?"

"I'm saying that your father is going to need ongoing care. More than just an occasional visit."

Alessandra cut her eyes at the doctor's shade, but held her tongue.

"He's going to be here for at least a month. We'll move him to a rehab facility to help with mobility." She sighed. "Your dad is almost seventy. A break like this," she paused, "it's life-altering. Some patients never fully recover. I need you to understand that. Compounded with the TIAs...You'll need to think about what you want to do once they release him from rehab. I can have a social worker get in contact with you, offer you some options."

Alessandra nodded, numb. A month? *I can't stay here a month.*

Dr. Clark rose and placed a hand on Alessandra's shoulder. "Do you have anyone to help you?"

Alessandra shook her head. "No." Her thoughts raced. What was she going to do?

"I'll be sure to have the social work office reach out."

"Thank you," she whispered.

"It would be helpful in planning your father's care to get a much fuller family health history."

Alessandra's brows rose.

"We want to rule out as much as possible. Often health issues are genetic, generational. We don't want to only treat what we see, but what caused us to see it." She offered a tight smile. "Someone will be in touch," she added, and walked out.

Alessandra let her head fall back against the chair cushion and closed her eyes. Inherited? Generational? Were visions and voices part of the mix? She shuddered slightly. She didn't have a clue.

· · ·

Alessandra recounted as best she could what the doctor had said as she and Zach walked to the parking lot.

Zach opened the passenger door, helped Alessandra into her seat, took Jeremiah's belongings from her, and put them in the back seat. Once she was settled, he handed her the bag of food he'd purchased at the cafeteria, then got in behind the wheel. "Hope you like Chinese," he said, then put the car in gear and eased out of the hospital parking lot. "So the doctor thinks that something other than tripping down the stairs is behind your father's fall?"

Alessandra sighed. "Apparently." She adjusted the bag of food on her lap. The aroma of chicken lo mein and shrimp fried rice wafted from the bag. Her stomach rumbled in response. "You mind if I eat a bit in your car? I'm way past starved."

Zach chuckled. "Go right ahead."

Alessandra opened one of the white containers of lo mein and took a hearty forkful. She hummed in appreciative relief.

"Actually, I think I'll join you. In this weather, driving at five miles per hour, it's going to be a while to get back. I'll take an egg roll."

She dug in the bag, took out an egg roll.

"You mind slathering that in some hot mustard?" He threw her a quick look and a smile.

"My go-to condiment," she said. One more thing they had in common. Music *and* hot mustard.

Steven hated hot mustard. Yet Traci had always teased her about Steven, especially when she'd first started working at his gallery. She'd said it was beyond her mental faculties to figure out how Alessandra could not get together with him. He was tall with basic good looks. Intelligent. Hard working. Bougie. *To him, "Netflix and chill" are curse words*, Alessandra had teased. He had all the qualities she'd been groomed to look for.

Alessandra took the teasing in stride and would tell her bestie that Steven was a good guy beneath his custom suits, and they'd laugh some more. But when it really came down to it, she didn't want to cross that line. If things went south, it would not only ruin a relationship but potentially screw up her finally blossoming career. Over time, Traci slowly changed her tune. *You're totally right about Steven*, she'd said one evening over drinks. *You've started to change*, she'd remarked. *You look for things with meaning now. It's all in your photographs, your* real *photographs, which by the way you need to do something about*, she'd added. *And to be honest, I surrender, Steven really is all facade. All show and not much substance, especially for a brother.*

She wasn't always this way. In truth, she'd been groomed most of her early life for a man just like Steven. It wasn't until her solo girl's trip to the Caribbean—Jamaica, Bahamas, Grenada, and Antigua; her birthday gift to herself a little more than a year earlier—where she'd photographed the beaches, villages, historic churches, and hidden places and talked with the locals about their lives and the history of the islands that she'd begun to question her own existence in the world. Ironic that it was a simple getaway that pried open her eyes. It was after that trip that she'd stopped straightening her hair and instead let it do its natural wild-and-curly thing.

She tore at the packet of hot mustard with her teeth and squeezed the contents over the egg roll, placed it on a napkin, and passed it to Zach, studying him in the dimness a moment longer than necessary.

They pulled to a stop at the light.

"Thanks." He took a big bite and hummed in satisfaction. "You have any history in the family of whatever it is the doctor is talking about?"

She shook her head. "Not that I know of. I'm not even sure what she's looking for." She took another plastic forkful of lo mein. "I mean, my family is just me and my father since my mom passed. No siblings." Saying the words out loud cut a hole in her spirit. "I barely remember my grandparents, and my parents never really spoke about them. My mother seemed totally disinterested in the past or where she'd come from."

She frowned, stared into those yesterdays.

Anytime she'd ask her mother about her grandparents or where she'd grown up, Jessica would wave her pale, manicured hand and tell her that the only times she needed to worry about were the right now and the future.

"Past isn't going to get you anywhere," Jessica would say. "Black folks' past is riddled with trauma and pain and destruction. Women raped and babies taken from them. Men beaten, tortured." She shook her head, her features creased into a tight mask as if she was seeing something beyond her own words. "Not our life."

She huffed, turned her bright smile on her daughter. "The future, young lady." She wagged a finger at Alessandra. "Eye on the prize."

So Alessandra took her mother at her word and kept her sights straight ahead.

"What about your dad?"

Alessandra blinked away the memory. "Umm, I...don't know," she said, inching toward the realization of just how little she knew about her own family. She'd grown up taking her mother's proclamations as gospel. She frowned.

There was that one time, though, she must have been about nine or ten, when she'd walked into the den and her father was going through papers in a wide wooden brown chest, about as long as she was tall. When she asked what he was doing, he'd smiled at her, and his eyes had seemed to glow with excitement.

"Come on over here, Ali. Let me show you."

Just as she'd gone to stand next to her dad, her mother came to the doorway.

"Jerry! Nothing in there for Alessandra to see. We agreed." She'd almost stomped her foot. "That's not *our* life." She walked over and shut the lid. "Dinner's ready," she said, giving her daughter a pointed look. Alessandra darted out of the door. She didn't remember ever seeing the chest again or what was in it.

Funny that she would remember that now.

She and Zach spent the rest of the drive nibbling the food, critiquing the music that piped through the speakers, and challenging each other's musical mastery by upping the ante with tidbits that only true jazz connoisseurs would appreciate, all against the rhythmic background swish of the wipers and the silent fall of snow. It was everything it should be, had been, would be. It was...*familiar*.

By the time they arrived at Alessandra's home, a good three inches of additional snow covered the walkway to the house.

"Wow." Alessandra stepped out. Her feet sank into snow above her ankles. Her father's car was barely visible. "A challenge for the morning, but I'm sure there're some young kids who need the money," she said with a smile, then covered her yawn.

"Well, at least let me help you to the door."

"That you can definitely do," she said, looking up at Zach with a smile.

They inched along to the front door, laughing and holding on to each other to keep from either sinking knee-deep or tumbling over into the snow.

"Thank you," Alessandra said over her laughter, then sobered. "For everything."

"Not a problem."

She held her breath. Under ordinary circumstances, like if this was the end of a great date instead of what it actually was, it would be the moment for the good-night kiss. But this entire day, meeting Zach Renard and all that had followed, was anything but ordinary. Her pulse raced at a clip. The hair at the back of her neck tingled. The only light was the moon that slid between the bare branches of the trees. *Stay on da path. Don't stop.* The howling grew.

Alessandra gripped the stair railing, lifted her chin to listen.

"Wind's really kicking up," Zach said, cutting off her confusing thoughts. "Hopefully we won't have any power outages." He hunched his shoulders up to his ears. "Better get inside."

She blinked. Swallowed and forced a smile. "Thanks for everything."

"Get some rest." He turned to leave.

"Good night," she called out.

Zach waved without turning around, bending his body into the wind.

Stolen, 1839

More bark from the sea for the fire. Laughter. Young, carefree bodies smell of salt and sand from hours of swimming in the ocean. Strong brown, muscled legs run toward the surf... then, screams. Shouts. Shots.

...

So dark we can't see no faces, only hear the wails and cries and moans from fear, pain, loss, and beatings circling around us like buzzards. Stomachs clench from hunger and the stench of our surroundings. Every now and again, a man with heavy boots throws buckets of salt water over us, again and again, seeming to enjoy our screams. Filth, he says over and over until I think it may be our name.

My tears will no longer come, only the heaving of my sadness. Why have they done this, taken me away from Mama and babu, away from my beloved? The elders always told tales of the men with skin like the moon coming onto the beaches at night and stealing away bad boys and girls. They warned about wandering too far from the village, of being alone in the bush or on the beaches.

I am not a bad girl! I am not. I was not alone. I didn't wander. I did not! Why? The words echo in my mind. I refuse to scream them.

Even on the few times they march us into the sunlight from the dark hole that they keep us in, I do not scream for my mama and babu or for him. I will not let these men with skin of the moon know my terror and loneliness. Babu always warned me never to show fear to those who could do you harm, man or beast.

In circles they make us walk, round and round, our eyes stinging from the blaze of sun, bodies weeping from sores,

weak from hunger for real food, lashed to each other by rope—
until I am not.

He cuts the rope that tethers me to the woman in front
and the girl behind. I can run now. Fast. Fast as the panther.
Away. Home. But my feet remain bound by the rope. He grabs
my arm and pulls me away from the others. I dare to look back
at my bound sisters as I stumble over sand and rock and my own
feet. What I see in their eyes terrifies me more than the grip
on my arm or the why I was taken. Perhaps this is my blessed
end, I pray.

The room is small, crowded; table, mat for sleeping, pails
with water, but no weapon that I can see. He cups his hands
into a pail and splashes his face with water. Come. Louder.
Come! He cups his hands into the water and pours it over my
shoulders. I expect the sting of salt, but it is only cool, clean
water. Wash. My hands dive into the cool water and I splash
and splash it over me, my face, my tangled hair, my bare
breasts, my thighs, the thicket between my legs, enough clean
water to cover my tears until the pail is empty.

He laughs, points to a chair, and orders me to sit, then
turns away to a table stacked with bottles and glasses. He
pours a brown liquid into a glass and hands it to me, then takes
one for himself. Drink.

Liquid fire burns my throat, boils in my belly, stings my
eyes. The coughing won't seem to stop, and it only makes him
laugh. He finishes his brown fire and pours more for me. Drink.

The room moves away from me, cloudy like the sky before a
storm. Drink.

Drink.

The rope that binds my ankles is cut. I can run now. But
the room sways around and beneath me. The locked door moves
from one spot to the next, making it impossible to reach—to

open—to run. The bearded face above me weighs me down into the mat, into the soil beneath, below the earth into the fires that pierce me, split my body and soul. My mouth opens to scream and scream, but there is nothing but the memory of sound. My voice is stolen.

But not my spirit.

I never return to my sisters in the dark, but remain in this new prison with clean washing water, bread, meat, fire down my throat and between my thighs. One day I will run like the wind.

I will.

CHAPTER FIVE

Alessandra found clean sheets in the hall linen closet and made up the bed in what was once her old bedroom. She took a long, hot shower, then went to the kitchen and heated up the rest of her Chinese food.

While she sat at the kitchen table, picking through her lo mein and shrimp fried rice, the events of the day popped in and out of her consciousness like five-by-seven photos, one after another, before scattering like a deck of Polaroids being dealt. She spread more hot mustard on the rice.

Suddenly she felt famished, as if she hadn't eaten in days, maybe weeks. She shoved forkfuls of food into her mouth, barely chewing. Grains of rice fell onto the table, and she scooped up every single one with her fingers. Her head spun. Her limbs felt heavy, her temples throbbed. She tried to push to her feet, but her legs were so weak she couldn't stand.

Then, as quickly as the sensations had overtaken her, they were gone. Her heartbeat, by degrees, returned to normal. She squeezed her eyes shut, slowly opened them, and gazed around the room. The stove. The fridge. The sink. The circular wood table. The overhead cabinets. One by one, they each came back into focus.

She pressed her forehead into her palm. *What is happening?* It was as if…she didn't know what "as if" meant. She couldn't put it together to make sense. Was she losing her mind?

What if she was predisposed to that TIA thing the doctor spoke about? Maybe she was having some kind of "event."

She shook her head, dropped her fork on the table, stunned to see there was nothing left but a faint trail of hot mustard on the white plate. She stared at the liquid remnants, not even certain that she'd eaten.

Finally, she pushed to her feet and took her plate to the sink. She turned on the faucet and watched the water rush over it. Mindlessly she soaped and rinsed the utensils, hoping the ordinary task would center her somehow.

This was maybe the third or fourth "episode"—or whatever the hell it was—since she'd returned to Sag Harbor.

She frowned, thinking, then turned off the water. She was frightened. It had been years since she'd last felt like this. When she was little, her mother had simply told her they were just bad dreams. "But I wasn't sleeping," she'd insist. And her mother would whisper, "It used to happen to me when I was a girl, but I grew up and they went away—just like shoes that don't fit anymore." Her mother smiled and insisted that she would be just fine.

Her mother—as always—was right. She did "grow out of it," and the last episode was after her mother died. Until recently. Maybe being back here was what triggered them. But what would account for the episodes before she arrived?

She dragged in a shaky breath as she dried her hands on the black-and-white striped towel. What she needed was a good night's sleep. The strain of the day was playing tricks on her. She was stressed and tired. That's all.

. . .

The morning brought with it a fairy-tale world of winter white so brilliant that it lit the overcast sky.

Alessandra stretched beneath the soft cotton sheets, blinked against the light spilling through the curtains, and realized that what had awakened her was the sound of a running motor. She tossed the floral-patterned quilt aside and got out of bed. She went to her window, which faced the front yard, and lifted the curtain.

She squinted against the glare that bounced off the crystal-white snow. *Zach.*

Her head jerked back in surprise even as a smile curved her mouth. For a moment, she allowed herself the fantasy that this was nothing unusual at all, that Zach outside her home barely after sunrise was an experience that was expected because he belonged there as much as she did.

No! She blinked. Stepped back from the window.

She turned away, went into the bathroom, and splashed water on her face. After a quick freshening up, she dressed in a navy sweatshirt, matching sweatpants, and her boots. She grabbed her coat and her Nikon camera on the way out the door.

She cupped her hand over her eyes against the glare of the sun bouncing off the snow, then took a quick set of candid shots in rapid succession. She lowered her camera. "Morning," she called out from the top of the porch.

Zach cut the motor on the snowblower, then wiped his forehead with the back of his gloved hand and looked up.

Snap. Snap.

"Morning. Sorry if the noise woke you." He lifted his chin toward the camera in her hand. "Capturing the moment?" he asked with a grin. "Am I gonna be famous?"

"Maybe." Alessandra walked down the salted steps toward the smile that beckoned her. She stopped halfway along the path where Zach met her. "One of the kids would have done this," she said in mock reprimand, then folded her arms in front of her to ward off a frigid blast of wind. "I thought we agreed."

"Oh you did, did you?" He chuckled. "I tend to take care of things that look like they need taking care of. When you get to know me—"

Alessandra's breath hung in her chest.

"It won't bother you half as much." He smiled, and his dark eyes crinkled at the corners.

She swallowed. "Oh, so you're assuming that I'm going to 'get to know you.'"

He leaned his head slightly to the side and studied her from beneath those thick, dark lashes. He ran the tip of his tongue along his bottom lip. "Well," he gave a light shrug, "to paraphrase the famous words of Zora Neale Hurston, 'I can't understand why anyone would deny themselves the pleasure of my company.'"

She laughed. "Music, food, literature, yard work—a regular Renaissance man."

He winked. "I can get with that."

She shook her head. "Well, the least I can do is offer you some coffee. Come on inside."

"Yes, ma'am."

She turned toward the house and tucked in a smile.

"Have you had breakfast yet?" She hung up her coat, then eased out of her boots and walked to the kitchen. Zach did the same.

"No, actually I haven't," he said, following her into the sun-drenched space.

"In eternal gratitude for plowing me out from under, I will whip us up a full breakfast." She took a bow.

"Anything I can do?"

"Nope. I got this." She walked over to the fridge and pulled it open. She stood there for a couple of minutes, willing the near-barren interior to magically bloom with everything needed for a fancy breakfast.

No time to stop. They catch my scent if I stop. Got to eat along the way. Just got to stay low and small til I can find my way home.

"Everything okay?"

Alessandra blinked. Her heart pounded like racing feet. She gripped the handle of the refrigerator door and closed her eyes, swallowed. "Uh, yeah." She took out the three lonely eggs, then pulled open one of the vegetable trays and found half a tomato, a slice of onion, and a green pepper. There was a small package of cheddar cheese that was just enough to make a difference. *Plenty*. Her body jerked.

Zach came to her side. "Let me help."

She ran her tongue across dry lips, glanced away. "Uh... since you insist." She forced a smile. "You can get the coffee going. I could definitely use a cup."

"Coming right up."

As she placed the omelet items on the counter, she watched Zach from the corner of her eye. He moved his long, athletic body with a comfortable ease around her father's kitchen—*her* kitchen. He knew where the coffee can was, the filters, the mugs. There was that tight knot in her stomach again. She still wasn't sure if she appreciated Zach or resented his familiarity.

She opened an overhead cabinet to look for a mixing bowl.

"The one to the left," Zach offered as he scooped coffee grounds into the filter.

Alessandra slid him a look. "I knew that," she snapped. She pulled the cabinet open, then took out the bowl and shut it with a bit more force than necessary. *Now he can read my mind, too*?

"Planning on going to see your father after breakfast?" He moved next to her, turned on the water, and filled the coffee carafe.

She held her breath until he moved away to pour the water into the coffee maker. "Yes." She rinsed the pepper and placed it on a plate with the onion.

"I can drive you again. I'd like to drop in and say hello to Jerry. If that's cool with you."

She turned toward him, planted her hand on her hip. She squinted. "Don't you have to go to work...or anything?"

"I make my own hours."

She studied him for a moment and tried to remember if he'd mentioned what he did for a living. "What is it that you do again—besides this and that?" She diced the green pepper, onion, tomato, and the slices of cheese, then cracked the eggs into the bowl.

"I study communities."

She angled her head toward him and frowned. "What does that mean?"

"I'm an anthropologist. Ethnography is my specialty." He gave a slight shrug of his right shoulder, then looked her in the eyes. "I travel around the world to study communities, tribes, families. I interview people and chronicle history. Tell the stories of forgotten people."

Alessandra's brows rose. "Ohhh, okay. That sounds… amazing," she said in a hushed kind of admiration. Her photographic eye visualized the faces, snapped pictures of the hills and valleys, coves and tiny obscure villages, family reunions. *Snap, snap.*

"Is this ethnography something you do on your own, or is it like a real job?"

Zach laughed, and she glimpsed that hint of a dimple in his right cheek again. "Yeah, it's a real job. I'm contracted with the Smithsonian in DC, but I do take on private projects from time to time."

Alessandra turned her attention to the ingredients in the bowl. Zach reached above her and grabbed the skillet from the hook on the rack, moved behind her to open the fridge. He took out the tub of butter and added a dollop, then turned the flame on low.

Alessandra watched the flame grow brighter, but it was the inexplicable heat of Zach's nearness that was as sensual as it was disturbing. The fork she held clattered to the floor.

Zach bent to pick it up, tossed it into the sink. "You okay?" he asked quietly. He lightly put his hand on her shoulder.

"Alessandra…"

Her gaze rose to meet his. She dragged in a short, shaky breath. "S-sorry," she sputtered. "Um, was lost in thought." She forced a smile.

"About your dad?"

"Yes," she said almost too quickly. "He told me we needed to talk," she managed. "Just didn't like the sound of that."

"Try not to worry. The truth is, you two do need to talk at some point."

"What's that supposed to mean?" She snatched a clean fork from the drawer and whipped the eggs into submission.

"Only means what I said. Been a long time. Stands to

reason…" He let the rest hang in the air.

She studied him while she continued to stir the eggs but didn't respond. Zach Renard was…was standing too damned close to her.

He gently clasped her wrist to cease her egg-beating. "Why don't you let me finish this up? Have a seat. The coffee is almost done, and I've been told I'm a master with tossing some eggs in a frying pan."

"Sure. Be my guest," she conceded, giving her the excuse she needed to get away from him.

Mindlessly, she walked to the kitchen table and sat down, still caught up in the residue of confusing sensations.

Zach placed a mug of coffee in front of her. Her eyes rose to land on the concern in his.

"Wanna talk about it?"

She shook her head. Where would she even begin, anyway? As much as she felt in her soul that she knew Zach Renard, in reality she didn't. She didn't need him thinking she was some charity case who required taking care of—as much as she inexplicably wanted him to take care of her.

"I'll be fine." She forced a smile and wrapped her hands around the mug of coffee. She lifted it and took a sip. Perfect. *Figures*.

Moments later, Zach set a plate with half of a perfect omelet, accompanied by a single slice of just-right toast in front of her.

"Thanks."

Zach sat opposite her, and she noticed the tapered hairline and the perfect short, silken twists that gave him an urban-chic vibe.

"How'd you sleep after being back here for the first time in so long?" He forked some eggs into his mouth and chewed.

"Actually, I slept well." Her brow tightened at the

realization. "Best sleep I've had in months, to be honest."

"Hmm, even though your return wasn't for the best of reasons, it seems to have a bit of a benefit."

"I guess." She bobbed her head in agreement. She took a bite of toast. "Your grandmother…has she always lived across the street?" She dug into her memory, trying to remember a "Renard."

"Yep. For as long as I've known her." He winked. "Why?"

"Renard…I don't remember the name."

"Oh, my grandmother's last name is Oweku."

Alessandra's eyes widened in recognition. "Mrs. O!"

Zach chuckled. "Yep. That's her."

"Wow. I remember." She bobbed her head and squinted as she spoke, as if to bring the image into focus. "She and my mom would talk from time to time, from what I can recall," she said slowly, reaching for the memories. "I'd see her sitting on the porch every now and then. Always with a book in her hand."

"Sounds about right."

"How is she?"

"Probably outlive us all," he said, his voice laced with amusement.

"Hmm." She finished off her breakfast and washed it down with coffee. She pushed back from the table and took her plate and Zach's to the sink. "More coffee?" she asked from over her shoulder.

"No. I'm good, thanks." He scooted the chair back and stood. "I better get out there. Car still needs to be dug out." He paused a moment. "Or the offer to drive you still stands."

"Um." She turned to face him, considered declining. "I'd like that. If you don't mind," she said, surprising herself. "But I'm sure you have other things to do beside run me around town," she quickly added to offer him a way out.

"I make time for the things I want to do."

Her heart thumped.

He checked his watch. "About an hour? I can come back for you then."

"Sounds good."

He gave a brief nod, grabbed his heavy coat from the back of the chair, and walked out.

Alessandra finally exhaled.

CHAPTER SIX

"So, tell me some more about this ethnography thing," Alessandra said as they drove along the silent road to the hospital. "How did you decide that's what you wanted to do?"

"Hmm. Bunch of reasons, I guess. I was always curious about stuff, worrying my folks to death with questions about everything. My grandmother was a kind of novice history buff, collectibles mostly."

He smiled wistfully. "I think I was about twelve going on thirty. Our class went on a trip into New York to the Natural History Museum. The evolution of humanity and what happened to the dinosaurs fascinated me. The little cards under the pictures only gave the minimum of information. But the one that totally caught my attention was a prehistoric family." His tone grew introspective.

"Something clicked, I guess, and I came to realize those were our ancestors. What stories could they tell about the times they lived in? What was it like? Humph." He half smiled. "Read everything I could get my hands on—and then, my senior year in high school, I was combing the shelves of the library and I found a collection of works by Zora Neale Hurston, mostly her nonfiction work, anthropology studies. She embodied everything I only imagined I could be." He shrugged. "Went to Howard for undergrad, Moorehouse for my master's, then Columbia University for my doctorate."

"Wait." She held up her hand and tipped her head to the side. "So you're *Dr.* Zach Renard?"

Zach chuckled, nonchalantly shrugged his left shoulder.

"Get. Outta. Here." She slapped her thigh and laughed.

"No biggie," he said with a grin.

"So says you. That's pretty major. I barely got my BFA."

"Photography was your discipline, right?"

Alessandra nodded. "Photographic journalism, to be specific."

"So, how have you applied your book learnin'?" he asked, his tone teasing. "I see you don't go far without your camera." He nodded toward her bag.

"There are images everywhere. Never know when the shot will appear. I wish I could say I have a lot more shots than I have, but…"

"But what?"

"I had dreams of bringing back the whole *Life Magazine* vibe." She laughed. "So much for dreams, right?"

"'What happens to a dream deferred?

> Does it dry up
> like a raisin in the sun?
> Or fester like a sore—
> And then run?
> Does it stink like rotten meat?
> Or crust and sugar over—
> like a syrupy sweet?
> Maybe it just sags

like a heavy load.
Or does it explode?'"

He turned to her and winked.

"Langston Hughes," they said in harmony.

"You *are* full of surprises," Alessandra said.

"I fancied myself a poet at one point in my life," he said with a very bad British accent. "Wasn't much good at it, though." He shrugged. "Too analytical, I guess. Not much creative juice flowing through these veins."

Alessandra had a flash of strong sinewy muscle that rippled when he moved. She shifted in her seat.

"Anyway, you were telling me about your photography."

"It's been a struggle, although things have gotten better over the past few years. I started out freelancing, mostly, and that had its pros and cons. I mean, I could pick my assignments, but they weren't always regular. And living in New York City," she blew out a breath, "is beyond expensive, but I love it there. The vibe, the twenty-four-hour everything," she said, laughing. "Then I met Steven James, a gallery owner. He liked my work and offered me a job as curator at his gallery. Nothing like having a steady paycheck, but I did miss my autonomy."

"What's your specialty?"

"Hmm, most of my work is urban, candid shots of humanity at work, but I really enjoy capturing moments, ya know? I've traveled around the country during one tense Black moment or another. Literally." She snorted derisively. "That list is long."

"Isn't it always," Zach murmured in agreement.

"What I'd truly like to do sometime is travel—to Africa. See the real history." She sighed. "I went to quite a few of the protests the year that George Floyd was murdered. Breonna Taylor, Ahmaud Arbery..." Her voice trailed off. "I have stacks of images of the crowds, the faces, the passion, the history in their eyes. And a complete collection of still photography of empty Times Square, Penn Station, the streets of Manhattan during the pandemic."

"What did you do with them?"

"They're in boxes at my apartment in the city."

"Dreams deferred," he intoned, and gave her a sidelong glance.

"Not entirely," she slowly admitted. "I'm actually preparing for my first solo show in a little under six weeks." She paused.

"Really? That's great."

"It should be. This will sound crass, but my dad being in the hospital is stressful in more ways than one. I was already having a hard time trying to figure out what to include in the exhibit. This is my big break, what I've been working for. The gallery owner and manager, Steven, really wants me to come back sooner rather than later."

"Hmm. That's a decision only you can make."

She sighed.

"I could show you some of the photos I have of my trips," Zach said, drawing her back. "I promised myself that by the time I'm forty, I want to have visited each of the African countries."

"That's ambitious. How much time do you have?"

"Five years." He grinned.

Seven years separated them. *No wonder he comes off as more...settled.*

"I know my photos aren't as good as yours. No one ever offered me an exhibit," he teased, "but—if you're interested."

Her mouth lifted into a smile. "Definitely."

• • •

Jeremiah's eyes were closed when Alessandra and Zach entered. His chest rose and fell in a slow, regular rhythm. The *beep* of the machine monitoring his vital signs kept the beat. He moaned softly.

Alessandra took slow steps toward his bed until she was at his side. "Dad?" she said quietly.

His eyelids fluttered. His gaze slowly focused. "Ali."

"Hey," she said softly. "How are you feeling today?" When they'd checked in, the nurse said her father had had a tough night, but he was on more pain medication now.

"Hmm," he murmured. "Better. They fixed me right up though," he said, his words coming like molasses, thick and slow.

Alessandra lightly squeezed his arm. "Zach's here to see you." She stepped aside to let Zach enter Jeremiah's frame of vision.

"Hey there, son. I see you found my little girl."

Zach chuckled. "Something like that. Good to see you, Jerry. Got to get you well and out of here."

"So I can beat you at the next game of checkers."

"Aw, you know I let you win, right?"

"Ha! You wish."

The two men chuckled.

Watching the brief but warm exchange between them, Alessandra realized how misplaced her annoyance with Zach was. He was a decent guy who seemed to really care about her father, and her father cared about him. *And* he was *fine…*

She lifted her camera from the case, adjusted the lens, and took several rapid shots of the two of them laughing and teasing each other. The smile on her father's lips and the light in his eyes made him look years younger. She lowered her camera for a moment, studied the scene without the benefit of a close-up lens. Zach had done that for him. Something warm shifted in her center.

Jeremiah's eyes drifted closed, then opened. "Need you to go through the papers, Ali," he was saying, seeming to forget that Zach was right there. "Everything is taken care of. Everything you need to know."

Alessandra drew closer, frowned. "What papers, Dad?"

His lips moved, but he was only mumbling at first. "Hmm, you can ask your mother. She'll know," he finally said.

Alessandra's heart nearly stopped. "Mom? Dad, Mom's—"

"The papers. Hmm. Those are important. Take care of it." He let out a long moan. The skin on his face tightened.

Alessandra gently gripped his arm, her heart racing in an erratic beat. She'd never seen him like this before, a look of fear and vulnerability in his eyes. "I'll call the nurse," she said urgently and pressed the call button on the side of the bed. She patted his shoulder and forced herself to breathe.

Moments later, the nurse came in. "Everything okay?"

"I don't know. He started telling me to talk to my mother, who's been dead nearly fifteen years, and then he started moaning in pain."

The nurse came around to the side of the bed and checked the tubes that dispensed the pain medication. "I'll speak to the doctor and see if she wants to make any adjustments." She offered Alessandra a sympathetic look. "Sometimes the pain medications…make the patient a little confused."

Alessandra nodded.

"Let your dad get some rest. I'll be sure the doctor sees him."

"Thank you." She sighed and gave her father one last look. Satisfied that he seemed to have settled, she gathered her purse and walked alongside Zach out of the room and toward the elevator.

"You okay?" Zach asked quietly.

"I don't even know where to search for papers or what to do with them if I found them," she mumbled, frustrated and confused. She swung her face toward him. "He talked about my mother as if…"

The elevator doors slid open. "It's the meds, like the nurse said," Zach offered. "Tomorrow will be better."

· · ·

When she got back to the house and finally checked her messages, there was one from Steven, wanting to know when she planned to return and continue curating the photographs for her exhibit. He ended his message with a reminder of how much this show would mean to her career and of all that he'd done to make it happen.

She flopped down onto a side chair in the living room and closed her eyes. Her show was less than six weeks away. She had tons of photos but no plan, no vision for how to make a story out of them. She needed to go home, but she couldn't leave. Not yet. Frustration burned her eyes. She tugged on her bottom lip with her teeth.

Her cell phone chimed in her palm. She looked at the screen. Traci. She pressed the green talk icon.

"Hey girl."

"You could sound more enthusiastic," Traci drawled. "How's your dad?"

Alessandra recounted the visits with her father, his cryptic comments, and his reference to her mother.

"Damn. Well, he's been through a lot, and it's probably like the nurse said, the meds can play tricks on the patient, ya know."

"Yeah," she said absently.

"What else is going on?"

"Got not one but three calls from Steven about the exhibit."

Traci let out an expletive. "What are you going to do?"

"If it was as simple as just coming back into the city and showing him what I planned to put up, that would be easy. But I don't have a clue. I've been paralyzed ever since Steven told me he would sponsor an exhibit of my work. It was messy before I left, but now with my dad…" She let her thought trail off.

"Sounds like self-sabotage, sis. The old imposter syndrome. There's a niggling part of you that doesn't believe you deserve this."

She sighed. "Maybe. Probably." She frowned. "I *do* want my work to say something. Sure, I've taken some amazing photographs—individually. But as a whole, it's just a jumble of pictures. Now I can't even concentrate, and I can't dance around Steven much longer." Her stomach knotted with dread. "I could blow it all. Everything that I worked for— wanted."

"You're not going to blow it. You'll figure it out. Besides, I want to be the one to write the exclusive article on your artistic debut."

Alessandra snorted a laugh. "I hope not to disappoint you."

"You won't, and you won't disappoint yourself either. You got blackgirlmagic, sis. You can do this. I'll be praying for your dad."

"Thanks."

"Hey, listen, the other reason for my call is that I did a bit of digging on Zach Renard."

Her heart thumped. "Why?"

"'Cause my girl is out there with some strange man and

I want to know who he is. Besides, like I said, the name sounded familiar."

"Anndddd?" she sang the word. Traci had a habit of burying the lede, as they said in her field of journalism, and she definitely made a short story long.

"Girl, Zach Renard, *Dr.* Zach Renard is one of the premiere anthropologists in the world. But that's nothing. I mean it's something, but his other claim to fame is the international list of women he's been connected to in pursuit of his research. In other words, the boy next door is an international playboy with degrees up the ying-yang. Oh, and I've seen pictures. The brother is fine."

Alessandra didn't know if she should laugh, cry, or be worried by Traci's news report. She opted for option four: not to worry about it. She'd come back home for a reason, and it wasn't to get involved with some man. "Thanks for the update, sis."

"Anytime. Just be careful. As notorious as he is for his work, he's equally as notorious for leaving broken hearts behind."

"Humph, that's comforting. Anyway, gotta run."

"Talk soon. If you need me in the meantime, just call."

"I will. Bye." She dropped the phone in her lap and let her head loll back.

Playboy? Broken hearts? String of women? She stared up at the ceiling. None of that jibed with what she'd seen of Zach Renard. But maybe that was the lure. At least now that she was aware, she'd be sure not to let that smile, dark eyes, and helpful hand get her mind all twisted.

She picked up her camera from the table and checked the shots she'd taken at the hospital. Seeing Zach with her father did not translate into the picture that the rest of the world saw of him. But hey, what did she know—and why should she care? She was here for her father. That's it.

Her father's words about "looking for papers" rolled through her head. It would help if she knew what papers he was talking about. But him mentioning her mother as if she was in the next room was what really freaked her out.

She pushed up from the chair and went to collect the plastic bag with her father's belongings. She slid open the bag and pulled out his boots and put them in the hall closet, then hung up his fleece coat and took out his pants and shirt. She checked the pockets before taking them to the laundry room and removed some crumpled receipts, two single dollars, and a loose key.

She turned the key in her hand. It was definitely old and slightly rusted. She shrugged; it was probably from his hardware store. She tossed it into the bowl on the table by the door before heading off to do laundry.

. . .

Before she knew it, she'd been back for more than a week. Most of her hospital visits barely lasted more than a few minutes before her father drifted off. Anytime she asked about which papers to look for, he'd wave off the question and ask her to find out what was on the menu for lunch or dinner, depending on the time of day. She stopped asking, figuring that maybe it was the meds that had had him talking that day.

He seemed to be stable now. They'd adjusted his meds. Maybe she could run back to Manhattan for a couple of days and get some work done—she bit down on her thumbnail— and if anything came up while she was gone, Zach was around.

Zach. She exhaled. He certainly made being back in Sag

Harbor more than bearable. She'd grudgingly begun to look forward to seeing him each day, even if only for a few minutes.

Zach had a calming presence. When her thoughts were scattered all over the place, he was able to help her see a path forward. She guessed it was because his work required direction and organization and the ability to look at a big picture and recognize all the pieces that made it whole. When Zach was around and she experienced an "episode," they didn't seem as frightening—and that was a problem for her. The more time she spent in his company, the more he didn't seem like the kind of man Traci had told her about. *Part of the charm, part of the charm*, she reminded herself.

She'd driven herself to the hospital today, beginning to feel that—although he didn't say anything—she was taking advantage of Zach's generosity and leaning on him a little too much. Something that she never liked to do. Besides, she couldn't imagine that the only thing he had to do with his free time was shuttle her back and forth like a car service. Needing other people was not her thing. When you did, you lost.

Now that she was a regular face at the hospital, she didn't stop by the nurses' station when she arrived, but breezed by and went straight to her father's room. When she pushed the door open, she gasped in alarm. Her heart banged in her chest. Her gaze raced around the room, trying to make sense of what she *wasn't* seeing.

She whirled away and ran back down the hall to the nurses' station. Breathless with fear, she pressed her fingertips into the countertop. Unimaginable scenarios played in her head. She leaned so far across the counter that she was practically on the other side.

"My father! My father, Jeremiah Fleming. Where is he?" Her voice cracked. Her frantic gaze swept the space.

One nurse turned away from the computer monitor, rose from her swivel chair, and came over to Alessandra. Her voice was low and calm. "Your father was taken down to X-ray, Ms. Fleming," she said in the pace and tone one would use with an agitated child. "He should be coming back up shortly. You're welcome to wait in his room if you want, or in the lounge."

Alessandra felt a tremor of relief flow through her, so palpable that she almost cried.

She swallowed. "Thank you," she managed. Dragging in a breath, she turned and walked back down the hall.

She leaned her elbow on the arm of the chair and rested her chin on her fist. The thought of losing her father… A shudder rippled along her spine and opened a hole in her center that she had not expected. She'd just gotten him back. There was still so much for them to talk about, to remember and fix.

She shook her head, tossing the disturbing feelings away. She turned her focus toward the window that looked out onto the snow-covered treetops, and her thoughts drifted back to Zach Renard. She felt that if she told him what had been going on with her over the past few weeks, he would understand. But she wasn't quite ready to cross that line yet, especially since she wasn't sure what *was* happening to her—real or imagined. Besides, she and Zach were ships passing in the night, heading in opposite directions.

The door opened, and an orderly pushed the bed carrying her father into the room.

Seeing him was like sitting in front of a warm fire. "Dad," she said on a breath.

The orderly wheeled the bed into place, locked the brakes, then checked the monitoring machine. Done, he gave Alessandra a brief nod and walked out.

Alessandra came to the side of the bed.

Jeremiah reached out and patted her hand where it gripped the bed rail. He smiled lovingly. "It's so good to see you every day, Ali," he said almost wistfully. "I got a confession to make." He paused, glanced away, then looked at his daughter. "I guess I've been dragging things out because I figured once I told you everything, you wouldn't have no reason to hang around."

"Dad…" She didn't know whether to feel comforted that he wanted her here every day or annoyed that he'd been stringing her along when she had a life back in New York that she'd abandoned.

"Some things I need to tell you."

"It c-can wait," she sputtered, in a combination of wanting and not wanting to know.

"No. Can't wait. Done waited too long as is."

She held his hand, and her soul ached. She was a little girl again, holding on to her daddy as they walked into town for ice cream, sitting on his lap asking questions about the music he was playing or the book he was reading. Her throat clenched. When had that all ended?

"I could have done better as a father after your mother passed. I know you think I blame you for what happened. Maybe in the beginning, I did. Had to blame someone." His chest heaved. "Wasn't never your fault. You got to understand and believe that."

"Dad, I—"

"Hush. Listen. I realized too late that the reason I was so hard on you about everything, especially about you leaving, was…because I couldn't stand the thought of losing you, too." His water-filled eyes stared into hers. "I'm sorry, baby girl. You got to forgive me."

"Dad—dy." Her voice cracked. "I shouldn't have stayed

away. I was just so…"

"I know." He patted her hand. "I know. And it's all right," he crooned. "It's all right. You're here now, and you can set everything straight."

"What do you mean?" She leaned closer, held his hand a bit tighter. He had to tell her—today. Now.

Jeremiah dragged in a shaky breath. "Your mama decided when you were just a baby that she would do whatever she needed to protect you from the world, from the hurt out there. From all the ugly we'd lived through." He took a breath. "I didn't always agree. Felt it was important to understand where you belong in the world. Acting as if the past don't exist don't make it less real; putting it behind ya don't make it go away. Your mama didn't agree." His eyes fluttered closed.

Alessandra stiffened, Ms. Edith's words coming from her father, too. Jeremiah tightened his grip on her hand.

"She started to kinda come to terms with it, realized it wasn't fair to you cause it was startin' to make you 'uppity,' as the folks used to say." He chuckled. Coughed. "After we lost her, I pretty much didn't care. Nothing seemed important. It was a struggle getting from one day to the next, never mind looking backward." He coughed again. Sighed.

"I'm so sorry, Daddy," she said in a broken whisper. She laid her head on his chest the way she used to when she was a little girl and scared. The sound of his steady heartbeat always soothed her. His description of her mother, she now understood all too well. Alessandra'd had that same uppity, entitled attitude as her mother. It was the thing that drove her to ignore her father's wisdom the night of that party.

Besides, what was more important; listening to her inner voice or having her way? She'd opted for having her way and lost her mother in the process.

"Your mama and me, we didn't always agree on how to

raise you. I think I let her have her way 'cause I loved her so much, wanted her happy, wanted *you* happy. I understood your mama." His chest shuddered. "She was terrified."

Alessandra lifted her head and looked into her father's eyes. "Terrified? Of what?"

He patted her shoulder, lowered her head back to his chest. "Terrified that if she wasn't the picture of the 'new Negro,' the one accepted by white folk, that she'd wind up like her parents, and their parents—struggling, poor, discarded, dying of heartache and body-breaking work. For your mama, there was no in-between." He paused. "And terrified of the dreams." The words hung in the air between them. He slowly shook his head. His brows creased. "Visions," he murmured, more of a question than a statement.

"Dreams?" Her heart thumped. *Visions?* All kinds of impossibilities ran through her mind.

"She'd wake up shaking and crying, soaking wet. Said she was there, back there. Men were after her. Water. Fire. Whips." He sighed. "Her mama and her mama's mama used to have them, too. Rumor was your mama's people could see all the way back to where we'd come from." He snorted a laugh. "Your mother didn't want no part of it. None. She figured that if she could bury it down, never talk about it, then somehow it wouldn't get passed on to you."

Alessandra's mind swirled. She tried to make sense of what her father was telling her. Her mother? Her picture-perfect mother?

"After you left, I picked up where your mama left off."

"What do you mean, where Mama left off? You had dreams too?"

His eyelids fluttered and closed. "Everything you need is right there in the house," he said faintly.

She stayed, with her head against the beat of his heart,

until she heard his breathing grow even and knew that he was drifting to sleep.

"All there," he murmured again. "Been saving it just for you."

CHAPTER SEVEN

Glass of wine in hand, Alessandra sauntered into the living room, went to the stereo, and put on Billie Holiday. The haunting refrain of the iconic *Strange Fruit* floated into the air. She sipped her wine, let the music and her father's revelations flow through her.

She wanted to dismiss it all as ramblings from the drugs that he was being given for the pain. But deep in her heart, she believed him. Needed to believe him so that she could begin to forgive him—and herself.

She'd do as he'd asked, look for what he'd left her in the house. But not tonight. She'd tackle that in the morning. She pushed up from the chair with the intention of fixing something for dinner when her cell phone rang. She picked it up from the end table and frowned at the unfamiliar number.

"Hello?"

"Ms. Fleming."

"Yes?"

"This is St. John's Hospital. Dr. Clarke asked that you come as soon as possible."

Her heart started racing. Her ears pounded. "What happened?"

"Please, Ms. Fleming. That's all I can discuss. The doctor will talk with you when you arrive."

"I'll… I'll be right there."

Her heart beat so hard and fast she couldn't catch her breath. She turned in a circle before she could gather her bearings, then grabbed her coat and bag and ran to the door, snatching up her father's car keys from the bowl on the hallway table. She darted to the car, which was once again covered in a light dusting of snow. It took her shaky hands three tries before she could get the key in the lock, only to discover that it was frozen.

Tears sprang to her eyes as she whirled around. The lights at Mrs. O's house were on.

She ran across the street and down the block. The cold wind whipped against her face. *Run. Don't stop. Run.* The inexplicable terror of being chased propelled her, kept her on her feet when she hit a patch of ice and nearly went down face-first.

She reached Mrs. O's door and ran up the three steps. She knocked. Pressed the bell. Knocked.

The door swung inward.

"I'm sorry to bother you—"

"Alessandra," Mrs. O said. "I'd recognize you anywhere… What's wrong, chile? Is it your father?"

Alessandra was shaking all over. "Y-yes," she stammered. "The hospital called. They said to come right away. I…the car…the lock on the car is frozen—"

"Zach!" Mrs. O called out. "Zach!"

His heavy footfalls could be heard on the steps. He appeared behind Mrs. O, a pair of very expensive headphones hung around his neck. He stepped around his grandmother.

"Hey." His brow creased. "What is it?"

"My dad," she croaked.

"Let me get my coat." He snatched his coat from the hook on the wall by the door and jammed his feet into his Timberlands. He gave his grandmother a quick kiss on the cheek, grabbed Alessandra's hand, and hurried to his SUV.

. . .

As the doctor spoke in the low, measured tones that were always the prelude to bad news on all the hospital dramas, Alessandra didn't even realize she'd gripped Zach's hand or that his whispered words: *Everything will be all right. I'm right here for you,* were the only things that kept her from falling. Her temples throbbed and the swirling in her stomach just wouldn't stop as the doctor's voice droned on. She blinked and blinked, but she was still there.

It was sudden, the doctor said. A massive heart attack. They did all they could, but…

The next few hours were surreal. Alessandra went through the motions, nodded as if she understood what was being said, and signed where they told her to sign. She was allowed into her father's room to say her goodbyes, and all she could do was weep uncontrollably and tell him how sorry she was over and over.

Zach finally peeled her away from her father's bedside. He held her tight against him, absorbing her shuddering sobs into his chest. He led her down the corridor onto the elevator and out to the car. He helped her into her seat and fastened her belt. He opened the door to the house with his key, eased her out of her coat and boots, led her up to her bedroom, and covered her with the heavy down quilt. Then he turned out the light and waited.

...

Morning arrived gray and unyielding, holding the day in an icy grip. Alessandra moaned, blinked against the dull light that filtered through the blinds. Her body ached. Her head throbbed. Why did she feel so awful? Maybe she was coming down with something—and then she remembered, and the cold reached deep inside of her and squeezed. She whimpered against the pain.

A rustling from the far side of the room startled her. She jerked up to see Zach rising from his post in the club chair by the window.

"Hey," he said gently. He unwrapped himself from the quilt he'd grabbed from the linen closet and walked over to her.

She looked up at him, confused. "What... What time is it?"

"Eight."

"In the morning?"

"Yeah."

She blinked against the graininess in her eyes. "You... were here all night?"

"Didn't think you should be alone. In case you woke up and needed me...needed something, I mean."

She pushed away the locs that danced around her face like ripples on a dark river and twisted them at the base of her neck. "Thank you," she whispered. "You didn't have to."

He ignored her protest and sat down on the side of the bed. "How are you feeling?"

She dragged in a long breath. "I wish I knew. I can't put it into words. I guess if my feelings were a photograph, it would be a dark empty space." She tried to smile and failed. Her eyes filled. She sniffed and turned her face away.

"I understand. I lost both of my parents."

She turned back to him, feeling her eyes widen. "Oh, I'm sorry. I didn't know."

"It was a long time ago." He stood. "I took a chance and darted out to my grandmother's house last night while you were asleep and brought over some food. Good thing, too. News said all the roads are closed. There was an ice storm overnight. Trees are down; we're lucky we have electricity. I'll fix breakfast and some strong coffee. Okay?"

She nodded, then wrapped her arms around her knees and rested her chin on them. The day before came back to her in waves. There were blind spots, though, things she simply did not remember, like how she got home or into bed. Clearly Zach had brought her here, but it was all a blur. The last thing she remembered clearly was sitting at her father's bedside asking for his forgiveness. And his words: *Everything you need is right there in the house.*

But what did that mean? Now she might never know.

She sighed deeply. Now what? She didn't have a damned clue. How was she supposed to handle everything? She had no parents to guide her. No family at all. She sniffed and blinked back a fresh flow of tears. All she wanted to do was burrow under the quilt and just sleep.

The sound of pots banging and water running tugged her out of her malaise. With great effort, she put her feet on the floor and stood. Her entire body revolted. She groaned, arched her back, and slowly turned her head left and right, heard it creak like an old door that needed oil. She took her robe from the foot of the bed. A shower wouldn't cure a damned thing, but at least she'd be clean.

She opened her bedroom door and stepped out into the night, stumbled over the long ragged skirt that wrapped around her legs, throwing her onto her hands and knees. *Get up. Get up.* The scent of seawater filled her nostrils.

"Hey, you okay up there?"

Alessandra crawled to the bathroom, reached for the knob, and pulled herself to her feet. She pressed her forehead against the frame of the door.

"Alessandra, are you all right? I heard something fall."

She turned, and Zach was standing there. She buried her face in his chest.

Alessandra and Zach sat side by side on the living room couch, with Alessandra wrapped tight in a blanket and Zach's arm looped around her as she periodically shivered against him.

He reached next to him on the coffee table. "Here, drink this." He held out a mug of chamomile tea. "It'll help." He set her breakfast plate on the table.

She side-eyed him with skepticism. Her hands poked out from beneath the blanket and took the mug by the handle. "Thanks," she murmured.

She closed her eyes and let the wafting steam bathe her face. She took a sip and gave in to the soothing heat that slid down her throat and spread through her belly.

"You wanna talk about it?" Zach gingerly probed.

Alessandra took another sip, sighed. "I'm not even sure what to say, or where to begin." She glanced at him with wide, sad eyes and slowly shook her head.

"Try starting with what happened this morning."

She pushed out a long breath, eyed him for a moment, the remnants of Traci's intel floating in her head. But exhaustion and simply needing a listening ear won. "You're totally going to think I'm bonkers."

"I'm a pretty good judge of character." He smiled. "And you may be a lot of things, Ms. Fleming, but I don't get the bonkers vibe."

Alessandra actually smiled and took another swallow of tea. "Okay...so...I got up to take a shower, and when I stepped out into the hallway...it was like I was someplace else. Like I was some*one* else. It was dark and I felt terrified." She drew a shaky breath and frowned. "For a second, I swear I could smell seawater. And then it was over." She shook her head and shivered, turned and looked at him. "See? Bonkers."

Zach studied her anguished expression. "Sounds to me like your mind, body, and spirit are trying to process your loss, Alessandra. The mind is an amazing organ and will do what it needs to in order to protect you."

Alessandra pursed her lips. "I suppose." She glanced at him. "Makes more sense than to think I'm hallucinating." She was thoughtful for a moment. "Ever since I was a kid, though...I felt things."

She swallowed, glanced warily at Zach, then looked away. "Sometimes I could feel someone's hurt or joy or sense something was going to happen—even if I didn't know what it was." Her brows tightened. "I would tell my mom whenever I was feeling *funny*, as I called it. But my mother would tell me not to let that foolishness get the best of me, and that when I started to feel those feelings I was to put them and the people that brought them on out of my mind."

She licked her lips. "It was hard trying not to feel, to connect with other people...but over time, I did. I put a lid on it. I guess that's why it's been hard for me to stay in relationships. The idea of connecting runs me off. The fact that my only friend Traci has stuck around as long as she has is an anomaly." She sputtered a broken laugh, dragged in a breath, and exhaled. "But...*it* started again—right before I left Manhattan—and got more intense when I came back here. Flashes of images, scents, dreams."

"Lot of sudden life changes, maybe," Zach consoled. "Sometimes we get overwhelmed by emotions and they come out in different ways. You did say you were struggling with what to do about your exhibit," he offered by way of an explanation.

Alessandra slid him another side-eye. "Only thing that makes sense of the senseless, I suppose." She stared into her cup of tea. "Besides my mom and Traci, you're the only person I've ever said anything to about it," she confessed.

Zach regarded her for a long moment, then gently squeezed her shoulder. "Thank you for trusting me. I won't ever dishonor that."

He stood. "Try to eat something," he said, lifting his chin toward the plate. "I have some things I need to take care of. I'll come back later to check on you." He looked into her upturned face. "You'll need to make plans," he said softly.

She swallowed. "I know." She gave him a tight-lipped smile, then he grabbed his coat and left.

Alessandra sighed and reached for her plate on the coffee table. She pushed the eggs and hash browns around, then took a forkful and realized just how hungry she was.

Plans. Her heart jumped. She didn't know where to begin or what to do. Her throat clenched. When her mom passed, her dad had taken care of the details. All she was good for back then was tears and heavy doses of guilt. She bit down on her bottom lip. *Plans.*

She closed her eyes for a moment, tried to think.

We wait till dark. When dey sleep. More of us den dem.

Alessandra's eyes flew open. She gripped the arm of the couch, glanced around as if expecting someone to be there. The smells of dank wood and seawater filled her nostrils.

She leaped up from the couch as her heart pounded, nearly knocking over her plate. She blinked rapidly and tried to get a grip on what she'd heard—or thought she'd heard—but it was like steam.

Fragile. There and then not.

CHAPTER EIGHT

Alessandra pressed the heels of her palms into her eyes. She should at least call Traci and let her know what had happened. But who she wound up calling was Ms. Edith.

"Oh, chile, I am so sorry. So sorry," Ms. Edith soothed through the phone.

"Thank you." Alessandra exhaled a long breath. "My head is just a mess. Can't think straight."

"I'm sure it is. I know it's not easy. But I'm glad of one thing: you got to see your daddy before he made his transition. That's a good thing. May not feel like it right now, but it is."

"I'm glad, too. I wish I'd had more time to talk with him, smooth things over. I just feel like there was so much that still needed to be said."

Silence hung between them for a moment.

"What else is it, sweetheart?" Edith asked, seeming to sense Alessandra's distress.

Alessandra hesitated, debating on what and how much she should say. "Ms. Edith...ever since I got here, things have been happening to me. Well, not happening *to me* exactly, but I'm feeling things that I can't really explain." Her voice cracked.

There, she'd said it, and it was too late to take the words back.

"Things? What kinda things?" Edith asked, her tone soft and even.

"It's so hard to explain."

"I got all day. Try me."

After nearly an hour of fits and starts and backtracking and trying to make sense, Alessandra finally sighed in resignation. "That's it. I know it doesn't sound right. Does it?" she asked, the pitch of her voice tinged with hope. And now she'd confessed to Ms. Edith, her tight circle of secrecy was widening.

Ms. Edith blew out a long breath. "My great-grandma used to have what the old folks called 'spells.' Times when she was outside of herself."

"Oh, Ms. Edith, I—"

"Hush. Just listen. My great-grandma Yula was born into slavery in North Carolina. Worked in the cotton fields better part of her life. Story goes that from the time she could walk and talk, she was 'different.' She could tell when the weather was changing—would start crying and shaking. If someone was coming to visit the plantation, she'd pace and moan for hours. She'd take on other folks' sickness if she was around them.

"When she got older, she would set 'round and tell stories of things she couldn't know nothing about 'cause she wasn't there; like how our people got taken, and about the ones that fought back, or that the crop was gonna fail at the next plantation. Some even said that Yula could see the paths for escape that guided several slaves to the North, even though she'd never left the plantation.

"The few times I was with her…" Edith sighed. "I just got this warm, safe, trusting feeling. One time she told me how I'd leave home one day and travel far, and it would be hard but I would find a wonderful man who would love and take care of me until the day he died. And then she stared off like she was wont to do. 'His name be Charles,' she'd said. And it was." Edith sniffed. "That was the last time I saw her."

Alessandra got a slight chill. It was as if Ms. Edith was talking about her.

"What I'm saying is, my great-grandma 'sensed' things. She could feel the joy and pain of others, 'see' things that nobody else could see. Know stuff. My mama told me that Grandma Yula was born en caul, and family folklore claims that gave her the gift of sight."

Alessandra blinked back her surprise. Ms. Edith was her elder, and she wouldn't disrespect her by telling her that her mother had convinced her not to believe in none of that nonsense. But—

"I know you young people don't believe in all that. But sometimes…" Her voice softened. "There are things in this world that we simply can't explain. And not even that 'Google' thing can figure it out."

They both laughed. That much was true. Alessandra sighed a slow breath. "Thanks for telling me that, Ms. Edith."

Edith snickered. "I know you think I'm an old lady running my mouth, but every now and again there's some gems in all the sand I toss."

Alessandra smiled. "I'll keep that in mind, Ms. Edith."

"Now, you up there with the world on your shoulders. Give me the address."

"What?"

"The address to your daddy's house."

"Ms. Edith—"

"I know what you gonna say, 'You don't have to come here,'" she said in a high-pitched singsong tone. "And you'd be right. I don't have to. I want to. So let me. Let me."

Suddenly Alessandra's eyes filled with tears that ran hot down her cheeks. Her chest and throat tightened and ached. Now that her dad had transitioned, she was an orphan. *An orphan*. No parents, siblings, grandparents, aunts or uncles or cousins. She was totally alone in the world.

The enormity of it slammed against her with tidal-wave force, knocking the air and anguish out of her lungs, spilling out between her and Edith.

"It's okay, chile," Edith cooed over Alessandra's muffled sobs. "It's gonna be okay."

Edith finally coaxed Alessandra into giving her Jeremiah's address.

"I'll be on the next bus," she promised.

Alessandra finally pulled herself up, collected her dish and cup, and took them to the kitchen. A wobbly smile teased her mouth as she soaped and washed the dishes. It would be good to have Ms. Edith around. She was the closest person to a mother that she'd had since she was fifteen years old, and she could use some mothering.

Plus, she had to admit that everything Edith had said about "the gift of sight" oddly felt right—a lot more right than Zach explaining it all away as heightened emotions or stress.

Her next call was to Traci, whose voice alone was like being wrapped in a blanket. She was relieved that Ms. Edith would be with her, and Alessandra promised to keep her posted with details and let her know if she needed anything before Traci drove out there in the next day or so.

Suddenly, Zach appeared in the kitchen's archway with a grocery bag in each arm. Snow dusted his wool cap and shoulders. His eyes glistened, and the smile that moved like a slow dance across his rich mouth settled in her center and two-stepped. When he saw she was on the phone, he pantomimed tiptoeing to the table, set down the bags, and mouthed that he would be back.

Alessandra rapidly shook her head in concert with her hand waving for him to sit. When she finally disconnected the call, shoved the phone back into her pocket, and turned to Zach, he was unpacking the bag.

"Your errands were to go grocery shopping?" she teased. She craned her neck to peek into the bags and across the table.

"I couldn't very well keep raiding my grandmother's fridge and pantry." He looked at her and winked. "It took a while with all the detours, but I made it into town. Not sure how long you'll be here." His gaze lifted to look at her, then returned to what he was doing. "Figured I should get all the staples and some extras." He placed a bottle of wine on the table and winked again.

"I can't thank you enough for all this. Really."

"I can think of something." He looked her in the eye.

Her brow creased. "What's that?" she asked, her tone skeptical.

"You can invite me to dinner." He took a whole packaged rotisserie chicken out of the bag.

"Oh." She laughed nervously. "Not a problem. I can do that."

"Cool." He finished emptying out the grocery bags. "Have you thought about what you're going to do in terms of plans for your dad?"

She dragged in a breath. "The hospital told me that they'll have my dad transported to the funeral parlor. I need to get over there and…"

Zach nodded.

"My neighbor Ms. Edith is coming. She's been like a mom to me."

"That's good. When?"

"I called her after you left and she ended our conversation by telling me she'd be on the next bus."

"Hmm, I can check the schedule and pick her up if I know what bus she'll be on. Hopefully, the roads will be cleared."

You don't have to was on her lips, but she'd come to realize that with this man, those words were futile. "Thanks. I'll call and check when she plans to leave."

Zach pulled out a chair from beneath the kitchen table and sat down. "Um, I know you have tons of stuff on your mind, but while I was driving I thought about…what happened this morning. There has been scientific research done—and of course there is anecdotal evidence—that links what happens with today's Black people as a form of generational trauma. The pain and events of our ancestors' lives continue to embed in our DNA—actually altering it."

Her stomach jumped. "So…you're saying that what's happening to me is in the makeup of who I am? In my genes?"

"I'm not saying it *is*, just that there are researchers actually looking into the generational effects of being stolen and forced into captivity and all that came with it."

She leaned against the sink and folded her arms, frowning as she tried to make sense of what he was telling her.

He took a breath. "Anyway, some of what you told me resonated." He linked his long fingers together. "In my travels and my research, I've come across hundreds of artifacts and historical documents from the Middle Passage crossing, the revolts and escapes of the enslaved, the Maroons who hid and survived."

"Maroons?" she asked.

"Yeah, sorry. Maroons are descendants of Africans across the Americas who formed their own settlements away from and out of the reach of slavery. They often mixed with the Indigenous peoples. The larger groups of Maroons were mostly in the Caribbean and Brazil, but there were also Maroon communities in North America, in and along the swampland bordering North Carolina and Virginia, and in parts of Louisiana. There were even Maroons in Africa made up of Africans who escaped the slave traders along the slave routes inside the continent."

Her head jerked back. "Really? I had no idea."

"Not many people do. Hundreds of thousands of us *did* escape, set up communities, and fought off slave catchers."

Alessandra slid into a chair opposite Zach. "You said what I told you made you think about all this, but I'm not getting the connection."

Zach exhaled. "The images of darkness, the smell of the sea, the feeling of being lost that you told me about." He paused. "The whole notion of the untold story and lost history. How you were saying you didn't know much about your family beyond your mother and father. As one whose life's work is just that—recovering our stories—well, your questions and struggle…" He shrugged. "Just made me think of some of the work and research I'd done in tracing ancestry."

He offered a wan smile, took her hand for a moment. "I'm sorry. I didn't mean to add more to the mix. Look, why don't you call your friend and find out what bus she'll be on, and I'll put these groceries away?"

Alessandra's heart was pounding so hard she could barely breathe. All she could focus on was Zach holding her hand.

Hers was on fire. Her lips parted, but nothing came out. The effect he seemed to have on her vacillated between pure annoyance and desire. Totally unnerving.

Zach smiled, let go of her hand, stood up, and began putting the groceries away.

Alessandra slid her hand toward her and tucked it between her thighs. *Bad move*. Her eyes fluttered closed.

"You okay?"

She swallowed, snapped her head in his direction. "Yeah. I'm good." She got up. "I'll call Edith," she said, her voice sounding faraway to her own ears. She hurried out of the kitchen.

Alessandra went into the living room, walked over to the window that looked out onto the backyard. As far as the eye could see, everything was covered in solid, glistening white. The long, icy claws of the century-old oak that sat sentinel in the center of the yard cut across the pale gray sky. She wanted to lift the window and drag in a lungful of the icy air to cool the heat that still flowed through her from Zach's simple touch. It had been a long time since she'd reacted to a man the way she did with Zach—if at all. Certainly not all jumbled and complicated.

She pulled her phone from her back pocket to call Edith, then stared at the black screen that sucked her into its depths, back into the dark hull of a ship.

The phone clattered from her hand to the floor. The air spun around in her chest. Slowly her vision cleared. She glanced at Zach.

His expression creased in concern. He strode toward her and clasped her shoulders. "What is it? What's wrong?"

Her rigid body grew limp and she leaned into him, pressed her head into his shoulder. Zach wrapped his arms around her and held her tightly against him.

"It's okay," he murmured into the riot of the cottony spirals of her hair. Gently he stroked her back. "It's okay."

• • •

Zach closed his eyes and inhaled her scent, allowed himself the momentary pleasure of holding her in his arms, feeling the soft curves of her body pressed against him. Comforting and protecting her.

From the moment they'd met, Alessandra Fleming felt familiar, but *not familiar* at the same time. From that first instant, there was a sudden, inexplicable aching, a longing inside him for her. It was something he'd never felt before, something deep and ancient, old as time itself. It made about as much sense as the sensations that Alessandra said she'd experienced since she'd arrived in Sag Harbor.

He didn't believe in all that "at first sight" foolishness. He was a scientist, for heaven's sake. He gathered evidence. He dealt in facts and things he could put his hands on, not this out-of-reach, elusive world that he'd stumbled around in. There was no reason for him to be this attracted to a woman he barely knew.

But he was. Every inch of him was.

All he could do now was return to what he was trained to do. Start with the problem: a beautiful, feisty, complicated woman drops into your life. What are you going to do about it? Are you going to run? Or are you going to stay?

"I'm...sorry," she mumbled against his chest. She lowered her head and eased out of his arms, and for some inexplicable reason, he felt as if someone had cut off his circulation. Her body melding with his had charged the blood rushing through his veins. Now the rush had ceased, and he wanted that feeling back again.

He lifted her chin with the tip of his finger and looked into her eyes. "Nothing to apologize for."

For several moments, they stared at each other, stunned, confused, searching for the answers that were just out of reach.

Zach cleared his throat. "Alessandra, I…"

He watched her slender throat move, the parting of her lips, the welcome in her eyes, and before he realized what he was doing, he pressed his mouth against hers.

He inhaled her sigh, felt her lips yield to his. When he cupped the back of her head and drew her tight against his mouth, her lips parted and the tip of her tongue teased his with sweetness.

His gut tightened. The hum of his groan strummed in his veins. A heady whirlwind of emotions carried him beyond the moment to something outside of himself. Something soft, welcoming him home, to the place he'd been searching for. But how was that possible?

"Zach," she whispered against his mouth.

The tenderness of her voice awakened him from the dreamlike space.

He blinked the here and now back into the room and, with a deep breath, eased away. "I…I shouldn't have done that." He shoved his hands into his jeans pockets.

"Why not?" Her husky voice sounded thready.

His pulse jumped. He gazed into Alessandra's eyes before drifting down to catch the rapid rise and fall of her chest. It seemed to match his.

"It's an emotional time. You're in a vulnerable place and—"

She cut him off with her mouth, wrapped her arms around his neck, and pressed against him until the throb between his legs pulsed like a heartbeat. He groaned.

Her fingertips pressed into his back, slid down and around to his front, and unfastened the button of his jeans. Then the lights flickered.

As first, he thought it was the jolts of pleasure that were shooting through him—until the room went dim and the house grew silent.

Alessandra jerked back, blinked in confusion, and looked around. "Did the power just go off?"

Zach walked to the end table and turned the switch on the lamp. *Nothing*. He flicked the wall switch. *Nothing*. "Thought we might have dodged a bullet, but it doesn't look like it. Be right back."

He strode out of the living room, opened the front door, and stepped outside. He dragged in a breath of cold air to clear his head and calm his body, then looked around. All the streetlights were out, and the lights that usually lit the front lawns of the homes were dark.

Moments later, he returned inside. "Power's out all over."

Alessandra plopped down on the couch with a shaky laugh. "And here it was I thought it was our sparks that shorted out the lights," she said. "Now what?"

He'd left the latch off da door.

After so many days of drinking burning brown liquid, it didn't make me dizzy and weak no more. Eating food and having clean water had strengthened me. I could stand and my knees didn't shake under me. I'd pretended I wuz 'sleep when he come to lay wit' me the same way I would pretend when Mama would come to check on me at night.

Mama. I eased toward the door and inched it open. My heart was runnin'. I stepped on the other side of the door. I could hear voices, men's voices, laughing in the distance. This might be my last chance. Had to take it.

"Help us." I runs to the side of the ship. On the other side of the water is home. I tries to climb up and over. "Help us!" Fall. The voices getting close.

Get up. Get up.

The bright white moon lights up the sails of the ship. Run! Jump! The faces of the others call out to me. "Help us." Run! Jump! No. I turns back and darts in between the shadows. If I kin get below...

Footsteps. Pounding closer.

Can't barely breathe, da smell so bad. So hot. Sick and dying bodies twisted and clinging to each other. Moaning, crying. Hard to see, to make out one face from the next.

I's lookin' for the big man named Cinque. He the one fight back when de moon-colored mens beat us. Got to be quick, quick 'fore he find me gone from dat room. I gots to crawl over des bodies and my stomach churning up hot liquid that burn my throat. Keep calling out Cinque name, hoping he answer. He got to answer.

Hard fingers reach out in the dark and grab my arm, hold on tight. Squeeze. I tighten my eyes against the dark till his face come clear. It him. It him. I gives him the nail I done stole, press it into his hand.

I hears my name. He coming for me. I gots to run.

Father taught me mighty lessons while we hunted, how to hide in the bush and make my body small and still, how to tell a poison berry from one good to eat or to scale a tree, to carve a spear from a tree limb, to hold my breath tight in my chest so I won't alert the wild to my presence. He warned me that to keep the animals off my scent, I must stay near the water. But the big water has drowned the scent of us.

How will they find us that have been taken across the big water and bring us back home? How? Babu! Mama!

"Go! Go!" the big man say.

I gathers my skirt, pick my way through the dark and over the bodies till I can get above. See the moon. Smell the sea.

Run!

CHAPTER NINE

"Gram!" Zach called out.

He'd promised Alessandra that he'd be back once he checked on his grandmother. He stomped his snow-crusted boots on the rubber mat and shut the door behind him. The scent of something warm, spicy, and mouthwatering greeted him.

"In the kitchen."

He took off his coat, hung it on the hand-carved wooden coatrack—passed down through generations—took a look around, and chuckled. He stepped out of his boots. His grandmother had already set out her battery-operated lanterns, an assortment of candles, and the battery-operated hot plate. She might be pushing ninety-five, but she was sharper than some thirty-year-olds, and she didn't miss a beat.

Zach found his grandmother stoking the woodburning cookstove that he'd sprung for a few years earlier after a severe storm left them without power for more than a week. His grandmother insisted that all the modern gadgets were useless without electricity, but you couldn't go wrong with some wood and matches. Of course, she'd been right. It took him a while to hunt down one that would fit in the kitchen and get it installed and the exhaust vents cut, but it had well been worth it on numerous occasions.

She was sprinkling some of her fresh-cut herbs into a large pot simmering atop the cast-iron plate. Steam rose and wafted round her face. He came up behind her and gently kissed her proffered cheek. He peeked over the neatly coiffed, waist-length silver braids twisted up on top of her head toward the source of heaven in a pot. "Mm, smells delish. You have enough for an army, Gram."

Grandma O gave the simmering stew one more stir and sealed the contents with the pot lid, then turned to her grandson. Lifted her chin to look him in the eye. "Just in case this thing lasts a while," she said, wagging a slim finger at him. "Besides, with no power I got to use up the perishables in the fridge," she said in her musical voice that was a melding of indistinct dialects she'd made uniquely her own.

She patted his arms and tipped her head toward the foyer. "Set up the lights and the candles for me that I left out there on the hall table. You know where I like 'em."

"Yes, ma'am."

He chuckled to himself. Eccentric though she might be, truth was, if it hadn't been for his grandmother, he might as well have been an orphan. He couldn't count the number of times when, barely a teen, he'd boarded the last bus from New York to Sag Harbor. Alone. Afraid. At night. But he knew that no matter what, his gram would take care of him. He'd be warm or cool as the weather dictated. He wouldn't be hungry. He'd be safe. Until the next time.

He shook his head. Those were memory lanes that he preferred not to travel along. Years away, self-care, and the nurturing from his grandmother had put them in the distance, but every now and again they surfaced, and that twisting feeling in the pit of his gut would cut off his air.

It was much of the reason why he traveled so often, dabbled in unfulfilling relationships. Of course, a great deal of it was work-related, but beneath the surface he constantly needed to put distance between himself and the scared and lonely boy he once was. Stitching together and uncovering the stories of others gave his life meaning, and coming to hang with his gram did the rest.

"All done." He pulled out a chair with a spindle back from beneath the rectangular wooden table and sat.

Grandma O wiped her hands on her orange-and-white apron, poured boiling water over a tea bag in a sky-blue coffee mug that Zach made for her one summer at camp when he was about twelve. The handle had broken off years ago, but Gram refused to toss it.

She lowered herself into the chair opposite him. "You eat?"

"Yes, ma'am. I'm fine." He gave her a wink.

"Hmm." She took a sip of tea. "How's Jerry's girl doing?"

Zach blew out a breath. "Shaken. Sad." He lowered his head, twisted his lips in concentration.

"What else?"

He raised his gaze; shoulders rose and fell. "That's pretty much it."

Grandma O cupped her mug. "How long I known you?"

Uh-oh. He tucked in a smile, knew what was coming. "Since before I was born."

"That's right. Know you better than you know yourself."

He mouthed the words along with her, having memorized them over the years.

"Don't get cute," she warned with a wag of her finger. "You not too old for me to get the switch."

He snickered. She'd been threatening him with a switch for as long as he could remember. The mysterious switch had yet to materialize.

"Anytime you do your lips like that, you got somethin' on your mind. It's Jerry's girl," she stated more than asked. She sipped her tea and watched him over the rim of the mug.

Zach leaned back from the table, angled his head to the side, and stretched out his long legs. "Still reading minds, I see."

"Readin' signs is what you mean."

He linked his fingers on his lap, frowned. "I... She's interesting." He twisted his lips into a half smile and stole a look at his grandmother from beneath his lashes.

"Interesting?"

He sighed. "She's different. Complicated."

Grandma O nodded. "I remember her. Her ma used to dress her up like she was going to a party every day." She chuckled. "Little Alessandra used to run up and down in those pretty dresses like a horse let out da barn. Sweet chile. Changed though when her mama died."

"Changed? How?" He leaned forward.

She pressed her lips together. "Used to fuss with Jerry. Loud. Some nights I'd see him sitting out on the porch at night waiting for her to come home. Anytime I'd ask about how things were going, he'd just give me a sad smile and say 'growing pains.'" She released a slow breath. "Then she was gone. Moved out." She sipped her tea.

Zach's brows flicked. "Hmm. She said things were strained between them for a while, but when she was in that room with him...none of that mattered. Ya know?" He looked to Gram for confirmation.

"Maybe now she's ready."

"Ready?"

"To put the pieces of her past together."

When he tried to press her on what she meant, she waved her hand in dismissal, a sure sign that she would add nothing more. But then she surprised him when she did add more.

"Her ma and me, we used to talk some days. She'd sit right where you sittin'. I'd tell her how I came to be here... my family. And she said her ma had told her things, too, but she never paid attention. She didn't want to hear about 'hard times,' but she wished she had with her ma gone; all her family really. Only people she had left was Alessandra and Jerry. She'd started searching, though. I helped."

Zach's brow tightened. He leaned forward. "Helped? How?"

"Don't know how far she ever got. But I pointed her in the right direction. Showed her how to find out about her people." Her gaze drifted away. "Then she was gone. Terrible. Just terrible."

She sighed heavily, shook her head, then pushed up from the table and went to the stove to check on the stew. She lifted the pot from the heat and placed it on a towel on the counter. "I'm going to take a nap. Help yourself. And...take some to Alessandra." She smiled, patted his shoulder on her way out of the kitchen.

He wanted to ask his grandmother what had happened to Alessandra's mother, since he was reluctant to ask such a question of Alessandra. But if it was meant for him to know, at some point, he would.

CHAPTER TEN

Alessandra contacted Edith and promised that she would call as soon as the roads were clear and power was back so that Edith could make her travel plans. She'd been informed during her call to the hospital that there would be a delay transporting her dad to the funeral parlor until the power returned.

With this item checked off her list, she held her breath and decided to call Steven, only to realize that her phone was at 5 percent and it was almost dark.

She fished through her tote bag, took out her charger, and put on her coat and boots. She got the keys to her father's car and went out into the twilight.

There was a stillness in the air that was too quiet. The kind of quiet in scary movies just before something or someone jumped out of the bushes. She snickered at her own silly thoughts.

Alessandra wiggled the key and, after several tries, was able to get the icy lock to turn. She pulled open the door and climbed in. The old leather seat snapped, crackled and popped beneath her weight. Her breath drifted in the chilled air like tiny apparitions. She stuck the key in the ignition, said a quick silent prayer to the car-engine gods, and turned.

The engine sputtered, hesitated, put up one last effort at refusal before it hummed to life. She smiled in relief, turned on the interior lights, and looked for the outlet to plug in her power cord. But of course that would be too easy. Her father's twenty-year-old Buick had a cigarette lighter outlet. She groaned, tossed her head back, and closed her eyes.

My father had a cell phone and probably used it in the car. She lifted the cover of the storage compartment in the arm rest. Gum. Batteries. Pack of tissues. Pens. She shut the cover and pulled open the glove compartment. Owner's manual. Registration. Insurance card. *Bingo!* Car charger.

Alessandra plugged one end of her charging cable into the car charger, then inserted the charger into the cigarette lighter outlet and attached her phone. She beamed and breathed a sigh of relief to see the lightning bolt icon letting her know her phone was charging.

She settled deeper into the seat and tucked her arms around her body. A part of her was mildly relieved that she could blame the weather on her inability to take care of the final arrangements for her father. The longer that part of her world stayed in the distance, the longer she wouldn't have to think about what would come the day after.

She closed her eyes and leaned back against the headrest. Her thoughts swirled, leaping from one crisis to the next. What would she do now? What about the house? She was an orphan. She had no one. The realization was beginning to become an unwanted refrain. There was just so much to do, here and back home. What about her exhibit? God, just thinking about screwing that up set her stomach fluttering.

Time. Her time was running out, on all fronts. Without

her work, without a family, who was she anyway?

Her throat clenched, and she blinked back the sudden sting of tears. How could it even be possible to be the last of your entire family? If she left the earth tomorrow, who would be there to tell the story of her family?

She snorted a laugh, looked out into the deepness of the descending night. *She* couldn't even tell the story of her family. She didn't know a damned thing. How sad was that? Beyond her mother and father...she was...it?

She leaped up and gasped at the sudden tapping on her window. She pressed her hand to her chest.

"Jeez, you scared the hell outta me." She lowered the window.

Zach poked his head closer. "Why are you sitting in the car?"

"Phone was dying. Used the car charger."

"Hmm." He nodded in understanding and came around to the other side, then opened the door and got in. "Nice and toasty in here." He lowered a plastic bag with a casserole dish down between his feet. He rubbed his hands briskly together, then cupped them to his mouth and blew.

Cocooned in the warmth, surrounded by the dark, Alessandra felt her pulse quicken at his closeness. She shifted in her seat, reached for her phone. "Just about done," she murmured, mildly surprised. Guess she'd been sitting there ruminating longer than she realized. "What is that?" She tipped her head toward the plastic bag. "Smells incredible."

"My grandmother made an enormous pot of Kedjenou, a traditional chicken stew. She insisted I bring some to you."

Alessandra smiled. "Please tell her thanks." She paused a moment. "Traditional?" Her brow rose in amusement.

Zach chuckled. "From the Ivory Coast."

"Is that where your family's from?"

"Generations ago, that's where we were from."

"Oh," was all she could manage. She studied him for a moment, then looked away. "At least you know that much." She turned all her attention on the steering wheel, anything but looking at Zach. His soap-and-water scent, mixed with an underpinning of something rugged, confused her thoughts and made her stomach do that funny flutter thing it did whenever she was nervous and had to explain something that she really couldn't.

"I just found out my grandmother knew your mom."

Alessandra swiveled her head in Zach's direction. "Makes sense," she said, hoping she sounded casual and not like having someone close by who knew things about her mother freaked her out. "They *were* neighbors," she added.

"You said something about not knowing much about your family."

"Mm-hmm."

"I think I know part of the reason."

Alessandra swallowed. "Okay, I'm listening." Her fingers curled into a fist.

"Your mom didn't want to know anything about the history of your family. Or maybe 'acknowledge it' is a better term."

Alessandra pushed out a long breath. "I know. I mean, I think I do. Sort of," she murmured. She told him about the day back when she was a kid and her father had wanted to show her some old family stuff of her mother's in a chest, and how her mother had walked into the room and put the kibosh on that. "And back in the day, what Mom said went. End of story. Literally."

A wistful smile passed across her lips. "The reasons why were never clear. Just that the past needed to stay there." She shrugged. Sighed. "It was almost as if she was afraid of something or…ashamed."

"Could be both or none of the above," Zach said. "Too often family history is forgotten because we grow comfortable at having 'arrived.' The pull and tug of everyday life, middle-class life…traditions get lost." He adjusted himself in the seat and turned to Alessandra. "History, especially family history, is sometimes like a game of telephone. The story starts off one way, and by the time it passes hands and ears, bits and pieces have changed until it's a new kind of tale."

"So…how do you ever know the truth?"

"That's where I come in. I dig and research and interview and read until I find the original source, or as close to it as possible. Then I put the pieces back together again."

"Then it sure is a good thing I met you, isn't it?" Alessandra teased, then licked her bottom lip. "All my life I've felt like I was always running away from something, heading somewhere."

"Hmm." They were quiet for a moment. "What do you think your father wanted to show you in that wooden chest?"

She shook her head. "I have no idea."

"Do you know where it might be?"

"Maybe in the house somewhere, but… I have no idea. Forgot about it…until recently. Why?"

Zach glanced at her for a moment but seemed like he didn't want to push the point. He exhaled. "Nothing."

Alessandra stared out into the night. What did her mother try so hard to keep from her? One of the last things her father had said to her was that it was time she knew. To honor his hope for her would be to dishonor the wishes of her mother. But if she didn't, she knew she would keep running in the dark, seeking and searching but never finding the light.

"Phone charged?"

Alessandra blinked away her musings, looked down at

her cell. "Yep. Guess we should go in." She turned off the car and dropped the keys in her pocket. "And in case I didn't mention it, I'm starving." She flashed a smile.

Zach chuckled. "There's plenty, and you're gonna love it. Promise."

. . .

"Oh. My. Goodness." Alessandra sighed with delight, ladled another spoonful of stew into her mouth, closed her eyes, then chewed and swallowed with reverence. "I will get down on my hands and knees to your grandmother."

Zach chuckled, then dipped a corner of sourdough bread into his bowl and took a bite. "Told ya."

Candlelight flickered between them, casting soft shadows around the room and creating a mystery of their faces.

"But seriously, I will definitely have to go over and thank her."

He glanced up from beneath his curled lashes. "We can make that happen." He picked up a napkin and wiped his mouth. "Feeling any better?"

"Humph, guess it depends on what you consider better. I am 'better' when I don't think about anything, turn my feelings off." She snorted a laugh. "I guess maybe my mother was right about not allowing myself to tap into that part of me." She lowered her head. "It protects you," her voice cracked, "if you don't feel."

"Is that what you want, who you are? 'Cause from everything that you've told me, you want to know about what's been kept from you. To know about yourself." He reached across the table toward her clenched hand but didn't take it. "Let go. Tap into that part of yourself that you've avoided for all these years."

Her nostrils flared as she sucked in air and fought back the sting of tears. "It was my fault," she uttered above a whisper.

"What was?"

Silence.

"Alessandra…" He gently squeezed her hand.

"I was a spoiled fifteen year old. Whatever I wanted, my mother made sure I got it: best clothes, shoes, hair always done and ready for the runway. She made sure I belonged to the right clubs in school and in the community. She and my dad argued about me a lot. My dad… He said my mother was doing too much, that she wasn't teaching me to be responsible."

Alessandra tugged in a breath and slowly exhaled. "I was at a party. Dad didn't want me to go. Mom overrode him. I'd been drinking. The crowd at the party was older. This boy, a senior, he tried…a little too hard. I called my mom, told her she had to come get me. I know she heard the fear in my voice." She swiped at the tears slipping down her cheeks, sniffed. "It had started to rain. Hard." She squeezed her eyes shut. "I stood outside on that porch for more than an hour."

She blinked fast to stem the tears, but failed. "She…never came. She had a heart attack while she was driving…crashed." Her fingers curled into fists. She bit down on her bottom lip.

"Alessandra…I am so sorry. So sorry." This time he covered her hand with his own.

"If I hadn't insisted on going. If my dad had been firmer." She pounded her fist on the table. "My mother would still be here! It's my fault." She snatched her hand away from Zach's hold. "I believed my father blamed me and I couldn't forgive myself, so I took it out on him. Gave him hell. I guess a part of me blamed him for not…stopping me. I don't know.

"And he, in some part of himself, blamed me, too. At least that's what I believed." Her voice broke. She swiped at her eyes. "But…but when I went to see him in the hospital, he told me he didn't and that I had to believe him. He loved me. I… I let myself believe that we could finally be father and daughter again."

She bowed her head, and her shoulders shook with her sobs.

Zach got up from his seat, came around to where she sat, eased her to her feet and flush against him. He cradled her in his arms, closed out the world, sheltered her, whispered soothing sounds into her hair, and held her through an expulsion of pain, loss, guilt, and confusion.

She lifted her head up to him. Her eyes ran over his face, questioning, needing. Her lips parted ever so slightly, but she couldn't form words.

"Alessandra?" he whispered her name as a question as his gaze moved like a soft breeze across her face.

She stroked his jaw, slid her fingers behind his head, raised up, and pulled him to her lips.

CHAPTER ELEVEN

The flickering light from the candles danced along the walls and across the floors, casting shadows, sparking imaginings, and giving the world around them an ethereal quality. Being held by him, kissed by him, stirred to her soul by him, added to the dreamscape.

Moving with him as one through the deepening shadows of her father's home, Alessandra led Zach up the stairs to her bedroom.

The thin veil of darkness separated them from the world, closed them off even as it joined them together.

Alessandra backed into her room leading Zach by the hand, her pulse thrumming in her veins. She'd neglected to put a candle in her bedroom, she realized. The only light was the bare haze of moonlight that had pushed its way through the weight of gray clouds. The only sounds were their own breaths, the swish of clothes coming undone, the sucking of skin, soft moans, and ragged groans.

The loss of heat had settled around the house, but it was not the growing chill that raised goose bumps along her flesh. It was the melody of Zach's fingertips that played along the column of her spine, the song his thumbs drew from her throat when they brushed and teased the peaks of her hardened nipples and made her skin sing in the deep, plaintive voice of Billie.

Their clothes fell away in pieces until they were skin to skin, their bodies humming in harmony.

Alessandra murmured his name against his mouth and pulled him down with her, sinking into the cotton comforter that cocooned them in its thickness. In this moment, the rumors about him didn't matter. If this one night was all there would be, she was okay with that.

Zach stretched out, turned on his side to face her. She felt, more than saw, the heat of his gaze. She cupped his jaw in her palms and drew his mouth to reunite with hers.

His tongue teased the entry of her mouth, sending silken shivers rippling through her, then slid in and out in a rhythm that throbbed all the way down between the dampness of her thighs. Her bud hardened, twitched as the tips of his fingers teased it before slipping two fingers inside her, making her walls weep with joy.

She moaned. Her hips arched even as she gripped the sheets in tight fists.

"Alessandra," he whispered like a psalm between the hot kisses he dropped along her neck behind her ear, down to the rise of her breasts. He adjusted his position so that he was on his knees between her thighs, his fingers still playing a concerto inside her walls.

Zach leaned forward, stretched his tongue to flick across the tip of her taut, dark nipple.

"Ahhhh." Her body quivered from the soles of her feet to the top of her scalp. "Ohhhh!" Her head whipped from side to side, her pelvis rose and fell.

He pushed her legs wider apart, then draped her knees over his shoulders, sacrificing her to his control.

Sparks zipped up and down her limbs, through every loc on her head. She was on fire.

Zach's talented tongue twirled against the slickness of her folds. She screamed and her body stiffened as if electrified before succumbing to the uncontrolled tremors of release. Her fists pounded the mattress. She cried out to the Lord over and over again until the words were only the movement of her lips.

Zach slowly moved up the length of her body until he was looking down into her eyes. Sweat slid across her hairline. Her entire body shimmied with aftershocks.

He kissed her tenderly. She tasted the salty sweetness of herself on his lips, cupped the back of his head, and dragged him into a deep, penetrating kiss, her tongue dancing with his. His deep groan slid down her throat and pulsed in her chest. The throb of his erection pressed against her, barely restrained, but still he held back.

One single thrust and he would answer the question that had hovered in the corner of her mind from the moment they met: what would Zach Renard feel like all the way inside her? His questioning gaze swept her face and settled on her eyes. Waiting. She smiled. Her thumb brushed his bottom lip, and she kissed him with an urgency of anticipation.

With a skill attributable to a gymnast, he kept her splayed and vulnerable beneath him while he leaned over the side of the bed, rummaged in the pocket of his jeans, found his wallet and a condom.

"Let me," Alessandra uttered on a raspy breath. She took the packet from his fingertips, tore it open with her teeth. She used her elbows to inch to a half-sitting position and reached for him. As much as she wanted to go from zero to one hundred in seconds flat, she turned sliding on a condom into an art form.

By torturous degrees that sparked hisses, sighs, and groans from Zach, Alessandra used her fingers and her mouth to sheathe him.

By the time the barrier had reached near the hilt, Zach's erection was so hard and heavy that the thought of having all that inside her both terrified and thrilled her. She eased back, stroking and caressing him until she was supine, then looped her legs across the bend of his arms into a perfect *V*.

"Skills," Zach growled low in his throat, his smile illuminated by moonlight. His broad frame loomed above her. He gripped the insides of her parted thighs.

Alessandra opened her mouth to speak, but her words hung in her throat as the first, single thrust pressed against her cleft and spread her tight, slick opening. Her eyes widened, then slammed shut when her insides yielded and Zach slid into the heart of her.

Zach expelled a long, deep groan, and they remained still for several moments as the sizzling connection charging through them rendered them immobile.

Alessandra dug her fingertips into Zach's hard biceps to assure their shared reality. The swirling, pulsing, breath-stealing connection that sealed them lifted them beyond the moment and propelled them to a space with no boundaries, one that electrified and shook them.

By degrees he began to move inside her, slow, deep, and steady, his breathing expelled in short, tight bursts. With every roll of Alessandra's hips and every one of Zach's thrusts, they whirled. Their cries and groans mingled and rose in harmony with the drumbeat of their rhythm. A rhythm as old as the universe and perfected between them through the ages that pulsed and intensified with each hungry kiss and caress.

Alessandra's mind swam along the shores, fluid and free, raced toward that horizon. She rode the ebb, flow, and power of the waves that rushed against her, washed over her, consumed her. She clung to him, called out his name in a voice she did not recognize as her own. Tighter she held on as the rush intensified and her mind spun.

Zach moaned deep inside her ear, flicked the inside shell with his tongue. The heat of his breath sped through her limbs, ignited her blood, and set off a series of sparks that slid in and out and up and down her body until she was consumed by the flame that licked her skin and steamed her insides.

"Ahhhh!" She buried her face in his chest when he rotated his pelvis against her and his erection hit her spot. The tingle started on the soles of her feet, curled her toes, and snaked up the back of her legs and thighs. Her insides snapped tight, opened, snapped again and again until her body shook with the power of her climax.

Zach scooped his arms underneath her, pulled her closer, absorbed her tremors even as he caused more and more with each deep thrust and groan until Alessandra was certain she'd pass out from the pleasure.

His hard, muscled body tensed. He dragged in a ragged breath as the pace of his strokes quickened.

"Alessandra!" He plunged deep inside her, every muscle in his body straining.

She draped her legs tightly across his waist, her arms around his back, and bound him to her, accepting all that he had to give until they were both satisfied.

Their hitched and heaving breaths skipped around and between each other until they harmonized. Tenderly, he stroked her hair away from her face, kissed her temples while she melted against him, tasted the saltiness of his skin against her lips.

It was new, exhilarating, and exciting. The comfort and ease that they found in each other was not born of a single moment, or even an hour, but rather, over time. Yet she knew that could not be.

Alessandra listened to Zach's heartbeat, felt the warmth of his breath across her forehead, the weight of his thigh draped across her body, and experienced a kind of joyous peace that was inexplicable. Yes, the sex was off the charts — but it was something else, something more than a physical connection.

She angled her body a bit so that she could tip her head up to look at him. When she found his dark eyes staring at her, she suddenly felt herself sucked into the depths of him to a place she could not name, but she knew he was there, too. Could he see it?

Zach brushed his thumb across her bottom lip. "Are you okay?" he softly asked.

She nodded. "You?"

Zach chuckled lightly. "Let's just say…very."

Alessandra felt her body flush with heat. She turned more on her side so that she faced him as a tremor skittered up her spine.

"I don't usually…do this," Alessandra managed.

The corner of Zach's mouth curved upward. "Do what exactly? Have out-of-this-world sex with a man who," he paused, "who knew he wanted this to happen from the moment he met you?" he said, the words seeming as much a surprise to him as a revelation to them both. He blinked, looked into her eyes.

"Yes." She laughed nervously. "Crazy, right?"

"Yeah, a good kind of crazy." He pressed his mouth to hers, teased her lips with his tongue. "That we need to seriously investigate." He rolled on top of her, braced his weight on his forearms. "What do you think about that?" he said, while dropping hot kisses behind her ear, along her collarbone, and between the valley of her breasts.

Alessandra's breath caught in her throat when his tongue flicked across the peak of one tender nipple, then the other. She moaned when his lips covered the dark bead and laved it gently with his tongue. She trembled, felt wetness build between her legs, and as if reading her mind, Zach slipped his hand between her parted thighs and let his fingers check for themselves.

She sucked in a quick gasp of delight. The hum of her moan vibrated between them.

Zach slowly slid two fingers in and out of her to the rhythm of the rise and fall of her pelvis.

"You like that?" he whispered in her ear, then nibbled her neck.

"Yesss. Yesss."

"Look at me."

Alessandra's lashes fluttered. She glanced up into his eyes. Her lips parted, and all the air hung in her chest as he slid deep inside her.

"How 'bout this?" he groaned.

"Ahhhh!" Alessandra cupped his jaw in her palms, lifted her hips to meet his thrusts, and kissed him with a hunger that shook them both.

CHAPTER TWELVE

Alessandra lay curled in the arch of Zach's arm, pressed herself as closely against him as physics would allow. Her mind was still spinning; her heart, though it had slowed to normal, still seemed to race; and that giddy sensation in the pit of her belly was still there.

Zach pulled the quilt up to cover her shoulders. He gently kissed the top of her head, and they fell into a deep, satisfied sleep.

Sometime later, Alessandra stirred, unsure of what had woken her. Blinked. The glow of streetlights and the beginnings of daybreak peeked through the window. "I think the power must be back on," Alessandra whispered. "Light's coming in from the window."

Zach moaned softly, twisted his head toward the window. "I do believe you're right. Streetlights are on."

She rolled to her left side and spotted the bedside clock that was flashing 7:16, the time the lights had gone out.

The real world was a light switch away, and she wasn't quite ready to turn it on.

"Hey, why don't you stay here? I'll check on the heat and warm up some more of my grandma's stew. Cool?" He sat up and reached for his clothes, tugged his shirt over his head, and put on his boxers and jeans.

"If you insist," she teased, burrowing under the covers.

Zach laughed. "I'll be back in a few. Once the heat kicks back on, it'll warm up pretty quickly."

"I thought we did a pretty good job of warming the place up."

He glanced at her over his shoulder and grinned. "Funny, I was thinking the same thing." He leaned down, gave her a slow, deep kiss before pulling away. He swallowed, looked at her for a long moment, as if wrestling with the answer to an equation, before he pushed to his bare feet and sauntered away.

The moment she came out from under the blankets, chill bumps ran along her arms and up her back and hardened her tender nipples. She took a deep breath, wrapped her arms around her body and popped up out of bed, then darted across the cold wood floor and into the hall bathroom.

She flipped on the light, and the face that stared back at her in the mirror was almost unrecognizable. Her long dreadlocks that had been twisted neatly atop her head were splayed across her shoulders like a cape, but more than that they seemed electrified, each loc vibrating with energy. Yet it was her skin and her eyes that drew her closer to the mirror.

Her skin radiated from beneath, giving her usual light-copper glow a deep red undertone, as if she'd spent hours in the sun. Her rather ordinary—at least to her—brown eyes glowed at their center as if a small flame had been struck behind her irises.

She leaned closer, blinked and blinked, then ran her fingers through her hair before splashing cool water on her face. She peered at her reflection again and smiled. It had been a long time since she'd been with a man. She'd forgotten how great sex could stimulate the outside as much as the inside.

Alessandra stepped back from the medicine cabinet mirror to get a better look at her body. For the most part she looked the same, except that her breasts seemed higher and heavier. Her nipples were dark and large, the manicured thatch of hair between her legs glistened, and her entire body had the same red sun-kissed glow.

She drew her bottom lip between her teeth. Stared one last time, then did a quick but diligent washup before going back to the bedroom.

. . .

Zach was rattled. That was the only way to put it. He stared without seeing the water level on the boiler until the hum of the motor snapped him out of his daydreaming. He brushed his hands on the thighs of his jeans and headed back upstairs to the kitchen. He set the correct time on the digital clock of the microwave, then turned on the stove to warm the pot of stew.

He braced his hip against the side of the sink and folded his arms. Alessandra was… He didn't have the right words. He dragged in a breath and felt it shake in his chest. That's how she made him feel, unsteady, as if the world was shifting under his feet. When he was cocooned in the wet heat of her, it wasn't just blow-your-mind sex, it was…surreal.

Rationally, he knew he'd been in Alessandra's bedroom, in her bed, in the middle of a power outage, clinging to her body—but he hadn't been. They hadn't been. Something had happened. As new as the first time between them was, it wasn't. It was like a reconnecting—or something. But how could that be possible?

He shook his head. It sure felt that way.

The aroma of the simmering stew awakened the hunger pangs and dragged him to the here and now. He opened the pot cover and hummed deep in his throat, and a slow smile moved across his mouth.

He took two large bowls from the cabinet and ladled heaping portions into each, then placed them on the table. He turned off the jets and went back to Alessandra's bedroom, where he found her sitting on the center of the bed, legs folded, hair streaming around her face, wrapped in a thick, pale-blue robe. She turned her head toward him and smiled.

His breath clung in his chest. Was this what they meant when they said, "takes your breath away"? He swallowed. "Hey." He leaned on the frame of the doorway. "Soup's on," he teased.

Alessandra languidly unwound her legs and stood. Her robe fell open, revealing just enough to raise the temperature in the room.

Zach's jaw clenched as he watched her walk toward him. Too slow, his body was telling him, but his eyes could watch her forever.

Alessandra stepped right up to him. Only a heartbeat separated them. She lifted her chin, and when she looked into his eyes, the electric energy rode through his limbs until the tips of his fingers tingled.

He angled his head, cupped her cheek in his palm. His gaze ran back and forth across her face, hoping to make sense out of what was happening. He couldn't.

"If we stay in this room, we might starve to death," he

teased, and ran a finger along her bottom lip. Her lashes fluttered.

She raised her hands, palms upward, moving them alternately, up and down like a scale. "Stay in bed and starve? Or…eat to be able to make love another day?" she said dramatically. "Hmm."

He leaned down and kissed her, absorbed her giggles. He threaded his fingers through her hair and cupped the back of her head, then deepened the kiss, savoring the tease of her tongue against his. When he pulled back, they were both breathing hard.

Zach cleared his throat. "Let's eat. We're gonna need our strength."

• • •

"Oh. My. God." Alessandra's eyes closed in bliss. "This is sooo good. Better than the first time, if that's possible." She shot a grateful smile to Zach as she spooned in another mouthful of the stew and savored the pop of herbs and spices that danced on her tongue. The meat was so tender it seemed to melt in her mouth. "Tell your grandmother," she chewed and swallowed, "that she needs to market this. She'd make a fortune."

Zach chuckled. "She won't even tell her only grandson what's in the recipe."

As she ate opposite Zach with the soft light of the new day behind him, the flavors that exploded in tiny bursts in her mouth were so familiar. Like this moment, the two of them sharing a meal. She'd tasted the stew before. Of course that was ridiculous. She couldn't even pronounce the name.

That's what was so crazy about everything having to do

with Zach Renard. There was a comfort, an ease, a trust that flowed between them, which normally took time to cultivate between two people, especially for her. Her relationships were few and very far between, and the men who stayed beyond a few weeks ultimately walked away because they couldn't deal with the walls she erected and her unwillingness to view them as no more relevant than the inanimate objects she focused her camera lens on.

She was used to it. It was easier that way. It was her normal. But there was nothing normal or ordinary about her and Zach. That was about the only thing she knew for certain, and it absolutely terrified her. But why be afraid of something that you knew wouldn't last, wasn't meant to last? Attachment was not in her MO, and, according to Traci, it wasn't in Zach's, either. She expelled a short breath. Enjoy it for what it is, while it lasts. End of story. Right?

"Everything okay?"

The soft-spoken question cleared her head. She blinked Zach into focus. "Absolutely." She dropped her spoon into her empty bowl and wiped her mouth with a napkin. "That was delicious."

Zach smiled. "I'm sure Grandma O will be happy to hear that." He got up from his seat and took their bowls to the sink.

She watched him move with ease around her father's kitchen, and that old flick of annoyance tried to ignite.

"I, uh, don't want you to think that I," she stared at her linked fingers, "do what happened with us on a whim."

Zach dried his hands on the dishtowel and turned toward her. He rested against the lip of the sink. "I work very hard not to, either," he said. His gaze landed on her face.

Alessandra ran her tongue along her bottom lip. She felt the erratic beat of her pulse in her throat. Her gaze flitted from Zach's steady one to the table, to her fingers, and back to him. "I know this may be kind of late to ask, but... Are you involved with anyone?" Traci's warning echoed in her head.

He pursed his lips and shook his head. "My work makes it kind of hard to maintain a steady relationship."

"I see." She found it hard to breathe over her racing heart. "Makes sense."

"You?"

"No," she said on a breath. "There's no one. Work keeps me busy, too," she added.

He held her gaze for a moment before lifting her hand to his lips. "Two adults, right?" He placed a kiss on her knuckle. "I should check on my grandmother." He pushed off from the sink.

"Sure. Of course."

"Your boiler is working fine. The entire house should be good and toasty in no time. Food in the fridge is still fine."

"Thanks." She licked her lips and stood.

They walked to the front door. Zach took down his coat from the hook and put it on.

Alessandra had a sudden, intense sensation of looming emptiness. She clenched her fingers into fists. "I'm going to call the hospital and see how soon they can transport my dad to the funeral home. Gotta give Ms. Edith a call, too."

Zach stood in front of her, almost looming over her in that moment. She felt tiny and vulnerable, yet towering and invincible all at once with Zach so close. Her throat clenched and burned and she could feel the onset of tears sting the back of her eyes, but she didn't know why.

Zach looked into her eyes. He cupped her cheeks in his large hands. "I'm not sure what's happening between us." His mouth quirked into a half smile.

"Neither do I," she said on a cracked whisper and

wondered if this was part of his routine or if it was real.

Zach exhaled a slow breath. "We'll figure it out," he said. It was as much of a question as a statement. "Two adults…"

"Yeah." She smiled.

Zach leaned down and kissed her, long and deep.

The next thing she knew, she was standing in the doorway of her father's home in a blue bathrobe, watching Zach Renard walk away with her heart running behind him.

Run.

Keep running. So dark can't see my hand in front of my face. Stay close to the water. Hide my scent.

I hear shouts. Screams. Flames from the lanterns dance in and out of the brush like fireflies. Stay low and small. Don't stop.

Run.

Thick mud sucks at my feet, grabs my ankles. Bug bites sting my skin. Branches slash my face, catch in my hair.

Run.

Shouts of my name drowned out by the pounding in my chest. Men behind me. Around me. Searching. I can feel them.

Lightning flashes across the ocean. The roar of thunder shifts the mud beneath my bare feet. Rain starts in drops, rattles the leaves. Harder, faster until the water from heaven blinds my eyes and hides my footprints. Erases my escape.

Thunder bangs its fists in victory against the sky.

Voices dim. Flames from the lantern no longer dance.

Run.

Hide.

I remember Mama showed me how to build a hut to blend with the world. Build from the earth, she said. I gather armloads of fallen branches and leaves to rest on and shelter me from the rain. The towering trees and underbrush will protect me. If I curl myself up small, I can stay warm. Too dangerous to start a fire. When the sun come up, I will start again. Don't know how to get back home, but I gots to keep going.

A weak sun peeks through the branches and leaves and bathes my raw skin. I listen for sound of heavy boots and hard voices, but don't hear nothing but the sweet chirp of birds, rustling of leaves from creatures that scurry from hiding places in search of food.

My stomach aches from emptiness. As quiet as I can, I creep out from under my roof. I tries to remember all Mama and Baba taught me about the woods, how to survive, how to avoid the poisons that pose as pretty leaves and shiny berries.

With my scent washed clean from trackers, I can move away from the water and deeper into the woods, stay low, find food.

Find a way home.

CHAPTER THIRTEEN

Alessandra disconnected the call, a smile on her face after having talked to Miss Edith for just a few minutes. Edith had confirmed she would be traveling out the very next day. Alessandra had already spoken with the hospital, and they'd transported her dad's body to the funeral home. Her appointment was at one, which gave her time to shower, find something to wear, and straighten up the house. Company was coming.

She tugged on her bottom lip with her teeth. Staying busy since Zach had left earlier helped to keep her distracted from the night she'd spent with him. Each time she took a breath, she could still smell his scent seeping from her pores.

This was *so* not her. Jumping into bed with a man she barely knew. And being the aggressor at that.

But with Zach she felt a boldness, a freedom unleashed, a longing that she'd never truly experienced before. To have Traci tell it, Alessandra was stuck in the time warp before free love and access to birth control. She'd dated the last guy, Jackson, off and on for nearly a whole month before they'd finally had sex. That was a little more than two years ago.

Not that she didn't *want* to explore, see what other men were like, "So you can have something to compare it to," as Traci had sarcastically counseled. It's that she was selective, she'd insisted.

"You're damn near thirty years old and can't count to five," Traci had teased, more times than Alessandra cared to remember. What Traci'd said was true, though. Her playing field was a bit limited by today's standards.

But the truth was, she was searching for one person who could touch her where no one else could, to make her realize, *this is it. The way Zach had*, a voice in her head murmured. She flinched at *that* crazy thought. *Get real, girl.*

She finished putting the washed and dried dishes in the overhead cabinet, then pushed the white Swiss-dot cafe curtains aside to look out the window. Everything was as quiet as Christmas Eve, although she did catch a glimpse of two intrepid travelers inching their way down the slick street. She craned her neck a bit to see farther down the road to Zach's grandmother's house. Lights shone in the windows.

What was Zach doing right this minute? Was he thinking about her at all? Did he feel the same quivering uncertainty that she did? To be honest, she'd say he was as stunned as she was.

Alessandra let the curtain fall back into place and headed upstairs to strip the bed and get the linens washed. When she stepped into the doorway of her bedroom, her breath caught in her chest as snapshots of her night with Zach, of them twisting in the sheets, of flesh slapping against flesh, of their moans and cries, flashed in front of her eyes. Over the thudding of her heart, a slow heat wound its way along her limbs and settled in the pit of her stomach.

Her lids fluttered closed, and she silently repeated her

mantra. *Get real, girl.*

She stomped across the room. Soon she would be done with this place and with Zach Renard. After her father's funeral and figuring out what to do with the house, she was heading back to Manhattan to resume her life. Her real life. She had a show to put together and more work than she wanted to think about at the moment. And she supposed Zach would go back to doing his research.

She tugged the sheets off the bed and emptied out the pillowcases, gathered the smooth, rumpled cotton in her arms. She drew the linens to her nose, closed her eyes, and inhaled. A pearl of peace filled her, so exquisite that tears filled her eyes. She sniffed, wiped her eyes, and marched off to the washing machine.

• • •

"Gram!" Zach called out as he shut the door behind him. He stepped out of his boots and hung up his coat.

"In the kitchen."

He walked down the narrow hall, the shiny wood boards creaking under his weight.

Grandma O was sitting at the kitchen table, sipping on a cup of ginger tea. She glanced up briefly when Zach entered.

"Spent the night out, I see." She took a sip of tea.

Zach cleared his throat. "Uh, yes. We got to talking and—"

She held up her hand to stop him in mid-sentence. "You're a grown man. Do grown men things." She put her cup down and looked him dead in the eyes. "She's going through a time right now. Easy to be soft to anybody that shows care and kindness. Don't take advantage of that. Not that you would," she quickly added. "You wasn't raised like that. But keep it in mind. Don't make all of what she needs to do more complicated because you toss yourself in the middle of things."

Zach pulled out a chair and sat. He leaned back and looked at his grandmother from beneath his lowered lashes. He folded his hands across his stomach. "It's not like that."

Gram's brow rose in an arch of sarcasm. "Really? That's what every man who didn't realize it has ever said." She tucked in a smile, then flattened her palms on the table. "So... what is *it* like?"

Zach sucked in air, then slowly exhaled. A frown creased his brow. "I'm not sure. I'm completely aware that we only just met." His eyes tightened at the corners. "But I swear, Gram, I feel like I've always known her." His gaze jumped to his grandmother. He tossed his hands up. "Can't explain it."

Grandma O studied the expression on his face. "This may sound like some ol' woman talking ol' folklore and ol' myths, but son," she stretched her hand across the table and he put his hand in hers, "sometimes there're some things that cannot and should not be explained," she said in the musical lilt he loved to hear. "They simply exist, yeah, like the meeting of two people who share something only with each other—their unified spirits."

Her voice lowered. "We have a belief from back home: in this life, there is only one soul that is truly meant to meet with yours. Sometimes the souls come together early in life, sometimes late; sometimes they meet repeatedly through and across time." She offered a soft smile.

Zach angled his head to the side. "Was it like that for you and Gramps?"

Grandma O's eyes lit up. "Oh yes." She nodded slowly. "Oh yes." She sat back. "She doesn't realize her purpose yet," she whispered. "Alessandra."

Zach blinked. "What?"

"That is why you were put in her life. In her path. Just as I was put in the life and path of her mother."

· · ·

Alessandra's hands were clenched in her lap. It was only Zach's gentle pressure on her arm that kept her from leaping out of her seat. The practiced words from the funeral director, used for those held in the grip of grief, droned in a slow melodious tone. A macabre lullaby. She tried and failed to fully process what he was saying about oak or cherry wood, velvet or satin lining, family photos, type of service, open or closed, suit and shoes.

"I know this is a lot to take in, Ms. Fleming," Mr. Hawkins soothed. He slid a glossy pamphlet across the table toward her. "The information will give you all the details about our various packages." He half-mooned a smile.

"Thank you," she murmured.

"Why don't you look it over and call me in the morning with your decision? We'll need a deposit and if there is any… insurance to…cover the costs."

Alessandra swallowed over the knot in her throat. "Thanks," she mumbled again.

Zach helped her to her feet.

"I'll call in the morning."

"Of course. Hawkins Homegoing Services is here for you in your time of need."

Zach ushered her to the exit with a gentle hand on her back.

The sudden slap of the frigid afternoon air jolted Alessandra from her malaise to her reality. She gripped the frame of the door, bent in half and dragged in shuddering breaths.

Zach cradled his arm across her back, held her close. "It's okay. Just breathe. Take a minute. I'm here. I got you," he gently intoned.

"I...didn't know it would be so hard," she said, her voice cracking. She gulped in another breath, braced her hands on her knees, then slowly straightened. She turned toward Zach. "Pretty sure I couldn't have gotten through that alone. Thank you."

"You could've done it if necessary. You're a lot tougher than you give yourself credit for, but I'm glad I was here so we wouldn't have to put my theory to the test." He kissed her forehead. "Come on, let's get out of this cold."

He'd parked his SUV in the near-empty parking lot. They gingerly walked across the slick concrete to his vehicle.

Alessandra sat pensive, staring out of the passenger window, as Zach pulled into traffic.

"There's some work I need to get done on this project I'm contracted for," he started, "but I don't think you should be alone right now."

"I'll be fine. I need to...take care of things, make some decisions." She morosely held up the pamphlet, then dropped it in her lap.

They stopped at a red light.

"How about this?" he tried. "Bring your laptop, cell phone, whatever and come hang out at my grandmother's house. She's great company and loves looking after people."

Alessandra turned to him with a smirk on her lips. "Bringing me to meet the family already?"

Zach looked into her eyes; his tone sobered. "Would that be a bad thing?"

Alessandra's lips parted. She glanced down at her folded, gloved hands, then back at him. Swallowed. "I'd like that."

"So would I."

. . .

Alessandra turned the key in the door and stepped inside. Zach was right behind her. She turned to him the moment she heard the door shut.

He tugged the multicolored wool cap from her head and freed her riot of hair, the tendrils tumbling around her shoulders. Her breath hitched. His intense gaze danced up and down her body as he unfastened her heavy coat.

Alessandra shrugged out of it, letting the coat fall to the floor.

Zach cupped her chin in his palm and tilted it upward. When he lowered his head to meet her lips, Alessandra felt weightless. The feel of his mouth, the taste, the passion, lifted her. She looped her arms around his shoulders and melted into his kiss.

Zach gathered her flush against him, melding their bodies into one continuous line of desire.

Alessandra pulled away, breathing heavily, her eyes shot with light. She licked the taste of him from her lips, then took his hand and led him to her bedroom.

CHAPTER FOURTEEN

"Gram!" Zach called out. "You decent? I have a guest," he added over a chuckle. "She's gonna be thrilled to see you. Watch," he whispered as he helped Alessandra out of her coat.

The homey aroma of warm rising dough filled the air, already bathed with scents of cinnamon.

"Decent!" came a lilting voice that made the single word sound like a song. Grace Oweku appeared in the archway, all five foot five of towering strength. She was dressed in a multicolored flowing caftan that reached her ankles, and her bare feet moved soundlessly toward them. Silvery hair was plaited into two thick braids and pinned on top of her head.

She stopped a few feet in front of where Alessandra stood. Vanilla spice floated around her. Piercing brown eyes, lit from deep within, settled on Alessandra.

Alessandra's urge to bow as if confronted by royalty quickened her pulse and muddled her greeting.

Grandma O blessed her with a smile that unwound the knot in her gut.

"All grown up," Grandma O said. "Just look at you!" She stepped forward and took Alessandra's hands in her own smooth brown ones. Her expression sobered. "I am sorry for your loss."

"Thank you."

Grandma gave Alessandra's hands a squeeze before letting go. "Come. Come inside. I'll fix you something to eat." She turned away with the elegance of a ballerina.

Alessandra stole a look at Zach, who winked and mouthed, "I told you so."

Alessandra grinned, shook her head, and followed Zach into the kitchen.

"Zach brought over some of your stew. It was delicious." She pulled out a chair and sat.

"There's more if you like. I was fixin' up some sandwiches. You like sourdough bread?" She turned from the sink. "Homemade. Fresh out of the oven."

Alessandra's brows lifted. "Sure. Um, can I help with anything?"

"No. No." Gram waved away the offer. "Zach, act like you have the manners I taught ya. Take the sliced chicken and turkey from the fridge."

Once he'd done so, Grandma O placed the bread on the table. "Help yourself." She stood over the spread. "You look like her."

Alessandra glanced up. "Ma'am?"

"Your mama. You look like 'er when she was about your age. She was a lot fairer than you in complexion but," she smiled, "same face."

Alessandra blinked, cleared her throat. "Some people say that," she murmured. Images of her mother flashed in rapid succession—always perfect. She may resemble her mother, but she could never be Jessica Fleming.

Grandma O placed a bread knife on the table. "Sat right where you sittin'." She lifted her chin toward Alessandra.

"She…came here?"

Grandma O nodded.

Questions tumbled in her mind. "When?"

"From time to time. We'd talk. 'Bout you, her life, questions."

Grandma O picked up the knife and cut four thick slices of the warm bread. "Fix what ya want," she said with a lift of her chin toward the contents on the table.

"I don't remember my mother coming here."

"Hmm." She shrugged, slathered mayonnaise on her bread. "Maybe wasn't for you ta know."

Alessandra snorted a sigh. "Just one more thing to add to the list of things I don't know about my family." She glanced around the kitchen. At some point, Zach had quietly slipped out. Inwardly she smiled, realizing that he was entrusting her with the one woman he trusted more than anyone in the world. The realization warmed her.

Grandma O layered her bread with sliced turkey, tomato, and lettuce, then cut the loaded sandwich down the center, the lettuce crunching under the blade.

"Your mama was not a simple woman. She was all circles and squares and angles." She bit into her sandwich and chewed as if every bite was manna from heaven.

Alessandra's brows tightened. "What are you saying?" She heard the tinge of frustration in the pitch in her voice. She'd been raised to respect her elders, but Grandma O was talking in riddles and it was straining her fragile patience.

Grandma O wiped her mouth with a paper napkin. "Your mother was finally coming to terms with wanting to understand who she was, where she come from."

The knife Alessandra was using to spread mayo on her

bread clattered to her plate. "What?"

"Spent most of her life trying to be something she would never be—accepted in a world that didn't see her as equal. Didn't matter none what school ya 'tended, who ya people was, how light-skinned or how straight ya hair." She chuckled. "She come 'round, though," she added in that musical lilt. "At least real close."

Alessandra wasn't sure what she was hearing over the thudding in her chest, or even what it was she wanted to know.

Grandma O spoke her words slow and deliberate. "Eat. Listen," she cooed. "She wanted to be everything that *her* mother was not—at least to her way of thinking. Wanted to be as far away from what happened to her as possible." She took another bite. "I'd catch glimpses of her running you off to school, sometimes in the village at the market. But as lovely looking as she was, how perfect her outward appearance, there was…an emptiness."

Alessandra almost slammed her hand on the table, but her home training, which this woman seemed to be questioning, held her back. "What are you getting at? You can't just *say* things about my mother—"

Grandma O held up a slender hand, the lines on her palm dark and deep. Alessandra felt as if she'd been shoved. Whatever words she wanted to toss hung in her throat.

"I only tell you the truth of what I saw and felt, and what your mother shared as she began to accept who and why she was," she said, soft as a nightly prayer. "She had to start forgiving first and let go of the guilt."

Alessandra tugged in a breath, rested her back against the chair. Thoughts and images of her mother rushed around in her head, swirling like raked leaves captured by a sudden wind. She caught glimpses of her smile, her voice, the lift of her hand to shield her eyes from the sun. Her lips tightened.

Her mother was her champion. Whatever she'd wanted, her mother made sure that she had it, even when it went against the wishes of her father—which was often. The more her mother gave and the more she bent to Alessandra's wants, the more Alessandra wanted. Her expectation of having her every need met had surely cost her mother's life and furthered the wedge between her and her father. She'd lived with the weight of that guilt every day.

Did her mother regret how she raised her daughter? Did she begin to feel guilty about the way she'd dealt with her father? Was that it? How would Alessandra ever know for sure?

Alessandra only felt the gentle touch of Grandma O's hand on hers. Her eyes were clouded with doubt and confusion.

"Let it out," Grandma O said in a whisper.

Alessandra's sobs shook her, tossed her around in a maelstrom of hurt, regret, and loss. At the center of it all, she knew she was the cause.

"Your ma did what she always thought was best," Grandma O said, poking through the darkness. "That's what mamas do. Most times we get it right. Sometimes we don't." She squeezed her hand. "I did my best with my own daughter." She sighed, gave a little shrug. "Didn't turn out like I imagined. But," she held up a slender finger, "I got my boy Zach."

Alessandra sniffed hard, coughed. She swiped at her wet cheeks, reached for a napkin and mopped her face. "Sorry," she mumbled. "Seems that's all I do lately."

"Ha. Why sorry? Sorry to feel?" She turned the word into three syllables. "Wouldn't be human if you didn't feel. At least none that I'd want to be involved with my grandson."

She offered a smile.

Alessandra sniffed, snatched a glance at Grandma O, but steered away from the implications of her comment. Instead she began, "The night my mom died…" she swallowed. "I'd begged and begged to go to a stupid party." She wiped at her eyes, frowned. "There was this guy I liked." She snorted a laugh. "I didn't tell them that the party wasn't in the Village. It was on Sullivan Island. I was going to meet my friends in town, and one of the older guys planned to drive."

She licked her lips. "The guy I was so desperate to see didn't even show up. Everyone was drinking. It was getting late and the boy who drove us said he wasn't ready to go. I started to panic. It would take me hours to get home, and it had started to rain. What choice did I have?" She turned imploring eyes on Grandma O. "I called my mom. The last thing she said to me was, 'Stay put, I'm coming to get you.' She never made it."

She paused, her breath heaved and tumbled in her chest. The knot in her throat burned like acid.

"I've played those words millions of times in my head. Every misstep I've ever made, every choice: 'Stay put, I'm coming to get you.' But…she's not." Her voice cracked.

"No. She's not. But you are here."

Alessandra's gaze flew to meet a steady brown-and-gold one.

"Your mother was human. With human faults and worries and strengths and doubts. It took her many years, but she'd slowly begun to come to terms with the choices she'd made, the ties she'd cut, the unknowing she'd done. A couple of months or so before she passed, she'd started a search for her people. I helped her."

Alessandra's eyes widened.

"She said as she watched ya grow, indulged ya, molded

ya into the image that she believed would be accepted in the world, she was comin' to realize that it was all false."

"What…made her change? Do you know?"

"Your dad. She felt she'd lost him. He'd told her he couldn't live how they'd been living. Pretending to be people they really weren't." Her lips pursed tight at the word. "And something had to give or he would leave."

Alessandra's brow creased. Her lips parted, but she didn't speak. Her dad was going to leave her mother, leave her? She couldn't believe that. She scoured her memory trying to recreate her parents' relationship, to pinpoint the moment when her father had had enough. She couldn't. One more thing her mother didn't want her to know… She didn't know how she felt about that—how she felt about this version of her mother that was slowly materializing.

"Of course, you know your dad was the only surviving child of his parents, and his parents died when he was barely a teen," Grandma O said, breaking into her thoughts. "Family was important to him, and he could not reconcile with the fact that your mom didn't want to know no parts of hers."

Grandma O sighed, gave Alessandra a gentle smile. "She wanted no parts of the past with all its hurt and loss and ugly and unspeakableness. She didn't want none of that ta touch ya. Evah."

Alessandra pressed a knuckle to the corner of her eyes to dam up the tears. Slowly she shook her head, blinked. Her voice cracked. "Do… Do you know what she found?"

"Some. She was trying to trace her line. How her family wound up here, of all places. Found some papers about her mom and her grandmom, bunch of other stuff in a chest she'd put in storage when she and your dad moved here from New York."

Alessandra leaned forward. "A chest?" Her voice

squeaked. "Do you know where it is, what's in it?"

"Mainly birth certificates, newsclips, letters, from what she showed me." She pressed her palms flat on the table. "There was plenty more, she said. She'd only begun to really go through the contents." She stared into Alessandra's eyes, challenging her. "But I never saw it."

Lips pinched, Alessandra spread her fingers toward Grandma O. "I need to know," she whispered. "I want to know."

Grandma O's rich lips curved into a smile. Her eyes picked up the light from overhead and sparkled. "Ya have at your beck and call an expert in what ya need." Her smile was sly and knowing.

Alessandra blinked. Understanding registered. She bit down on her lip to smother her grin. Sometimes what you needed and what you're looking for were right in front of your face. "You think so?" she softly asked.

Grandma tossed her head back and laughed. "I know so."

CHAPTER FIFTEEN

"Looks like you and my grandmother hit it off," Zach said a few hours later.

They stopped in front of Alessandra's front door.

She turned to him, looked into his eyes, nodded. "Yeah, we did. She said things that I didn't expect to learn about my mom, but it's only the tip of the iceberg." She licked her bottom lip. "She said you'd be the one to help me pick up where my mother left off."

The right corner of his mouth inched upward. "Did she?" He pulled in a breath. "I mean I can do what I can, in between my own work, but you'll need to do some of the heavy lifting." He shoved his hands in his pockets.

Alessandra nodded. "Fair enough." She unlocked the door and stepped in but stopped when Zach didn't follow. She tipped her head to the side. "Coming in?"

"I have some work that I need to get done. Dinner?"

"Sure. I'd like that."

"I can bring something in from town."

"Okay."

He leaned in and kissed her forehead. "Oh, did you get a time for Ms. Edith?"

"Yes. She said she should arrive by two tomorrow."

"Good. I'll pick her up. See you later."

She stood in the doorway and watched Zach walk away. Shutting the door, she toed out of her boots and hung up her coat. For a few moments, she simply stood in the middle of the foyer, knowing that she needed to do so many things but not sure which one first.

Her talk with Grandma O had unsettled her more than she'd realized. For too long she'd been wrong about everything she thought she knew. So now what?

Pick up where my mother left off. The woman she thought she knew, but clearly did not.

Alessandra went upstairs, the steps creaking slightly beneath her bare feet. She stood in the threshold of her father's bedroom. Tentatively, she pushed the door farther open—and in an instant, she was a little girl again, transfixed by her father as he sat on the window seat playing his sax.

When her father played, it seemed that he was in another world. His eyes closed, and his body swayed as if moved by a summer breeze. The notes were dizzying, tumbling, and darting between each other, daring to be caught and held by the listener. Alessandra would sit at her father's feet, watching and listening, amazed. Her love of music, and of the arts in general, was certainly something that bound them, even in ways that she was not connected to her mother.

Growing up, she would spend hours on Saturday afternoons with her father, listening to his collection of albums. It had become clear by her preteens that she had an affinity for the jazz vocalists, even though she couldn't quite carry a note in a sealed jar—and not due to a lack of trying.

She stepped into the room that she hadn't set foot in

since… She steeled herself and walked to the window. Her father's battered black sax case, with the edges so worn they'd turned a warm brown, rested on the flowered, padded seating. Kneeling in front of it, she flipped the thick silver latch and opened the case.

Her heart jumped. She pressed her lips into a tight line. With shaky fingers, she ran the tips of them across the sparkling gold surface, tracing the curves of the neck, then down along the bow to the bell. Her dad had taught her the names of the major parts, the ones that mattered, as she would never remember the six hundred that comprised a sax. Her father's reeds were lined up on the red satin like soldiers waiting to be called to duty.

She closed her eyes and could almost hear her father playing "'Round Midnight," one of his favorites. When she opened her eyes, her vision was clouded by memories and sorrow.

"I'm so sorry, Daddy. So sorry. I'm going to find out all the things you wanted me to know. What Mom finally wanted me to know. I promise."

· · ·

The sun had fully set by the time Zach pulled into the short driveway of his grandmother's home. One by one, lights from curtained windows began to dot the chilly evening.

His trip to tour the structures on Sullivan Island and the hours spent combing through documents and images at the Sag Harbor Historical Society had provided extra kernels of information to add to his research on the freed communities that had inhabited Sag Harbor. A community that had lived and thrived, fully independent of the rest of society.

Their descendants ultimately spread across the island. Some settled in Eastville or Azurest, creating the enviable beachfront communities of well-to-do Blacks, while those who moved farther north, south, and to the Midwest carried their stories and their culture with them.

The contract for this project came from a multimillion-dollar grant from the National Endowment of the Humanities, overseen by the Smithsonian. His research centered around the freed men and women along the coast of Sag Harbor, in particular the little-known Maroon communities. Were they real or myth?

He hopped out of his SUV, grabbed the backpack stuffed with files and copies of images, and went inside. Based on his preliminary research, he believed that this mythical community was very real indeed and that some of their descendants might still be alive and living in any number of places across the country. That was the hard part: tracking people down and then convincing them to tell their story.

He unlocked the front door and stepped inside. As always, the house smelled of something delicious, a combination of herbs, spices, and a wafting of vanilla.

He took off his boots and hung up his coat, then went in search of the aroma that wagged a come-hither finger.

Grandma O was not in the kitchen but ensconced in the living room in the overstuffed armchair. She had her glasses perched on the tip of her nose, and she was totally engrossed in a novel.

"Hey, Gram." Zach crossed the room, leaned down, and kissed her cheek. "Whatcha reading?"

She turned the cover toward her grandson.

"Hmm, romance." He quirked a smile.

She swatted his arm with the book. "Had a good talk with Alessandra today. I think I did." She kept the book open and placed it down on her lap. "Sweet girl. Confused. Sad. Curious. And ready."

Zach lowered himself onto the love seat, leaned forward, and rested his forearms on his thighs. "She…is all of those things."

"I did tell her that you would be the perfect person to help her find out the things she wants to know."

He tugged in a breath and nodded, trying to tuck in a smile. "Yes, you did."

Grandma O chuckled. "You stayin' for dinner?"

"I was, uh, gonna have dinner with Alessandra. Probably our last night together for a while."

She pursed her lips. "Hmm. Why is that?"

He gave a slight shrug, slouched back in the chair. "Her surrogate mom is coming in tomorrow to stay with her and help out with arrangements. Then it's the services." He licked his bottom lip. "After that," he blew out a breath, "I guess she'll be going back to Manhattan. She has an exhibit coming up. Her first."

Grandma O eyed him over the top of her glasses. "Hmm. The city is only a drive away, son."

"I'm sure she has a very full life back home."

"I'm sure she does." She pushed her glasses up the short bridge of her nose, picked up her novel, and continued to read.

Zach snorted a laugh and stood. He knew when he was being dismissed. He kissed her brow. "See you later."

"Probably not," she teased and winked at him when he glanced over his shoulder.

Zach grabbed his backpack from the foyer and jogged up the steps to his bedroom at the end of the narrow hallway.

He dropped the heavy bag at the foot of his bed, then tugged his sweatshirt over his head and tossed it in the wicker hamper by the window. He chuckled at the perfect swoosh. There was a time in his life when he'd envisioned himself in the NBA. He'd played in high school and during his freshman and sophomore year at Howard University until he'd torn his ACL. During his recovery, he dove into reading to pass the time, and it was the work of Zora Neale Hurston, in particular, that had sparked his interest in ethnography.

He shucked his jeans and dropped them in a heap on the floor before heading to the shower.

His initial plan was to bring dinner to Alessandra's, but since this might be their last evening together, he thought she might like to go into town to eat instead. At least, he hoped she would be up for it. He was even willing to ditch his usual sweat- or thermal shirts for an actual button-down if that would seal the deal.

A few minutes later, he was dressed and at the front door. "I'm heading out, Gram!" he called as he donned his black down jacket and stepped into his boots.

Grandma O emerged at the end of the long foyer. She folded her arms beneath her chest. "Take care of yourself, son. And Alessandra, too." She turned away and ambled back to the living room before he could ask what she meant.

. . .

Zach helped Alessandra into his vehicle, then came around and got in. He fastened his seat belt, then glanced at her, giving himself a moment to simply take her in without ogling. Her long, sugar-brown locs were twisted into an intricate style atop her head with pinpoints of tiny seashells adorning them. And her skin...always dewy soft, that pouty mouth with a hint of something glossy and coral-perfect against the sweet honey of her complexion. But it was her eyes, always her eyes; bold, piercing, deep fanned by those thick lashes…

"Zach?"

He blinked, cleared his throat. "I hope you don't mind us going out instead of staying in. Thought you needed a change. Ya know."

She angled her body toward him and smiled. "Not at all. You're right. Besides the hospital and your grandmother's house, that's pretty much been it for me. I hope the place isn't too fancy. I only brought one dress. Not much in the way of 'going-out' clothes."

"Don't even worry about it. I think this is the first button-down shirt I've put on in months." He chuckled.

Alessandra grinned, unfastened the top button of her coat. "It's been years since the last time I had dinner in town." Her smooth brows squeezed together in thought. "Must have been about seventeen. Me and my dad, actually." She lowered her head. "We talked about my last year of high school and what I wanted to do when I got to college. If I was thinking of majoring in photography. I didn't even know he knew I was interested in photography, at least not as a major." She slowly shook her head. "But I should have known." She frowned. "He gave me my first camera. I just… I was so caught up in being a spoiled brat…"

Zach reached over and patted her balled fists. "You were a kid. A teenager. They are known for being smart-asses, rebellious, and basically awful to live with. For the most part," he added. The comment earned him a half smile.

"I was definitely all that and then some. I only wish I could say all the things to my dad that I should have said." She sniffed, but didn't cry. She dragged in a lungful of air. "A do-over, ya know."

"You have the chance for that do-over by doing what your

dad always wanted and continuing what your mom started."

She looked him in the eye and nodded. "Yeah," she said on a whisper. "I do." She paused. "And I'd like your help."

He threw her a quick glance. "No doubt. That's my thing, ya know." He winked at her.

She chuckled and gently squeezed his arm. "So I've heard."

. . .

Sag Harbor Village resembled a picture-postcard winterscape. The row of shops and restaurants, the Grenning Art Gallery on Main Street, were lit with twinkling lights and the remnants of the December holidays, now more than a month in the rearview. The cobblestone streets were still slick with ice in some spots, and crystal icicles hung from awnings and bare tree limbs. Humps of snow were piled at the curbs in an array of sizes and shapes.

Couples and families clung together as they gingerly inched along the cleared pathways.

"Here we go." Zach pulled open the door to Page at 63 Main.

"Niiice," Alessandra hummed, stepping in and scanning the decor. It was a mix of nouveau and old, with brick walls and dazzling chandeliers, floor-to-ceiling windows, and circular tables covered in white linen. Glass bowls with dancing flames served as centerpieces.

"The food and the service here are great," he said, his hand at the dip of her back. "I try to come here whenever I'm in town." After stopping at the hostess podium, they were showed to a tucked-away table near the towering nine-pane windows, giving them an almost movie-like experience as the passersby and twinkling lights crossed, frame by frame.

"My name is Jasmine and I'll be helping you this evening," their server said as Zach helped Alessandra out of her coat.

He leaned close to Alessandra's ear as he slipped the coat down her arms. "That dress is hot," he whispered, eyeing the burnt-orange knit dress that hugged her body with a dangerous dip in front.

Alessandra glanced over her shoulder at him. "Why, thank you," she said with a wicked grin. "I'm happy you approve." She eased into her seat.

"Hmm," he murmured and took his seat.

Jasmine placed a drinks menu and a dinner menu in front of each of them. She signaled, and a busboy arrived and poured water into their glasses.

"Would you like to order drinks while you review the menu?"

Alessandra eyed the drinks menu for a moment, then looked up at Jasmine with a smile. "I think I'll try the mango spritz. Sounds like fun."

Zach chuckled. "I'll have a bourbon on the rocks."

Jasmine gave a short nod. "Coming right up."

Alessandra settled in her seat and glanced around. She linked her fingers together on the table. Her short, manicured nails were unadorned. "So, Mr. Renard, what have you been up to today?"

His eyes lit up, and he launched into the treasure trove of artifacts that he'd collected on his trip to the Historical Society and the documents from Sullivan Island. "It would have been great to have you with me. I could have used some of your expert photographic skills."

Alessandra smiled at his enthusiasm.

When their drinks arrived, Zach raised his glass. "To everything you need and want," he softly said, staring into her eyes.

Alessandra smiled. "To tagging along on your next adventure." She glanced at him from beneath her long mascaraed lashes.

They touched glasses and sipped.

"I'd like that." He lifted his chin toward the menu. "No matter what you choose, you won't regret it. Promise."

She grinned. Her eyes roamed the menu. "Wow. Everything does look delicious. Any recommendations?"

"Hmm. We could start with the fried calamari and steamed mussels as appetizers."

"Sure. Perfect. I haven't had mussels in ages." She looked at the menu again. "And…what about…the Mosner grass-fed veal rib chops?"

"Yes! And a night at Page would not be complete without their seared sea scallops."

Alessandra giggled. Her eyes widened. "Yum."

"Absolutely. We can share. Best of both worlds." He winked.

"I can definitely get with that."

As promised, the service was excellent, and the food was out of this world. They dined and laughed and drank and laughed some more.

Zach recounted his travels to Africa, to Sierra Leone where he could trace, to a point, his own family lineage. "I was able to get as far back as," he frowned in thought for a moment, "about 1880. I do know that my great-great-grandfather was captured. But I haven't been able to pursue that line of inquiry as far as I would like. I got pulled into the Smithsonian project. That's taken up the last four years of my life," he said with a crooked smile.

Alessandra nodded, urging him to continue.

"There's something…soul-moving about returning to the

continent. Spiritual." A faraway look came into his eyes. "To move from one place to the next and to feel like you belong, like you've come home." His brows tightened. "Faces and smiles and eyes and noses that look like yours everywhere you go." He heaved a breath, and his focus returned. "I had a chance to sit with tribal leaders in some of the older villages nestled in the hills, to listen to their stories and observe the rich culture up close. The vibrancy and energy aren't visible to the eye, but they're felt deep in the soul." He smiled thoughtfully. "At least they were for me."

"Wow. That sounds so amazing," she said with a tinge of wonder in her voice. "I have to make it a point to take a trip *home*."

"You won't regret it."

"So, is that where the name 'Oweku' comes from?"

Zach nodded. "Yes, the family name on my grandfather's side. On Gram's side is Native American, then there's the Creole from my father's side. I'm like a box of chocolates," he added with a chuckle.

And very tasty, she thought but didn't say. "Did you know your grandfather?"

He pursed his lips and slowly shook his head. "No. He passed away before I was born."

"I'm sorry," she whispered. "So," she breathed, switching gears, "tell me about some of your other adventures."

"I've traveled all through the South collecting stories and artifacts. One of my personal passions are the stories of the Maroons—I mentioned those before." Alessandra nodded. "Anyway, all along the coast of the Deep South and the shores of the Caribbean, Africans who were able to escape their captors hid in the marshes and swamps, fortified themselves against intrusion, often under the protection of the Indigenous people. In today's lexicon, they would be considered 'living off the grid.' They hunted, grew crops, married, raised families, even developed their own dialect— and all without relying on the outside world." He took a swallow from his drink. "Part of my research is uncovering the myths and legends around a Maroon settlement here in Sag Harbor."

"Here? Really?"

Zach nodded. "There are signs, documents, artifacts that I've been putting together." He talked a bit more about his trek through Europe with its ancient architecture and museums, full of many treasures that were questionably obtained.

By the time their dessert of toasted almond and cherry biscotti arrived, Alessandra felt as if she'd been given a whirlwind tour of the globe. The dinner ended with a glass of wine and a toast to possibility.

• • •

They stood at her door as she fished for her key. "You were absolutely right about the restaurant. The food was out of this world." She looked into his eyes. "The stories were amazing, but…the company was the best part of the evening."

He stroked her chin with the pad of his thumb. "Anytime," he said softly.

She turned from him and unlocked the door. Zach didn't second-guess. He followed, shutting out the world as he closed the door behind him.

I ties what's left of my skirt higher round my legs to make it easier to walk. I walk and walk til the sun peak its highest in the sky, til it began to sink and I keep walkin'. Couldn't hear the lap of the ocean no more, only the faint smell of salt-washed air and something else.

I duck down low, hide between the thick green growth and fallen limbs. I make a space so I can see. I cover my mouth quick to quiet my gasp when I sees two peoples walkin' through the brush.

The lady she be dark, dark like me, with thick wooly hair that stand out on her head like a crown. The other be a big man with a bare chest and long black hair that hang down his back in a thick braid. Two people with color that's not chained up or beaten or scared lookin' in the face. They ain't runnin'. Theys walkin' like theys free!

I thinks that maybe they can help me, get me home. The lady stops and touches the arm of the man. She turns to where I be hiding, lookin' and lookin', and starts comin' to me. I thinks I should run but I is too scared and weak from hunger. I curl up tight, try to make myself small.

The lady come and kneel down, peel the bushes aside. Her eyes be wide when she see me, but then she smile. She say some words but I don't really understand. She stretch out her hand to me and say some more words, sweet-sounding words like my mama. My heart hurts in my chest and I feel the tears stinging my eyes. The lady keep talkin' soft, almost like a song that Mama would sing at night. I don't understand all the words, but I don't feel scared. She reach in the pocket of her skirts and pulls out a red round fruit and stretch it to me. I so hungry I feel faint. I takes it. She smile and nod her head. The man just stand there watching. His chest shine in the sunlight.

The fruit is sweet and crunches between my teeth. I eat

it til there's nothing left but the sticky juice on my fingers. The lady laugh. The man smile. She reach out her hand to me again. Smile.

This time I take it.

. . .

This place deep in the woods, shadowed by tall trees, wild bush and deep rich soil, is filled with people that look like me, dark-brown and black skin, wide noses and lips, hair that rises to the sun or twisted in braids like back home. I touch my own hair that has become thick with sweat and dirt and leaves. Then there are men and women and some children with skin the color of copper with straight black hair and eyes of onyx. There are no huts of dried mud with roofs of straw, but wood rooms with passages that swing open and close. There are hollowed-out spaces of earth, caves, where discovery from the outside is not possible.

The woman who found me is Sarah. She says the word "Sarah" over and over, slow, until I knew it was her name. In her hut of wood, she bathes me and washes my hair with warm water and a bar of something sweet. She is gentle, whispering words I do not understand as the tears drip from my eyes into the barrel of water. This is my first kindness in so very long.

Sarah wraps me in a towel and smooths coconut oil over my limbs until my skin smiles and shines. She drops a cool white shift over my head, the fabric soft against my skin. I sit on the hard wood floor, between her thick thighs, as she tenderly combs the tangles from my hair and braids it into two heavy ropes that hang down my back, while I eat a thick soup of meat and potatoes. Then I sleep and sleep.

As time goes by, Sarah keeps me close, tucked to her side as she moves about this village of happy brown and black bodies, stopping at wood huts to talk with those inside. She works with the other women gathering fruit, making potions, and cooking the meals. She points to me and says "Sadie" and smiles. From then, wherever I go in the village, the tribe smiles and says the word "Sadie." I take this new name for this new place.

The children play, running and chasing, squealing in laughter. The sound is so sweet. It can sometimes make me smile. The men come and go, bringing slaughtered animals to be cooked over open fires. The women gather bright fruits and green vegetables that they prepare.

It is like home. Almost.

Slowly I learn and speak the names: Joseph who acts as the head of the tribe; Sparrow, the best hunter with the dark eyes and black hair; Martha the midwife, Janie who looks after the children, John, and others I can't name but come to know.

Sarah tells me no one can bother us here. "We are free."

Would free get me home? If I left this place, would my free be stolen again?

. . .

Two moons have come and gone, and the sickness has come with it. When I take my weekly bathing, I see the growing roundness of my belly. Sarah sees it too.

She sits me down and puts my cheeks in her palms, looks deep in my eyes. It will be good, she says. It will.

But the pain that rips through me after five moon passings, screams that tear through the walls of the wooden room, the sound bathing the women who tend to me—I cannot believe that it will be good.

Until it is.

My own sobs soften, replaced with the tiniest of cries, then a wail that lifts my heart with a kind of joy that I cannot explain.

Martha washes away the remnants of birth that cover my thighs and applies something cool and slippery in the place where the baby had come.

Sarah sits next to me with a wrapped bundle in her arms and hands me my child.

The room is silent except for the roaring of my heart. I feel the warmth of my child resting on my swollen breasts. The birthing women stand round me as I peel back the cloth that wraps my child to expose their face, the pale, round face with pink cheeks, cherry lips, and a crown of curly hair the color of wet sand.

My heart stops. My breath hitches. Nooooo. And then my girl opens her eyes, my eyes, and I dive into them and feel a kind of bonding love that fills my soul, and I promise us both that it will be good.

I will make sure of it.

CHAPTER SIXTEEN

"Barring any more traffic or blocked roads, we should get to the Jitney stop right on time," Zach said as they drove down Main Street.

"Good," Alessandra replied absently, adjusting her trusty camera on her lap. She was quiet for a moment. "It's hard to put together that so much has happened in such a short period of time. Coming home. Seeing my dad. Losing my dad. You. Us. Things I once believed all coming undone." She slowly exhaled. "You're gonna love Ms. Edith, though," she said, switching gears from her moment of introspection.

Zach focused on the road. "Looking forward. If she's anything like what you've described, I know she and Gram will hit it off."

Alessandra laughed. "I know, right?"

"And about everything else," Zach shot her a quick glance, "it's all going to be okay." He gave her a wink, made a slight right, and turned into a side street across from the Jitney stop. "Should be pulling in any minute." He put the SUV in park, unsnapped his belt, and hopped out. Alessandra did the same.

Zach slid his arm around her waist. She blinked in surprise and quiet delight that Zach would put their involvement on display in front of the woman who was like her mother.

What did it mean? Nothing—it meant nothing. He simply didn't want her to slip. That's it. Right?

They crossed the street and joined the waiting assemblage. The Jitney pulled to a stop moments later, and the passengers filed out.

"There she is!" Alessandra raised her hand above her head and waved, aimed her camera and snapped. Then stopped. Her mouth dropped open, her eyes widening. "Traci!" she squealed.

Alessandra and Zach wove their way around the crowd. Traci squeezed them both in a tight hug, kissing cheeks, laughing and jumping with happiness.

Her heart swelled with so much joy, it spilled from her eyes.

Edith wiped Alessandra's tears away.

"Why didn't you tell me you were coming?"

Traci laughed. "Wanted to surprise you. Moved some stuff around—and *bam*, here I is."

The two friends laughed and hugged some more.

"I'm so glad to see you," Alessandra whispered in Traci's ear.

"I know, girl," she whispered back.

"Oh my goodness. I'm so sorry. Ms. Edith, Traci, this is Zach Renard." She turned toward Zach and did all she could to act as if her heart didn't head off on a gallop every time she looked at him.

Zach turned on his global charm, flashed that dimple and the Hollywood smile that crinkled his eyes. He stuck out his hand to Edith and then Traci. "I feel like I already know both of you."

Traci tipped her head to the side and tucked in a smile. "I could say the same." Her right brow inched upward.

Alessandra nudged Traci in the side. "Lemme get a group shot of your arrival," she said to Traci and Ms. Edith. She waved them into a clear spot. "Say…Sag Harbor!" She took a few shots before Zach chimed in.

"Let me take one of all three of you, then I'll collect your bags and get us out of the cold," he offered.

Alessandra handed over her camera. After a few quick shots, he returned her treasure and lifted a suitcase in each hand.

Alessandra linked an arm through Edith's and Traci's. "This way, ladies," she said, leading them toward the SUV with Zach bringing up the rear.

• • •

Zach hid his smile as he drove back to the house listening to the women laugh and talk all at the same time, their voices weaving in and out of each other's in an odd kind of harmony. It was a sort of magic that he'd experienced for the first time at his grandmother's house when she would have the ladies of the quilting circle come over. They would talk in all kinds of soothing accents, from the molasses sounds of the South to the lilt from the blue and green waters of the Caribbean to the rapid clip of the North. Over and under each other, in and out the same way they stitched, finding and piecing the right pieces together to create the whole.

Zach pulled into the short driveway of Alessandra's home and everyone piled out. "I'll take the bags in," he said to Alessandra in a low whisper. "Then I'm gonna head out. Let you ladies get settled."

"Settled. Oh my goodness," she said in a hushed voice. She tugged on her bottom lip with her teeth. "I wasn't expecting Traci. Well, at least not today. I mean, we have the space—if we use my dad's…bedroom." Her brow creased.

Zach twisted his lips in thought. He placed the suitcases in the foyer and kissed her forehead. "I'll be back," he said to Alessandra. "Ladies, great meeting you both. I know you all have a lot to talk about, so I'm going to leave you to it."

"Nice to meet you, too," Edith called out from the club chair in the living room that she'd quickly commandeered.

Zach cupped Alessandra's elbow. "See you later." He closed the door behind him.

"So this is it, huh?" Traci said, moving slowly through the space, taking in the home, with its solid mahogany mantels and framing, bay windows, and overstuffed comfy furnishings. The wood floors, worn in some places, still retained their regalness.

"Yep, this is it," Alessandra said, feeling a moment of pride. "Moved here when I was about seven. Big change from living in the city. Parents never really talked about why, but I always guessed it had to do with money." She glanced around. "But my mom was determined to bring the big-city shine to Sag Harbor." She shoved her hands into the back pockets of her jeans. "I fixed us up a late lunch," she said, turning the topic away from the past. "Y'all got to be starved."

"I know I am," Traci chimed.

"Ms. Edith, you want to eat in here or in the kitchen?"

Edith smiled. "Chile, you know me and kitchens are best friends." She pushed herself up from the chair. "Lead the way."

Alessandra took the store-bought rotisserie chicken from the oven, which she'd kept on warm, and placed it alongside bowls of seasoned green beans and saffron rice and a pitcher of iced tea. She was so happy that Zach had the foresight to get her kitchen stocked. *Zach*. Inwardly she smiled, even as a twinge of "too good to be true" teased her consciousness.

"What's that look?" Traci quizzed before mouthing a forkful of rice. She arched a brow.

"What look?"

Edith chimed in, "*That* look." She snickered.

Two sets of inquiring eyes stared at her.

Alessandra shifted in her seat. She waved her hand in feigned dismissal. "Y'all are seeing things."

"Mm-hmm," Traci murmured.

"Fine," she huffed, as if giving in after hours of interrogation. "Maybe it is about Zach." There—she'd said it. "He's…"

"Special," Edith filled in softly.

Alessandra put down her fork. She licked her bottom lip, then held it between her teeth. "He is," she said on a breath. "From the moment we met," she said, bringing that first night into focus. "I can't explain it."

"Sometimes ain't nothing to explain," Edith said. "It just is. Told ya that."

Traci reached over and patted Alessandra's hand. "And the brotha is fiiine! Whoo girl."

Alessandra laughed as her cheeks heated. "It's so exciting…and scary. But I have no idea where it's going—or if it's even going anywhere. Look, it's temporary. In the moment. He has a whole other life." She slid Traci a meaningful look. "And I mean, I can't live here. I have a life and a job in New York." She blew out a breath. "Not to mention my show. Just the thought of it is giving me anxiety."

"Nothin' is promised," Edith said. She took a long swallow of iced tea. "Sometimes all you can do is step out on faith." She dipped her head toward Alessandra, then took up with finishing off her lunch, but not before asking about "arrangements" for her dad.

The funnel of pain that she'd kept corked when Zach was around came loose and began to spin in her chest. For a moment, she couldn't breathe until she felt Edith's gentle hand on her shoulder. Her eyes were clouded with tears.

"It's all right, chile. Cry. It's all right," Edith soothed. "Good cry helps wash out what hurts ya."

Traci came around on Alessandra's other side and put her arm across her friend's shoulders. "We got you, girl."

"I...stayed angry for so long. And for what?" Her voice cracked. "Now...I'm starting to find out things about my mom that make everything even worse. I was so unfair to my dad," she cried, and covered her face with her hands. "Now I can't make it up to him. It's too late."

"It's never too late to do what's right," Edith said, practically echoing the words Zach's grandmother had shared.

Alessandra sniffed hard. Traci grabbed a paper napkin and shoved it in her friend's hand.

"You gon' be all right." Edith stood. "Come on and help me clean up this kitchen," she said to Traci. "Then we can figure out what we gon' do. Okay?" She threw her gaze from one to the other. Traci nodded her assent.

Alessandra wiped her eyes and forced a smile. "Okay," she whispered.

"I am, like, the worst hostess," Alessandra groused after putting the last dish away. "Your bags are still in the hall. Let me show you where to put them, and you can relax after the ride and *food*," she added with a grin.

Edith dried her hands on a towel, then covered her yawn

with the back of her palm. She walked toward the living room. "Scuse me." She chuckled. "But if it's all right by you, I can settle in for a quick nap right in that chair. Humph," she hummed. "Reminds me of a chair that my grandma had."

She walked into the room with Alessandra and Traci following, and lowered herself into the club chair.

"She would settle down in that chair of hers, all thick and soft with stuffing, and put me on her lap." Her gaze wandered as a smile bloomed. "She'd stroke my hair and make soft cooing sounds in her throat, tell me I was a special child and was gonna be a special woman. I was free, and one day I was gonna travel far from home and make a new life. Told her I didn't wanna leave her. She just laughed, said we all hafta leave sometime." Edith pulled in a breath, blinked. She laughed lightly. "Long time ago," she said on a sigh.

"Are you sure you'll be all right taking a nap in the chair?" Alessandra asked, kneeling down at Edith's side.

Edith waved her hand. "Go on now. I'm fine. If I can spend days riding on a bus, sleeping on hard benches, this here chair is heaven on earth."

"At least let me get you a quilt," Alessandra offered. She got to her feet.

"That would be fine." Edith settled in the chair, linked her fingers across her stomach, and shut her eyes.

Alessandra crossed the room to the built-in cabinets where her mother always kept the table linens, Christmas ornaments, and extra quilts. She took a quilt that was a brilliant abstract of orange and gold and red and gently placed it over Edith. She lightly squeezed her shoulder as Edith's eyes drifted closed.

Alessandra and Traci tiptoed out.

"Ms. Edith sure is something," Traci whispered.

"Yes, she is. I know riding on that bus for almost two

hours wasn't easy on her. She's no spring chicken. I want to make her as comfortable as possible, which leads me to my somewhat dilemma."

"What?"

"Well, there's my bedroom, a small guest room, and my dad's room."

"Okay?" Traci asked with a questioning frown.

"I didn't know if either of you wanted to sleep in my dad's room...I mean..." She hunted for the right words.

"Ohhh. I get it. My tagging along kinda messed things up. Look, I," her voice squeaked, "could stay in your dad's room." Her expression twitched.

"No. *I* should. It's just that I can barely step in the room for any length of time. Went in there and...it was tough. I guess it's a combination of hurt and guilt. Ya know."

"I totally get it. Hey, I can sleep on the couch. Ms. Edith can take the guest room. No worries." She squeezed Alessandra's arm.

Alessandra sighed. "I guess." Her cell phone vibrated in her back pocket. She pulled it out, and instant sunshine lit her cheeks. "Hey," she practically sighed into the phone. "Oh. Really? Are you sure? I mean if it's okay with your grandmother." She laughed. "I think so, too. Okay. About five. Great. Thanks so much. See you later." She almost blew a kiss into the phone but didn't. She shoved the cell back in her pocket. "Guess what? Problem solved."

"The knight in shining armor to the rescue?" Traci teased with a knowing smile.

"Whatever," she giggled. "Anyway, he said that his grandmother would love some company her own age, and they have plenty of room. I know that Ms. Edith and Grandma O will get along great. We're all invited for dinner."

Traci tipped her head to the side and squinted at her

friend. "I need a knight to solve some of my issues," she said with a grin. "He have any brothers? Besties? Distant acquaintances?"

Alessandra laughed. "Girl, please, like you want to settle down."

"I would with the right man. But until then, I'm here for you, sis. So, what do we need to do?"

"Find my father's insurance policy so that I can give the information to the funeral home. I should have done it right away, but—"

"Hey, don't worry about all that. We'll get it done. Where do you think he kept his papers?"

"In any one of these drawers or cabinets." She looked around and waved her arm. "Or maybe upstairs. Take your pick."

"We can start this evening, after Ms. Edith gets settled. But until then, you can tell me everything about Mr. Tall, Dark, and Sexy. Humph, boy next door. Right out of a romance novel!"

They both laughed, then tiptoed out of the room and into the kitchen, where they had a good old-fashioned girl talk at the table.

CHAPTER SEVENTEEN

"This is so nice of you to have us over, Mrs. O," Alessandra said. "This is my best friend Traci Howard and my second mom, Edith Samuels. Ladies, Mrs. Oweku."

"Welcome. Please call me Grace," she said to Edith, "and you, young lady, can call me Grandma O," she said with a sharp nod in Traci's direction. She led the guests into the front room. "Always loved a full house. Come on and make yourselves comfortable. Son, bring the tea from the kitchen. Only takes a minute to catch a chill in this weather."

"Yes, ma'am," Zach said, caught Alessandra's eye, and winked. "Coming right up."

"And I have something a little stronger for later," Grandma O said in a conspiratorial whisper. Her eyes picked up the overhead light and sparked with mischief.

Edith slapped her thigh. "A woman after my own heart!"

The two elders laughed, and Alessandra and Traci shared a tickled side-eye.

Zach returned with a wide wooden tray laden with a teapot of hot water, cups, teabags, spoons, and a saucer with lemon slices.

"This is nice," Edith said. "My Charles and me used to have tea before bed." Her smile was wistful.

"How long were you married?" Grandma O softly asked.

"Forty years. We had a good life; hard sometimes, but good," she said on a sigh of satisfaction.

Grandma O turned all of her attention on Edith, and before long they were hip-deep in stories of their lives in a world very different from the one they lived in today and shared laughter at their escapades in navigating a world that didn't see them. They had all but forgotten the younger generation.

"Let's leave these young folks, Edith. Let me show you around, show you where you'll be staying while you're here."

"Staying? Here? You sure? I could be a serial killer." Her eyes crinkled at the corners.

"If you are, it be the most exciting thing to happen around here in a long time!"

The room broke into laughter.

The two elders rose from their seats. Grace took Edith's arm and leaned her head close. "Now, I was thinking…" Her voice trailed off as they left the front room.

Traci looked at Alessandra. "Well, that's settled," she said, grinning.

"Told you they would hit it off," Zach crowed. He put the used cups back on the tray. "Can I get you two anything before dinner?"

"No. I'm fine."

"Me, too," Alessandra said, looking up at him and hoping that her eyes conveyed how much she appreciated him.

He walked out with the tray.

Traci flopped back against the couch. "He's really nice," she said softly.

"Yeah, he kinda is, right?"

They laughed.

"Did you let Steven know what's going on? You might have to postpone the show," Traci gingerly hedged.

Alessandra heaved a sigh. "No. And I know." She sadly shook her head. "Needing to be in two places at once is killing me softly. I have to be here. And I need to be there. I don't want to blow my big opportunity."

"Avoiding the inevitable is fruitless. He needs to know so he can determine how to go forward. You, too."

Alessandra squeezed her eyes shut. "I know," she groaned. "That's what makes this even harder. If I blow this, there's no telling when another chance will come. I feel torn. I ran from here to build the career that I've finally gotten in my sights, and the irony is that being back here is what could derail it all."

"Some advice?"

"Sure."

"No matter whatever else is out in the world, you only have family—the one you're born into, and the one you make. You can keep taking pictures until you can't anymore. But this time—this *now* in your life—if you blow it, it will be that picture that never gets developed. You need to be here for your dad and for yourself." Traci shrugged. "I'm just sayin'."

Alessandra's eyes crinkled at the corners with her smile. "Look at you, sounding all wise and whatnot." She paused. "But you're right. I feel this pull to be here." Her brows knitted as she looked at her friend. "And my father wanted me here to find out whatever it was that has been kept from me all my life."

Traci covered Alessandra's hand. "Then I think you have solved your own dilemma, my friend."

Zach returned and stood in the doorway with his coat on.

"I'm gonna run into town, meet up with my research buddy; he's only here for a couple of days. I should be back in time for dinner, but if not, start without me. See you ladies later," he added with a smile. He winked at Alessandra, turned, and left.

"Research buddy?" Traci quipped. "And who might that be?"

"No clue." She frowned. "As much as I feel I *know* Zach"—she paused a beat—"I really don't."

"Yeah. I get that. I mean there is a big difference between having a...I don't know...soul-filled connection with somebody and *knowing* them. That part takes time."

"Yeah, that's true." She sighed.

Grace and Edith returned, laughing like old friends.

"Where's Zach?" Grace asked.

"He said he had to go into town to meet his 'research buddy,'" Alessandra offered.

Grace snorted a laugh. "That's what he told you, huh?" She laughed again. "Gotta be that Morgan." She shook her head, even as a warm smile lit her eyes. "Those two been thick as thieves since they were boys. Got into more trouble! Humph. Turned out all right, though, thank goodness. Both of 'em." She pulled in a breath and looked around. "Get him on his phone and tell him to get hisself back here *and* bring Morgan with him for dinner. Period."

Alessandra's eyes widened. "Yes, ma'am."

Traci bit down on her lip to keep from laughing.

"Good." She turned to Edith and linked her arm with her new friend and started out of the room. "Now you was telling me about..."

Traci focused on Alessandra. "Well, I suggest you get on the phone and call your man *and,*" she held up a finger, "let's just put the good vibes out that this Morgan dude is half the man Zach is."

"Traci!" Alessandra cried, feigning shock. She pulled her cell from her back pocket. "Be on your best behavior."

Traci winked. "Always."

. . .

Zach pulled his hat from his head and shoved his gloves into the pockets of his jacket as he walked into the steamy interior of Night and Day, the local bar/restaurant that served *the* best burgers.

"Zach, haven't seen you in a while," Rachel, the hostess, greeted. "How are you?"

"I'm good. Been running around. Back for a little while."

"Great. You want a table or seat at the bar?"

"Actually, I'm meeting Morgan."

"Morgan." Her entire expression softened. "He hasn't arrived yet, but I can get you a table."

"I think the bar will be cool. Thanks, though. Point him in my direction when he gets here."

"I sure will."

Zach gave a short nod and headed toward the bar. Morgan and Rachel had been a thing for a short while. She wanted commitment. Morgan Chambers was a lot of things, but committed to a woman was not one of them. Fortunately, they'd parted ways on good terms. Zach attributed it to Morgan's charm.

He slid onto the barstool and was approached by the bartender.

"What can I get you?" He wiped the bar top with a white rag and slid a bowl of mixed nuts in front of Zach.

"Hennessy on the rocks."

"My man!"

Zach swiveled on his seat toward the familiar salute. He rose with a big grin on his face and embraced his childhood buddy. "Hey, brotha."

They stepped apart and shared the handshake of the day, followed by a tight fist pull to the chest.

Morgan sat next to Zach. "Whatcha drinkin'? Hennessy?"

"Of course." He chuckled.

The bartender slid Zach's drink in front of him.

"Make that two," Morgan said.

"So, what brings you back to this little neck of the woods?" Zach asked.

"Needed a break from DC, man."

"Wouldn't have anything to do with a woman, would it?" Zach teased.

"Bruh, you wound me." He paused. "But yeah."

He chuckled and shook his head. "Some things never change."

Morgan's drink arrived. He raised his glass. "To the day that things change."

Zach tapped his glass against Morgan's. "To change."

They sipped.

"How's Grandma O?"

"Feisty as ever."

"Remember that time she chased us all the way around the block yelling she had a switch?" Morgan said, laughing at the vivid memory.

"Right!"

"She coulda been a track star. I swear I could feel her breath on my neck. I knew if she caught my sorry ass, I was in trouble!"

"At least you got to run home. I had to listen to the lecture on the error of my ways for hours and how I was putting a stain on the family name with my foolishness." He shook his head, took a sip of his drink. "I would have opted for a beatdown."

"Ha. Right. I know she wouldn't have really beat us. It was the thought of it, though—and the humiliation of being caught by a grandma!"

They broke into laughter.

Morgan sipped his drink. "So, what's been happening? You on another project, or what?"

"I am." He took a beat. "Met someone." He side-eyed his friend.

Morgan angled his body toward Zach. "Ohhh. And?"

Zach exhaled. "It was sudden. Intense and complicated."

"Complicated is my middle name. So…let's hear it."

Over drinks and handfuls of peanuts and a platter of hot wings, Zach told Morgan about Alessandra Fleming from the moment they met right up to when he left her in the care of his grandmother. "I'm not sure why we hadn't crossed paths when we were coming up. I guess when you and I were kids, girls were the last thing on our minds. And by the time I was old enough to care, she was still too young for our circles. At some point she moved away. But," he paused, "there's this crazy feeling that I have when I'm around her. It's like I've always known her." He turned to Morgan with a questioning frown tightening his brow.

"Damn, bruh." Morgan finished his second drink. "Sounds like it might be something. 'Might' being the operative word. I mean, you're always traveling." He gave a slight shrug. "And she's gonna eventually go back to her life…"

"Like I said, complicated. Plus, with her recently losing her dad, who knows if any of this is real or reaction?"

Morgan tipped his head toward Zach. "There's that."

Zach's cell vibrated. He pulled it from his pocket. Smiled.

"Speaking of." He pressed the talk icon. "Hey, everything cool?" He listened. Laughed. "Of course she would say that. Tell her we'll be there in about a half hour. See you soon," he ended softly. He stared at the phone for a moment, a faraway look on his face.

"Yep, you're hooked," Morgan said, snapping Zach out of his reverie.

The corner of his mouth curved upward. "I just might be." He slid his phone back in his pocket. "And you are commanded by the queen of the castle to come for dinner. She's cooking."

"Grandma O cooking? You don't have to tell me twice. *And* I get to meet this lady that has your head on swivel? Let's roll."

CHAPTER EIGHTEEN

Dinner at Grandma O's was a raucous affair. The six-foot dining table was covered end to end with platters and bowls of steamed red snapper, seasoned cabbage, rice and beans and sweet bread, and jugs of iced tea, coffee, and water. Laughter, over and under conversation, danced from one end of the room to the other.

Edith shared harrowing stories about her trip up north that had them all on the edge of their seats, then of her early days of loneliness in a strange city. But then she met her husband, Charles Samuels. He was sitting in the pew in front of her at Abyssinian Baptist Church one Sunday afternoon in late May. The same church where, six months later, they said "I do." She knew that with Charles she could endure anything, and that she could make a new family in a city that wasn't lonely anymore. "After Charles passed, I didn't think I'd ever really feel whole again." She paused and sent Alessandra a loving smile. "Then I met Alessandra here. I got the daughter I never had."

Alessandra blew her a kiss, knowing that she'd lost count

of the ways that Ms. Edith had seamlessly stepped into the shoes of a mother and looked after her, even when she didn't know she needed looking after.

Morgan and Zach, on the other hand, had the group in stitches with tales of their antics as kids and of Grandma's unending threats to their very lives.

Grandma O merely *tsk-tsk*ed at her characterization. "All that scolding and threats musta worked. You two turned out half okay," she said with a shadow of a smile.

"Two halves make a whole," Morgan quipped, raising his glass.

The diners sputtered with laughter.

Alessandra let her gaze wander from one animated face to the next, laughing at the jokes and becoming wide-eyed at the tales. This was what family felt like. It had been so long since she'd felt this way, embraced in a cocoon of love and feeling safe from the world, belonging to something outside of herself and her work. She'd walked away from the only family she'd had. And she would always regret her choice. But tonight, she was reminded that family was more than a connection by blood. *The family you're born into, and the one you make*.

With them at her side, the next few difficult days would be bearable—and the future as well. She wished she had her camera with her to memorialize this moment.

She sipped her tea and listened to Grandma O tell about the early days of Sag Harbor, the history of Eastville and Azurest and the Black and Indigenous inhabitants who had been there long before the community had its name, living and building together in harmony. In its early days, Grandma O explained, Eastville was a whaling town, a place for adventurers looking for economic opportunities. The center of the town was St. David A.M.E. Zion Church. "Freed people built it back in 1840. Folklore says that the church may have been part of the Underground Railroad. Now I know most figure the Underground Railroad was about slaves escaping from the South. But they was up here, too, many of 'em brought here with their masters." She sighed.

Suddenly, Alessandra's temples pounded, the air swirling in circles in her chest, the word "Run" repeating over and over in her mind. *Hide. Make yo'self small. The wood plank closed over our head. Dark as pitch. Smell of damp earth and rot fill my nose. I think they must be able to hear my heart banging. Mama cover my mouth with her hand so I don't scream when a rat run over our feet.*

Alessandra blinked, looked around, but everyone was engrossed in listening to Grandma O. She reached for her glass of iced tea and took a shaky sip.

Slowly the sensations dissipated, and she felt calm again.

"One of the Church's first preachers was a known abolitionist, J. P. Thompson," Grandma O was saying. "Story goes that the trapdoor near the pulpit and one under the library was used by those running for freedom."

Having heard Zach's tales and discoveries and now Grandma O's, she knew that she had to uncover her own family story. It was here. She could feel it. "Totally fascinating," Alessandra murmured. She turned to Zach and lowered her voice. "I can see how easy it is to go down the rabbit hole to find answers."

He bobbed his head in agreement. "Researching history, to borrow from Forrest Gump, 'You never know what you're going to get.' That's the excitement."

She was beginning to accept and manage the sudden onslaught of images, sounds, and scents, maybe even to need them. They no longer frightened her, but rather, offered a path to something just beyond her line of sight. The possibility of what she might discover excited her the way an image did as she waited for it to slowly take shape in photographic solution. "Hmm, you might be right."

· · ·

"It's all settled," Zach said, close to Alessandra's ear while he moved next to her on the couch. He stretched his arm across its back and let his fingers drift to her shoulder.

She angled her head to look at him and once again felt that quick tug in her stomach and thump in her heart. She swallowed. "What might that be?" she quipped, hoping to slow the steady racing of her pulse.

"Gram convinced Ms. Edith to stay here. Traci can stay in your spare bedroom, and we...can stay in yours. If it's cool with you," he quickly added with a lift of his brows.

Alessandra grinned. "Seems like you have it all figured out." She leaned closer, gazed up at him from beneath her lashes. "We'll have to be very quiet," she said in a hushed voice filled with innuendo.

He cupped her cheek, leaned in. "I'll do my best," he said, low in his throat.

Approaching voices separated them.

"Son, why don't you go on over to the Fleming place and grab Edith's bags so we can get her settled?" Grandma O instructed.

"Yes, ma'am." He got up from his seat. Alessandra did the same.

"Thank you so much for dinner, Grandma O," Alessandra said. She walked toward the coatrack.

"Yes, it was delicious," Traci added, following suit.

"And I don't want you to worry about 'the arrangements,'"

Grandma O said softly. "Me and Edith are going to take care of everything."

"Oh, please, you don't have to do that," Alessandra implored.

"I'm sure I don't. But I want to."

"And so do I, sweetheart," Edith added. "You just concentrate on you."

"I'll call over to the homegoing parlor and get everything set. I'm figuring we can have the service on Monday and a repast right here."

Alessandra felt a sting in her eyes and a knot in her throat. This woman barely knew her, and yet she was willing to do so much. She sniffed. Swallowed. "Thank you," she whispered, her voice cracking.

Zach put his arm around her shoulder. "It's going to be fine," he said softly. "And it's okay to let folks who care about you help."

She tugged on her shaky bottom lip with her teeth and blinked hard. She nodded. She wasn't alone. She was surrounded by people who cared about her. "Thank you," she said on a breath, to everyone in the room. "For helping. For...being here."

"That's what friends and family are for," Edith said.

"Now go on, do what I told ya. We have things to do," Grandma O said.

Morgan gave Grandma O a hug and kiss. "Good to see you and thanks for dinner."

"Don't stay away so long next time."

"I won't. Promise. So nice to meet you, Ms. Edith." He kissed her cheek. "You two stay out of trouble," he said, wagging a finger at the elders.

"Boy, go on," Grandma O said, chuckling, and waved him away.

The four young people got into their coats and boots and piled out of the house. Traci and Morgan lagged a few steps behind Alessandra and Zach and talked in hushed voices.

"Those two seem to have hit it off," Alessandra murmured to Zach as she unlocked the front door.

"Morgan is generally not so obvious," Zach said, stepping in behind Alessandra.

She took off her coat and her boots. "Meaning?" She turned to look at him.

Zach gave a light shrug. "Hmm, he's not the ongoing conversation type. Plays it close. Reserved." He snorted a laugh. "Traci must have flipped a switch."

"She *does* have a way about her," Alessandra said lightly. Traci was a no-holds-barred woman. When she saw something or someone she wanted, she went after it—and it was becoming quite clear that Traci wanted Morgan. She held in a laugh. He had no idea what he was in for.

"Are you two coming in, or what? You're letting all the warm air out," Alessandra shouted, stepping into the foyer.

The newly minted duo laughed and trooped inside.

"I'll get Ms. Edith's suitcase," Alessandra offered. She walked off and returned several moments later with the suitcase to find Zach flipping through her dad's album collection and Traci and Morgan seated hip to hip on the love seat.

Zach glanced over his shoulder. "Your dad has an amazing collection."

Alessandra set the suitcase down and walked to his side. "Yeah," she said softly. Warm childhood memories drifted through her mind. Saturday mornings had been theirs, once upon a time. Her's and her dad's.

He'd always test her knowledge with trivia questions about what they were listening to—and more often than not, she got them right. Sometimes he'd open his sax case, take out the instrument, gaze at it with a kind of love, then play along with some of his favorites. When she was older and began to develop her own tastes, they would debate for hours about instruments versus vocals.

Why had things gone so wrong between them? She blinked against the sudden sting in her eyes. "Yeah," she murmured again.

Zach tipped up her chin with the tip of his finger. "You okay?"

She tucked in her lips and bobbed her head. "Um, you should probably get the suitcase to Ms. Edith."

"Sure thing. I know we kind of agreed that I'd stay here. But don't you need some space? Spend some time with your friend?"

Alessandra placed her hand on his arm. "I think so. If you don't mind. We can see each other tomorrow." Her gaze glided across his face.

Zach leaned down and kissed her lightly on the lips. "Whatever you need."

"Thanks."

He kissed her again. "See you tomorrow." He turned to the couple on the couch. "Okay, partner. I'm out."

"Yeah. Yeah," Morgan said on a breath and reluctantly stood up. "I need to roll, myself." He cast a look in Traci's direction. "Call you."

She nodded, then crossed her legs. "Whenever you're ready," she said in sweet invitation.

Morgan chuckled. "Great to meet you, Alessandra. And I'm real sorry about your dad. He was a real cool dude."

"Thanks."

"You girls don't stay up too late," Zach teased as he slipped on his coat.

Alessandra sat on the arm of the chair next to Traci. "And you two stay out of trouble," she countered.

"Always!" Morgan said over his chuckles. "Good night, ladies." He opened the door.

Zach stepped out behind Morgan. "Have a good night." He closed the door behind him.

Alessandra glanced down at Traci from her position on the love seat. "So, um, what's this vibe I'm getting between you and Morgan?"

Traci dragged in a breath and slowly exhaled. She tugged on her bottom lip with her teeth. "Hmm," she said in a low tone. "He's definitely got something." Her brow arched. She turned to Alessandra. "Know what I mean?"

Alessandra grinned. "Do *you* know what you mean?"

Traci slowly shook her head back and forth, but a wide smile crept onto her face. "Gurl, gurl. Humph, humph, humph."

Alessandra swatted Traci's shoulder. "I don't think I've ever seen you like this, my sister."

Traci tilted her head to the side and pursed her lips. "And I could say the same thing about you, miss. I've been in a room with you and a guy you were involved with—and trust me, sparks like this, there were none."

Alessandra smiled wickedly, then frowned. "Damn. Speaking of no sparks…"

"What?" Traci asked.

"Steven. I totally forgot to call him. Shit…" She pulled her cell from her back pocket and groaned when she saw the three missed calls and an unopened text. "I don't even know what to say to him," she murmured. She dropped her hands to her sides and looked at her friend for a miracle of words. "He's done so much for me, and this show has the potential to truly launch my career. But I swear… I don't know how

I'll be ready, and I'm going to let him down."

Traci's sleek brow flicked upward. "The truth." She gave a light shrug. "Sis, Steven was never 'the one.' As much as I figured he was your type…" She shook her head. "Nope. But he *is* your employer, and more than likely he gave you this major career opportunity because he kinda likes you more than because you take great photographs—though you *do* take great photographs. We both know that. I mean, he's a good-looking guy, nice job, decent personality. But…when you want to build a life with someone, it has to be more than the surface stuff. Ya know?" She pressed her fist to her chest. "You have to feel it, deep inside. And I'm kinda getting the vibe that Zach is somebody that could mean something in your life."

Alessandra's neck craned back, and her eyes tightened at the corners. "Who are you and what did you do with my best friend Traci?"

Traci laughed. "I'm just sayin'…"

"Uh-huh, saying what?"

"That maybe…we're all actually grown folk and need to play our role. You need to call Steven and put your cards on the table so that he can make some decisions. That's the grown-up, professional thing to do."

Alessandra blinked fast enough to cause a breeze. "What in heaven's name did that man say to you?"

She sighed. "Nothing in particular and everything at the same time." She shook her head in confusion. "He made me *feel* something. Know what I mean?"

Alessandra smiled at her longtime friend. "I sure do."

Traci ran her tongue along her bottom lip. "So, in the meantime, putting all this new touchy-feely stuff aside for a minute, be about your business and call Steven?"

Alessandra looked at the screen of her cell phone, then

dragged in a long breath and released it slowly with her answer. She lifted her chin. "I'll be back." She walked out and climbed the stairs to her bedroom to make her call.

"If your expression is any indication, I take it the call didn't go well," Traci said when Alessandra returned.

Alessandra slowly sat down. "He was…very empathetic about my father and making arrangements and everything. But when I told him that I was nowhere near ready for the show in the next four weeks, he flipped. I mean, ballistic."

Traci made a face. "Damn," she whispered.

"I can't even put together everything he actually said. He went from shock to fury to blame to how much he'd done for me, the risk that he took, and the financial support he put into sponsoring my show." She rested her head back against the cushion of the couch and closed her eyes. "That was brutal, and not even so much what he said, but that I'd let him down—and myself."

"Listen, sis, life gets in the way. No way you could have seen this coming."

She exhaled a slow breath. "Yeah, but if I'm honest, I wasn't ready *before* my dad passed."

"Hmm. So what's the bottom line? Date change?"

She glanced across at her friend. "Cancelled. Period."

"Oh damn, girl. For real?"

Alessandra nodded.

"I'm so sorry."

She sighed. "Everything happens for a reason. My father brought me here, back home, and I feel in my spirit that, as hard as losing him is, I'm supposed to be here to find out what my mother didn't initially want me to know." If she was honest, not having the show was a kind of relief mixed with panic as to what her future held as a photographer. Yet, on the other hand, her life was now filled with new possibilities, exciting ones.

She now had the chance to find her roots, to pull back the curtain that separated her from the life her mother didn't want her to know about and why. Her skin tingled.

Something—someone—was out there, just waiting for her to find them. She just knew it.

Out in the world, Mama calls me Ella. The family, not of blood, but of common good, call me Ella. Our villagers call Mama Sadie for her safety. But at night Mama whispers my real name, the same as hers, the one she keeps in her spirit. To remember.

"Pass it on," she whispers to me each night before we sleep, and she tells me the tales of home—our real home. Tells me I got to learn to read and write so I will know and pass it on.

When Mama first came to this place, she was protected by woods and swamp and the villagers who sheltered her from the men who wanted her return. For many weeks, she hid during the day in a deep tunnel beneath the home of the village doctor until her rounding belly, with me tucked inside, made it too difficult and dangerous.

I am raised in a village of people who love and protect each other. During the days, the women cook and prepare the meals, sew clothes, play with the children, teach us the letters and numbers in a small room at the center of the village, laugh with each other, and worship on Sundays. The men tend to the houses, make repairs, bring in meat and fish and supplies, talk late into the nights in warm, deep voices that cover us with a blanket of protection.

Mama got a shop in the back of our place to fix up the ladies' hair now. She make nice-smelling oils and grease for they scalp to smooth the thickness. She make it special in a big vat out back. House always full of ladies comin' in one way and goin' out another. Saturday be the busiest day. Ladies want to look dey best on Sunday.

Mama braid and twist, comb and smooth, hum to herself while she work, a faraway look in her eyes.

I ask her how she know to do all that with hair, make up the grease to twist the kinks and curls into crowns? She say she learned from her mama and her mama learned from her mama, and my mama show me how to mix the oils and melt the fat and sprinkle it with herbs and flower petals.

Most days as she works, I play with the other children and help the elders cook and plant and harvest. As time goes, some of the families move away, but before a new moon could rise, another family would take their place. Come from all over, hoping for a better life like the kind we got here, I 'spose.

Seem like every day the village grow, but not really. It is us children that was growin'. Wasn't right for us girls to run 'round with the boys playin' tag and go-seek, skippin' off to sit under the houses and share pieces of hard candy no more. Dem elders always sayin' to us girls, "Stop yo' runnin', no yellin', fix yo' skirt, smooth yo' hair." Dem elders want us girls to sew and sweep and tend to the food.

I like runnin' cross the pond, splashin', searchin' for bugs, cleanin' chickens and huntin' for rabbits.

But as far back as I can think, I knew I was different, from the bronze color of my eyes and my skin that was not like Mama's or the women, men and children in the village, skin the color of weak tea drowned in milk that stung after long hours in the sun. My hair slides between my fingers and doesn't rise like a dark halo toward the sun.

Why am I not like you, Mama? I ask, holding her deep-bark-colored arm in my hand. The difference between our skin like sunrise and nightfall. You are of me, from me. That's all that matters, she say.

But when tightness fills the air of the village and the horses whinny and the cocks crow and Mama tells me to hide in that place where she'd hidden those years ago, I peek out and see men with skin like mine and wonder. Am I of them?

CHAPTER NINETEEN

The next few days flew by in a flash of preparations, notifying people, and shopping. Alessandra was on her way out of the door when Zach was on his way in.

"Hey, not leaving on my account, are you?" he teased.

"No. Have to take care of some things. I've got my marching orders from your grandmother."

He grinned. "I can imagine. Need any help?"

"No. The generals have everything under control."

Zach angled his head to the side. "What's wrong?"

Her stomach fluttered. She glanced down at her booted feet. Yes, the preparations had been draining, but what was truly exhausting her were the dreams.

Ever since her call with Steven, she'd dreamed of nothing but flashes of rushing water and running feet, hiding from something unseen, her heart racing, even as she peered into the darkness searching for...what? She couldn't be sure. At times, she felt the comfort of strong arms around her; at others, she felt herself free falling into darkness only to tumble into the light and onto a bed of downy softness. Over and over, different versions of the same thing, until she finally woke up drained and confused. Even though she'd begun to manage the visions when she was awake, it was the dreams that were so powerful.

Alessandra pressed her palm to Zach's chest. "I'm good. Just a bit tired."

"Too much girl talk?"

She forced a smile. "Yeah. Listen, I need to follow Grandma's orders. I don't want her coming after *me* with a switch!" She leaned in and kissed him on the mouth. "See you later." She brushed by him and out, but what she wanted to do was turn back around and tell him about her dreams, have him ease her mind and her spirit.

But deep inside, she knew that the only person who could find what she sought was herself.

When she returned home, Traci was busy in the kitchen, whipping up something that smelled delicious.

"Hey, something smells good."

Traci glanced over her shoulder. "Home fries, grits with cheese, and catfish."

"Gurl, gurl. I sure forgot you could cook." She joined Traci at the stove and sniffed in delight. "How much longer?"

Traci laughed. "About twenty, twenty-five minutes."

"Cool. I need to find a suit and stuff…for my dad."

Traci stopped stirring the grits. "You good with that?"

Alessandra nodded. "Yeah, I'm fine. I need to do this. Ya know."

Traci arched a skeptic brow.

"Besides, I've been ordered by Zach's grandmother to get it done," she said, with a lift of her right brow. "She's going to take the clothes to the parlor."

Traci nodded. "Everything's gonna be all right," she said, lullaby-soft.

"I know. I know," she whispered. Then she turned and headed up to her father's bedroom.

· · ·

"I see you ladies are busy," Zach greeted as he walked into the kitchen. He came around to where his grandmother sat and lightly kissed her cheek before doing the same to Edith.

"Just about done. There's breakfast in the oven if ya hungry," Grace said. "You left out pretty early this morning."

"Went into town. I had to meet with the archivist at the library. Needed to get some research done before the library opened."

"Sounds important," Edith said. She took a sip of her tea.

"It is," Grace said, pride ringing in her voice. "Tell her. Go 'head. He's written books, too, *and* he's a doctor. Not a medical doctor, but one of those doctors that studies things. Well, go 'head and tell her."

Zach shifted the backpack filled with documents on his shoulder, amused and embarrassed by his grandmother's effusiveness. "I study communities, the history of the people and their culture. I'm working on a project for the Smithsonian about the early beginnings here in Sag Harbor of freed Blacks and the Indigenous tribes. Most of the available history centers around the white families that settled here and on Sullivan Island. There's much more to the story, and it's my job to put the pieces together."

"That's what you do for your work?" Edith asked. "Investigate and tell stories?"

Zach chuckled. "Something like that."

"Hmm. I'd like to see some of what you do one of these days."

"I'll be sure to make that happen, Ms. Edith. Gram, I'm going to take my plate upstairs."

"So long as you make sure you don't leave no dirty dishes up there," she warned.

Zach bit back a smile. "Yes, ma'am." He got his plate from the oven, grabbed a fork and napkins, and headed to his room.

"Sometimes you just hafta remind these young people what's what," he heard his grandmother murmur to Edith. Zach chuckled and climbed the stairs.

Once in his room, he placed his aluminum-foil-covered plate on the table by the window and dropped the backpack on the floor.

Part of his research was to document the existence of Maroon communities along the eastern seaboard. He believed, from what he'd begun to uncover, that his original theory was correct. Somewhere here on the island, there had been a thriving Maroon community that, for reasons unexplained and only vaguely referenced in documents, disappeared from the land and from history.

He planned to change that narrative.

He brought his plate to his desk and opened the backpack. He'd been able to get copies of newspapers dating back to the mid-1860s, as well as copies of diaries from several of the female gentry. He was confident that he'd be able to glean information about the *real* comings and goings from the diaries. Much of his interest and focus centered on a slave ship that ran aground in 1839 off the shores of Sag Harbor.

He spread his notes and photocopies on the desk. His gaze homed in on the artist's rendering of the schooner *La Amistad*. He picked up his magnifying glass for a closer look. The fine detailing of the ship, its ragged sails still fluttering in the wind, and the rawness of the barely clothed ebony bodies that lined the deck, all backgrounded against the whitecaps, were as clearly captured as by an actual photograph.

He peered closer, moved the magnifying glass slowly across the image. He could almost make out the features of the dark faces. One small image, almost hidden by the shadows of the foreground, begged a closer look. It was the only image that was not shirtless. Rather, this captive seemed to wear some sort of nightshirt. Their features were finer than the others', and the thick bush of hair hung below the narrow shoulders. If he was a guessing man, he'd conclude that it was a woman. But, much to his frustration, no more than that could be determined by the rendering.

The centerpiece of the etching was the hero of the centuries-old tale, Sengbe Pieh, known better as Cinque. Much had been made of Cinque, the de facto leader of the enslaved revolt. It was he who had led his fellow captives to take over the ship, he who became the spokesperson for them all during the historic trial. But Zach's research hinted that there were parts of the story that were untold, folklore that claimed someone else was involved in—and possibly responsible—for freeing Cinque from his chains, the event that led to the takeover of the schooner.

Zach's instincts, combined with myths and legends, along with the ship's manifest that indicated that not all the captives that were brought on board *La Amistad* disembarked, led him to believe that there was much of the story that remained untold.

Most historians theorized that it was merely a recording error or that one of the captives had died en route and was tossed overboard. He had as well—but not anymore. That flame in his gut had ignited further when Alessandra had told him about her "experiences" since arriving at her father's home.

He needed to hear more about Alessandra's experiences. If she would open up to him. Trust him with this.

He was a scientist. He was guided by facts. But he had also been raised by a woman who was equally as adamant that the spirits of their ancestors lived within them. They guided, they anchored, their DNA flowed in their progeny's veins, lived on through them.

As much as his training wanted to discount all that, throughout the course of his work in documenting oral histories, and having listened to similar stories of the power and legacies of the ancestors from every corner of the Black diaspora, there was a part of him that believed.

After all, everyone was a descendant.

CHAPTER TWENTY

Alessandra stepped into her father's bedroom. The scent of him, something woodsy and clean, still lingered in the air. As always, her attention was drawn to his sax case, which rested by the window seat. She sighed.

She crossed the room, the old wood flooring squeaking lightly beneath her feet, and opened his closet. She wasn't sure what she expected, but the sudden visual of her father's life lined up in a neat row in front of her engulfed her, clenched her throat, and sent tears slipping from her eyes.

With reverence, coupled with waves of nostalgia, she ran her hand along the dress shirts in varying shades of blue with a few white ones thrown in, recalling the times that her dad would get dressed for a meeting or a visit to her school, his shirts starched until they could stand on their own. Work shirts of red-and-black plaid in cotton and fleece dominated the lineup, but there was also a sports jacket with actual patches on the elbows.

She smiled. It was his favorite jacket. He said it made him look like a college professor instead of the owner of the local hardware and supply store.

There were several pairs of slacks and well-worn jeans. At the end of the row were two suits, one gray and one black. Her heart thumped.

He'd purchased that black suit when they buried her mother. Now it hung like a talisman, a dark reminder. She'd been standing at the edge of his bedroom door the morning of the funeral, wanting to go in but afraid that he would turn her away as he'd done since *that* night. The black suit had been laid out on the bed, eerie without a body to fill it.

Her father just stood there, staring at it as if he expected something to happen. Then his broad shoulders slumped and began to shake, and something akin to the sound of a wounded animal slowly rose, strengthening, filling the room with an anguish that defied explanation.

She'd shoved her fist to her mouth to keep her own pain from escaping as she'd watched her father collapse to his knees and sob until there was no sound left in him. She'd spun away and run to her room, shutting the door, the vision of her strong father on his knees and broken behind her.

The next time she saw the black suit, there was a body in it, moving, bending, but it remained as lifeless as it had been when it was sprawled on her father's bed.

Alessandra swiped at her eyes, again and again, until her vision cleared of the tears—and the memories.

The gray one. Dad would look good in the gray one.

She lifted it from the rack, held it for a moment to her chest, inhaling the dissipating scent of her father, then selected a pale-blue shirt and a blue-and-gray striped tie. She took the garment bag from its hook on the door, shut the closet, and went to his dresser to pick out socks and underwear. On top of the dresser was his everyday watch, a good old Timex. Her father had sworn by it. She picked it up and ran her finger along the worn brown leather, smiled to see that the second hand continued its rotation. He'd want his watch with him.

She placed all the items on the bed, unzipped the garment bag, and put everything in. Shoes! She went back to the walk-in closet, scanned the choices. Her father had one pair of "good shoes" behind a row of work boots, track shoes, and his slippers.

She bent down to pick up the black leather shoes, which were going to need a shine, and spotted the edge of something wooden tucked at the back of the deep walk-in closet.

Her pulse quickened. Memories swirled. She froze.

"Food's done!" Traci called from the kitchen. "Come get it while it's hot."

The doorbell rang in the distance.

"Hey, Zach's here," Traci shouted. "Says his grandma is ready to go."

Alessandra blinked as the hold released. Slowly she rose to her feet. Whatever was back there would have to wait.

She headed downstairs, heart thumping.

"There's plenty," Traci was saying to Zach as Alessandra entered the kitchen.

"Just finished eating. I'm stuffed. But thanks." He turned toward the door. "Hey." He smiled. "Didn't mean to rush you, but the ladies want to get moving and I'm the designated driver."

"No problem," she said, her voice barely audible.

Zach frowned. "Everything okay?"

Alessandra licked her dry lips. She nodded. "Got a bit shaken going through my dad's things, that's all." She forced a smile. "Here." She held the garment bag out toward Zach like a roadblock. "Shoes need shining." Her voice broke.

Zach took the bag and draped it over the chair before

gathering Alessandra to him. He held her head against his chest, stroked her back. "It's okay," he whispered into the dark twists of her hair.

Alessandra squeezed her eyes shut, and the image of that old wooden chest bloomed behind her lids. She could see her mother standing in the door of the den telling her father that there wasn't anything in the chest her daughter needed to know about. Her father gave in, and she didn't recall ever seeing the chest again.

Until today. She was sure of it.

After Zach had taken the clothes and left, she pulled out a chair and sat with Traci at the kitchen table. Her friend placed the tray of catfish and the bowls of grits and home fries on the table.

"I found something," Alessandra blurted out as she spooned food onto her plate.

"What?"

"The box, the chest that my father showed me years ago, the one that my mother basically said was none of my business…"

Traci stopped filling her plate. "And?"

"I didn't get a chance to look inside yet."

Traci's eyes widened. "So what are we sitting here for? Let's go." She pushed back from her seat and stood.

Alessandra held up her hand to slow her steamrolling friend. "As much as I want to see what's inside, a part of me is kinda…ya know. There must have been some reason that my mother didn't want me to see what was in there. Right?"

"But your dad didn't feel the same way."

Alessandra sighed. "I know." She stared at the food on her plate, took a forkful of catfish and chewed slowly.

Traci sat back down, leaned forward. "Look, you told me that Zach's grandmother had been talking with your mom and that your mom was beginning to think differently about things, right?"

"Yes."

Traci gave a light lift of her shoulder. "So maybe going through whatever's inside won't be betraying her memory," she said gently.

Alessandra blinked. A slow, crooked smile curved her mouth. "How well you know me."

"Gotta be good for something besides making a kick-ass breakfast." She pointed to Alessandra's plate with her finger.

"Girl, please, you're one of the most highly regarded editors in the publishing biz. That's major."

Traci feigned humility with a short bow of her head. "Well, there's that, too," she said.

Alessandra lifted a forkful of home fries to her mouth. "To kick-ass breakfasts and best friends taking over the world."

"You got that right!"

...

Alessandra felt out of body. Her mechanical smile was more from good upbringing than from emotion. It settled on faces she did not know or recall, thanking them for coming and feigning remembrance of the array of mourners who echoed, "The last time I saw you..." There was a bottomless reality that had settled in the center of her being. All she could feel was Zach's presence, a hand on her shoulder, warmth at her side.

The image of the glossy cherrywood casket, perched in a place of honor, floated in and out of her vision like a photograph shot out of focus.

The voice of the reverend mouthed words in a soothing baritone, but Alessandra could not make sense of them. All she heard were the notes of her father's saxophone and the soft rasp of the last words he'd uttered from his hospital bed. *Everything you need...*

Voices cried in her head, calling to take the day back, the years back, the relationship back. She wanted the time back to make it up to her dad for blaming him, for the guilt she felt, the guilt that closed her heart to him and made her run.

I'm so sorry, Daddy. I'm so sorry.

She didn't realize she'd said the words aloud until she felt the warmth of Zach's hand clasp her fisted one and Traci's head rest in comfort on her shoulder.

She was an orphan now. No mother. No father.

A tear slid down her cheek. But she wasn't alone.

. . .

Grace and Edith had outdone themselves for the repast. The dining and kitchen tables were lined with platters of steaming food, a mix of African, Caribbean, and Southern cuisine: flying fish, yams, rice and peas, fried and fricasseed chicken, turkey, honey ham, spicy collards, string beans and deep-dish mac and cheese, pies and cakes.

"Thank you so much, Grandma O, Ms. Edith," Alessandra said, her voice thick. "I don't know—"

"Hush," Edith said, lifting Alessandra's chin with the tip of her finger. "You're not alone," she said, seeming to understand the words that Alessandra had thought but not spoken.

Alessandra dragged in a long breath to settle the tumbling in her stomach.

"Family isn't always blood," Grace added softly. "You remember that. Hear." She turned and assumed her role as hostess.

Zach eased along Alessandra's side. "You good?"

Alessandra angled around to look at him. "I don't know. I think so." She sighed, shrugged. "Limbo."

He fingered a loc of her hair and gently tucked it behind her studded ear. "I'm not going to fill your head with a bunch of platitudes. All I'm going to say is that I'm here for you—whatever that means for you. Okay?" he whispered, looking steadily into her eyes.

Alessandra tucked in her lips and nodded.

The late afternoon meandered into early evening. Her dad's friends and acquaintances mixed and mingled, stopped to share condolences and anecdotes about Jeremiah.

"Did you know your dad was the best chess player at the senior center?...Jerry had one sense of humor. Always had his staff at the shop in stitches...was a big history buff, used to work with the library...give you the shirt off his back... loved your mama...talked about you all the time...how proud he was of you..."

She smiled, nodded, thanked, hmm-ummed, and uh-huh'd her way through the stories and faces. By the time the last guest left, they all blended into a bright, abstract tapestry, stitching together the image of the father she wished she'd known.

CHAPTER TWENTY-ONE

Traci crossed her ankles and raised her glass of wine to her lips. "Long day." She studied Alessandra over the rim of her glass. "You okay? I know it couldn't have been easy."

Alessandra nodded slowly. "Yeah," she said absently. "I can't thank you enough for being here for me."

"Girl, where else would I be? I'm your ride or die, remember?"

They lifted their glasses.

"Steven was noticeably absent," Traci commented.

Alessandra sighed. "He sent flowers and condolences. It's fine," she said, resigned to her and Steven's new dynamic— which was none. But there were more immediate, pressing matters.

She frowned a moment, leaned into the back cushions of the couch. "There were parts of me that thought I knew my father. The part that believed him to be indifferent to me growing up, overbearing, especially after my mother passed, ya know. It seemed that after my mom he had free rein to put a stop to everything."

She sniffed. "I'd convinced myself that he was just being hard and mean." She lowered her head. "To make myself feel better. Then we talked that last day at the hospital and…he was not the man I'd taken a picture of and locked in my mind all those years ago. Then, today, one person after another came up to tell me a story or share a small memory of him." She blinked back the sting of tears. "Damn shame that he had to die in order for me to see how he really lived, who he really was."

Traci leaned over and patted her hand. "But you have, and that's what's important. You build new memories."

Alessandra offered a semblance of a smile. She let her gaze roam the living room. "At some point, I need to decide what to do about the house."

"Hmm. True. Did your dad…leave a will or anything?" Traci asked, halting between each word.

"I haven't got a clue. I was lucky that his insurance papers were in the desk." She paused, frowned. "Everything happened so fast. I'll have to go through his things."

"Speaking of things, maybe a will or house papers are in that chest you found."

Alessandra sucked on her bottom lip. "True. I've put it off long enough." She set her glass down on the end table and got to her feet. "You coming?"

"A family mystery?" Traci hopped to her feet. "Don't have to ask me twice."

• • •

Zach had sent his grandmother and Edith to bed. Much as they'd protested, he'd known they were bone-tired from the droop of their eyelids to the yawns they tried to hide behind smooth brown hands.

He moved through the rooms collecting the last of the half-filled glasses of iced tea and lemonade, paper plates, and forgotten flatware. He filled the last black garbage bag and took it to the cans out back, then went to the kitchen.

Years ago he'd asked his grandmother to let him get a dishwasher installed for her, but she'd insisted that washing dishes was therapeutic. While the suds and water rushed over her hands, she'd look out the window over the sink, watch the comings and goings of the neighborhood and let her mind wander, stopping on a happy memory or letting the waters wash away some trouble that was nagging at her. By the time she was done, she'd been reborn, she'd insisted.

He'd always thought that was just his grandmother's last stand about more gadgets in her house, but he'd often found, as he stood at her sink, his hands soaping and rinsing, that the task really did release his mind from the tensions, questions, and challenges of the day.

He added more soap to the cloth and slowly swished it in circles along the surface of the plate, then turned it over and repeated the process. The water rushed over it, and the suds swirled along with his own thoughts. He understood much of what Alessandra was going through. Although the circumstances of the loss of his parents was different, it was a loss nonetheless.

His parents had died long before the house fire that took their bodies. They'd been taken away from him years earlier, by a love of work and drugs that had ultimately proved more powerful than their love for him or themselves. A kind of void that opens inside the soul when one loses a parent that is never really filled again. He was sure that much of the reason he traveled the world and chronicled the stories of others was to fill that space.

As improbable as it seemed, meeting Alessandra had begun to fill the hole. He didn't feel as if dragging in enough breaths would fill the gap in his spirit—just a gentle inhale of her scent and he felt almost complete. Almost.

His thoughts bubbled and flowed to the surface: the moments shared between him and Alessandra, the connection they seemed to have, the spark they ignited in each other.

He adjusted the temperature of the water, gazed out the window to the patch of stars scattered beyond the glistening treetops. He smiled, seeing her eyes light up when she talked about her work or challenged him on his knowledge of jazz singers. She had him beat on that score, he had to admit. They spent word-defying times together in bed, but there was a part of Alessandra that he could not reach. Even though there was an inexplicable sensation of knowing each other, there was a veil—thin, almost see-through—that separated them.

It was as if she was trying to be whole, to see her full self—but couldn't.

If she were to put into words what he was thinking, she would likely say she was an underdeveloped photograph, a picture out of focus. There were parts unknown, parts that hovered around her, daring her to reveal them and, in turn, to reveal herself.

Zach chuckled, shook his head, and dried the last dish. He stacked it in the cabinet with the others. That was the researcher in him whispering in his ear. According to his mantra, everybody had a story to tell, whether they realized it or not.

He wiped down the sink, turned, and scanned the kitchen. Surfaces cleared, floors swept, everything in its place. Just the way his grandmother liked it. He hung the dish towel on the hook above the sink.

Alessandra had a story to tell. It was inside her, and when she allowed herself to listen, she would be able to speak the words and step fully into who she was. She'd closed the door to her family and its past. Tragedy had brought her back—not only to bury her father, but to unearth all that had been hidden.

For reasons that he had yet to explain, they had been brought together. Some of the answers, he was sure, would be uncovered by the documents he'd collected. How they connected to Alessandra, he still wasn't certain. It was only a feeling. Nothing he could prove. Yet.

The rest Alessandra would have to discover on her own. He wanted to be there, though, for every step that she'd allow him to take with her.

He turned off the kitchen light and headed up to his bedroom. Grandma was right: washing dishes *was* therapeutic.

• • •

Alessandra and Traci sat cross-legged on the thin, red-and-gold area rug in the middle of Jeremiah's bedroom. The heavy wooden chest sat tauntingly between them.

"Kinda looks like one of those treasure chests from a pirate movie." Traci grinned, eyes wide.

Alessandra rolled her eyes. "Really, Traci," she snarked.

"Well…you gonna open it or what?" Traci tossed back, unmoved.

Alessandra heaved a breath, leaned forward, and twisted the metal latch—only to realize that there was a lock beneath the wide leather flap.

Alessandra frowned.

"What?"

"Needs a key."

"Damn. Really? Gotta be around here somewhere."

"Right." Alessandra scrambled to her feet, planted her hands on her hips, and looked around the room. "Nightstand." She crossed the room, her footsteps, no longer padded by the rug, teasing the creaks out of the floor.

She sat on the side of the bed, pulled on the gold-plated knob of the drawer, and slid it open. She lifted papers, envelopes from utility companies and old prescriptions, pens, crumbs, and a granola bar, but no key. She shoved the drawer closed, stood, rounded the bed, and repeated her efforts in the second nightstand. Again she came up empty.

"Dresser," she announced. She hopped up, turned around, and went to the six-drawer dresser. It had a cabinet on the other side and was topped with an oval mirror. The entire thing took up one half of the wall. It must weigh a ton.

Methodically, Alessandra checked each drawer, careful not to make a mess of her father's neat rows of socks, shorts, t-shirts, and pajamas. Was he always this neat and organized? She frowned. She couldn't remember. Her dad seemed to always be working, listening to his music, playing his sax, or trying out a new recipe, which drove her mother crazy. But somehow he knew where everything was.

It was her mother, as put-together and efficient as she appeared, who would, without fail, ask, "Jerry, did you see my…?" or, "Jerry, did you move…? I know it was right…" And, like magic, her dad would appear with an amused smile on his face and whatever item had vanished, or he'd call out over the beat of Coltrane, "In the bottom drawer on the left, sweetheart."

Maybe her dad *was* the one who kept the house from spinning out of control, while her mom sat on this board or that, ran to one community event or the other, had lunch with Jack and Jill members, took trips to Manhattan to shop, and made sure that Alessandra never had a hair or a word out of place.

Her father had always balked at the excess, at the indulgences that her mother showered on her. Closed his eyes and shook his head when Jessica prattled on about an upcoming social event, dinner, or luncheon.

"Only the best people will be there," she'd always qualify.

"Whatever that means," her father would reply.

"It's the way to make connections, especially for Alessandra. Those are the people she needs to cultivate."

"You make people sound like a product to be purchased."

"No, a seed to be planted."

"Instead of planting new seeds, how about knowing your roots?"

Jessica would frown, then, and her warm-vanilla-toned skin would tighten around her hazel eyes. "Nothing but ugly and pain in those roots, running and trying to belong somewhere. We have the chance to plant something new and beautiful. We finally belong, Jerry. I did that. We don't have to run anymore, or be run off!"

But Alessandra had run anyway—and had then run right back to where she'd started.

"Alessandra…" Traci lightly tapped her shoulders. "You okay?"

Alessandra blinked. She pressed the tips of her fingers into the polished hardwood of the dresser. "My mother and father were so…different," she said in a faraway voice. "My dad was a simple, hardworking man who loved his music and his family. That was enough for him."

She gazed into the mirror atop the dresser and saw a brown version of her mother's face in her reflection. Her mother worked tirelessly to ensure that her daughter had the "best" life at any cost, even at the expense of her marriage, and that Alessandra was accepted by those her mother deemed acceptable.

Alessandra had bought into it, loving the clothes, the trips, the pampering, the parties. *Alessandra is going to have everything we didn't, that my folks and your folks didn't.*

"I always sided with her," Alessandra whispered.

"Huh?"

"My mother. I always sided with her against my father." She blinked back the memories. "I knew that if I did, I could get whatever I wanted—she would make sure of it. My dad would insist that she was ruining me for the real world. He was right," she whispered.

"You don't really believe that, and neither do I. You've come a long way, baby." Traci winked.

Alessandra smiled at her friend, scanned the room again. "Let's find this key."

Traci leaned her weight on her right leg, crossed her arms, and tipped her head to the side. "We could just break the damned thing."

Alessandra looked at Traci from beneath her lashes and pursed her lips. "Last alternative, okay?"

Traci shrugged. "In all the mystery movies, the key is always taped under a drawer."

Alessandra slid her a sideways glance and laughed. She wagged a finger at Traci. "You are very funny, but you might be right." She returned to the nightstand and pulled out the drawer. She dumped the contents on the bed and turned the drawer over.

"Well, I'll be damned." Alessandra peeled off the beige tape, used for sealing boxes, and there was a key. She held it up.

Traci offered a smug, self-satisfied smirk. "See, maybe now you'll stop turning up your nose at me and my ID channel and *CSI* marathons."

"I doubt it." She got back down on the floor in front of the chest.

Traci sat next to her. They gave each other a quick, expectant look.

Alessandra stuck the key in the lock. She jiggled, twisted, stuck it in, pulled it out. No luck.

Traci cussed. "So much for that."

"Well, you're no Sherlock Holmes," Alessandra snicked.

They braced their backs against the side of the bed, stared forlornly at the chest.

"We could always go back to Plan A: break the damn lock."

Alessandra sighed. "Yeah…wait." Her pulse raced. She scrambled and darted toward the door.

"What?" Traci called out.

"Be right back."

Moments later, she returned, smiling broadly and holding up the old, rusted key she'd found in her dad's pants pocket when she'd first arrived. "This is the key. I just know it."

CHAPTER TWENTY-TWO

Zach turned on the overhead lamp, sat at his desk, and reached for the stack of folders on top of the short file cabinet. The label in clear block letters read MAROONS. He flipped the file open. To fully appreciate the Maroon settlements scattered across the Eastern seaboard and the shores of the Caribbean, one had to accept that the once-enslaved Blacks had escaped, becoming fugitives from slavery and hiding themselves in fortified settlements outside the plantations in the woods and swamps. Others were freed and came together to build their own separate community, independent of the white world.

These Maroon settlers built homes, places to worship, schools, and stores. They grew their own food, developed their own economics. They were tight-knit. Many of the Maroon colonies interacted with the Indigenous people — and even married them. Some had limited interaction with the colonists. However, they were extremely protective of their community and were fierce fighters against an enemy that sought to re-enslave them.

Most of the documents that he'd located on Maroons and maroonage pointed to Brazil, Haiti, Jamaica, Suriname, Florida, and the Carolina coast. But there were lines tucked within those documents that alluded to a possible Maroon village that sprang up off the shores of Sag Harbor, the village that ultimately birthed Eastville, Azurest, and St. David AME Zion church. The documents that he'd gathered on the slave schooner *La Amistad* fit with his theory that someone, the unaccounted-for fifty-third captive, made their way to the Maroon village—right here in Sag Harbor.

Zach used the magnifying glass to study the handwritten script of the diary of Charlotte Holcomb. According to the census documents, the Holcomb family were the wealthy elite, having built several homes on Sag Harbor and made their money from the booming whaling industry. Charlotte Holcomb was the young daughter of Lizbeth and Lucas Holcomb, and the only heir to their fortune. Sickly in her early teens, she took to writing, documenting the day-to-day activities of the townspeople and the longings of a young girl.

What drew Zach's interest were her sporadic references to "the Negroes in the woods." He was particularly interested in a location that hinted it was just beyond the main perimeter of Sag Harbor Village, the area that was now the community of Azurest.

The library's historian had been kind enough to make copies of several pages of Charlotte's diary that were still legible.

Sunday, May 1855
  Dear Diary,
  Church as usual this morning. For a place that boasts joy and happiness, the boring somber sermon about hell and damnations drained the light out of me as usual. I never understood why we need to be reminded about the

fires of hell and the afterlife. Ms. Martha Southgate moaned and sobbed as usual. I was bored. Jimmy Hunterfield promised to meet me behind the schoolhouse once service was done.

Jimmy is the cutest boy in town and his daddy owns the general store and his mother is the headmistress at school. They are important and that makes Jimmy important. When I become his girl, I will be important, too, not just the daughter of Lizbeth and Lucas Holcomb! Besides, snotty Phyllis Smythe will choke when she sees me on the arm of Jimmy. Today is going to be our first kiss.

. . .

Monday May 1855

I waited and waited and Jimmy never showed up. Why would he lead me on like that? Play with my heart?

I was too upset and ashamed to go home. So I told Mama that I was going to pick flowers for my teacher's desk.

When the morning sun started to arch toward afternoon, I left from behind the school and started walking. I kept walking so I could cry in private away from the nosy church ladies and irritating girls.

When I finally stopped and took measure of my surroundings, I was on the edge of the woods. I could smell the swamp water, thick and gummy. Things I couldn't quite see rustled the leaves above and the bushes below. The towering trees blocked out the sun. Only thin rays made it to the ground, making shadows dance on the rocks and leaves. That's what I thought I saw at first, a shadow.

I'd never been this far from town. I heard about it. I heard my father say that dangerous negroes hid in these woods, and redskins who would take our scalps.

I heard a hard rustle and footsteps. I knew I was going to wind up scalped or, worse, ravaged by a negro.

I hid behind a thick set of bushes. The steps got closer. I heard a voice, light and sweet, singing or humming, I could not tell. Then all of a sudden a bare pair of feet was right in front of me. My heart was racing so hard, I could barely breathe. But the legs were not covered in britches, but a smock the color of the bags used to hold grain. The feet stumbled backward and the body attached landed with a thud.

Right there in between the bushes, we looked in each other's eyes. I think we were both too scared to do more than hold our breath so as not to scream. But in the minute that our eyes locked, I knew I'd seen those eyes before. Years ago.

I was about nine or ten and I'd begged my pa to take me with him on a walk to the wharf to see the ships come in. He finally agreed, saying that one day the business would be mine and it might be time I saw how he made his money. We spent the afternoon watching the ships dock and unload supplies. Pa went to talk to one of the men that got off a ship. He looked important and handed my pa some papers.

My pa told me I had to wait for him in the office because he had some business to take care of with the men, and when he got back he would take me home. I waited and waited until I got bored. Probably not long but it felt like forever.

When I went outside, I saw my pa and a few other men heading out of town toward the swamp. What business could he have there? The only way for me to know was to follow along. Right? So I did, but far enough behind so that they didn't see me.

The group finally slowed, then stopped. They came face-to-face with five or six negro men. I ducked way down behind an overturned log.

"Looking for a runaway wench," one man shouted. He shook a paper high over his head. "Property of Mr. Percival Hammer. Tell us where she is and we'll be on our way."

I covered my mouth to keep from crying out.

The negro men drew themselves together and raised their sticks and farming tools high over their heads. One negro shouted, "Ain't no runaways here. We free!" They moved toward my father and his friends, who backed up. "Not looking for trouble. Just want this runaway gal. She been gone a long while. Her master done finally come back to fetch her." "Ain't no runaways here," the negro repeated. "Don't let us find out you niggers been lying," my father said, all the while backing away.

I scrambled to my feet and started back, but somehow I got all turned around. The path was gone. The sound of voices was gone. I just knew those negroes was going to find me and cook me for supper. I was too scared to keep going and too scared to stop. It would be dark soon. I pushed through the brush, catching my dress and tangling my hair in the branches. I walked and walked and then space opened in front of me. It looked like a small town in the middle of the woods. How could that be? The houses looked like the frail old ladies from the church that may blow down with a good winter wind. But what stopped me even colder was all the negroes. They were sitting on barrels, going in and out of those frail houses, children playing and laughter. Living. Were these the free negroes that the man shouted about to my pa?

Then I saw the men that had confronted my father and his friends. Seemed like all the negroes and redskins in that little town came and gathered around them. Their voices only drifted to me as a steady hum.

I had to find my way back. Suppose they were planning to attack our town? I turned to pick my way through the bush and that's when I saw those eyes for the first time staring at me from between a thicket of weeds, and I never saw them again until yesterday.

It was a girl. A negro girl. Prettiest negro girl I'd ever seen. Her skin, her eyes and even her curly hair was all the same color of golden honey.

She scrambled to her feet and started to run. I call out to her. "Wait! Don't go. I won't tell!" That stopped her cold. She turned around, real slow. I got to my feet and brushed off my dress.

"My name is Charlotte," I say real slow in case she does not understand English.

"My name Ella."

. . .

Sunday July 1857
   Dear Diary,

   I should be happy, but I can't be happy. Ella is getting married today to that boy she's been mooning over and can't stop talking about. I tried to tell her she's too young to be a wife. She says she's seventeen and that all she wants is to be a wife. But what about your sewing and your drawing I ask her. She says she'll do that in between having babies.

   I suppose it would be all right with Ella getting married, but Winston wants to take her away to some place called Chicago. She said colored have a better life there with real jobs and don't have to worry about slave catchers. She said I should come with them. It would be an adventure, she says. Even if my folks did let me go, which they would never do, I probably wouldn't last long. Doctors say my heart is weak, getting weaker by the day.

   I never told Ella how sick I am or why I couldn't run too much or why I get tired from walking. So most times when I can sneak away after church, we'd sit by the water and talk. She told me once that her Mama escaped but that she could never really talk about it. That man that took her from her home and brought her here on a ship might still be looking for her. So her mama could never leave. She had to stay with the people who would protect her. Every time the people in her village hear about white men getting close, her mother hides and makes Ella hide too.

   We still have posters in town about runaways and rewards for capture, and sometimes I think back to the day in the woods and wonder if it was Ella's ma they were looking for. I never told Ella that one of the men that day was my pa.

   There were a few negroes and Indians, too, that lived in town and worked for the families there. They never caused trouble and no one troubled them. Ella said that's because "they free."

   Then why can't Ella and Winston be free right here? Ella's dream is taking her to Chicago with a husband. My dream is to live long enough to have my first kiss.

• • •

The rest of the entry was too faded to make out, and there were no more pages of Charlotte's diary that had been recovered, no more references to Ella.

Zach slid the copies into the folder and rubbed his eyes. The diary entries were the pieces of evidence that proved that an enslaved girl had escaped from a slave ship and found her way to the Maroon village. Her daughter's name was Ella, and Ella was due to marry someone named Winston.

He blinked. Peered closer. Read the words again. An enslaved girl had escaped a ship—what if it was *La Amistad*? His heart thumped. She'd survived, at least into her teens. He squeezed the journal between his fingers.

This was the kernel of information that he knew was out there, and he'd found it. Further down the rabbit hole, he was sure there were more answers. What had happened to Ella next?

• • •

By degrees, Alessandra leaned closer to the opened chest as if all that was contained inside might suck her into its depths.

"This is not a few birth certificates and some letters," Alessandra murmured, each word coming out as if she had to search for it. "Mrs. O said that my mom started sorting through a few things before she died...but nothing like this. This is not *a few things*."

The chest overflowed from end to end, and deep inside its womb were typed sepia and black-and-white pages, photographs, pieces of fabric, jewelry that appeared handcrafted in vibrant colors of aqua and sunshine yellow, hair ornaments, small, dented tins, the names and images long-ago faded, several leather-bound notebooks, and tattered news articles dating back decades.

Traci reached in and reverently ran the tips of her fingers across the treasure trove. "Oh my goodness. Some of this looks like it's hundreds of years old."

With deliberate care so as not to damage the contents, she lifted a flimsy piece of paper. It was a wanted flyer for a unnamed slave girl. There was a faint artist sketch of a young girl with large sad eyes and a mountain of thick hair that nearly obscured her delicate features. Reward $100.00. Property of Percival Hammer. The date was September 1839.

Alessandra's hand began to shake, rattled the paper like a leaf in the wind. The flyer floated from her fingers. Her heart pounded in concert with the sound of pounding feet that raced across the night, the small body breaking through brush and thickets, stumbling, falling in the mud, running toward—

"Hey," Traci whispered, placing a hand on Alessandra's shoulder. "You okay?"

Alessandra blinked and blinked to clear her head and vision. She swallowed, exhaled a shaky yes. "All this…my mother…she kept all this, kept it safe. And my dad, too." Her head snapped toward Traci. "Why did she want to hide it all?"

"First, we don't even know what all this is. Right? And until you—we—go through it, we won't know."

Alessandra heaved a breath. "You're right." Her gaze ran across the contents. "Some things look so old and fragile, they might fall apart."

"Then we have to be careful, don't we?"

"We'll just lay things out on the floor and the bed." She

pushed out a frustrated breath. "I'm trying to figure out, if my mother didn't want any part of her history, then why keep all this? Why?"

For the next hour, item by item, they gingerly lifted sepia photos, newsclips, advertisements, handwritten letters, pieces of clothing, journals from the padded cedar-lined chest and spread most of the treasures across the floor until the available space of the bedroom was covered in history.

The two friends sat back on their haunches and stared in astonishment at the extensive amount of material in front of them.

"Jeez, girl, just looking at all this gives me goose bumps, ya know?" Traci said. "Like I'm getting a backstage pass to a performance no one else will see. This is real-life history," she said on a breath.

Alessandra ran her tongue along her bottom lip. Her sleek brows rose and fell. She tucked a wayward loc back into her topknot. "It's overwhelming." Her eyes scanned the array, then she jumped up. "Be right back." She darted down the hallway to her bedroom and returned with her Nikon. She tugged in a breath, adjusted the lens, and began to take shots at varying angles, close-ups and at a distance, until she had a respectable representation of some of the chest's contents.

"Okay." Traci began counting off on her fingers. "We got the chest open. Got a bunch of stuff out. Took pictures. Now what do we *actually* do?" She shrugged helplessly. "This stuff goes back decades."

"Centuries," Alessandra whispered, then immediately knew what came next. "Zach."

"Zach?"

"Yeah. It's what he does. Retrieve and document and gather histories of people from all over the world."

"Well, just damn. You couldn't have made this up. He's

fine *and* useful."

Alessandra laughed, took a breath. "And then some," she added with a wicked wink. She pulled her cell from the back pocket of her jeans and called Zach. "I have some things over here that I need you to take a look at. A lot of things. Some very...*old* things," she said into the phone. "How...how soon could you be here?"

CHAPTER TWENTY-THREE

Ten minutes later, from the arch of the bedroom door, Zach scanned the patchwork of history that covered the floor while Alessandra's heart threatened to jump out of her throat.

"Whoa." He ran his hand across the short, neat twists on his head. "Where was all this?"

"Stored in that chest in the back of my father's closet."

He dropped his "go bag" of basic research tools on the floor and hunched down to get a closer look. "This is incredible." He turned his tight expression toward Alessandra. "It's beyond rare to discover a personal collection this extensive."

"What do we do? How do we go through it all?" she asked.

"First things first." His gaze did a slow dance over the treasure before them. "Many of these paper documents are so old that improperly touching them in the open air can begin to destroy them."

"But we had to pick them up to..." Alessandra began, mildly frantic.

Zach held up his hand. Smiled. "It's okay. From this point on, only touch the items with white gloves." He unzipped the bag and pulled out a pair of white gloves. "Like these."

"Church-lady gloves," Traci joked.

They laughed.

Zach slipped on the gloves and then stepped out of his sneakers.

On his hands and knees, he meticulously picked up paper documents and photographs, each accompanied by "My God," or "Incredible," or a sigh of pure amazement. He finally glanced up at the women, frozen in place, and his eyes lit up like a hearth in winter. Alessandra could tell he was in his element. It was clearly taking all his patience and years of training not to tear through everything at once. But he didn't want to damage anything.

"What you have here, from what I can determine, is a story of a family dating back to their arrival here in the United States. I'd have to tag and chronicle everything but— this is history." He beamed. Slowly he got to his feet. "I've been doing some research myself, and believe it or not, I think what I've found is connected."

Zach went on to explain what he'd been researching and the storyline that he'd been weaving about the captive who had escaped *La Amistad* and found refuge in Sag Harbor among the marooned Blacks and the Indigenous peoples. He pointed to the wanted flyer. "I found one just like it," he said slowly.

Alessandra frowned. "I don't see what you're getting at."

"Your mother, or maybe your dad, somehow came across or 'inherited' the same document along with everything else," he added, scanning the floor. "That can't be coincidence."

"Are you saying that this girl is somehow connected to my family?"

"Yes, I am."

Alessandra's eyes widened.

"Wow," Traci said. She placed a hand on Alessandra's shoulder. "This beats ancestry dot com any day."

Alessandra snorted a chuckle and rolled her eyes at the quip. "Sooo, what do we do now?"

"Go through every piece, one by one. Photograph, organize by date, and seal to preserve. Then we can go through each item in detail—put a timeline and story together. But don't touch anything else without putting on the white gloves. I'll bring over a couple of extra pairs. In the meantime, let me return everything to the chest. Now that they've been exposed to the air, some of the really old documents made from pulp can begin to break down. In the morning, I'll bring the rest of my tools of the trade." He gave Alessandra a wink.

Alessandra folded her arms and nodded in agreement. "Isn't there something I can do to help—anything?"

"Sure." He frowned a moment. "There should be one more pair of gloves in that bag."

Traci's phone chirped. She pulled it out of her pants pocket, checked the illuminated number on the screen, and a sly smile slid across her mouth. "'Scuse me a sec." She backed out of the room and out of earshot.

"Ten bucks it's Morgan," Alessandra said.

"Let's just say I'm not taking that bet," Zach agreed, laughing.

Alessandra grinned and slipped on the gloves. Zach took a small roll of treated paper and covered the interior of the chest.

"Now," he said, "let's start putting things back until the morning."

Traci popped into the doorway, beaming. "Um, I'm gonna change and run out for a bit."

"Oh?" Alessandra said, feigning confusion.

"Morgan's coming by to pick me up in about an hour." She smiled, wide-eyed. "You two good without me?"

"I think we can manage," Alessandra replied drolly.

"Cool." She spun away, then turned back. "I might be late…like, really late."

"Hmm." Alessandra's brows rose to a sarcastic arch. "Enjoy," she called out to Traci's rapidly retreating footsteps.

Alessandra and Zach looked at each other and cracked up laughing.

"So…looks like we have the house to ourselves," Alessandra said seductively.

Zach stopped in the process of placing a journal back in the chest. He slid her a look and a half-arched smile. "Are you propositioning me, Ms. Fleming?"

She leaned in. Her eyes roamed over the smooth lines of his chestnut-brown face. She stroked the short line of his scar with the tip of her finger, then pressed her moist lips to his and moaned softly against his mouth. "I believe I am, Mr. Renard."

For the next few hours, until they crumpled into exhausted laughter, Alessandra and Zach set out on a quest to imprint themselves on each other with every hot kiss, searing touch, tantalizing stroke, thrust, roll of hips, moan, groan, and entwining of limbs.

Zach flipped onto his back, breathing hard. He threw his arm over his eyes. "Damn, woman," he uttered.

Alessandra giggled over her attempt to catch her breath.

"Hope Traci didn't try to ring the bell, 'cause over your hollering we wouldn't have heard her," he snorted with laughter.

Alessandra playfully swatted his arm. "Like all your groaning, moaning, and singing my name—in soprano I might add—was all in my mind."

Zach roared with laughter. "Me? Soprano?" He laughed some more, then turned onto his side to face her. She rolled her head toward him and smiled. "I confess," he said from deep in his throat, "you made me see the universe, woman."

"We were there together," she whispered in return.

Zach heaved a deep sigh, smiled, and moved onto his back, stared up at the shadows that hovered on the ceiling, cast by the quarter moon that filtered in through the ice-covered branches.

As the euphoria of being with and buried deep inside Alessandra slowly released its grip on his mind and body, he closed his eyes and his thoughts drifted to the chest and its contents, as well as to his own findings. His pulse kicked up a notch as he ran over the possibilities.

He didn't believe in coincidence, but what he couldn't deny was that every step he'd taken had led him to the research project at the Smithsonian—which in turn had brought him back to Sag Harbor and tied him to Alessandra in ways that he had not yet fully discovered. If what he was beginning to believe, and if the contents of the chest bore out his theory, Alessandra would have a story to tell that she could have never imagined.

"Do you think we'll be able to put a story together…from the papers in the chest? Maybe finally understand my mother?" Alessandra asked into the darkness, as if reading his mind.

Zach reached for her hand, and their fingers entwined. "I know we will." He needed to, he thought, and fast—before he had to return to DC, then set off on his next project. And before Alessandra returned to New York and to her whole other life.

CHAPTER TWENTY-FOUR

Alessandra couldn't sleep. Her mind's eye continued snapping images of what they'd discovered, the pictures spinning and twirling in her head. She listened to Zach's steady breathing, then turned and checked the clock on the nightstand. It was almost two. Traci wouldn't be back until morning—or afternoon.

She snatched a glance at Zach and placed a featherlight kiss on his temple. He stirred slightly but didn't wake. Her heart leaped. What was happening? They'd gone from strangers meeting on a snowy night to sharing meals, secrets, and bodies. That sounded too much like...like a...relationship. But she didn't *do* relationships. They all ended badly—or, at the very least, quickly. This—whatever this was—would be no different.

She lifted the heavy quilt, shivered when the cold air hit her bare skin. Tiptoeing across the room, she grabbed her thick robe from the hook on the back of the door, put it on, and tied it tightly at the waist. She took one last look at Zach, inched the door open, and scurried down the hall to her father's bedroom.

Once inside, she flipped on the light and closed the door quietly behind her. Zach's bag was in the corner. She unzipped it and took out the pair of white gloves. Her pulse quickened.

She crossed the room, bent down, and opened the chest. A warmth enveloped her, and she felt a settling in her soul, a calm that replaced the anxiousness that had been with her only moments ago. Her eyes moved slowly over the contents. She was hesitant to disturb the papers again until Zach showed her how they should be handled. She reached for one of the leather-bound books and carefully opened the dark-blue cover that had faded to near white around the edges and spine, quietly praying that it wouldn't fall apart in her hands.

The front page read *Property of Ella* in a childlike scrawl.

Alessandra tucked her legs beneath her. She turned the page, and it crackled in response.

September 1857

Mama gave me this here book as a wedding gift along with all her potions and hair creams.

Are those the tins that are in the chest—Ella's mother's creams? Alessandra's heart thumped.

Mama never learn how ta read and write. A few words here and there but she make sho' I had my schooling. When she give me this book wrapped up in pink paper with a bow to match, she say I want you to write 'bout what happens, what happens here, what happens to you no matter where you go. Tell our story.

Every night that last year 'fore she pass, she share another piece of herself wit me and tell me to nevah forget.

Mama hung on long enough to see me married off to Winston. I'm grateful for that. Last winter was really hard on Mama. She kept saying she want to go home, 'way from the cold, sit under the sun on the beach with Kwaku. Told me they wuz in love and she was gon' find him if she could get back home. I always ask Mama if Kwaku was my pa, but all she ever say is she da one that brought me in the world and that's all that matter. I 'spose.

Winston work on our lean-to home every day after work at the store. He add bricks to the outside, fix the roof, add plank wood to the floor and build two rooms in the back of the house, he put hinges on the doors and seal the windows to keep out the draft.

By the time he done our house be the prettiest and strongest house in the village, even better than his own folks'.

Want your mama to be comfortable when we gone, Winston say. How I gon' tell him, much as I love him, I'm not leaving my mama while she sick. Cain't do it. So I just smile and nod.

When I get a chance to set by the water and talk with Charlotte, she say of course you can't leave your mama. That would be a sin against the commandments. Honor thy father and thy mother. I think Charlotte don't want me to leave no how. She like to tell me anything to make me stay.

Alessandra drew in a breath, frowned. Her mind spun, imagining the young Ella and her new husband, Winston, her mother who longed for the love of her life, and her charge to her daughter to tell their story. But who were they, and why did her own mother have this journal and all the other things?

Alessandra turned the pages. They were soiled and faded and the ink had run, making the words unreadable. Page after page until the next legible entry almost a year later.

January 1858

    Hard gettin' use to Mama being gone. I still hear her voice, feel her fingers moving through my hair. I convinced Winston we need to stay for a while longer, right here. We got us a pretty old house to raise some babes in. He workin' hard fixing up and building houses and shops. Got so much work, he come home so tired cain't hardly keep his head up to eat supper. I say how we 'spose to make babes if he always too tired.

    I busy myself with sewing clothes for the ladies and their daughters. Keep me plenty busy. I took the room Mama used for her hair salon and turn it into my sewing place. Plenty days my back room fill with ladies coming and going for fittings and picking up they finished pieces. Keeping busy keep me from wondering how long its gon' be 'fore I'm a mama.

June 1860

    Pain so bad, broke me in half. Winston pacing the floor like he gon' wear out the wood. Miss Clair and Miss James wit me the whole time the labor pains grip me. Sat wit me and dried my tears, while I watch the doctor wrap my baby in a white sheet. Say he real sorry and walk out. Was a girl, that one, like that one before. Next one a boy, then another girl. All come in this world and never take a breath. Figure I must be cursed. Doctor say my womb is weak, cain't hold a baby full.

March 1861

    Winston say its time for us to move on. Been near three years since Mama gone. He say we can start fresh in Chicago like we always planned. He say he can get a good job in construction and I can do well with my sewing. All I got to do he say is show my book of sketches 'round and ladies will come running.

    I finally say yes. Nothing left here but a big old pretty house full of lost babies and sadness.

June 1862

    Mama come to me sometimes. Sit right on the foot of the bed and talk. Tell me stories of home of running barefoot on the hard ground under the white hot sun. Tell me about her ma and pa how they wuz important people in her tribe. She tells me of Kwaku, how he tall and handsome with bright eyes that sparkle like stars in the night sky and how much she loved him and that they is together now. She remind me on those nights when she come visit to remember to write down what she tell me so I can tell my chil'ren. I say, Mama I ain't nevah gon' have no chil'ren of my own. Mama just smile, say in time. In time.

    When Mama don't come to visit I draw pictures of the place she call home and of Kwaku and her on the beach. Good thing too cause it's getting harder to see Mama. She like a mist after a hard summer rain. All I gots now is her voice, her stories and the pictures.

    Alessandra felt the twist of her heart in her chest. A knot clogged her throat as a single tear slid down her cheek. The emptiness, the hole, the loss of a mother never went away.

She felt Ella's hurt like it was her own. How did Ella's mother die? Was she buried somewhere here on Sag Harbor? Did Ella ever return?

She turned the page, and a wave swept through her like a storm churning up sand on a beach. There was a sketch of a young woman with long, thick hair braided in two plaits that hung below her shoulders. She was dressed in what looked like an ill-fitting shift, but it didn't take away from her beguiling beauty. Her features were soft with large eyes, full lips, and an open smile. She was holding hands with a man. He was tall, shirtless, muscular. He seemed to stare right at Alessandra, and her stomach seesawed. She ran the tip of her gloved finger across the image. A surge of something familiar that she couldn't quite identify settled in her center.

She stared at the picture for several more moments before turning the page, hoping to find the answers she sought, but the next legible entry was three years later.

May 1865

Just like Mama say. In time.

She come screaming and hollering into the world like she got a bone to pick with anybody in sight. Little brown fists balled up tight as a drum. Head full of ink black curls and wide dark eyes, just like Mama's. We call her Mae Ella cause she born in may.

For all her hollering Mae is a sweet baby, sleep right through the night, take the teat without a fuss and grow like a weed.

Just like I promised Mama, late into the night when I rocks Mae to sleep against my bosom I tells her stories of home, our real home, and I whisper Mama's real name so Mae won't never forget and Mama won't be forgotten.

Alessandra's heart swelled. She sniffed back tears of happiness. Ella finally got her long-wanted baby girl, just like her mother said. *In time*. She sighed, blinked back the sleep that threatened to lull her into its grasp. She rested her stiff back against the bed and continued to read.

January 1868

Life is different, good but different, here in Chicago. We live on what they call the Southside where the Negroes and poor white folk live. Winston still work hard but he got help now. Got his own little business fixing up folks' houses and making repairs in those buildings they call tenements.

But there are hard days, too, days when I miss back home, my friends and Charlotte. Word come to us that Charlotte pass. That hurt my heart something awful that I couldn't be there for her like she was for me all those years ago. I hope her passing was peaceful.

Back home we didn't worry too much about white folk most of the time. We ain't bother them and they ain't bother us. 'Cept those times they come lookin' for runaways and Mama and me had to hide.

Since Lincoln done made it official that Negroes is free everywhere, seem like more and more Negroes movin' in, squeezing in. Shaky wood homes going up on any patch of space, dusty gray and dull brown, held together by spit and hope, until there are rows and rows of 'em far as the eye could see. Nothing more than shacks, but there was a feeling among us that as ugly as things looked we wuz in it together.

And my beautiful baby girl make all the ugly go away. Between running behind her and keeping up with my sewing orders, life is 'bout as good as I kin expect.

October 8, 1871

Wuz the smoke that woke us. Women screaming. Men shouting. Windows rattling from the force of the wind that been whipping through the streets for days. Winston jump up out of bed, tell me to stay put. He would see what was going on. I grab up Mae Ella from her bed that Winston built with his own hands and pull her in bed with me. She fussing wanting to know what is happening. I tell her just hush, Papa went to find out.

Minutes later Winston come running back in the house. Ain't never seen that look on his face since that time back home when four white men from the town, carrying torches, come looking to burn us down if we didn't turn over one of our men they claim had their way with one of their women. All the men Negro and Indian alike circled 'round them with they sticks and hoes and pitchforks and swore them men wasn't taking nobody. White men point and say it was Winston's pa they was looking for. Winston's pa step to the front, told them men right to they face they was a liar. Last thing he want in life is a white woman. You gon' hafta kill us all if we don't kill y'all first, shouts one of the Negroes and they move forward in a tight knot, weapons raised. Flames dancing over the white men's heads. One of 'em musta got some sense and say, y'all niggers betta watch yourselves or we coming back sho' nuf. After what seem like forever, they walked away until their firelight disappeared but not before they toss one of them torches right next to the school house. Took out one whole side, like to take the roof before we got it under control, before it spread.

The terror of that night and almost losing his pa did something to Winston. Etched in his mind and on his heart.

Every time Winston see loose flames, that look would come back into his eyes. Like tonight.

Sirens shrieked. The roar of voices rose.

Fire coming, Winston say. Fire coming. Can see it blocks away. Sky lit up like hell on earth. Say it started on DeKoven Street in O'Leary's barn and got out of control. Wind carrying the flames from house to house. Coming this way, Ella. We gotta go. Gotta go.

We grab up everything we could carry in bags and on our backs, got in the old pickup truck and drove with the flames licking behind us.

The next thing Alessandra knew, Zach was gently shaking her awake. She blinked. Jerked up. "Fire! We have to go!"

"Alessandra." He shook her again.

Her heart continued to thump. She shook her head to clear it, looked into Zach's concerned gaze. He held her by her shoulders.

"They had to leave. Fire was everywhere." Alarm pitched her voice.

"Who had to leave?"

For a moment, her eyes were wild. "Ella and Winston and Mae Ella!" She looked down at the blue leather-bound journal that had slipped from her hand to her lap.

The room where she was slowly came back into focus, and the depths and fear of where she'd been slowly began to recede. And then she was back in her father's bedroom.

"Ella? Winston?" Zach sputtered, the surprise evident in his voice. He slipped on a pair of gloves and reached for the journal. "Alessandra, Ella and Winston were here," he said softly, looking Alessandra in the eyes. "They lived here in Sag Harbor."

Her eyes raced over his face. Her brow tightened. "*I* know. But how...do you know that?"

He got off his knees, sat next to her on the floor, and began to tell her of his own discoveries of Ella and Winston and the pieces he was beginning to put together.

They talked until the sky began to turn a soft peach, as they filled in the gaps of each other's tales until pure exhaustion claimed them and they dragged themselves away from the stories that were begging to be told.

They curled tight together in Alessandra's bed, tucked beneath the soft weight of the down comforter, and slept, their dreams merging together.

CHAPTER TWENTY-FIVE

T he next morning, she and Traci sat opposite each other at the kitchen table sipping their second cup of coffee over half-eaten bagels. Zach had left shortly after nine saying that he needed to go into Manhattan to purchase the supplies he would require to protect the artifacts and that he'd return later in the afternoon. Being the man he was, he offered to drive Edith back to Manhattan, and she reluctantly agreed.

Edith's departure was bittersweet. Alessandra felt like she was losing another part of herself again. But Edith promised that she was only a phone call away and would be back on the next bus if need be. She assured Alessandra that she would take care of her mail and check on her plants. After tears and hugs of love and thanks, Alessandra finally let Edith settle into Zach's car.

Zach lifted Alessandra's chin so that she had to look into his eyes. "It's gonna be okay," he said softly. "You're gonna be okay." He offered up a smile and lightly kissed her lips, then made Alessandra promise that she wouldn't disturb anything in the chest until he got back. She tacitly agreed with a kiss—

and her fingers crossed behind her back.

"That story about Ella and Winston…" Traci's voice drifted for a moment. "I'd read about that fire in school, and there were all kinds of rhymes about Mrs. O'Leary's cow. Always thought it was more fairy tale than real. But this." She exhaled, looked across at her friend. "Real people were there. Maybe *your* people," she whispered.

"Yeah." Alessandra sighed out the word. Her brows drew together. "It's like…going back in time, like actually being there. I can feel them, almost hear their voices in my head when I read." She exhaled, blinked, looked at her friend. "I promised not to mess with the actual papers and photographs," Alessandra said, finishing off her coffee. "I didn't say that I wouldn't read the diaries."

Identical sly smiles slid across their mouths.

"I won't tell if you won't," Traci said, crossing her heart.

"Let's go."

They jumped up from their seats and darted up to Jeremiah's bedroom.

"There are about four or five diaries, maybe more. Most of the entries aren't easy to read, worn away over time, pages missing." Alessandra hugged herself, then opened the chest and reached for the faded blue journal, then stopped. "Whoa. Hand me those white gloves, please." She pointed to the bag that Zach had left on the floor by the dresser.

"Right!" Traci retrieved the gloves.

Alessandra slipped them on and picked up the journal. "This is the one I had last night. This is Ella's," she whispered reverently.

She gingerly turned the delicate pages, grazing her gloved fingers lightly over Ella and Winston and Mae Ella's escape from Chicago.

"Where'd they wind up?" Traci asked.

"Gonna try to find that out," she said absently, as she scanned page after page of faded ink. Some of the brown-tinged pages actually crackled in her hand. She shot Traci a look of wide-eyed concern.

"Take your time," Traci whispered, as if speaking too loudly might make the pages crumble into dust.

"Here's one," Alessandra uttered on a breath of excited relief. "1879."

"Okay. What's it say?"

Alessandra began to slowly read the entry aloud, stumbling over the spelling and missing words.

Dear Mama

I sho wish you wuz here to see what I done made of myself after the fire in Chicago. Things were hard for a good long while, Winston moving us from place to place, city to city til we finally made our way to Oklahoma.

Alessandra's eyes flashed toward Traci.

Winston say we was gon' keep on going til we found someplace to set down roots. This is it. This feel like it, Mama, like home, our Sag Harbor home. Colored folks everywhere, colored folks running things. Proud colored folks.

Your granddaughter Mae Ella is blooming into a beautiful young lady. Smart too. Read and write and do numbers better than I ever could. Better than her daddy. Looks like you Mama. Same thick hair that gives me a fit to comb, and your wide eyes.

Alessandra absently stroked the thick ropes of her hair.

Stubborn too but she quick to smile. Makes friends easy.

I be sure that I pass on to her all that you pass on to me. Make sure she know who she be, who we be, and that we wuz here.

Next to raising up Mae Ella, the thing that fill my heart was the day Winston hung the sign over the door Ella and Daughter Dressmaking. Winston carved it hisself, etched my name right in it for all to see. He built my sewing tables and shelves for my fabrics and hair creams, too. All my drawing comes in handy when I draw up designs for the ladies to choose from. Mae Ella got a good hand and a good eye too. Guess she get it from us both and her pa, too.

I gots me a good man Mama. A good man and he worship the ground that Mae Ella walk on. She had him wrapped 'round her finger from the day I pushed her out in the world.

I miss you Mama I miss you so bad. So much I want to ask you, to tell you, to hear your voice, feel your fingers in my hair agin, listen to your stories about home. I ain't gon' cry. I have a good life, a loving husband, a wonderful daughter and a business to call my own.

I thank you Mama for all you taught me, even when I didn't want to learn. I understand that now that I got a chile of my own. I won't forget. Mae Ella won't forget neither. I promise.

Alessandra turned the pages, but there were no more entries. She sniffed and wiped at her wet cheeks. "Damn," she whispered. "I know," she gulped, "I know how Ella feels. Missing your mother is something you never get over, no matter how old you are. There's this, this empty space inside you that never gets filled. You just…find ways to walk around it, ya know." She blinked back the sting in her eyes, lowered her head.

Traci put her arm around Alessandra's shoulder, pulled her close and let her cry.

When her soft sobs subsided, she sniffled her apologies.

"Nothing to be sorry about, sis. You've been through it. I'm surprised you aren't crying 24/7. I know I would be," Traci added with a crooked smile. "It's going to be okay," she said softly.

Alessandra bobbed her head. "Yeah, I know." She puffed her cheeks, then blew out a breath. "That's all I can take for the moment."

Traci angled her head. "Huh?"

Alessandra straightened her shoulders. She licked her bottom lip. "I don't know how to explain it. I'm going to sound crazy."

"Nothing crazy about that part," Traci teased.

Alessandra almost smiled. She spread her hands on her lap. "Since I've been back home…a little while before I got here, actually, I've been…experiencing things, feeling things. I told you about some of it and just tossed it off as being stressed, but when we got the chest open," she paused, "I felt overwhelmed, like the air was being sucked out of my lungs and replaced with waves of heat. The pages that I read didn't feel like some random words written by some stranger. I was *there*." The word scorched the air. "The visions, the feelings…" Her gaze bored into Traci's. "After, I feel exhausted, drained. It's all so…real."

"Hey, listen," Traci said softly. "You're in a very vulnerable place right now. You're bound to feel things more deeply."

Alessandra gave a slight shrug of her shoulder. "I guess," she weakly conceded. "Seems more than that, though. But in any case," she returned the journal to the chest and shut the lid, "enough for now. What we can do in the meantime is look for my dad's paperwork on the house." She removed the white gloves. "I don't think it's up here, but maybe in the small room where he listened to and played his music."

"Seems like your whole family is totally talented in some kind of a creative way. Your mom had an eye for design, you art and photography, your dad music. Come from good genes, girl."

They helped each other to their feet.

Alessandra smiled. Something deep inside her soul shifted. The weight and legacy of her very existence settled and sparked through her like the flame that lights the furnace. "Yeah...I do, don't I?"

· · ·

Zach continued along Avenue of the Americas, weighed down with two large shopping bags in each hand, the bags bumping against his legs and thighs as he navigated around the late-afternoon congestion of bodies.

The towering office buildings sliced through the semi-gray sky, creating an archway that stretched along the length of the iconic thoroughfare.

When he was in New York, he usually tried to get into Manhattan, or "the City," as it was affectionately known, after Thanksgiving, for the lighting of the tree in Rockefeller Center, but with all that had transpired in the past few weeks, it hadn't been high on his list. And even though he was in one of his favorite cities, he was eager to get back and dive into the treasure that Alessandra had uncovered. He visualized himself tagging and chronicling the items within the artifact cases that he'd purchased. Much of what Alessandra had found in the chest was in an extremely fragile state, so he'd added an extra supply of acid-free paper to line the cases to his haul.

He turned onto Fiftieth Street toward the parking garage, lifted his shoulders to his ears, and bent into the burst of wind that cut around the corner. He was still having a hard time wrapping his mind around the thing that was happening with him and Alessandra. It was like something out of one of those romance-novels-turned-television-movies on Hallmark. Not that he would know anything about that exactly—just what he'd heard.

Hot air and car exhaust pushed out of the open garage entrance. He slow-walked down the ramp, concentrating on keeping his balance and not losing his bags in the process. He turned right and down another ramp toward the ticket counter.

His thoughts churned as he eased out of the garage where he'd parked and into the waning twilight of the winter day. Waiting at the red light, his thoughts leaped to the evening and days ahead. His own research was sure to fill in many of the holes in the information, and once they were able to assemble all the pieces: the letters, journals, newsclips, photographs, combs, jars, and even pieces of fabric, the full body of an untold legacy would be realized. Just thinking about it sent a new rush of anticipation shooting through his veins.

That and the thought of getting back to Alessandra.

It had only been a few hours, but he actually missed her. *Crazy*. There was an energy that radiated from her and enveloped him in a kind of ethereal hold that he couldn't explain. The old folks would say, "Gal done root ya." He smiled.

Truth be told, he wouldn't mind if she did put some kind of Black-girl magic on him. Born of African tradition, to all those of Black diaspora, was the DNA of the descendants from the homeland. Their wisdom, cultures, spiritual understanding of Mother Earth, their own natural genius, and the use and power of herbs and prayer were transported to the shores of the Americas and the Caribbean and realized in its children. He believed that.

He'd witnessed it time and again as he traveled around the country and interviewed survivors of slavery or their descendants. He understood that it was in the *telling*, the passing-on of the magic, where the power lay. Alessandra had that power, hovering just beneath the surface of her consciousness. The power had begun to appear in the unexplained visions and her visceral reaction to reading the journals. All she needed to do was to let go and allow the power of her past to emerge through her.

If he said all this out loud to the average person, he would get serious side-eye. But there were so many who understood. His grandmother was one of them.

• • •

Grace was dozing in her favorite recliner by the window when Zach returned. He tiptoed into the room and pulled the handwoven Native American blanket up over her shoulders. She stirred. Hummed deep in her throat, like the beginning of a gospel song. Her eyes flickered open, and her lips pursed in contemplation while she focused on him. "Just getting in?" she finally said.

"Yes. Took a bit longer than I thought."

She dragged in a long breath. "How'd you make out?"

"Got everything I needed," he said and plopped down on the love seat. He stretched his long legs out in front of him and tucked his hands behind his head, then jerked forward and rested his hands on his thighs. "Gram?"

"Umm-hmm." She stifled a yawn.

"Remember when I came to stay with you full-time?"

"Of course. Best day of my life, even though your coming was under such sad circumstances."

He'd never seen his grandmother truly weep before that day. He'd seen happy tears and even sad tears now and again, but the weeping, the weight and heft of her anguish that Zach's parents were gone, was a burden that it did not seem she could bear. But Grace Oweku did bear it, as she'd borne so many other weights, and she never neglected to remind Zach that he was her comfort, the legacy of the family, her blood.

She raised him, loved him, scolded him, educated him, and freed him to go after his dreams in life.

"What about it?" Grace asked, prompting him back to the present.

Zach pulled in a short breath. "Do you ever think that if Mom and Dad had lived, *we* wouldn't be who we are?" He stared at her in earnest.

Grace shifted to a more comfortable position in the chair. "Don't have to think about it. Every step we take leads to another and brings us where we s'posed to be. You were s'posed to be on my doorstep that day so that you could be here now, doing the work that you do. You were s'posed to be out there the night that Alessandra arrived." She lifted her brow in emphasis. "Just like I was s'posed to befriend Alessandra's mama and lead her to where she needed to go."

Zach's eyes narrowed. "What do you mean?"

Grace sighed. She linked her fingers together across her stomach. "Jessica Fleming was a complicated woman, at war with herself, really." Her gaze drifted. "She come up during a time when colored folk was being accepted for all the things that didn't make us colored: straight hair, light skin, fine features, for being educated, well-dressed, belonging to clubs and organizations that declared you had arrived." She chuckled softly. "*Arrived where?* I always wanted to know. The goal for so many colored folks when she was coming up was to—what's the word—fit in?"

"Assimilate?" Zach offered.

She snorted. "Yes. That." She wagged a finger. "It was some kind of badge of honor to move into places where they didn't want us, get jobs they didn't want us to have, sit next to their daughters and sons, even show up on the television screen. Sure, it's our right to live and love and laugh just like anyone else. But too many went runnin' after that shiny thing in the window to prove their value, their humanity, at the expense of the richness of their souls."

She paused a moment. "The fact that Jessica was light, bright, damn-near white as we used to say, with what the folks call 'good hair,' surely the stain of an unnamed ancestor, only fueled her. She didn't see herself in the mirror as a reflection of the abuse that was brought down on her line, but instead as a doorway to a life she believed she deserved."

"What changed? You said she finally started asking questions."

"That chest that Alessandra found..."

"Yes."

"So happens one afternoon I was going 'round the neighborhood just asking folks if they had anything they might want to donate to the museum for auction, and to bring it by the following week. Jessica was home, invited me in, and offered me some sweet tea. She was always 'the lady, the hostess.'" Grace smiled in reflection. "She told me she had some things her family collected for years that she could offer, and asked if I wanted to take a look." Her gaze rose to meet Zach's. "It was the chest."

His lips parted, but he didn't speak.

"The instant I gazed on what was inside, something give way inside me, as if someone had stepped into my soul and spread their wings. For a moment, I couldn't say a word. I finally asked her had she gone through what was in the chest. She said not really, and that she kept it pushed away and out of sight. *The past is the past,* I remember her saying. *The past is the future,* I told her, *and you need to know that, understand it.* I asked her to promise me not to give any of it away. She waved a hand and said she'd put it right back where it had been."

Grace shifted in her seat again. "Must have been maybe a month or so later, Jessica come knocking on the door. She had a shoebox in her hand and asked if she could come in. That day was the first in a handful of times. She'd bring news articles for us to read, old letters from folks we didn't know. But what we did come to understand was that these were *her* people, *her* family, *her* history, as hard and ugly and beautiful as it was. Told her she couldn't let it die by pretending it didn't happen and she needed to add her own story for her daughter." Grace slowly shook her head as the memory rolled through her. "Don't know if she ever did," she finally said with a heavy sigh. "I went south that summer, to visit my cousin, and when I come back I heard she'd passed away in that awful accident."

Zach simply blinked in astonishment. "Do you think Alessandra's mom may have added to the chest or written things down?"

"She might have." Grace smiled. "That's why you're here, son, to help put the pieces of the story together," she said with a knowing lift of her brow. "Alessandra's—and maybe yours, too."

CHAPTER TWENTY-SIX

Alessandra opened the door to the room off the living room that her father used as an office for his business and his wind-down space where he'd play his sax, listen to music, and read while sipping a bottle of beer.

Another wave of nostalgia and a bit of regret met Alessandra at the door. She wished she'd had more time. She wished she'd allowed herself to fully love her father while he was here. She wished she could turn back the clock and make things right. None of that was possible, not in actuality, but in some way the past was going to set the future straight. Of that she was growing more certain.

Traci stepped in behind her and stood in the center of the room with her hands on her hips. She looked around. "These cabinets and wall units are amazing," she said in awe.

Alessandra smiled, a twinge of pride filling her. She lifted her chin toward the unit that took up the entire side of the far wall. "My dad made all of these pieces. That one, the unit with the books, he let me help."

Traci's head jerked back in surprise. "Get out. For real?"

She came to stand next to her friend.

"He let me hand him the slats of wood. Sometimes he'd let me hammer in a nail." She chuckled. "When it was time to varnish, I got my very own brush." She gazed off into the distance, then ran her hand down the smooth side of the varnished wood. "I was only about seven, maybe eight. My dad would hold my hand and show me how to paint the varnish on in smooth strokes so that it wouldn't bubble."

Alessandra lifted a volume of Jean Toomer's *Cane* that was next to *Passing* by Nella Larsen.

"Girl," Traci said, almost breathless as she took in the impressive collection of original editions, from Harriet Jacobs's *Incidents in the Life of a Slave Girl* to Alice Walker's *The Color Purple*, Zora Neale Hurston's classic *Their Eyes Were Watching God*, to her novels, essays and short stories, the half row dedicated to James Baldwin and to Barack and Michelle Obama's memoirs. She ran her fingers along the spines of the books. "This is like great sex for a booklover like me. Almost," she qualified with a wink.

Alessandra laughed. "Yeah, my dad was a book and music lover bar none. I'd forgotten how many books he had." Her gaze scanned upward.

"Probably worth a pretty penny," Traci mused, returning the volume to its rightful place. She spun away. "Where do you want to start?"

"I'll look through the desk. Those two chests," she said, pointing, "have drawers along the top and at the bottom. The two doors in the middle open to the pullout shelves that have his albums and playbills from shows."

Traci sat cross-legged on the floor. "Sis, if we weren't cool like real blood sisters, I would knock you over the head, stash your body in the attic, and make off with allll these goodies! Damn. This is puredee heaven."

Alessandra laughed. "So the only thing standing between me keeping my books and albums and me winding up on the side of a milk carton is our sisterhood."

"Yep." Traci nodded. "Yep."

"Girl, just start looking," Alessandra said with a dismissive wave of her hand. She sat at the desk and pulled open the center drawer by its brass knob. The velvet-lined drawer was filled with envelopes, slips of paper, and stationery. She picked up the square box of notecards with a small trumpet embossed in gold on each, took one out of the box, and turned it over. BLUE NOTE JAZZ CLUB, 131 WEST 3RD STREET, NY 10012, COLLECTOR'S EDITION. She didn't remember her father being the letter-writing type, but as she was discovering day by day, there was so much she didn't know about her dad.

She slowly leafed through the envelopes, taking out contents and returning them. For the most part they were paid bills and receipts for purchases for the house. She opened the right-hand drawer that held a hanging rack with actual file folders. These, it turned out, contained the paperwork for the store.

"Hey, think I got something," Traci called out, and wiggled her behind around on the floor to turn toward Alessandra. She held a sheaf of papers in her hand encased in a clear plastic envelope.

Alessandra got up and moved over to Traci. She took the envelope, sat next to her friend, and pulled the papers out, turning them right side up to read. One was several pages of contract lingo for the new roof, another for replacement storm windows. She flipped through a few more bank statements, then the deed to the house in her father's and mother's names, and the mortgage papers from the bank.

Alessandra drew in a breath, took a quick look at Traci, then carefully read the mortgage papers. "Looks like the house is fully paid for," she finally said after several long minutes, and continued to scan the pages. She blinked several times.

"That's a good thing."

She rested the pages on her thighs. "The house is worth 1.5 million dollars, T," she said, a bit breathless.

Traci's brows rose to her hairline. "Say what?"

"Yep." She handed the paper to Traci and pointed to the figure.

"Damn," Traci said on a breath. "A fully-paid-for million-dollar home. Whew."

"My head is spinning." Alessandra tugged on her bottom lip with her teeth. "Still need to find a will or something. Make sure that whatever Dad wanted to do with the house and the business is done."

Traci squeezed Alessandra's hand. "Then we have to keep looking."

They spent the next hour searching every nook and cranny in the room: each shelf, each drawer—and came up empty. They plopped down on the floor, tired, hungry, and feeling defeated.

Alessandra blew out a long breath. "Has to be around here somewhere. Just don't know where. What I do know is that I'm starved. Let's get back to this later. Maybe he slid it in between the pages of one of those hundreds of books like in the movies," she said over a weak laugh.

Traci draped her arm across Alessandra's shoulder as they walked out. "Or...maybe there's one of those walls that open to a secret chamber," she teased.

Alessandra chuckled. "Anything is possible at this point." She closed the door behind them in concert with the ringing of the front doorbell.

• • •

Alessandra opened the door, and her spirits instantly lifted. Zach dropped the shopping bags at his feet, crossed the threshold, and slid an arm around her waist.

Zach's brows creased. He studied her face with a kind of wonder. "I knew I was missing you. Just didn't realize how much until right now."

Alessandra tilted her head back a bit to look into his eyes. Her mouth softened. "I can't wait for you to show me how much," she said in a rough whisper.

Zach leaned down and covered her mouth in a kiss that quickly had them both humming with longing. He pulled her tight against his body, and she molded to him.

The loud clearing of a throat came from behind them. Reluctantly, they eased back from each other. Alessandra turned, shoved her hands in the back pockets of her jeans, and looked at her friend in wide-eyed innocence.

"Umm, could you two close the door? You're letting in all the cold air…not that you would notice," Traci teased, then spun away.

Alessandra and Zach broke into laughter. He shut the door.

"What's in the bags?" She picked up one. Zach took the other three.

"The cases for the artifacts, some more gloves, labels, acid-free paper, pens, tape." He gave a light shrug. "Tools of the trade."

"I guess you can leave them in the front room for now. Traci and I were getting ready to fix something to eat. Hungry?"

"I could eat," he said over a chuckle.

The three sat around Jeremiah's table over double-thick roasted chicken sandwiches on sourdough bread and tall glasses of iced green tea while Alessandra explained to Zach what they'd found and what they hadn't.

"Whoa. One point five." He took a long swallow of tea.

"Yeah," Alessandra said on a breath. "But not what I needed to find, which is my dad's will."

"Did your dad have an attorney?"

Alessandra frowned. "Good question. I'm not sure. I would think that he probably did. I just don't know who."

"Maybe time would be better spent finding his attorney. If he wrote a will, his attorney would have it."

"Good point. I'll take another look through the papers."

"I noticed a Rolodex in your dad's desk drawer," Traci offered, and took a bite out of her sandwich.

"A what?" Alessandra asked.

"Rolodex." Traci chewed, swallowed, and smiled. "Pre-technology. Names, numbers, and addresses on little cards on a spinner thing, organized by the alphabet." She took a swallow of water.

"Why do you even know that?" Alessandra asked.

"Some of the old heads at the publishing house still have them." She shrugged.

Zach and Alessandra looked at each other and grinned.

"Everybody's good for something, right?" Traci said, before finishing off her sandwich. "Um, Morgan called me while you two were canoodling." Her lashes lowered. "I have a last one-night stand tonight with Morgan. He's going back to DC, and...I need to get back to the office. Said he'd drop me off in Manhattan on his way, so I took the offer." She covered Alessandra's hand with hers and gave a light squeeze. "You know I'd stay forever if I could."

"I know. Don't even worry about it. I'll be fine. And as

soon as I can get the situation with the house settled, I'll be heading back, too."

Zach shifted in his seat but kept his gaze fixed on the last few bites of his sandwich.

Traci must have noticed the change in the air, because she stood and took her plate and glass to the sink. "I'm going up to pack," she said from the sink. She washed her dishes and turned off the water, then gave them a tight smile as she walked out.

"So you'll be going back to New York?" Zach asked, his voice sounding strained.

Alessandra swallowed. "I have to, at some point. I do have a life in Manhattan. And," she added, "you have your work."

He licked his lips. "Then we should make the most of our time together—and get to work. I'll be upstairs setting up."

Alessandra watched him walk out, heard him rustling with the shopping bags before going upstairs. She sat there for a few moments. What did he expect? That she'd stay forever? Here? What was he offering? A few hot nights, knee-wobbling kisses, and…? She didn't know, and as much as Zach Renard was all about uncovering lost stories and lives, he had yet to uncover any intentions when it came to the two of them.

She got up from her seat, took the plates and glasses to the sink, and went upstairs.

When she entered the room, Zach was unpacking the shopping bags. She leaned against the frame of the door, crossing her arms tightly across her waist and her legs at the ankle.

"I do have to go home," she said quietly. "Even though my show has been canceled, I still have a job—I hope—and an apartment, friends, responsibilities," she went on, as much to convince him as herself.

He briefly glanced up. "Of course."

Her heart thumped. "Any thoughts about…us?"

Zach stopped unpacking. He turned fully toward her. "That's all I think about," he confessed. He drew in a breath, angled his head to one side. "When I wake up, move through my day, when I go to sleep at night."

Alessandra warmed from the soles of her feet to the top of her head. "Me too." She unwound her body.

Zach crossed the room. "So, what are we going to do about it?"

"Figure it out? I'm willing if you are."

His warm gaze moved slowly across her face. "I could be persuaded." He brushed her bottom lip with the pad of his thumb, drew in a long breath, and slowly exhaled. His brow furrowed. "This thing between us…"

"I know," she whispered as if reading his thoughts. "Can't explain it."

"This is so new, but it feels…"

"It feels like forever," she said on a breath of wonder. She stared into his eyes, needing him to confirm what was stirring in her heart.

Zach nodded. "Yeah. Like forever." The corner of his mouth lifted. "Crazy, huh?"

Alessandra lifted her gaze and slid her arms around his waist. She rested her head on his chest as he drew her to him.

Their hearts, one beat behind the other, slowly began to synch until they beat in unison.

"Everything that has happened since I came back home has been crazy. Finally reconciling with my dad after all these years only to lose him."

He held her tighter.

"The dreams…or visions, whatever they are that I've been having, this inexplicable connection that you and I have, finding the chest...the hidden history, the questions—this house." She dragged in a breath, tilted her head back to look at him. "You can't make this stuff up."

Zach gave a light chuckle. "It may seem bizarre and out of the ordinary, but in my line of work, so much of what has happened these past few weeks is pretty commonplace—everything except finding you." A slow smile bloomed, crinkling his dark eyes at the corners. He lifted a stray loc of her hair away from the side of her face and tucked it behind her ear. "That's the best part."

...

"Hey girl, I'm sorry I can't stay longer," Traci said from the doorway to the kitchen later. "But I'll be checking in, and if you need me, I'm here in a heartbeat."

"I know. Thank you for everything, T."

The friends hugged tightly.

Traci glanced over Alessandra's shoulder to where Zach stood. "You take care of my girl," she ordered with a wag of her finger.

Zach came to Alessandra's side and draped his arm across her shoulder. "Plan to." He lifted his chin toward Morgan, who was coming up the front steps. "And don't put a hurt on my boy," he teased.

Traci winked. "That's half the fun."

"Hey, good people," Morgan greeted. He bussed Alessandra's cheek and shared the brothers-only handshake with Zach. "What's good, man?"

"Everything." He smiled.

"I hear that." He focused on Alessandra. "Sorry to take your friend away and leave you in the hands of this guy," he joked.

Alessandra grinned. "I kinda like those hands." She tugged on her bottom lip with her teeth and looked up at Zach. He winked.

"Make sure he keeps you happy. If not, I'm only a phone call away." He playfully chucked Zach on the shoulder.

"I don't think that'll be a problem, but thanks for the offer," she said over her laughter.

Morgan turned to Traci. "Ready, babe?"

"Yep."

Morgan picked up Traci's suitcase and shared a pull-to-the-chest handshake with Zach. Traci and Alessandra managed one last hug, both sniffing and trying not to cry.

"I'll call you, girl," Traci said over her shoulder as she descended the front steps.

Alessandra and Zach stood in the doorway until the taillights of Morgan's SUV disappeared into the night.

"I could use a drink," Alessandra said on a breath as she turned away and walked back into the house.

Zach closed the door. "Easy or hard?"

Alessandra looked at him and cocked her head to the side. "Mr. Renard, that is a loaded question."

He chuckled. "Wine or something stronger?"

"Wine. I want to keep my head relatively clear. I really need to locate the name of my father's attorney and go through some of the items in the chest *and* after a long—hard—day…" She came to stand in front of him and wound her arms around his neck. She leaned up and pressed her mouth softly against his, then let her tongue run along his bottom lip. Zach hummed deep in his chest.

"Listen, woman," he said, snatching her tight against him, his voice rough and low, "keep that up and we won't make it out of this living room."

CHAPTER TWENTY-SEVEN

Zach sucked in a quick breath as Alessandra shimmied out of her navy-blue sweatpants and kicked them aside. "Who said I wanted to leave?" she purred, pulling her T-shirt over her head.

Zach felt his mouth curve upward. He unbuttoned and unzipped his jeans, then tugged off his sweater. Alessandra eased in front of him. She hooked her fingers into the loops of his jeans and tugged them over his hips, down his thighs to his feet until she was on her knees in front of him. She glanced up, a wicked smile teasing her mouth. Her eyes darkened, then lit with the fire that burned for him.

Her tongue teased. He hissed in air from between clenched teeth and gripped her shoulders. Again, this time along the length of him. Slow, steady, circular until his thighs began to tremble and his moans turned to low growls.

Her lips encircled.

"Ayyy—!" His fingers dug in and gripped the wild tendrils of her hair.

Again.

His knees weakened.

Her tongue trailed the underside of his erection, stiffening it to the point of near pain.

Zach groaned, an almost wounded sound. He pulled himself free, his fingers still wrapped in her hair, forced her to look up at him. Her eyes were mere slits, her smile triumphant.

He bent, scooped her petite frame in his arms, and lifted her until their mouths were inches apart. "I'm afraid, woman, that you'll pay dearly for that."

She pressed her open mouth to his and suckled his tongue as it danced with hers. "I'm hoping you're a man of your word," she whispered against his lips and hooked her arms around his neck as he carried her to the couch.

He sat her down and hovered above her for a moment, then knelt and pressed his palms against her knees to spread her thighs wide. "Do unto others…" he said, his voice thick, an instant before he parted her folds.

Alessandra's head fell back against the cushion of the couch. A tremor ran up the inside of her thighs and stirred the center of her being.

A flick, a tease, a lick, a suckle.

She moaned, gripped, whimpered, shook, dug her fingers into his bare shoulders.

Zach draped her legs over his shoulders, then eased her thighs back toward her breasts. She was there for the taking, vulnerable, incapable of halting the total and complete submission of her body to his velvet tongue.

Zach reluctantly eased away and relished for a moment the look of pure angelic rapture that captured her face. Her eyes were closed, her skin flushed, her swollen lips moist and parted, hair splayed across the back of the couch. Her breath came in short, tight bursts.

He slowly moved up her open and exposed body, planting hot, wet kisses along her fevered flesh, until he reached her breasts. His mouth replaced her hands and drew her taut dark nipple between his lips, flicked it again and again with his tongue until she cried out his name and dug her fingers into his back.

Zach deftly moved along the length of the couch, stretching her out before him. He moved above her. She draped one leg across the back of the couch and the other around his back.

Zach dragged in a breath. He reached out, stroked her cheek with the tip of his finger until her lids fluttered. She tightened her leg around his back and drew him to her.

A guttural groan rose from the depths of his throat as she thrust her hips upward and he had no choice but to obey the demands of their longing.

Their cries melded into a single note, rose and fell in harmony with every stroke, every roll of hips, each hungry kiss, building in intensity until the very air they breathed was electrified.

White light enveloped them, spun them into a funnel of time and space back to yesterday, to all the days, months, years, decades, centuries before. They saw each other, again and again, across time until they were back on the sandy beaches of Mendeland where they first made love beneath the towering veil of the kapok tree.

That time, that instant, they experienced together again in this moment, a moment so powerful it exploded into a million stars. They each dove into the gaze of the other, and their lives, their memories, and their souls merged.

And they knew…the inexplicable.

. . .

They lay together, their arms and legs twisted around each other, Alessandra feeling like she desperately needed the anchor of Zach's limbs to keep herself from flying away.

Zach grabbed the quilted throw from the arm of the couch and covered them. She didn't speak, didn't trust what she might say.

Alessandra tucked her head into the dip of Zach's shoulder. His arms encircled her again. Their breathing slowed.

"We were there. Together," Alessandra finally whispered, the images of past and present still swirling in her mind. "I... saw you."

Zach's jaw tightened. "I... It felt like a dream but real at the same time." He drew in a long breath and slowly released it.

Alessandra stroked his back. She stared into the darkness. The kaleidoscopic images of time spun and danced across the ceiling. "I know," she whispered.

CHAPTER TWENTY-EIGHT

"It all seemed like it was an extension of my visions or dreams," Alessandra murmured against his chest.

"Since the first time we made love," Zach began picking his way through the swirl of the out-of-body experience, "there was always this feeling that we'd been together before. But that's crazy, right?"

She adjusted her body closer to his, as if to burrow beneath his skin. "I know. I mean, we didn't know each other...before." It came out as more of a question than a statement.

"What if we did?" Zach said suddenly. "What if..." He paused, frowned. "I mean—I don't know what I mean."

Alessandra angled her head up a bit to look at him. "Whatever it is, it feels right." Her gaze trailed across his face.

He bent his head and kissed the top of hers. "Yeah. It does."

...

After some time of basking and murmuring in the afterglow of their surreal lovemaking session, Alessandra and Zach finally dressed and returned to Jeremiah's bedroom.

"How can I help?" she asked as they walked toward the chest.

"While I write up the descriptions and secure the items, you can take photographs before they're sealed and after."

"Not a problem."

"You can use my camera."

"I'd rather use my Nikon. Be right back." She hurried off to her bedroom and returned moments later with her camera and extra film tucked in the pockets of her sweatpants.

Zach had dragged the chest to the center of the floor and donned his white gloves. "Can you empty out the shopping bags, please? I'll need the index cards and the felt marker, and I'll start with the acid-free sleeves for the loose papers, newsclips, and photographs. We can work our way up to the journals and artifacts. Those will go in the plastic cases."

"Aye, aye, captain," she teased with a mock salute.

He snorted a laugh. "Funny. Once we get them labeled, we can organize them by date and create a timeline."

Alessandra nodded eagerly.

Zach drew in a breath and slowly exhaled. "Okay, let's get busy."

Zach gingerly lifted some of the most fragile documents from the case and laid them out on a roll of white paper, similar to the paper from a doctor's examination table. Alessandra took the "before" photos and closeups to catch as much detail as possible. Zach used a small magnifying glass to reexamine the documents, then wrote up a card and slipped them into the plastic sleeves. Alessandra took more photos.

They worked in tandem for nearly two hours, in between

murmurs of awe and fascination and sharing looks of wonder.

"Hmm," he murmured absently, intent on the news clipping in front of him about one J.B. Stradford, one of Tulsa's most influential Black entrepreneurs. This particular article in *The Tulsa Star* touted the grand opening of The Stradford Hotel at 301 N. Greenwood in 1918. It was said to be the largest Black-owned and -operated hotel in America, the towering achievement of Stradford, who'd amassed a fortune from his more than two dozen rental and rooming houses, pool halls, and shoeshine parlors. "Check this out."

Alessandra leaned closer. "Wow," she sighed as she scanned the clipping. "Wonder how much he'd be worth now."

"He'd probably be up there with the Gateses and the Buffets of the world." He slid the article into a plastic sleeve and taped the card to the front.

Alessandra snapped a photo.

"The key to generational wealth is ownership of land," he continued. "It's one of the reasons why those in power wanted to make sure that Black people never owned anything. The result is centuries of poverty. The city of Tulsa was a beacon of what was possible for free Black people, and it scared the hell outta white folks."

Alessandra pursed her lips. "So, about generational wealth... Um, like I was saying, I found the papers for the house—and it's worth 1.5 million."

Zach stopped what he was doing. He slowly turned his head in Alessandra's direction. "Why the look? It is good news, isn't it?"

"That's just it. I have no idea. I mean, the house is totally paid for, my dad owned it outright, but what I haven't found is his will. That's what Traci and I were doing earlier. No luck. Next step is to try and see if I can find an attorney's name."

"If you can't find it here, someone at his shop might know."

"True."

He paused a moment. "Once you find the attorney and the will turns the house over to you, which I'm pretty sure it will, what then?"

Alessandra blinked, looked away. "I haven't thought that far ahead. To be honest, Zach, I'm living day to day at this point."

"Yeah. I get it."

"But...if Dad did leave me the house," she said, slowly and deliberately, "it would give me roots." She swallowed, tossed him a sidelong glance from beneath her lashes.

He rocked his jaw. "It would." He continued to scan documents.

"You mind if I get started on the journals while you work on the papers?" Alessandra asked, shifting the topic from what the future could be to what the past was.

"Sure. Put the information on the card: beginning and ending dates, owner's name, and tape the card to the outside of one of the plastic boxes."

She gave a short nod. "Simple enough." She moved closer to him, tucked her legs crisscross, and took out the journals that she'd had a chance to read. She labeled them accordingly and placed them in protective boxes.

"Hey, look at these." He held out on his palm a stack of papers of varying sizes tied together with a thin leather string. "Letters. I think."

Alessandra inched closer. "Welllll," she urged wide-eyed, "let's see."

Carefully, Zach untied the age-old knots of the leather string, and it shredded in his hands. He flicked away the flakes of leather from his gloved fingers. One by one, he laid the crackling, yellowed pages on the white paper. All of the edges were ragged, as if they'd been torn from a book.

"Check for any dates. We'll line them up that way."

They leaned in, scanning the faded ink for signs of any dates, and began to organize them as best they could.

"Looks like the same handwriting," Alessandra noted.

"Yep."

They glanced at each other and smiled with anticipation.

"Get some pictures before we touch them anymore, on the off chance that they fall apart," Zach said.

Alessandra took several shots of each. There were about fifty pages in total. She carefully lifted the page dated 1893 and began to slowly read, Zach looking intently over her shoulder the entire time.

I saw him for the first time when I come home from working at Mama's sewing shop. I was so tired from the hours of fittings and hand stitching, I could hardly lift my feet. What I want to do with my free afternoons is paint my pictures, but Mama says the business will be mine one day and I need to learn it. Out front the sign already says Ella and Daughter Dressmakers. She says you sometimes have to wish things into existence.

Alessandra stopped short. She flashed Zach a look. "This must be Ella's daughter," she said in a tight whisper.

"Yeah," he agreed with a nod. "Go ahead. Finish."

She squinted a bit.

Mama is funny like that. She has all those old timey sayings and ways. Like how she'll come sit on the side of my bed and tell me all about her mama, and how it was growing up and how her mama made her promise to never stop telling our stories. Share them with the children. Write down what we can, what we remember. Mama must of said that a million times. Sometimes at night, though, Mama would whisper her name in my ear, our ancestor, tell me to keep her name in my heart and in my spirit and never forget. Guess all that talking must have stuck with me, too. I've been writing for as long as I can remember.

Mama swears by her homemade hair pomades, that my grandma, that I never got to meet, taught her how to mix up. Our new shop is on Greenwood Avenue…

"Tulsa!" she and Zach said in unison.

…on the street with other colored businesses, lined up one after the next: bank, churches, two school buildings, barber, grocery store, shoe repair. Tulsa even has a theater now for musicals and plays. Folks say that Greenwood is the most prosperous colored town in the country. And Mama says we have to dress the part.

The next pages detailed a beautiful yellow dress that Mae Ella planned to wear to a dance. Alessandra could feel the love between Mae Ella and her daddy, and her heart ached with missing her own father.

My dad doesn't show affection like Mama. He works and works, says very little, lets Mama run the house and look after me. But I always have a feeling that no matter what, my daddy is there in the background watching over us.

Alessandra's throat burned.

The dance is in three days and Mama said she'd do my hair. Mama said my hair is too long and too thick for that wave style I showed her in the magazine, but she said she'd press and grease my hair and use the curling rods. I can't wait.

A page was missing. Alessandra groaned. She went to the next paper on the lineup.

Anyhow, he's new around here. I can tell because everybody know everybody and I don't know him. He slowed his horse and tipped his hat to me. Gave me a nice smile that made my stomach feel all funny, and fluttery.

Wonder if he's here to stay or just passing through. Lou Ann and Estelle might know.

Us three, me, Lou Ann, and Estelle pinky swore that we would not accept any invite from the fellas in town. We're going together so we can "test the waters" as Estelle says.

...

I only told Estelle because Lou Ann can't hold water least lone a secret.

I met up with Carter last night behind the church and we kissed. Lord forgive me, but I didn't want to stop. Before I knew it my blouse was undone. I'm probably going straight to hell. I kept telling him to slow down, but when he asked me if I was sure I wanted him to slow down, I said no.

Ever since the night of the spring dance, me and Carter Hopewell been sweet on each other, maybe even from the first time I saw him up on that horse.

He's older. All finished with school a few years back, so I was surprised to see him at the dance. He said since his pa was feeling poorly, he'd escorted his sister Mabel. I thought that was the nicest thing.

We danced a few times and he fetched me a cup of punch. He has the smoothest caramel-colored skin and eyes to match. I have to look up to talk to him. That's kind of nice. But I swear I could feel my daddy's eyes on us the whole time.

Lou Ann and Estelle backed me in a corner and pressed me to tell them every detail about how it felt dancing with Carter Hopewell. Were his eyes really that pretty up close? Did he smell like soap? The good kind, Estelle wanted to know.

When it was time to leave the dance, Carter asked me if he could see me sometime. I said I figured it would be all right if he come 'round to Mama's shop and introduce himself. He said he'd do that.

It'll be the best day of my whole life.

The entry abruptly ended.

"Oh no." Alessandra scanned the pages in front of them. "What happened at the dance?"

Zach chuckled. "We may never know. Only imagine." He kissed her forehead.

Alessandra pouted. The next letter was many months later. "This girl is going to drive me nuts. Where are the missing pages? I want to know every detail."

Zach tossed his head back and laughed. He put an arm around her shoulder and rested his head atop hers. "I love listening to you read. I feel like I'm there."

"So do I." She glanced at him. "And I don't mean because of the words in the letters and journals, but really *there*. Ya know." She frowned. "Like when you and I…" Her voice drifted off.

"I do. After what happened between us earlier…" He let the words and the memory linger.

She held his gaze for a moment, then cleared her throat and picked up the next page.

September 1894

I know I love Carter. He's all I think about. Mama says I better get my head out of the clouds and stop messing up her customers' orders.

Thing is all I want to do is be with him. When I try to explain it to Mama she told me the story of how she fell in love with Papa. She said she was about my age and they lived in a place called Sag Harbor in the North. They was Maroons. Something like what we are here, she said, all to ourselves, making our own way, not depending on or fearing any white man. 'Cept they lived in the woods surrounded by marshland and woods. Train tracks separate us from the white folks here in Greenwood.

Mama said the minute she rest her eyes on Papa it felt like her heart stopped beating and she couldn't breathe. She had this faraway, soft look on her face like she was back there in that moment and I saw my Mama different. She wasn't just my mama who ran her business and who tended to me and Papa's needs. Most times she's so tired from working, she can barely smile or give me a hug. But she always has enough strength at night to tell me stories about her life as a girl and about my grandma who was captured and brought to America to be a slave and we wasn't never to forget. Her mama told her and she would tell me and I would tell my own.

Her voice always broke at that part of the story. But it was the story about her and Papa that had me seeing my mama, not just as my mama but a woman with feelings that ran deep. She knew what it was I was feeling 'cause she felt it for my papa. Still did, she said. She said every time pa walks through the door her heart still races and she feels all warm inside. She said that feeling can make you do things you are not ready for. As much as the body says yes, I got to remember to say no.

What if I'm ready? I asked her. Mama's brows rose and a smile lifted her mouth. She patted my thigh and laughed a little bit. When you really are ready, you'll know, but don't let Carter get you there until you know for sure. Ya hear.

I don't know about all that, but I'm going to try.

January 1895
I'm a woman now.

"Uh-oh," Alessandra murmured and flashed Zach a look.

A real woman that been with a real man. I can't even find the words to describe what I'm feeling. I wish I could tell someone about all that's running through me, the fire, the wetness between my thighs.

Caint let Mama find out. She'd have one fit, even though I think she might of been with Papa before they got married. And Papa, Lawd knows he'd probably shoot Carter right in the middle of Greenwood Avenue.

Mama's words keep coming to me: "Don't let Carter get you there until you know for sure."

What if Mama was right and it was Carter's sweet talk and sweet tasting lips what made me think I was ready?

Carter never told me he loves me. Why not?

Alessandra looked at Zach with pursed lips. "Men," she grumbled.

"What?" Zach asked, sounding offended.

Alessandra rolled her eyes. She picked up another page. "April," she said. "I think. The ink is so faded."

Mama hasn't been feeling too well lately and Papa says I'm going to need to help out more at the shop. Don't know how much more I can do. But with Mama ailing and me working every free minute at the shop I hardly have time for Carter. He says he understands, but if I give him too much time to be without me, one of those girls that's always sniffing around him will sho' nuf catch his eye. Where's that gonna leave me?

Every evening pa comes to the shop after work to fetch Mama, cause it's getting hard for her to walk. She says it's nothing and waves me away whenever I try to help her out of her sewing chair. But when Papa comes she just glows and smiles and does whatever he asks in that soothing deep voice of his.

*Funny to think of my folks being in love like that,
"doing it." They share something secret and special, a
happiness that they bring out in the other. That's the
kind of love I want with Carter. It's what I feel
for him. I wish I could say he feels the same.*

*He says he cares about me and I'm the only
girl for him. That's about it.*

There were several more pages, but the paper and the ink
were too degraded to be able to make out the words. Zach
said that he might be able to raise the lettering back at his
lab in the Smithsonian.

April 1895
*The winter was wicked on Mama and the spring
not much better. Mama can barely stretch out her
fingers and her knees are worst.*

*She says it feels like the cold crept into her
bones and froze them solid. When she tries to move
them, they creak like rusty metal. Doctor Phillips
says its arthritis from years and years of plaiting
hair and sewing and sitting for hours and hours.
He gave her some salve to rub on her joints and
it has the whole house smelling like camphor. But
whatever it takes for Mama to feel better. Daddy
dotes on her like a kid with a new puppy. Most
important thing, Doc Phillips says is to keep her
joints warm and not to sit for too long in one place.*

*My heart aches to see my strong, unbreakable
Mama wince in pain, force herself to smile and grit
her teeth with every step she takes. But even with all
that's going on, her only worry is me and Papa and*

getting my wedding gown done in time.

"A wedding!" Alessandra's heart soared. Had Carter finally come through for Mae Ella?

Each night before I turn in, I sit on Mama's bedside and listen to her stories. With the stiffness in her hands she can't write anymore, so I do it for her. I write down her words.

Last week Papa brought home a present for Mama. He said he'd been working on it for months. A place to keep all her treasures and her mama's and her grandmama's. It is the most beautiful chest I've ever seen.

Alessandra and Zach both inhaled a sharp breath.

"This chest." Alessandra exhaled, and her eyes settled on the intricately carved chest. "The only way my parents would have this chest is if—"

"It's your family history that's inside," Zach finished for her.

Alessandra bit down on her bottom lip. "Maybe it came with the house," she said, scrambling for an explanation that sounded feeble even to her.

"You don't believe that. I know I don't."

She squeezed her eyes shut for a moment. "It's a lot."

"Yeah, it is." He paused a beat. "You have no idea how blessed you are. Most people can't trace their roots beyond their grandparents." He twisted his body toward her and took her hands. "If what I've pieced together about the arrival of *La Amistad* and the legend of the escaped African girl is connected to all this—as I believe it is—you'll be able to trace your legacy back to Africa and the ship that stole your ancestor."

Alessandra breathed heavily. The enormity of what he said was almost too much to take in, but maybe tucked into the stories she would find out who her mother really was.

"I was talking with my grandmother," he began slowly. "She told me that shortly before your mother passed, she'd started bringing over a shoebox with old pictures and newsclips, sometimes letters. A little at a time. The two of them would read and try to put it all together." He paused, stroked her cheek. "She was coming to terms with whatever had been holding her back, Ali."

Her lips pinched. She blinked and blinked. Her voice cracked. "I still miss her," she whispered. She rested her head on Zach's shoulder.

"I know. You always will. I still miss mine, even as absent as she was. My dad, too." He kissed the top of her head. "That hole never truly gets filled, but over time it doesn't feel quite as hollow."

She closed her eyes. "I filled up the space with distance," she said softly, "and resentment. Since I've been back, I *feel* her." Her eyes flew open. "All around me. Inside my soul," she said, her voice urgent and raw, "leading me…somewhere. From the moment I met you, reconciled with my dad, met your grandmother, found the chest…" She swallowed. "It's been this surreal journey. One moment it makes perfect sense, and the next it doesn't.

"There's the reality of what's right in front of me," she said, waving both hands toward the chest and what was spread out in front of them, "and then there's the inexplicable—the visions, the experiences, the dreams…the, the thing that happened between us."

His brows flicked. "Humph, there's definitely that. Look, why don't we take a break from all this?" He stood up, took her hands in his, and helped her up. He ran his hands across the ropes of her hair. "Get some air? Go for a walk, a drive into town?" His gaze moved across her face. "It's still early."

She slid her arms around his waist, leaned up and kissed him. "Yeah. Sounds good." Her lashes lowered. "Some fresh air will do us both some good."

"Let's get out of here."

Alessandra turned off the lights. They walked out, and she closed the door behind them.

• • •

"It seems so late," Alessandra said as Zach helped her out of his SUV. "But it's barely six."

"Winter always takes getting used to, even though it shows up every year," he joked.

Alessandra slipped her arm through the bend of his and they walked down Main Street, the cobblestones gleaming with salt that crunched beneath their booted feet. The night air was crisp but still, the branches frozen in repose. Twinkling lights from the rows of shops, boutiques, and eating spots lit the avenue like a holiday Hallmark movie.

"This *is* a beautiful town," Alessandra said, her words punctuated by puffs of steam. "I'd forgotten. Or maybe I didn't want to remember." She pressed closer to Zach's warmth. "Until I came back for my dad, my memories of living here were overshadowed with pain and loss. But…I'm starting to understand that all of it, the good, the bad, the in-between, are all part of my story. And by pushing this part of my life out of existence"—she stopped walking and looked up at him—"I've been doing exactly what my mother did for years."

She snorted a laugh. "There's a saying that a daughter will eventually turn into her mother. Ta-da!" She twirled her hand dramatically.

Zach chuckled. "If the saying is true, then I'm a pretty lucky man, because from everything I've discovered about your mother, she was beautiful, smart, complicated, dedicated to her family, and she adored you. You and your father were blessed to have her in your lives, flaws and all."

She nodded thoughtfully. "We were the blessed ones. We had my dad, just like all the women in the journals and in the letters. They all had good, strong, hardworking, loving men in their lives, who made sure that their wives and daughters and sisters could thrive and bloom." She lowered her head. "Even if they stayed in the background. No fanfare, just working quietly to stitch all the threads together."

They slowed in front of the Grenning Gallery, its bright orange-and-white awning and brick front reminiscent of a New England tavern. The expansive glass window framed stark white walls that featured a newly installed collection of Egyptian pottery and life-sized canvases of ancient Pharaohs in bold gold, deep russets, and azure blues.

"Wow," Alessandra breathed and stepped closer to the window. "Those are stunning. My dad used to bring me here sometimes when I was little," she said slowly, as the memory took shape. "I remember telling him one day—I must have been about ten or eleven—that one of these days I'm going to have my pictures in a place like this." Her smile wobbled. "He put his arm around my shoulders." Her brow tightened. "'You come from a long line of amazing women,' he said, 'and you can be anything that you want.'"

She blinked away the memory and looked at Zach. "My dad...he believed in me even back then. When I came home that afternoon, I was so excited, and I told my mother that one day I was going to have a gallery and show all my pictures. She laughed in that indulgent way of hers and said something like, 'Sure, sweetheart. That is a very nice hobby.'"

Zach offered a comforting squeeze of her shoulder. "A lot of parents have opposite views of what they want for their children. Clearly your mom wanted something solid for you, and your dad saw your creative side. In the end, you found your own way—a combination of both of them."

She blew out a breath. "I still want this," she said with a lift of her chin toward the window.

Zach leaned down and kissed the top of her head, which was covered in a blue-and-white-striped knit hat. "And there's no reason why you shouldn't. Plan for it. Make it happen. You told me you have tons of photographs at your apartment—and just think about all that you found at your folks' place. You could put together a phenomenal exhibit. Something significant."

"You really think so?" The old imposter syndrome that she always tried to beat back reared its ugly head. There was that tiny corner of her conscience that didn't believe she had what it took, didn't have the skill, the eye—didn't even believe she deserved to be happy. She knew that that was the underlying reason she couldn't get her photos together back in New York. Self-sabotage. If she cut herself off at the knees first, no one had to see her fail.

"It doesn't matter what I think. It's what *you* think," he said with a smile.

She tipped her head to the side and inhaled deeply. "You are absolutely right." Her pulse raced. "I'll find out the status of my dad's house, and then we're going to document every item in that chest and figure out how to showcase it," she said with renewed conviction, her mind already whirling with ideas. "As a matter of fact," she turned to him, "I'm going to call Grenning Gallery in the morning…just to see, to feel them out."

"That's more like it. Come on, let's get out of the cold and grab some dinner."

They walked past what was once B. Smith's restaurant.

"Such a shame," Alessandra mused as they paused for a bit in front of the darkened windows of the restaurant. "Beverly Smith was an icon for decades."

"Yes, Alzheimer's is an insidious disease. She was still young. But she left a legacy behind. That's all any of us can hope for, to be able to leave a positive mark on the world." He turned to look at her. "You can do it with your work."

"What about you? What do you want to leave behind?" she asked, as they continued down a pathway of twinkling lights.

Zach drew in a long breath and slowly exhaled a cloud of condensation. "I'm passionate about my work. I love collecting and documenting the stories of ancestors, tracing family lines and uncovering previously undiscovered artifacts that tell their own story, and it's what I believe I was meant to do. If we don't do everything possible to hear firsthand from survivors and descendants whenever it's feasible, and continue to work to uncover family treasures, court documents, ledgers, then a great deal of our history will be lost forever.

"They all tell a story. It's important. That is how I want to maintain legacy—putting together the pieces of Black families from hundreds of years ago, a forgotten community, making connections to people and places across time, land, and sea…" He stopped, snorted a laugh. "Wow. Sorry. I can go on a bit."

"I love…your passion," she said softly.

He studied her a moment, offered a half smile, then pulled open the door to Holliday's Bar and Lounge. "Food's great. Drinks are better," he said as she stepped in front of him.

CHAPTER TWENTY-NINE

"I know we've been focused on the house," Zach began after they'd settled down at the bar and ordered food and drinks, "but what about your dad's business? Have you thought about what you want to do about it?"

She put down her glass of water. "Fortunately, that's not as complex as the house. The space where Fleming Hardware and Supplies sits is bought and paid for as well. No lease, thank goodness. My father had pretty much stepped away from the day-to-day operations and left it up to Carl Howell to manage. Mr. Howell told me at the funeral that he'd love to stay on if it was okay with me. I told him of course, and that the only thing we needed to do was hire a bookkeeper, since my father was the one who kept all the records. Unless, of course, the will says something different."

"You do realize that your parents were building their legacy to pass on to you? Like I've said, home and business ownership are essential to generational wealth. It's one of the main reasons that African Americans have struggled so hard economically for generations, because land and property were kept out of our reach. There was nothing to pass on. All very intentional."

Alessandra breathed heavily. "I know." She shook her head in disgust. "Systemic. Hundreds of years. It takes a helluva lot of work to keep an entire race of people disenfranchised. For some, it's like their mission in life. And as much as we've gained…" She blew out a breath of exasperation. "One step forward, two steps back. There has been a visceral shift in this country that hasn't been seen since the days of the Revolution and Reconstruction."

Zach reached across the table and covered her tightened fist with his hand. He looked deep into her eyes. "That's exactly why it's more important than ever that our stories are told. Even as we sit here, there are movements across the country to ban books, to eliminate any conversation or study of race in the classroom. Voting rights are being stripped. The immigrant is turned into the greedy bogeyman that will steal jobs and destroy neighborhoods. History books are being rewritten to recast slaves as servants who came here to work and who lived well and were paid for their labor. There are climate deniers and conspiracy theorists who will say everything from 'the Holocaust didn't happen' to 'Sandy Hook was a lie' and 'the pandemic was a hoax.' Historians and scientists have become the enemy. It's disgusting."

"And frightening."

"Very." He nodded in agreement.

The waitress returned with their beers. "Food will be coming right up. The kitchen's a bit busy tonight. The owner said the first round's on the house to make up for the delay." She smiled and hurried off.

Alessandra's eyes widened. "Whoa." She lifted her long neck bottle of beer. "That will keep customers coming back."

Zach chuckled and lifted his bottle as well. "To free beer."

Alessandra tapped her bottle against his. "And to telling our stories."

"You were so crazy right," Alessandra managed, chewing her succulent burger. "What kinda magic fairy dust do they put in these things?"

Zach laughed. "I wish I knew. Secret of the chef. I remember one summer, about two years ago, there was a burger-eating contest, and the fifty contestants had to figure out the ingredients. Winner got free beer for a year."

"And…who won?"

He held up his hands and lifted his shoulders in a helpless gesture. "Not a soul."

"Dayum."

"Go figure."

They laughed.

Alessandra wiped her lips with the paper napkin. "I know you lost your parents in a fire." She lowered her gaze, then looked back at him. "But what were they like?"

"You mean when they were around?" His lips tightened, then loosened until they made space for the mouth of the beer bottle. He took a long swallow and studied the last few ketchup-drenched fries on his plate. "I mean, other than them both being consumed by their work, they cared about me, loved me—at least as much as they could."

"Of course they did. The same way my folks cared about me. As kids, we can't really see it. If the loss of my dad has taught me anything, it's that parents are just people. We want them to be perfect or fit some image of television parents." Her voice softened. "But they can't. That's not reality."

Zach smiled. "Look at you sounding all wise."

She fake-rolled her eyes. "And what about you? As much as you have some ambivalence about your parents' absences, you're walking in their footsteps—a passionate researcher who travels the world, doesn't set down roots, and allows his work to consume him." She arched a brow.

Zach drew in a breath and offered a half grin. "Of course, on a rational, logical level, that's all true. I've been fascinated with research for as long as I can remember." His expression drew tight, his eyes melancholy. "If I were to be honest, it wasn't the work," he swallowed, "it was that they left me—forever." His voice wobbled a bit. "Sure, I would run off to my grandmother's every chance I could get away, but it wasn't out of some lack of love from my parents—not in the traditional sense. It was…" He looked like he was searching for the words. "It was that I knew they were on some great quest and I couldn't go. Their lives together, their love, their work bound them in ways that didn't necessarily include me. As a kid, I convinced myself that they didn't love me."

"And now?" she whispered.

He ran his tongue along his bottom lip. "What's Maya Angelou's saying? 'When you know better, you do better.' I know better now. It's clearer. It still aches in places inside me that they're gone and that I can't tell them all the stories I've collected."

He pursed his lips a moment. "Funny, but what both you and I do, where we find our purpose, is in giving voice to people, places, and things that have remained voiceless. We compel the world to look back on what it has wrought and hope that when they know better, they'll do better."

"I… I never quite thought of it that way. But you're right." Her eyes brightened. "We do. And it's important."

He clasped her hand and nodded in agreement. "And that's why we must curate every item in that chest, and you

have to cull through all your photographs back in New York…
to tell the story, Alessandra," he said with an urgency that
raised the tiny hairs on her arms.

"I will. We will."

. . .

Zach pulled into Alessandra's driveway and parked. They
hopped out and walked to the front door.

"I'm going to check in on my grandmother."

Alessandra stopped with the key in the lock and turned
to face him.

"Then I'll come back. *If* you want me to," he added.

She puckered her lips for a moment. "Hmm, let me
mull it over." She leaned in and kissed him, then turned
and unlocked the door and handed him the key. "Whenever
you're ready," she said in a throaty whisper. "And tell your
grandma 'hello' for me."

He slid the key into the pocket of his jacket. His gaze
lingered on her face. "I will." He lifted his chin. "Go on,
you're letting in the cold air."

Her lids lowered. "But everything else will be very warm,"
she teased before spinning away and shutting the door.

Zach chuckled, slid his hands into the pockets of his
jacket, and walked across the street.

Alessandra closed the door and dragged in a breath.
Her gaze rose up the staircase and envisioned what they'd
uncovered. It was still almost too much to process. Yet the
question that still lingered was: Why was her mother so
adamant about forgetting the past? And, more importantly,
if these were her ancestors—which seemed more likely than
not—why wouldn't her mother want to celebrate that legacy?

She removed her coat and hung it on the hook, then shucked off her boots and placed them in the shoe rack. Zach's grandmother said that her mom had started to come around, but Jessica Fleming's epiphany had been cut short—and it was Alessandra's fault.

A pang of guilt tightened her chest. Things would have been so different if she hadn't insisted on going to that stupid party. If she hadn't been such a brat. If she hadn't found herself stranded where she never should have gone in the first place. If she had gotten a ride home from someone else. If. If. If. She sniffed.

Rationally, she knew that no one could predict that her mother would have a heart attack while driving to pick her up from a party that her father had insisted she not attend.

Her dad. Her mom. She'd had these idealized notions about her parents. Now, at almost thirty, she was finally beginning to see them for who they were, not for what she'd imagined them to be. They were simply human beings with perfections and imperfections, trying to do the best they could.

CHAPTER THIRTY

Alessandra stood with her face turned up to the pulse of the shower, her body unwinding even as her thoughts raced and twisted with questions, excitement, and uncertainty. If, in fact, the contents of the chest held the legacy of her family, what would the full story reveal? Did her mother add her voice? What if everything that she thought she had and needed in New York was here all along?

What about her and Zach, too? What was it really? When the dust settled, would they be anything more than two people inexplicably attracted to each other for the moment? Was it even real? But what would be the point? He was only passing through on his way to his next discovery.

She turned off the water and grabbed a towel from the rack, wrapped it around her body, and faced the medicine cabinet mirror. She used her palm to wipe away the fog. Her reflection was there but cloudy, the edges muted, the features indistinct. By degrees as the steam in the room began to dissolve, her face became her mother's—a browner version. They shared the same eyes, cheekbones, nose, mouth. Back in the day, her mother might have been able to pass in some circles, and although Jessica hadn't—directly—she certainly parlayed what her fair complexion afforded her. And while Alessandra shared the warm brown shade of her father, Jessica Fleming was determined to ensure that her daughter would never suffer the "consequences" of her color.

Was she only just now coming to this realization, or did she always know but didn't want to accept it? To do so would have meant taking her mom off the pedestal upon which she'd placed her—and where would that have left them both?

She tightened the towel around her body and padded down the hallway to her room. More questions than answers.

She languidly smoothed lotion on her damp skin as the questions continued to bounce around in her head. She dug around among the few items of clothes she'd brought along and pulled out a Black Lives Matter T-shirt. She harrumphed at the irony as she tugged it over her head and put on her trusty sweatpants.

She went downstairs and entered the room that was her father's sanctuary. Traci said something about maybe finding the name of the attorney on the Rolodex. She didn't remember seeing it on the desk, and as she suspected, it wasn't there. That would have been too easy. She pulled open the side drawer opposite the one with the files, and found a Rolodex beneath a stack of papers and hardware magazines.

She pulled out the contraption and laughed. "I'll be damned." She flipped the little white cards around on the spindle. Since she didn't have the name of the attorney, she would have to read each one. She rubbed her fingertip across her father's familiar boxy scrawl, each letter and number carefully recorded. It came to her then, a forgotten memory. Perhaps a Sunday afternoon, she thought, sunny. Dad was sitting in this very chair.

"Whatcha doing?" she asked, scooting beside him.

He turned, blessed her with his smile, and kissed the top of her head.

"Writing," he'd said.

"Writing what?"

He'd chuckled. "Names and numbers."

"Why?"

He smiled. "So just in case I forget," he tapped his temple, "it will be here to remind me. It's important to write things down."

Her stomach jumped. *Write things down.* Even her father believed in writing stuff down. Did her mother?

She dragged in a breath and began going through the hundreds of little cards. Sometimes she had to laugh. Some of the cards were so old that the phone numbers began with *Hy* for Hyacinth followed by the seven numbers, or *Sp* for Springfield. Jeez, there was probably a story to tell behind some of these phone numbers and the people on the other end.

History sure was all around her.

After about ten minutes, she came across a card with a business card stapled to it: *Wallace Newsome, Esq.,* with a Hempstead, Long Island, address and phone number.

She popped the card off the spindle. Why would her dad use someone in Hempstead instead of right here? If, of course, this was her dad's lawyer. She checked the time on her phone. It might be after hours, but there was no harm in leaving a message.

She tapped in the numbers on her cell phone. It rang once, twice, and someone picked up on the third ring.

"Wallace Newsome," the no-nonsense voice answered.

For a second, Alessandra was taken aback, but quickly got herself together. "Yes, hello. This is Alessandra Fleming,

Jeremiah's daughter."

"Oh, yes, Jerry's daughter. What can I do for you?"

"Are you my dad's attorney?"

"Yes, have been for years. Is everything okay with Jerry?"

Her eyes drifted closed. "My dad passed away."

"Oh, I am so very sorry," he said, sounding truly distraught. "I had no idea. I've been away and only returned this morning."

Alessandra swallowed. "Um, I'm trying to sort things out, and I can't find a will or anything that would let me know what my dad wanted to do with the house and his business."

"Then I suggest we meet and talk. I have Jerry's will. I can come to you in the morning."

Her heart thudded. "Of course."

"Is ten good for you, Ms. Fleming?"

"Yes. That's fine. Thank you."

"See you tomorrow. I'll bring everything with me. And again, my sincere condolences. Jerry…he was one of the good ones."

Her throat clogged.

"Good night," Mr. Wallace was saying.

She held onto the phone until the call finally disconnected. Hopefully, tomorrow she would have more pieces to the puzzle. She stood up from the chair, took one last look at Mr. Newsome's business card, then returned to her father's bedroom.

She slipped on a pair of white gloves and sat cross-legged on the floor. The stack of loose pages were where she and Zach had left them. Gingerly she reached for them and gently put aside the pages she'd read until she came upon Mae Ella's writing about her wedding to Carter in 1895.

Much to Alessandra's disappointment, the pages didn't contain details of the wedding, only the preparations, but they were just as eye-opening and entertaining.

CHAPTER THIRTY-ONE

1895

    My wedding will be the biggest wedding Greenwood has seen in years. Every female in town, young and old, wants a dress made for the occasion. The shop opens before sunrise and closes after sunset. Mama gives more orders than doing real sewing. I don't mind. With the pains in Mama's hands she can't do like she used to. But no one can take a measurement like Mama.

    Lacey come back to work after her husband Freddy run off with some other woman. Lacey's father say if he ever see Freddy Temple anywhere on earth he'd shoot him where he stood. The whole town believed him, too. Poor Lacey was humiliated. Who wouldn't be?

    She moved back home and came to the shop about three months ago to ask for her job back. Me and Mama was happy to have her. After the ladies that came to the shop finally stopped giving their condolences on the death of her marriage to Freddy, Lacey was just fine, and with my wedding coming in less than two months we needed all the help we could get. Mama had hired Sylvie Hargrove, but Sylvie was more pretty than talented. But she was good at keeping the fabrics and threads, making appointments and deliveries. She keeps things running smooth. Like Mama say, everybody can do something.

Now that Lacey is back and can take over more of the sewing and fittings, Mama is putting all her focus on my wedding gown. I told her I could do it, but she won't hear of it and she wouldn't allow anyone to help.

It just breaks my heart. I know how much pain she is in, sewing on all those tiny pearl buttons, adding the lace bodice and overskirt. The pinning, the stitching, but she never complains. All she ever says when she fits me each week is that I am her and Papa's angel and the most beautiful bride. It's my mama that's the real angel. I can't wait. I love Carter so much and I can't wait to have a family with him and a house full of babies.

Alessandra blinked away tears. She carefully looked through the worn journal for details about the wedding, but she couldn't find them. Young newlyweds. She probably had much more to do than detail her life.

Sometime much later, it seemed, Mae Ella returned to her writings, though.

1897
After hours at the shop, me and Carter try to

have a walk in the evenings after dinner. His barber shop Carter's Cuts doing real well, and with the town growing like it does, Carter said in a couple months' time he wants to open another shop. Rumor has it that the builder J.B. Stradford had plans to come to Greenwood. In the meanwhile Carter partnered up with Claire Fields Beauty Shop and bought a bigger place they could share. Ladies upstairs, men downstairs. And Ms. Fields buy much of her pomades from Mama. Carter say he going to make a good life for us and all the babies we would have.

But, the babies don't come. Been two years since we said "I do" and no babies. Mama say women in our line have a hard time bringing babies in the world, and I gotta be patient.

With Papa's hardware supply shop doing so well and his woodworking picking up, and Mama getting the help she need in the dress shop, and Carter's business keeps growing, we doing real good. Some folks say we is one of the wealthiest families in Greenwood. I don't know if it's true but it feels good to know people think so. I might be able to get back to painting and taking pictures. The paper and the camera and the flash can be costly but everyone I make a portrait for loves my work and recommends friends.

"A photographer…like me," Alessandra whispered.

"What did you find?"

Alessandra looked up. Zach was standing in the doorway. He walked toward her, careful of the artifacts on the floor.

She held up the fragile pages. "Mae Ella." She smiled

sweetly. "She got married. To a man named Carter."

He grinned and came to sit beside her. "Any other discoveries?"

She dragged in a breath. "Seems that Ella and Winston and Mae Ella and Carter were pretty well off. Mae Ella's mother isn't doing well, though," she said as if the worry was immediate rather than a century ago. "And the best of all: Mae Ella was a photographer—like me."

Zach smiled.

"I'm thinking some of those sepia and black-and-white photos might be some of Mae Ella's work."

"I'm thinking they are."

She ran the tip of her gloved finger across the ancient words. "Seems they're having a hard time having kids, too," she murmured and wondered when and if her time came, would she find the same trouble? "Hopefully, in all of this," she gazed at the wonders in front of them, "I'll find out what happened to Mae Ella, especially if they were there during the massacre."

Zach lightly squeezed her shoulder.

The couple spent the next few hours sorting and cataloguing the dozens and dozens of single sheets of writings, one more enlightening than the next about life in Tulsa, Oklahoma, especially the news articles that chronicled the blossoming enterprises in Greenwood.

Alessandra slowed when she came across the news clipping about the grand opening of the Stradford Hotel in 1918. Articles in the *Tulsa Star* touted Stradford's more than two dozen rental and rooming houses, pool hall, theater, and a sixteen-room brick apartment building. *The Crisis* covered W.E.B. Du Bois's visit in March of 1921 and wrote of his pride and admiration for what the people of Greenwood had accomplished.

"Black Wall Street," Zach was saying with a kind of reverence.

"Until it was destroyed," Alessandra intoned.

"Hmm."

Alessandra leaned back against the side of the bed. "I got in touch with my dad's attorney. He's coming in the morning."

Zach's eyes widened. "Did he give you any hint of anything?"

"No. Not really. Just that he would bring all the documents then."

"I wish I could be here for you, but I'm heading to the Smithsonian tomorrow. Hopefully the work and meetings won't take more than a couple of days." Zach pushed out a breath. "At least you'll finally know what your father's wishes were."

Alessandra rested her head on Zach's shoulder. Her father's wishes *and* her future.

· · ·

Alessandra looked around at the empty house. Today was the first day since she'd arrived that she was truly alone in the house and with her thoughts. It was a good thing. She needed to take charge of her life on her own. It was great, but too easy, to lean on Zach and depend on everyone around her.

She drew in a breath, pushed back from the kitchen table, and stood. She took her coffee cup to the sink. Mr. Newsome was due to arrive in about a half hour. She put on a fresh pot of coffee and waited.

When the front bell rang and she went to the door, her first thought was that the man standing there couldn't possibly be her father's attorney. Mr. Newsome wasn't old, bespectacled, stooped, or gray. And he certainly didn't look like a Wallace. He was tall and athletically built, with a golden complexion, thick dark hair that curled at his temples, and a smile that exuded confidence—and if he was thirty, she was Beyoncé.

"Mr. Newsome?"

"Yes. Good morning." He flashed a smile and hunched his shoulders against a blast of wind. "This is my assistant, Lillian Dunham. She'll serve as witness."

"Good morning," Lillian said.

Alessandra blinked, shook her head. "Please, come in."

"Thank you." They stepped around Alessandra.

"I really appreciate you coming out here," she said while closing the door.

He turned toward her, took off his leather gloves and stuck them in his pockets, adjusted the strap of his leather briefcase on his shoulder. "Not a problem. I'm very sorry to hear about Jerry."

"Thank you. Let me take your coats."

He set his briefcase at his feet, tugged off his black wool coat, and handed it to Alessandra. Lillian followed suit.

"So how did you first connect with my dad?"

He chuckled and followed her into the kitchen. "I was in town one day about three years ago, taking in the sights. I needed some supplies for the deck I was working on, figured I'd stop in. I got to talking with your father."

He pulled out a chair and sat at the table. Lillian sat next to him, flipped open her laptop, and settled in. "He asked what I did for a living," Wallace was saying. "I told him I was an estate lawyer, just getting started." He gazed off into the distance and grinned. He turned and looked at Alessandra. "He said, 'Son, I love to see our people doing their own thing. I want to be one of your first clients.'"

"Just like that?" Alessandra asked incredulously.

"Yep." He pressed his lips together and nodded. "I helped him draw up his will and reviewed all of the documents for the house, the business, and his accounts. Your dad is—was—very well-off. And now—so are you."

Alessandra blinked, gripped the edge of the table, and slowly lowered herself into a chair. "Well. Off? What does that even mean?" She tugged on her bottom lip with her teeth.

Wallace Newsome reached for his briefcase at his feet, clicked the lock open, and pulled out a thick folder of documents. He reviewed them one by one.

Her heart was hammering so hard she could barely hear what she was being told.

Her father's will bequeathed the fully-paid-for house and business to his only heir, Alessandra Olivia Fleming, plus the remainder of any funds from his insurance policies after funeral expenses, as well as a savings account totaling two hundred and fifty thousand dollars.

Alessandra sat speechless. The enormity of it all was a bit overwhelming. But what truly moved her was that even after years of estrangement between her and her father, he had left everything to her. Everything. An inheritance that she could have never imagined. She didn't know what to say or think at the moment.

"You'll have to, of course, hire your own accountant—and perhaps a financial planner."

Alessandra blinked him into focus. She cleared her throat. "Yes," she murmured.

"I take it you had no idea of your father's worth."

She shook her head numbly. "No. I mean I found the deed for the house, but…" She licked her dry lips.

He nodded. "You'll probably want to get it appraised again. The last appraisal was when I came on three years ago.

The house has definitely gone up in value since then."

"An appraiser. Okay," she murmured.

"There is one major stipulation," Wallace said.

Her brow tightened.

He flipped to the last page of the will. "Your father included a caveat. In order to claim any portion of what has been willed to you, you must agree to and sign indicating that you will not sell the family home, and that the home will be passed along to your children."

She blinked rapidly in response. "My children?" She laughed. "What if I don't have any?"

"Your father seemed to have thought of that as well." He cleared his throat and read from the will. "Should my daughter Alessandra Olivia Fleming not have children of her own, she must include in *her* will that the house and all its contents, including the family chest, will be turned over to Eastville Historical Society." He paused, looked across at Alessandra. "Do you know what chest he means?"

Alessandra swallowed. "Um, yes. Yes. I know what he means."

Wallace nodded. "Good." He inhaled and released a slow breath. "That's all of it. There are a few documents to sign to officially turn over the properties and give you access to the accounts. Lillian will serve as witness."

Alessandra nodded. "But I'd have to agree never to sell the house," she stated as much as asked as she looked at the documents in front of her.

"That's right."

It would mean that she'd be tied to the house, to the town, basically for the rest of her life and the life of her children—should she have any. Was that what she wanted? She had a life elsewhere. It was, however, only a two-hour drive—tops—away. She could keep the house, come in to check on it, maybe even get a caretaker. It was quite beautiful in the spring and summer. Yes. She could visit. Once she'd put together the pieces of the puzzle contained in the chest, there was nothing else to keep her here.

This thing between her and Zach would end soon. He'd go on with his adventures, and she'd return to the real world. Clearly, whatever had been happening since day one in Sag Harbor was out of the realm of reality, and being apart from Zach for the first time since her arrival would give her the space she needed to get this cloudy picture of her life into focus.

"Where do I sign?"

Alessandra closed the door behind Wallace and Lillian. Wallace had promised to get the finalized paperwork to her as soon as it was filed with the court. It shouldn't take long, he'd assured her, and had offered her legal assistance in the future should she need it.

Alessandra pressed her back against the closed door. Her gaze panned the space in front of her. This was all hers now, her responsibility. Her dad, despite their long estrangement, trusted that she would care for the home he and her mother had built. "I'm going to do right by you, Dad. I promise."

She pushed away from the door, walked into the living room, and wandered over to the extensive album collection. She found *Miles Davis Live at Newport Jazz Festival*. She smiled. Miles was one of her dad's favorites. He could go on for hours about the genius of Davis's playing.

She turned on the stereo, slid the album out of its sleeve, and placed it on the spindle. Expertly she lifted the arm and placed the needle with precision on the near-invisible groove. She smiled, listening—really listening—and hearing her father's enthusiasm as he'd explained the nuances of the master trumpeter. At the festival back in 1955, her dad had said, Miles had made new "'Round Midnight," Thelonious Monk's classic, balancing short phrasing and curling long notes. It was a performance that put Miles on the map and was touted to have ignited and reinvigorated the jazz sound, bringing it to a mainstream audience.

Her dad, of course, had been right.

After an infusion of jazz and conceding that her dad *may* have had a point about the instrumentalists, she grabbed her camera and laptop, tucked her locs under her wool hat, donned her coat.

She'd gotten a bit too comfortable with Zach driving her around, and it took a few wrong turns for her to get her bearings in her dad's car—combined with the fact that living in the city didn't require her to drive. All she could do was chuckle at the honk of horns at her slow-moving vehicle.

After circling the block several times, she finally found a space. Despite the chilly weather, the streets were bustling with pedestrians and drivers. But it was a workday after all.

She walked around the corner, onto Main Street, and stopped in front of the Grenning Gallery. She dragged in a breath and pulled the door open.

It was time for her to start making her own mark on the world.

CHAPTER THIRTY-TWO

More than an hour later, Alessandra floated out of the gallery. Her mind was ablaze. The curator had explained that the gallery generally showcased local artists who depicted sea- and landscapes or highlighted life in the Hamptons. However, what Alessandra proposed—mounting a show that chronicled the life and legacy of freed slaves and their descendants in Sag Harbor—would be a major coup.

The only downside was that the gallery was booked until the end of the year, with the exception of a two-week window at the beginning of March. If Alessandra was prepared, she could have those two weeks. Otherwise, it would be next year.

That only gave her two weeks to get everything together. She'd let her opportunity in New York fall apart. But what she was beginning to realize was that Steven's gallery was not where she was meant to be.

Everything had happened for a reason.

Without second-guessing herself on how she would pull this off, she'd agreed, and on the drive home was already visualizing how she would craft the story of what she now knew was her family. But first, she had to finish sorting the material—and maybe, just maybe—find the story of her mother in the process.

. . .

Alessandra returned home. She got out of her heavy outer clothes and boots and moved with a renewed purpose to her father's bedroom, taking her camera with her.

She stood for a moment in the threshold and took in all that lay in front of her, then got to work. Donning the prescribed white gloves, she continued sorting through the artifacts that still remained undocumented in the chest. She was looking specifically for information on Mae Ella and Carter and their lives in Tulsa. Were they there during the massacre? Did they survive? Did they have children? But they must have. They had to.

She opened the chest and removed some of the pieces of fabric and journals to get to several stacks of paper that were tied together with ribbon. She gently unknotted the faded blue ribbon on the first stack and was tickled to find it was pages of recipes for corn cakes, collard greens, banana pudding, chicken and dumplings, lima beans, black-eyed peas, fried chicken, smothered pork chops, fried catfish, and sweet potato pie—and even one for chitterlings.

She scrunched her nose. All of the ingredients, along with precise measurements, were included on each page in neatly printed handwriting, the ink fading in places. Fried catfish on Friday night was a favorite at the Fleming household. The flash of memory shook her. She swallowed and took a breath, then photographed each recipe and moved on to the next parcel of papers. She untied the washed-out yellow ribbon.

These were all headlines from newspapers. Her pulse skipped in her veins.

Tulsa Tribune
"Nab Negro for Attacking Girl in an Elevator"

TULSA WORLD
"State Troops in Charge: Barrett Heads Machine Gun-Armed Guards. Negroes Driven from Burning Black Belt"

THE DAILY OKLAHOMAN
"70 Negroes, 10 Whites Die in Rioting.
Tulsa is Quiet Under Rule of Troops"

The BLACK DISPATCH
"Looting, Arson, Murder"

The San Diego Union
"100 Dead in Tulsa Race Riots"

Tulsa Tribune
"County Put Under Martial Law"

She stared at the clippings until her vision clouded. Her throat was dry. There were no articles, only the horror of the headlines, carefully cut from papers. But even those were enough to inflame the imagination. Tears filled her eyes as a sudden and swift sensation of pure fear seeped into the marrow of her bones. The suffocating scents of smoke and gunpowder, the roar of voices, airplanes overhead, and shotgun blasts exploded in her head and stole her breath.

Flames. Screams. Bodies.

Run! Run!

Her body stiffened, then shook as if struck by lightning.

A cry rose from her throat as a man was struck by a bullet from an unseen assailant. He fell hard to the ground. A woman's scream echoed her own. She ran to his side, followed by a screaming young woman in yellow. *Papa!* Together, they lifted and dragged him into the back of the truck.

Run! Run!

The truck sped off in a cloud of dust and smoke as bullets peppered the ground and Molotov cocktails crashed through windows of the homes and businesses that lined Greenwood Avenue. Men, women, and children ran for their lives, leaving behind all that they'd built as their world erupted in flames and exploded all around them.

White men with guns, and sticks and axes and rifles, broke down doors, looted, destroyed—with glee.

Alessandra gasped, gulped air. Blinked. Pressed her palms to her eyes.

Her vision slowly cleared, even as her heart continued to hammer. She pulled off the white gloves to wipe the band of sweat that lined her brow. The muscles of her arms and thighs ached and burned, as if she had been lifting weights and running for hours.

She shook her head to clear it of the terrifying images, the sounds, the smell, the fear. She wasn't sure how long she'd sat there staring into the past that had bloomed to horrific life in front of her.

The room moved back into full focus. *I was there.*

She'd lived and breathed that horrible day as surely as she sat on the floor of her father's bedroom. Of course that wasn't possible. It couldn't be. But so much of what she'd been experiencing for the past few weeks was inexplicable. And trying to make rational sense of it would make her totally crazy instead.

She unfolded her aching legs and slowly stood. She felt momentarily unsteady on her feet. Her gaze ran across the damning headlines. She picked up her camera and took shots of each clipping. Following Zach's practice of detailing artifacts, she wrote up a small card describing each clipping, then put them back together, tied the ribbon around them, and returned them to the chest. She slid back down on the floor and leaned her head against the side of the bed. She closed her eyes.

Were these clippings collected by Mae Ella? Or someone else? There was no way to tell. There was no note of reference on any of the well-worn pages.

She exhaled slowly. These experiences were so visceral, they affected her physically, and she felt momentarily drained afterward until the feelings and the images fully dissipated.

Her cell phone vibrated in her back pants pocket. She shifted, lifted her bottom, and pulled out her phone. Zach's name appeared on the screen.

"Hi," she said on a breath.

"Hi. How are you?"

She paused a moment to collect her thoughts, then told him about Wallace, her trip to Grenning Gallery, and the invitation to mount a show—if she could get it done in time—and her newest findings in the chest that had sparked her latest episode.

"You have had some day," he said, emphasizing each word.

"Tell me about it," she said.

"Totally great news about your father's affairs. At least that's settled. And I'm so happy for you. I know whatever you put together for your exhibit will be amazing. Early congratulations." He paused. "The...episode...are you okay?"

Alessandra blinked rapidly. "It was so damned real, Zach." Her heart began to thud as the waves of fear flooded her senses again. "I swear I felt like I was there. I could hear the gunshots, the screams. I can still smell the smoke in my nose."

She closed her eyes for a moment, then opened them to look at everything in front of her. "But as I've been sitting here experiencing all this, I've decided that I'm not going to fight it anymore. I'm not going to run from whatever the past is trying to tell me. I spent my life fighting against everything that's been happening to me over the past few weeks.

"My mother led me to believe that digging into the past would do more harm than good, that it would be bad to allow it into my conscious. But even she came to a point where she couldn't, or wouldn't, run from truth anymore. I still don't know exactly why or if there was something specific that happened to turn her away from the legacy of our family, but I need to find out. The answers are here somewhere."

"Yes, you need this, and I'm glad that you're willing to make the leap."

For the first time in hours, she actually felt relaxed, as if she could cleanse her lungs with a deep breath of calm.

"There's still so much to do. But I'm feeling good about it. It feels right, ya know?"

"Yeah, I do," he said softly.

"I only have a couple of weeks to pull it all together for the gallery."

"You'll do it."

She sighed. "Enough about me. How are things going in DC?"

"Meetings are always boring," he said with a chuckle. "But we're making progress. The funders wanted an update on our projects, and we have a few more presentations to make—and sit through."

Alessandra laughed. "You'll be fine. When do you think you'll be back?"

"Hopefully in a day or two."

"Great. I can use all the help I can get. I still haven't found anything connected to my mother, and there's still so much to sift through in the chest."

"Listening to what you've accomplished on your own, you'll do fine. You know how to handle the materials, photograph, and document everything. You got this, 'young Skywalker,'" he said, in a very bad imitation of Obi-Wan Kenobi.

Alessandra giggled. "Yes, Jedi master."

They both laughed.

"I miss you," he said suddenly.

Her heart skipped. "Yeah," she sighed. "I kinda feel the same way."

After they'd disconnected the call, Alessandra took a look at the task in front of her and knew she'd need some fortification before she dove back in. With a minor grunt and a protest from her knees, she got up and went down to the kitchen to locate something quick to nibble on.

The haunting images still floated in her mind's eye as she ate a sandwich. Indelible photographs filling in the many cracks, secret places, and crevices of her existence. She felt on the cusp of answering the unanswered—but when?

Her gaze drifted to the window in front of the sink that looked out onto the front yard. Cars passed sporadically, but for the most part it was quiet. She glanced slightly upward at the shelves above the sink and smiled. Her mother's cookbooks still lined the shelf; she hadn't noticed until now. Her mother had been an amazing cook. She followed recipes to the letter and then added her own twists.

Alessandra remembered sitting with her mother in the kitchen one weekend. It was a Saturday, she recalled, because her favorite cartoons were coming on. Her mother was at the table with a cookbook on one side and a leather-bound notebook on the other.

Alessandra hopped up on a chair. "Whatcha doing, Mom?"

Jessica looked up, her hazel eyes picking up glints from the overhead light.

"Well, if you must know," she'd said, lowering her voice to a mother-daughter-secret whisper, "I'm reading the recipes from this book." She tapped the book. "And making them my own in this book." She tapped the pages of the notebook.

Jessica winked at her daughter. "One day you'll have a house and a family and make recipes of your own and can put them in your notebook." She playfully tapped the tip of Alessandra's nose, then went back to reading and writing.

The recipes in the chest.

Alessandra's pulse quickened, then settled. She pushed back from the table and went to the sink. She eased the store-bought cookbooks aside in order to pinch out the four leather-bound notebooks beside them on the shelf. She held them in her hands for a moment, then darted back upstairs.

Did her mother copy any of the recipes from the chest? Had she known they were there? Were any of them hers?

She hurried across the room, careful to sidestep the contents on the floor, and went to the chest where she'd returned the collection of recipes. She pulled on the white gloves and gingerly retrieved the packet of recipes. Meticulously, she untied the ribbon and slowly lined up the pieces of paper. Her heart thumped, then raced. She felt warm all over. Taking a breath, she reached for one of her mother's cooking notebooks and opened the soft tan leather-bound book.

Her breath caught at the sight of her mother's familiar scrawl. A surge of longing flooded her body. Her index finger reached out to travel across the words, as if by touching the blue ink she could, in a way, feel her. Her throat clenched against the burn in her eyes. "Mom," she whispered, blinking rapidly.

She sniffed, dragged in a breath, and brought the finger that had touched the words to her lips and back to the page. She licked her lips and began reading.

Her attention darted back and forth between the pages of recipes and her mother's writing. There were clear similarities. The catfish recipe was identical, as was the one for collard greens that included bits of potato. It wasn't so much that the recipes were similar; it was the measuring of ingredients that were identical.

What did it all mean? Had her mom found these and simply copied them, or was it something else—wise words passed down through generations? She shook her head in frustration, then put aside the first book of her mother's and picked up the next.

But it wasn't recipes spreading across the pale, blue-lined paper. It was something else entirely.

CHAPTER THIRTY-THREE

Alessandra brought the book closer to her face to ensure that she was actually seeing what she thought she saw.

Affixed to the pages of the notebook was an unfamiliar handwriting on yellowing paper. Page after page. Her heart beat so rapidly that her hand began to tremble.

Wait, what was this? Her frown deepened. Her mother had had letters from the past glued into her notebooks—in plain sight—all this time?

Across the top of the first page was her mother's handwriting.

These are the writings of my mother Olivia, daughter of Mae Ella and Carter Hopewell.

Alessandra tucked her bottom lip between her teeth. Her grandmother!

July 1921
  We've been on the road, the three of us, for the past month. Stopping where we could, relying on the kindness of strangers, staying a while then moving on. I think it's the nightmares that

keep us moving. Sometimes in my dreams I see myself running down Greenwood Avenue, flames and gunshots erupting all around me, and there's this pack of white men with rifles aimed at me, torches over their heads and they're running faster and faster. I'm trying to catch up to our truck that's pulling off without me. I hear myself yelling 'don't leave me!' My heart is about to burst with exertion. I can feel their hot hatred on the back of my neck and my screams wake me.

August 1922

It's been more than a year since that godawful day. So much horror. So much loss. Evil came to Greenwood, sure as my name is Olivia Hopewell. Even now I can still smell the smoke, hear the screams, the gunshots. At night I leap out of my sleep hollering, sweating and goose bumps running up my arms sure that the white men are at the door—coming for us. Mama used to sit with me in the dark, hold me to her bosom and swear that we were safe. I wanted to believe her.

She wasn't much more than a ghost herself after daddy passed. He hung on for two months after that gunshot blew a hole in his stomach. Doctors along the route of our escape to Oklahoma City did what they could. But he never really recovered. To see him fade away, grow weaker, thinner was a kind of pain that I have no words to describe. Oh god, that moment repeats in my mind, behind my lids. We were almost in the clear, truck all packed, but Papa went back for the chest. He hauled it onto the back of the truck when the shot rang out. Blood spouted from the center of Papa's body. He went down. If only he would have left it behind...

The *chest*. Now she understood her mother's vehement rejection of it. While it held the treasures of their legacy, it was also the source of immense loss. Sighing, she continued to read.

Mama tended to Papa hand and foot, night and day, no matter how weak and in pain she was. She fed him, bathed him, prayed with him. The awfulness of what happened in Tulsa had me believing nothing could ever be worse. Thought I couldn't hurt any more than I already did until Mama followed Daddy three months later.

I'm alone now.

She felt Olivia's loss as surely as if it was her own, a kindred spirit. That feeling of being alone in the world no matter how many people surround you was inexplicable. She assuaged her loss with work, capturing and preserving the lives of others as if theirs would supplement her own in some way. They never did, not really. Not until she'd returned home and reconciled with her father. Not until she'd met Zach Renard.

That echoing hollowness grew a bit more dim each day. The very things she believed she wanted no part of seemed to be the very things that she needed.

She sniffed, gently ran her gloved finger across the fading ink of her grandmother's script, then turned the page to another entry from Olivia.

June 1923

Life in Oklahoma City is hard, hard because it is lonely without my parents, friends, my community. I have work as a seamstress in a small dress shop. Keeps my hands and my mind occupied, at least during the day. It's the nights that still terrorize me. At least the customers finally stopped asking me about Tulsa—that day. Now they just give me sad looks. I'm used to it now. I'm just going to work hard, and save my money and move as far away from here and Tulsa as I can get.

I rent a room in the house of the local reverend and his wife. Reverend Barnard, who presided over both my parents' funerals, and his wife Cora invited me to stay in their spare room. "You need people around you that's gonna care for you," Ms. Cora had said, hugging me close as I wept over Mama's coffin. I suppose I must of said yes to her invitation because here I am.

July 1923

When I'm alone in my room I go through all the headlines from the newspapers. None of them could ever put to words what happened to us that day or the days and months, and now years, that followed. It's fresh like an open sore that won't heal. I try, but it's hard. So I just collect the headlines as a reminder, because I know the rest, the real rest of the story.

July 1923

At least I'm writing again. Sometimes. I promised Mama that I would. It was too hard at first, the trauma too vivid. But I know it's important, so I'm going to keep my promise. That's the least I can do to honor my mama and Papa and all the lives that were destroyed and lost. We must never forget.

Alessandra pressed the small notebook to her chest and shut her eyes. Images of Olivia running from the flames, seeing her father gunned down, losing him, and then her mother from grief, being alone in a strange new city trying to make sense of the senseless, scorched indelible imprints behind her closed lids.

It was overwhelming.

A part of her was beginning to understand her mother's adamant stance about leaving the past behind. It was ugly and painful. But there were beautiful moments too; there was love and happiness, and marriages and babies and hope.

Alessandra slowly opened her eyes. Her heightened need to know pressed her to find everything that she could. She wanted to discover if there was more about her grandmother, Olivia, who'd passed away before she was born.

With reverence, she turned the page. Her heart thudded. Her hand shook ever so slightly. The writing had changed. It was her mother's.

June 2004

When I came across my mother's letters in the chest, everything that I'd kept buried deep in my spirit rose to the surface like the smoke rising from the ruins of Tulsa. I'd struggled and fought most of my life with the images of a past that I didn't understand, the nightmares that took me to places I'd never been.

At night, at my bedside, my mother would whisper the stories to me that had traveled through the generations. Say her name, she'd whisper over and over. She told me it was our truth and that I needed to allow the spirits of our ancestors to continue to live through me and pass them on to my own children one day. I needed to remember so that I could tell our stories, she said. So that we would never be forgotten.

But I would not do that to my own child, saddle them with the weight of what had happened to our family. I vowed to start a new tradition, new stories, recreate who we were.

And I did, until I couldn't any longer. I couldn't. The visions. The dreams. Calling to me. The visions that have plagued me since I was a child.

Alessandra took a moment to let the words sink in. Her mother had hinted that she'd been "afflicted"—for lack of a better word—with dreams and visions when Alessandra began to exhibit some of the same symptoms as an adolescent, and Jessica had assured her daughter that the way to combat them was to not give in to them. Push the images aside. Do not give them life.

Alessandra squeezed her eyes shut and dragged in a breath. She sniffed hard and returned her gaze to her mother's testimony.

I knew that I couldn't keep turning away from who my family was, what they endured so that I could be here, no matter how much it hurt. All the things that I believed were important, meant nothing. I told myself and Jeremiah that we'd "arrived." But where? And to what? I realize now that I cannot deprive Alessandra of her legacy. But first I need to understand it all myself, what is inside me.

CHAPTER THIRTY-FOUR

Alessandra blinked and read the words again, then again. Her mother had had an epiphany, but she didn't live long enough to share her newfound acceptance with her daughter. She pressed her palm onto the fading ink of her mother's script.

Suddenly, her phone vibrated in her back pocket, jolting her out of the temporary shock of seeing her own mother's handwriting. She pulled out the phone and looked at the illuminated screen. Traci.

"Hey," she breathed into the phone.

"Just checking in. How are things?"

"Where do I begin?" She glanced at the notebook on her lap, then leaned her back against the side of the bed and closed her eyes. Images flashed like tiny explosions behind her lids. She brought Traci up to speed on the basic turn of events, then hit her with the bombshell of her mother's writing.

"Wait. What?" Her pitch rose. "Your mom's journals were right in the kitchen with the cookbooks? All this time?"

"Yeah," she said on a breath. "At first I thought they were only recipes…" She went on to tell Traci what she'd read so far.

"Wow, girl," Traci uttered in a whisper when Alessandra finished laying out her discovery. "Did you find out anything about where your grandmother settled?"

"I haven't gotten that far. I'm not sure if I'll find out in my mom's writings or in my grandmother's. It's crazy how the journal is set up. Some pages are from my grandmother, and then there'll be an entry from my mother. Almost as if my mom is responding in some way."

"Like a call and response," Traci said, cutting in. "Like church."

"Yes! Exactly. The writings from my grandmother were all loose papers, and my mom glued them onto the blank pages of the journal."

"Sounds like she was piecing the story together herself," Traci offered.

"I guess," Alessandra said, no longer sure of anything.

"Where's Zach?"

"In DC, for work. He should be back tomorrow or the next day."

"Well, you got a lot going on. If you need me, I'm there—just say the word."

"I know, sis. I'll be fine. I do need your help publicizing my exhibit. If you could get someone from Arts and Entertainment to cover—"

"Did you really have to ask? I got you."

They laughed.

"Anyway, I need to finish up a few things and head home. Guess who's coming to dinner?" Traci teased.

"Girl—Morgan?"

"Yep," she said sounding giggly.

"This is starting to get serious—for you," Alessandra added.

Traci exhaled. "I think it could be," she said thoughtfully. "But…you know me. We'll see."

"Hmm-umm. Don't break that man's heart," Alessandra half-joked.

"Ha! Anyway, chat soon. Okay?"

"Will do." She shoved the phone back into her pocket, pressed her lips together, and flipped the book back open. She slowly turned the pages until she reached a new entry.

September 1923

I'm not sure what it is I'm feeling. A part of me believes that being happy is disrespecting the memories of Mama and Papa. But happy just keeps bubbling inside me like a shaken bottle of pop. Every time I see Stanley Charles I get that bubbly feeling in my center. He comes to Reverend Barnard's church but not always. Other times I see him driving the truck for the lumber yard where he works.

Today was the first time we actually spoke to each other beyond polite hellos at church. He was walking toward the five and dime when he saw me. I swear I was standing stiff as a statue on the middle of the sidewalk, heart racing like I'd been running up through town.

Alessandra smiled. Funny, it was the same kind of reaction she'd had to Zach when they'd first met. She tucked her bottom lip between her teeth. All the women in the journals and letters, even in the midst of their trials and hardships, had found love—or love had found them. Unquestionable love. Was that where she was headed?

She blinked and refocused on the pages in front of her.

Stanley stopped right in front of me. I liked to pass out. He nodded his head and swept his cap off and squeezed it between his fingers. "Miss Hopewell, right?" he asked and kind of shifted from one foot to the next. I thought that was kind of cute.

His voice, up close, was low and deep with the soft melody of the South. I think I managed to respond because he smiled, and I swear, I don't know if it was the late afternoon sun shining down on my head or my empty stomach or having Stanley Charles this close that had me feeling lightheaded and unsteady.

When he said his name was Stanley Charles, as if I didn't know, he asked me, or rather told me, that I work at the dress shop and that he'd been meaning to stop in to say hello. Everything he said after that was a blur until I found myself accepting an invitation to dinner.

I ran his name over in my mind and across my tongue. I liked the taste of his name in my mouth.

"Grandma!" Alessandra laughed softly. Seemed as if the women in her family were always getting hit by that lightning bolt. She drew in a breath and smiled dreamily. The way she and Zach had gone from zero to one hundred in such a short time still had her questioning herself and her race down the fast lane. But the truth of it all was that she couldn't imagine things any other way between her and Zach. It was as if they were simply destined to find each other.

She blew out a breath. "Getting too philosophical, girl," she murmured. She turned to the next page.

October 1923

Stanley's kiss is as sweet as I imagined. I'm sure First Lady Cora Barnard stands in the window, peeking out from behind the frilly white curtains whenever Stanley drops me home. But I don't care. I want to feel again, to be held again.

    Being with Stanley makes me remember I'm alive and not just a shell. For so long I didn't believe it was possible to really smile again, to feel just a tiny bit of joy. But the cold hand that has been around my heart is loosening its hold. I'm starting to feel hopeful that happiness and love are still possible.

Alessandra held the book to her heart and inhaled the words, let them flow through her, become part of her. Behind her closed lids, the images of her ancestors manifested with life. They might be gone in body, but they were part of her, in her blood, in her DNA. The biggest trial in her life was missing a gallery exhibit. Nothing compared to what the women of her family had endured.

She owed it to all of them to tell their story—a story that was her own as well.

CHAPTER THIRTY-FIVE

The meeting room began to clear of the dozen or members of the various grant projects. Chairs scraped against the wood floors, the attendees a confluence of scholars from several disciplines who murmured together in low voices as they made their way out.

"Great work, Zach. I'm really pleased with the mapping and oral collections of the Maroon settlements," Horace Mann, the head of the project, said.

"It's important work," Zach said, gathering his notes and closing his laptop. He glanced up. "I'm glad that more than you and I believe in it."

"Once this project is complete, it will be a major addition to the Smithsonian. Believe that."

Zach offered a half-moon grin. "That's the plan."

Horace clapped Zach lightly on the back. "How long are you in town? Maybe we can get drinks later."

"Yeah, I'd like that. Actually, I may need a few hours free first. I'm still working on my own little side project, tracing my family history." He snorted a laugh as they pushed open the heavy glass doors and into the corridor. "I've been starting and stopping for years. Work seems to keep getting in the way."

"Ha! I know how that can be. Making any progress?"

"Yes, finally. I think," he said on a breath. "I'm going to spend a few hours at the National Archives. I finally was able to get an appointment to do some genealogical research. Maybe we can grab drinks around seven? That will give me a solid five hours."

"Sounds good. Hotel bar?"

"See you there."

The National Archives was a short walk from the Smithsonian, and his hope was that he'd be able to narrow down his familial search prior to 1880. He didn't want to let his mind race too far, but from piecing together what was in the Fleming family chest and his own research, he was slowly beginning to believe the impossible.

He checked in at the front desk and was directed to the genealogical research division and set up at a work station.

He took his laptop from its carry case and placed it on the desk, booted it up, and clicked on his family's zip file icon.

A series of three dozen files lined up on the screen, labeled by family member, location, and date. He double-clicked on the most recent folder. Images, data points, graphs, and notes filled the screen. He'd gotten as far back as 1880 and knew that his family originated in Mendeland—what would become Sierra Leone. The slavers that stole hundreds of Africans and transferred them to *La Amistad* had taken them from the interior villages and beaches and transferred them to the barracoons or depots at Lomboko, a slave trading port, where they were held until they were transferred onto ships that would take them to a life of terror and servitude.

He quickly scanned the notes in the file to reorient himself with the material, typed in some additional comments, then turned on the microfilm machine and began his search.

For several hours he dove into the artifacts, blocking out everything around him, rapidly reading and taking notes as each click of the dial flashed another black-and-white image, article, letter, or bill of sale.

His eyes began to feel grainy as he continued to peer at the worn lettering and the often out-of-focus imagery.

Just as he was about to call it a day, he stopped, peered closer. It was a letter, torn around the edges, ripped in places and pieced together like a puzzle, then photographed.

December 1840

It has been seasons since the wench escaped. No amount of bounty has turned her up. I have searched land and sea. She plagues me in my dreams and haunts my days. Times I feel I will go mad. Perhaps I am mad. Those weeks that I held her in my cabin, her only cry beneath me was the wretched name Kwaku. Oweku. Kwaku Oweku. Over and over. Those were the only words she would utter, no matter the beatings, or the food, or the clean water to drink and bathe.

Zach's breath seized in his chest. His right temple pulsed. Oweku. *My God.* He continued to read the few words that he could make out.

I believe I am cursed by what I have done. I can no longer keep food down, incontinence torments me. I am not a man any longer, unable to bed even the most tempting of females. I satisfy myself with drink and memories of her. Sometimes in the throes of mental anguish, I think that if we were reunited, my torment would finally end. I know that my days grow short. If I am to enter the afterlife, this is my confession.

The notations from the researcher indicated that the letter could not be authenticated, but it was believed to be written by a slave-ship captain named Percival Hammer, who had spent more than a year in search of a runaway girl. The letter had been uncovered among the ruins of a small home on Sullivan Island. The next slide was an image of the wanted poster signed by Percival Hammer.

Zach inhaled a long breath. He'd seen Percival's wanted poster. This letter was one more bit of evidence. But most startling was that the girl, whom he was certain was Alessandra's ancestor, had known and was in love with Kwaku Oweku—*his* great-great- (and then some) grandfather, though their union was never to be. His grandmother had the names of her and his grandfather's lineage in her Bible. Kwaku's name was among them.

This was the piece he'd been missing.

For several moments, he stared at the screen, the words blurring, his mind twisting and turning. His ancestor. Alessandra's ancestor. Together. In the past. The two of them together, in the present.

He shook his head. Could it really be?

His finger trembled ever so slightly with excitement as he hit the print key. He gathered up his belongings and snatched the printed pages from the machine, signed out at the front desk, and ran more than walked back to his hotel. Drinks with Horace would have to wait for his next visit.

He made a quick apologetic call to his colleague, then checked the train schedule. If he left now, he could make the six-fifteen Acela and be back at Penn Station by nine thirty. With any luck, he could then catch the last Jitney to Sag Harbor. If not, he'd take a car service. This couldn't wait until tomorrow.

He needed to see Alessandra tonight.

• • •

April 1924

Dear Diary,

I couldn't ask for a more perfect day. The sun was high. The sky was cloudless. I wore my mother's wedding gown. As much as I blame the chest for my Papa's death, I knew that it held treasures. My mama's dress was among them.

Reverend Barnard presided over our wedding. When Stanley looked at me with so much love in his eyes and slid the simple gold band on my finger, my only regret was that Mama and Papa weren't there to see that I'd found my piece of happy at last.

I'm married now! And I'm going to make the best life I can for me and my husband. Stanley is a good man. A kind and loving man, and I know Mama and Papa would approve.

Stanley has been working extra hard over the past year to save up for a little house. In the meantime, we will stay with his folks.

I feel happiness.

Alessandra grinned. *Love wins again!*

There wasn't a wedding dress in the chest, and she wondered what might have happened to it. She'd seen her mother's wedding gown. Could that have been it? Curiosity and desire pushed her to keep reading, but her eyes and body needed a break.

She sighed, unfolded her legs, and achingly pushed to her

feet. Her knees protested. She arched her back and rotated her head to loosen the tight muscles in her neck and shoulders. She removed the white gloves, planted her hands on her hips, and surveyed everything in front of her. She needed some space to clear her head and put all that she'd uncovered into perspective, and working with her photographs usually did the trick.

She took her camera and laptop downstairs so that she could work in the dining room while she grabbed something to munch on.

She sure wished she had some more of Grandma O's soup. Her mouth watered. Unfortunately, she would have to settle for a grilled cheese sandwich and some iced tea.

She made quick work of fixing the sandwich, then went to settle down to work. She powered on her computer, attached an adaptor, and inserted the memory card from her Nikon into the slot. After a bit of whirring, the images began to appear, one after the other, until they filled the screen and spilled over to the next.

Her breath caught as the untold story of her family, in all its pain and glory, unfolded in stark black-and-white images. She pressed her hand to her chest in reverence as she studied each frame, doing what she could to sharpen the focus when needed.

Shifting smoothly into the art of her craft, she meticulously began captioning each image using identical fonts, moving the frames around on the screen by date — as much as possible — until they began to speak.

Her pulse quickened as the story of her ancestors started to unfold, their voices whispering in her ear. But — there were still pieces missing. Who was the young woman who had escaped to freedom and launched her family legacy in America? Her name, only whispered between mother and daughter, remained unknown. And she still needed to thread together her grandmother Olivia's and her mother Jessica's stories.

As she worked, she made notes on an app on her computer, indicating any inconsistencies and noting any images that she might need to reshoot for clarity. There were still many items in the chest that had not been photographed—the tins, the pieces of fabric, the newspaper headlines, and her mother's journals. Those were on her to-do list.

As she studied the images, made some adjustments and additional notes, her skin tingled, and excitement pulsed in her veins. She realized that what she was doing was so much more than shedding the shackles of her insecurities. She was settling the debt owed to her ancestors.

"Yes!" she said aloud.

Not taking any chances, she saved her arrangement on the computer's hard drive, on a flash drive, *and* to the cloud before leaning back in the hard wooden chair with satisfaction. She'd had her share of computer mishaps in the past.

Now she only had about a week and a half to finish photographing and documenting, then get the photos printed and framed for mounting. She shook her head. She needed more time. Time that she didn't have. Somehow she'd pull it off. She would.

Her cell phone vibrated. She tugged it out of her back pocket.

"Zach. Hi."

"I'm glad you're still up."

"Sure. I've been working. Why, what's wrong?"

"I'm on my way back. I found something."

She felt the urgent excitement in his voice. "What? Tell me."

"Too much for a phone call. I need to show you. I should

be there in about another hour or so—just got into Penn Station."

"You're an awful tease. But in that case, I have my secrets, too."

"Good," he said in a low voice. "We'll spend the night uncovering secrets."

She laughed. "I like the sound of that. Hurry," she said, her voice dropping to a husky order.

"Before you know it."

CHAPTER THIRTY-SIX

The mood-altering tones of Billie Holiday's "God Bless the Child" floated through the space as Alessandra waited for Zach later that night. She hummed along, letting her lids drift closed and the music move through her.

The next thing she knew, a buzzing noise disturbed the flow of music. She blinked. Sat up. Shook her head. The buzzing again.

Oh damn! It was the door. She tossed the blanket aside and jumped to her feet. She darted across the living room, out into the hallway, and to the front door. She slowed her step, schooled her expression, and calmly opened the door.

All calm and pretense flew away with the cold wind that whirled around him. Her heart thumped, and warmth snaked through her veins.

Zach dropped his bag at his feet, cupped her face in his gloved hands, and brought his mouth to meet hers.

She grabbed handfuls of his heavy coat in her palms and pulled him across the threshold. He shoved his bag in with one foot and shut the door behind him with the other.

Alessandra laughed. She snatched his ski hat from his head and tossed it, then unzipped his down jacket. He shrugged out of the coat and it fell to the floor, along with his leather gloves.

Zach chuckled deep in his throat. "We're leaving quite a trail," he said, nuzzling her neck. "Your scent is making me crazy." He suckled the soft skin of her collarbone, then slid his hands under the hem of her nightshirt and expelled a groan when he found her naked as the day she was born underneath.

Alessandra grinned wickedly and continued to back them into the living room, helping Zach part with his clothing along the way.

By the time they reached the couch, her nightshirt was being pulled over her head and Zach was stepping out of his jeans and boxer shorts.

They tumbled, kissing, stripping, and laughing onto the overstuffed cushions of the couch. Alessandra looped her arms around Zach's neck and poured herself into their kiss, settling her body beneath his weight.

Zach caressed her hip and down her thigh before sliding his hand beneath it to kiss the inside of her knee. She shivered. He smiled and continued a leisurely pursuit along the satiny skin until he reached her center. Alessandra gasped. His tongue flicked. The tips of her fingers dug into his shoulders.

Zach clasped her hips in his palms and brought her inescapably to his mouth.

• • •

Later, wrapped in blankets on the couch, sipping wine, they read and reread the document that Zach had uncovered at the National Archives.

They looked at each other in astonishment.

"This m-means…" Alessandra stammered.

"It means that my ancestor and yours were together—a couple. Percival Hammer tore them apart. But karma…" he said.

Alessandra blinked rapidly. She swallowed, ran her tongue along her bottom lip. "The writings from the young girl who escaped…" She looked into Zach's eyes. "It was her—the one who longed for Kwaku."

Zach nodded slowly.

Alessandra's eyes inexplicably filled with tears as the enormity of it all began to settle in her soul. "It seems ridiculously impossible but inevitable at the same time," she said slowly.

Zach draped his arm around her shoulder. "I didn't understand how I could have been so quickly attracted to someone." He ran the tip of his finger along her cheek, looked into her eyes. "It's never been my thing, ya know."

She nodded, fully embracing the romance-novel trope of instant attraction. She'd never believed it was real or possible until she met Zach. She took his free hand and brought it to her lips. "Destiny," she whispered, the word as much a question as a statement.

Zach pulled in a long breath. "It took centuries," he murmured.

Alessandra slowly nodded, still working out the enormity of it all in her mind. Her ancestor—the unnamed young girl—and Kwaku were to be wed. The cruelty of slavery tore them apart, and for more than a century their spirits lived on through their progeny until they could be reunited in her and Zach. It sounded utterly insane. She glanced at Zach.

But here they were, and there was no other explanation.

. . .

Cuddled in bed, over coffee and bagels the following morning, Alessandra read aloud the entries from her grandmother's and mother's journal.

"So my grandmother married my grandfather Stanley in Oklahoma City. But," she flipped a page, "he had bigger plans and moved them to Philadelphia." Her gaze ran over the words, looking for key phrases or clues, then back to the beginning. "This is my grandmother's entry from, umm, looks like 1925." She settled into the curve of Zach's shoulder. The tips of his fingers trailed lightly across the swell of her breasts, barely covered by the pale-green sheet. She swatted his hand. He laughed.

April 1925

The long drive across country is hard but exciting. Stanley said that if we drive without stopping we could reach his cousin in Philadelphia in about twenty hours. I think that's a crazy thing to do since I'm not a good driver and Stan would have to do the trip alone. But he insists that it will be fine. He said we will stop along the way. See some sights and move on. He says we should be in Philadelphia in a week.

I haven't told Stanley yet, but I'm pregnant. Again. This is the second time since we've been married. Losing that first baby was about the worst thing next to losing my parents that I'd ever experienced. Don't know if I can go through it again. I should have told him. Now I'm afraid.

Alessandra's breath hitched. "Oh no." She glanced up at Zach.

He gave her shoulder a gentle squeeze and kissed the

top of her head.

"It seems that the women in my family have a hard time carrying babies," she said in a faraway voice, her unspoken worry resurfacing. She swallowed.

"Times were different then," Zach soothed.

"Not enough. Even with advancements in medicine, Black women still have the highest maternal and infant mortality rate in this country. The highest of any first-world nation."

Zach's brows flicked. He nodded in agreement. "In my travels across the globe, it still astounds me how 'underdeveloped' we actually are in so many respects."

"Humph. That's a whole other conversation," she groused.

He smoothed her hair.

She turned the page. Her gaze flashed toward Zach. "My mother!" Her smile was shaky.

June 2005

I promised myself that I would start to write more, or at least more frequently. But the truth is my hands are full with committees and volunteer work and looking after Jerry and Ali. I wasn't sure that I wanted to move to sleepy Sag Harbor after living in Manhattan, but Jerry convinced me that we'd have a better life here and provide a better life for Ali. So I agreed. And he was right about so many things. I don't often give Jerry enough credit for being right.

Jerry is steady. My anchor. Without him, I know that I would simply float away. His love for me helps to keep the dreams and visions at a distance. But I know that I can't continue to deny or ignore my past.

I opened the chest today. When I lifted the lid, something swept over me, a warm breeze, a breath of memory. My skin tingled, and my heart thumped. The sudden sensations scared me. I started to shut the cover, but I couldn't tear my eyes away from what was inside. Long buried curiosity resurfaced.

There was just so much! Papers and papers and books and odds and ends and fabric and tins of hair pomade, photos, newsclips. Even a wedding dress. It's like a tiny museum.

I have no idea where to begin with all this or if I should stir up the past.

When Mrs. O came by asking for donations, I brought down a small shoebox of items from the chest. I can't put to words the look on her face—alarm, surprise, awe. She told me she wouldn't take them and that I really should go through everything because they looked important.

Alessandra saw her mother's beautiful face—and even the uncertainty in her eyes—as Jessica broke her own vow and shared her secrets. How must she have felt during that moment of decision? As uncertain as Alessandra was about what was happening with her and Zach? "Your grandmother told me about that visit," she murmured.

Zach nodded. "I think it was the start of your mother coming to terms with herself," he said gently.

Alessandra pulled in a breath and rested her head against the beat of Zach's heart. She turned the page. It was another one of her grandmother Olivia's entries, glued into the book. Slowly, she began to read.

January 1926

I couldn't have asked for a better way to begin a new year. Today we crossed the threshold of our very own two-story brick house on Warnock Avenue. Community is busy and reminds me of back home with all the Negroes owning homes and running businesses.

After living in a fourth-floor walkup for almost a year, this was a blessing in more ways than one.

I only wish that we could have blessed our new home with a child. Third one lost. Just thinking about it breaks me.

Stanley says he's happy with just the two of us, but I know better. I feel less than a woman. I keep myself busy with my work as a seamstress, pay is good and business is non-stop. Stanley still works in construction and recently got a promotion to foreman. Life is as good as it can be I suppose. We're real comfortable.

April 1926

I'm afraid to lay with my own husband for fear that I'll conceive and lose again. He thinks I don't love him anymore. That's not it. But I can't seem to find the words to explain to the man I love what the pain of losing a life growing inside you does to your mind and your body and your spirit. There's a mourning. A grieving that dims but doesn't quite go away. And what remains is the fear that it will happen again.

So I turn my back to him at night, shrink from his kisses and his touch. We are more like roommates than husband and wife. Divorce crosses my mind. I love him enough to let him go, so he can find a woman who can give him the family I know that he wants. But our families don't believe in divorce.

So we just exist in the same space. Instead of reaching for me now, Stanley reaches for his whiskey at the end of a work day. Sits and sips and sits and sips in the small room off the kitchen, *sometimes sleeping there until the sun comes up, then he goes to work and starts all over again.*

Alessandra sniffed back her sadness. She could only imagine the grief that hung around her grandmother. At least she knew how the story ultimately turned out—with the birth of her mother, Jessica. She only wished that she'd been able to whisper in her grandmother's ear to just hold on, that joy would find her in time.

She turned the page. "From my mom," she said, "2005."

I grew up loving and resenting my mother and father. I had dreams of pretty clothes and shoes and attending parties like the ones I saw on television and in the magazines. Like the ones that the white girls went to, the clothes they wore. But my mother was a maid working for a wealthy family in Chestnut Hill and my father cleaned toilets and washed floors at the local hospital.

My mother told me when they first arrived in Philadelphia from Oklahoma that she had a wonderful job as a seamstress and my father was a foreman at a construction company. But when the Depression hit, it hit the white community hard, but it smacked Negroes even harder, she'd told me after one of my silent treatments on being refused a new coat. She was let go from her job and so was my dad. Businesses closed all over, and whatever savings they had went to food and trying to keep the house from falling down around them.

It took my mother almost a year to find a job as a maid. Took my father longer than that, she'd told me. In my mind back then, they should have tried harder.

I was a certified brat. All I knew was that the depression was supposed to be over and my mother was a maid and my father came home every night smelling like Pine Sol.

Alessandra scoffed, shook her head. "Sounds like I got my bratty honestly," she said with regret.

Zach chuckled and kissed the top of her head. As he listened to her read the entries from her mother, he tried to grapple with the notion of the two of them together. Every scientific bone in his body rebelled against fate and coincidence and fantasy. But it was data and science and research that proved who they were and where they'd come from.

For reasons that outweighed the findings of any scientific journal, the roads that their ancestors had traveled, the trials they'd endured and survived, were so that a long-ago promise between two young people would be fulfilled. Was their destiny truly predetermined? What about the laws of self-determination, free will? The scientist in him balked at something that couldn't be quantified.

Yet, his years of work and study of oral histories and of the importance of telling and documenting family histories were for this very outcome. What would have happened if Alessandra's ancestors hadn't reminded each of their daughters to tell their stories so that they wouldn't be forgotten? And there was no ignoring the undeniable connection between him and Alessandra.

As he listened to her reading, he was both lulled and enthralled by the throaty cadence that brought to life the voices, places, and events. They were no longer something to be found in history books or on the History channel. They *were* them.

He gently pulled her closer against him and deeply inhaled the enormity of it all.

A sudden silence pulled him from his reverie. He angled his head to look down at her. "What is it?"

Alessandra dabbed at her eyes and cleared her throat.

"1938," she whispered. "The year my mom was born."

Zach lightly squeezed her shoulder.

After so many years of hoping, crying, and praying for a miracle she is here. My baby girl. My Jessica. As much as I love and want to protect her, her very existence reminds me how she may have been conceived.

Alessandra flashed a worried look at Zach. She turned her gaze back to the words in front of her.

Stanley had been drinking, more than usual. He sat in the chair by the window, staring and drinking.

Alessandra's voice became unsteady, her words hesitant, but she kept reading.

I asked him did he want some dinner and he began shouting about how the only thing I want to give him is food. It was more an accusation than a question. I turned to walk away, feeling that this rage was different from the others that had become more frequent.

Before I could leave the front room, he grabbed me, twisted me around and gripped me by the shoulders. I could feel his fingers press into my bones. "Why don't you love me no more," he slurred. "I do. I do, Stanley." I was scared. Scared of my own husband. His eyes were glassy and it was like he didn't really see me. He started to cry as he lifted my skirt up over my hips and tugged on my panties. I think I told him to stop, not like this, but I'm not sure. Maybe I only thought the words.

When he was finished, he sank to the floor, taking me with him. He grabbed me around the waist and buried his head in my lap, sobbing and saying he was sorry. He was sorry.

"Oh God," Alessandra whispered. She swiped at a tear that slid down her cheek, blinked hard to clear her vision. She swallowed hard.

2005

I was snooping around in my mother's things one afternoon. Hoping to find some loose change. I must have been about ten. Instead, tucked between her slips and girdles, I found two folded sheets of paper with my mother's handwriting on them. I was sure I'd stumbled upon some treasure, or maybe some real explanation why we were so poor. Instead, I found the way I'd come into the world.

It took me a while to fully understand what I was reading. I couldn't connect the man my mother wrote about to the man who doted hand and foot on my mother and treated me like fragile china. He never had a harsh word. I never saw him take a drink.

I never told my mother what I'd seen. How

could I? I wasn't supposed to be in her things. My father had passed away two years earlier. I couldn't confront him. So I buried that ugly piece of knowledge and swore an oath to myself that I would never speak of the past. Ever. I would never go looking for answers. I would rewrite my history the way it should have been, the way I wanted it to be, the way I deserved. No one needed to ever know that I was stained. And if I could bury that, then I could bury the visions and the dreams, too.

Alessandra was openly weeping now. Her slender shoulders shook. Zach held her tighter, crooning softly to her. Every fiber of his being ached at hearing her sobs and feeling her pain. He might not be able to erase the past, but he could do everything in his power to make sure Alessandra never experienced hurt or heartache again.

"Now I know why…" Her voice broke. "It makes sense now." Her tear-filled eyes looked up at Zach. "Did my father ever know why my mother was the way she was?"

"I think," he said slowly, "that even if he did, he still loved and adored her *and* you."

She sniffed hard, wiped at her eyes with the edge of the sheet. "My mom spend most of her life trying to get as far away as she could from that part of her life, from the way she was raised to the way she was conceived. She wanted to erase it all with how she lived her life."

Zach pulled in a long breath. He tenderly stroked Alessandra's cottony ropes of hair. "But she didn't," he said softly. "She kept the chest, she kept the contents. As much as she may have wanted to bury it all, there was still a part of her, a part in all of us, that is tied to the past—to those who came before us. She may have been able to put a lid on it, literally, but she came to realize that it wasn't right or possible."

Alessandra tucked her lips in to keep them from trembling and blinked back a new wave of threatening tears.

Zach took the journal from her limp fingers and turned it facedown on his lap. "Maybe this is enough for now," he said gently.

Alessandra visibly swallowed. She shook her head. "No. If there's more, I want to know what it is. It's only a few more pages."

"Fine. Let me, then." He turned the book over to the final pages. "This is your mom."

Alessandra nodded. "Go ahead."

"2007. Funny how me and Jeremiah met," Zach began.

Alessandra sat up a bit straighter. She leaned over, her eyes following the words as Zach spoke.

I was waiting at the bus stop on Main Street. It was pouring, and I'd forgotten my umbrella. And here comes this gorgeous man, tall and lean and brown. He hurried over to me and held his large black umbrella over my head. Said a beautiful lady like me shouldn't be a victim to Mother Nature, he said. He had the most amazing big white smile and sparkling eyes. Still does.

I think I was hypnotized by those eyes. Next thing I knew, we were a couple. Mama loved him on sight. We were married a year later in a simple but beautiful wedding at the local church. I wore my mother's wedding gown that had been handed down generations, a simple satin gown with lace at the collar, across the waist, and around the hem that brushed my ankles. With a few alterations, it fit like it was made for me. Mama'd kept it wrapped in paper and linen inside the chest.

Hopefully one day I can pass it on to Ali. It is such a beautiful dress.

Alessandra blinked, frowned. "I don't remember seeing the gown in the chest," she said, sounding almost panicked.

"Maybe your mom put it in storage so that it wouldn't get damaged."

"Hmm, maybe. There's a picture of her and my dad on their wedding day in the album. She *was* in that dress," she said in a kind of awe. She dragged in a long breath. "Go 'head. Finish."

We had and still have a good life. I know I'm not easy to live with, but Jerry—he takes it like a champ. I couldn't ask for a better man at my side. The only thing that was missing for years was a child. We tried. Lost two.

"Again," Alessandra murmured.

"Hmm," Zach agreed and continued to read.

I'd given up. I filled my life with work as an administrative assistant while we lived in New York. But the thing that always terrified me was that, at some point, Jerry may turn into a man like my father had become that one horrible night. I did everything I could to make sure he had a beautiful home, a loving and giving wife, and then out of the blue, I was pregnant. A late in life baby, my GYN doc told me with a big smile on her face. I think I jumped into bed and didn't get out until the pains started nine months later. I was not taking any chances. And of course Jerry took it all in stride with a wink and a smile. And not one of my outrageous requests I made of my husband was denied.

When Ali was born, it was the greatest day of our married lives. I promised myself that she would have everything that I didn't have growing up, the best of everything, no matter what. Jerry insisted that we could give her a better life away from the craziness of New York City. I fought him tooth and nail but finally gave in when he brought me out here and showed me the house that he said could be ours if I only said yes. So, here we are, ten years and counting, and he was right.

Anyway, I need to finish up this entry and help Ali get ready for this party that she insists on going to.

Alessandra inhaled a sharp breath.

"I can stop," Zach said quietly.

Alessandra's nostrils flared, sucking in air. "It's o-okay," she stammered, "go on. I have to hear this."

There's so much I need to tell my darling girl. It's time. It's long past time. I should have been whispering the ancient stories in her ear each night so that she would know and remember and pass them along. It was wrong of me. But I intend to make it right. Jerry was right about that, too. Dammit!

I'm not sure why this memory unfurled inside me today. I suppose I've finally gotten to a place of acceptance of things, about myself and my family. The afternoon talks with Mrs. O helped me to see the importance of things.

They looked at each other and smiled. Zach continued.

The women of my family were strong and smart and amazing and enduring. It was terribly wrong of me to keep that part of who we are from Ali. I think I've finally come to a place where I can talk about things. Let go of my own concocted hurt and self-absorption, and stop believing that the visions and the dreams were something to fear.

I can still hear my mother's voice at night, telling me the stories of who we are, how we had come to be. The one that sticks out most of course is the story of when we were taken on the beach, how a young couple was separated by flesh but not by spirit. My mother would whisper that she lived inside each of us, waiting to go home and find her one true love.

His name was Kwaku, my mother had said, and her name was Ayah. Say her name, she'd whisper before I would drift off to sleep. She survived so that you could live.

Ali is the embodiment of all our ancestors' greatest dreams. She needs to finally know that. Say her name, my sweet Ali. Ayah.

"Ayah," they whispered in unison.

Zach held Alessandra protectively against his chest as she wept, her breath stuttering in her chest as she gulped and expelled her sobs.

As much as she'd wanted to unearth the truth, reliving the loss of her mother as a result of her own selfishness remained a wound that she was unsure would ever fully heal. The one consolation, however, was that now she knew, now she understood Jessica Fleming and the dynamics between her mother and father. Her spirit ached for her mother and the weight that she'd kept buried inside her for all those years. It ached for her father, who had bent to Jessica's will and kept her secrets.

Perhaps her mother's conception did occur the way her grandmother wrote. There was no excuse for what her grandfather appeared to have done. Her one hope was that perhaps it was another night, a night of love and reconciliation. That was the "truth" that Alessandra chose to believe.

She drew in a slow breath and released it, listened to the calming beat of Zach's heart, the steadiness of it. She closed her eyes.

So much had changed in her life since she'd gotten that phone call at the gallery. She'd made an attempt at amends and rediscovered a father she never truly knew—and a mother whom she thought she did, but had been wrong.

The voices and visions that had been reawakened inside her served more of a purpose than to make her think she was going crazy. They took her on a visceral journey, guided her bit by bit through the incredible tale of the ancestors whose blood flowed in her veins: Sadie, Ella, Mae Ella, Olivia, Jessica, all born of Ayah, stolen from her homeland, sold, beaten, raped, language disavowed, but survived, only to see her descendants' businesses and homes burned.

Loss upon loss, yet they too endured to allow Alessandra to become, to tie the threads of their lives back together, to tell their amazing story of resistance, persistence, hope, and love.

And then there was Zach Renard, descendant of Kwaku, brought into her life because they were always destined to be together when the moment was right. It was inexplicable; yet here they were.

"That first night I saw you standing in the snow," Zach said quietly, nudging Alessandra from her reverie, "and you looked at me—something happened. Like a shock of recognition." He frowned a bit, breathed deeply. "I consider myself your basic decent human being, but," he paused, "with you I had this overwhelming urge to be with you, to help you, to…protect you."

He drew her closer. "While you were coming to terms with your family's past, so was I. Piece by piece, the unthinkable began to emerge. When I confirmed that there was a woman on *La Amistad* who had escaped, I knew in the marrow of my bones that she was connected to you. At the time, I just didn't know how. When the name Kwaku came up in my research and I remembered the name in the family Bible," he paused, "all my scientific training went out the window."

He chuckled lightly. "It's all been a giant jigsaw puzzle that we've been putting together piece by piece." He looked down into her upturned face. "Now it's complete, the circle is unbroken. We were led to each other." He slowly lowered his head until his mouth was inches from hers, giving her the chance to back away if she wasn't ready.

Instead, she leaned in. She pressed her mouth against his until their lips parted, their tongues met and teased and danced, stirring the embers in their souls.

Zach's long fingers stroked her shoulder, down to her waist and across her hip. He hooked his hand under her thigh and lifted it to drape across his hip. She sighed, felt herself opening, softening once again.

Zach broke away from the kiss, but his mouth continued to work along her collarbone, down to the rise of her breasts. He paused, suckled the warm brown skin, let his tongue slide along the softness until he reached her nipple, which rose to meet him. He took it between his lips, let his tongue flick it, lave it, suck it, until she began to whimper and moan.

Her draped leg rose higher up his hip. She pressed her body tighter against him, felt the pulse of his erection between her legs. He groaned out her name. She reached down between them, seeking him out. She wrapped her fingers around his length and stroked him with maddening slowness. He let out a curse. She smiled.

He squeezed her firm behind and took her offered breast fully into his mouth. Her body arched as if shot with electricity. He sucked a bit harder. She whimpered, and her strokes quickened. Their rapid breathing heated the air around them.

In a skilled movement, Alessandra flipped Zach onto his back and straddled him. He grinned. Her hair fell around her face and shoulders, her eyes gleaming. She braced herself on her knees and lifted up just enough to place his stiff erection at her opening. He held her hips in his large palms. His eyes were so dark they were like midnight during a moonless, starless night. His lips parted.

By torturous degrees, she slowly lowered herself onto him. Her breath stuck in her chest as he began to fill her. Her neck arched back. Zach reached up and cupped her breasts in his palms.

She gasped when the swollen head of his penis touched the furthest reaches of her insides.

They both froze, held in the grip of sensation, as a wave of unimaginable pleasure coursed through their bodies.

Zach lifted his pelvis, thrust once, twice, again.

"Ohhhh, ohhhh," she cried. Her fingers dug into his shoulders, the veil of her hair fell around them, shielding them from the world.

She drew in a deep breath and rocked against him, drawing a low growl from deep in his throat. She lifted, lowered, lifted, then wound her hips in a circle that had Zach nearly speaking in tongues.

Zach held her firm against his thrust, meeting her every move with one of his own.

Lights seemed to flash, and warm air blew around them. They sighed and moaned and held each other, unaware of everything around them except each other and a past that they now knew they shared, beginning centuries ago on a white sandy beach, beneath blazing sunshine with crystal-blue water as far as the eye could see. Laughter filled the air as two young brown bodies darted along the shore, raced back to the line of trees where they could not be seen by the elders.

Kwaku pulled young Ayah, his wife-to-be, into his muscular arms. They laughed, breathless and excited. Ayah made sure no one would see her as she boldly lowered the slim green-and-yellow band that covered her breasts. Kwaku's dark eyes sparkled, his nostrils flared. *You are so beautiful*, he whispered. *By the next moon, you will be my wife.*

He reverently kissed the rise of her breasts before returning her top to its rightful place. *And we will have many children and I will love you for all eternity.*

Ayah smiled shyly at her husband-to-be, her heart bursting with young love. *And I you*, she said before they sealed their promise with a kiss.

They drifted back from the shores of Lomboko to a bedroom in Sag Harbor, their own lips locked in a deep kiss until the images, but not the memory, faded.

Having talked and cried, made love, then talked and cried some more, the couple showered, dressed, bundled up in their coats, and trooped over to Zach's grandmother's house. Alessandra had impressed upon Zach her need to hear from his grandmother's own lips just what she and her mother had talked about all those years ago.

Grace was sitting in her favorite paisley chair by the window, intent on her latest romance novel. She barely looked up when they entered.

"There's some hot chocolate and apple pie in the kitchen," she said absently.

"Gram, Alessandra needs to talk with you."

Grace slowly put down her book and removed her glasses. She placed both on the circular table next to the chair. A slow, knowing smile moved across her generous mouth. She folded her hands in her lap and tipped her head slightly to the side.

"Finally put it all together, I suppose," she said mildly.

Alessandra lowered herself onto the love seat. Zach sat next to her. Alessandra leaned forward. "Please tell me what you know. What did you and my mother talk about? What finally made her change her mind? You're the only one who knows," she said, her voice beginning to break. "Why didn't you tell me?"

Grace drew in a breath. "It was not my story to tell, sweetheart," she began slowly. "You needed to *want* to find out—on your own, the same way your mother did, not have me shove things down your throat that you might not have been ready to hear or understand."

"I'm ready now," she insisted.

Grace nodded, settled more deeply in the thick cushions. "My husband, God rest his soul, used to always tell me about his great-great-uncle Kwaku and how he'd been taken and brought to America."

Zach reached for Alessandra's hand and gave it a gentle squeeze.

"He said that according to family folklore, Kwaku spent all his days in slavery searching for the one who'd been betrothed to him. Our family didn't know the girl's name."

"Ayah," Alessandra whispered.

"He never found her." Grace sighed. "All he had left of her was a piece of her skirt, green and yellow. It was said that he'd torn it when she was snatched. It was passed down through Stanley's family. I have it upstairs in my treasure box."

Alessandra's heart pounded. There was a swath of green-and-yellow fabric in the chest.

"That day when I stopped by your house to get donations," Grace continued, "your mom brought out a shoebox of odds and ends. Old things. Ancient. But my heart nearly stopped when I saw that piece of cloth. It wasn't torn, mind you, just old, and it looked like some kind of band."

Alessandra and Zach shot looks at each other, both

recalling the surreal experience of being on the beach with Ayah lowering her breast covering. Alessandra pressed her hand to her chest in the hopes that it would slow down her racing heart.

"I told her those things looked too important, too special. She looked at me as if she was surprised that I believed there was value in the shoebox. 'There's plenty more of this stuff where this came from. A whole chest,' she said."

Grace snorted. "I told her that she really needed to keep those. They looked like family heirlooms and should remain with family. 'Heirlooms tell our stories,' I told her. She kind of shrugged. 'I have a few,' I said to her. 'Love to show you sometime if you want.'" She sighed.

"To be truthful, I never thought she'd take me up on my offer. Then, one day out of the blue, she rang the bell. She had a bigger box this time.

"One of the first things I showed her was the matching piece of fabric. She didn't make the connection until I told her the story of Kwaku. Your mother got still as stone when I told her our family folklore." Grace closed her eyes. "She said, 'Her name was Ayah.' When I looked at her, she was crying. Quiet tears. Almost a cleansing."

"Gram, all this time you knew!" Zach said.

Grace looked forlornly at her hands. "Like I said, son, it was not my story to tell."

Grace blinked back the past and focused on her grandson and Alessandra. "We talked for quite some time that day and the days that followed. Each time, she would share a bit more about the stories that were passed down to her and why she'd kept them from you. What frightened her were the visions and the dreams. She didn't see them as a means to remember, but as something to be afraid of."

Grace pursed her lips a moment. "Nightmares. We

talked about that, too. The visions and the dreams were calling on her to resurrect them, not bury them." Grace smiled. "Your mother was a ball of conflicting knots. But she finally got unwound." Her gaze softened. "She was accepting her family's past as part of her own *and* yours, and realizing that it couldn't be shoved forever in a chest and forgotten."

Her lips tightened. "The last time we spoke, she promised that she was going to tell you everything."

Alessandra's bottom lip trembled. Her throat was so tight she could barely swallow. "She never got the chance to," she murmured.

Zach looped his arm around her shoulder. "It's all good now, though," he whispered.

She nodded against his chest, then inhaled a long breath and exhaled her vow. "I'm going to do what my mom didn't have a chance to do and what my dad always wanted. I'm going to tell our story the best way I know how."

CHAPTER THIRTY-SEVEN

"I'm pulling my hair out," Alessandra said into the phone as she used a magnifying glass to closely examine some of her photographs. The process of paring down the extensive collection of artifacts to only the essential pieces was exhausting. "This week has been crazy trying to pull everything together. I'm running out of time and energy," she groaned.

"This is not your first rodeo," Traci assured.

"Humph, maybe not, but it's my first solo as an artist. If I had my way, I would use everything. I actually have all the artifacts mapped out on my storyboard, but the gallery doesn't have the space, so I'm in the dreaded position of having to decide what to cut."

Traci chuckled lightly. "Some artists would kill to have *too* much inventory for a showing."

"Hmm, that's true." She sat back on her heels. "It's usually the other way around. Thankfully," she said in a faraway voice as she examined one of the hair pomade tins, "Zach was able to get the order in for the frames, and I'll be able to use the display cases that he seems to have stock in," she added with a chuckle.

"See, you got this! Speaking of got this, I got you with our best A&E staff writer, Laura Martin, who will cover the opening. She's going to need some time either before or after the opening to sit with you for an interview. I know the day of will be crazy, so maybe afterwards?"

"Sure, whatever works. I'm just thankful to be able to do any of this. To have it covered by *The Times* is a mega bonus."

"You know that once this show hits you're going to be the new 'it' girl in the art world."

Alessandra drew in a slow breath. "Maybe," she softly conceded. "I spent all that time trying to find a story to tell, and now I just want the story I've been given told. I want people to understand and appreciate my family's journey of 'arrival,' the determination and bravery that it took for Ayah to escape and survive, birthing generations that would never have existed without her. I want the visitors to grasp the need for and incorporate the practice of passing on our stories. If I can, then I'm good with that."

"I have no doubt, sis. No doubt at all. Anyhoo, I'll see you next week. If you need anything in the meantime, holler."

"Will do. Oh, before you sign off, what's the latest with you and Morgan?"

Alessandra smiled at her friend's girlish laugh.

"As surprised as I am to realize, we are still 'a thing'! Can you imagine?"

Alessandra laughed. "Barely. But I'm totally happy for you. You need someone solid in your life."

"Oh, because you're so überhappy with Mr. Wonderful, you want me to fall in line," she teased.

"Girl, I want every woman to have a man like Zach in their lives, especially the women I love—like you."

"You may be getting your wish," Traci whispered. "I've been holding on tooth and nail, but—I'm falling hard and I can't seem to stop it."

"Don't stop it," Alessandra softly urged. "Fall. I can guarantee Morgan will be there to catch you."

. . .

The last three days leading up to the opening of Alessandra's show were a whirlwind of activity. She'd hired a small U-Haul to transport all of the pieces, and it would take at least two days to hang the photographs and set up the cases.

"Your show is going to be the event of the year," Zach said. He deposited two canvas bags of clear plastic cases on the floor, then plopped down on a dining room chair and placed the newspaper on the table.

The local paper ran a full front-page cover story about the opening, announcing that parts of Sag Harbor's untold history and its earliest inhabitants would be on display, presented by former resident Alessandra Fleming.

Alessandra took a quick look, catching the picture of her face looking out. She frowned. "Jeez, where did they find this photo?" She picked up the paper and looked closer. "This is from my high school yearbook," she said with appalled laughter.

Zach chuckled. "And you haven't aged a bit," he joked.

"Very funny." She dragged in a breath and looked at him with a mixture of excitement and terror. "It's really happening," she said.

Zach nodded. "Yep."

"I want this exhibit to do my family—all the families—

justice. Ya know, it can't only be a bunch of pictures and 'stuff.' I want people to leave with a greater understanding of history, of course, but also of the importance of family."

Zach got up from his seat and came to stand in front of her. He lifted her chin with the tip of his finger. "They will." He lowered his head and kissed her. "They will."

. . .

When Alessandra stepped out of Zach's car the night of the opening, it was akin to a nominee walking the red carpet at the Oscars. The Grenning Gallery was lit up, and lines of people stood outside waiting to get in. A life-sized photo of her stood in the window, and the waiting crowd began to buzz in anticipation as she approached.

"Oh my goodness," she whispered, as Zach took her arm. She blinked in disbelief as cell phone cameras took silent pictures of her entrance and waved to her like she was a celebrity.

"This is your night, babe," Zach said in her ear. "Enjoy every minute."

"Somebody important must be here tonight," Traci teased from behind her, walking with Morgan and Grace and Edith.

The gallery owner, who was working the front door, pulled it open to let Alessandra and her guests enter.

"Welcome! This is so exciting," she enthused. "I can't remember the last time we saw this much anticipation for an opening. What a way to kick off Women's History Month. Come in. Come in." She signaled to an assistant. "This is Stephanie. She'll get you settled in the back with some refreshments, and I'll open the reception to our guests in about ten minutes." She smiled brightly.

"Oh my goodness," Grace said, looking awed by the display.

"All this for our girl," Edith responded.

On the white walls, the storied and heroic history of Alessandra's family spoke to the room, whispered their tales. The framed photos, wanted posters, and news clippings were set about in chronological order. Situated throughout the space, atop three-foot white pedestals, were the Lucite cases that contained pieces of fabric, journals, tins, combs, and shoes, along with a replica of *La Amistad*. As visitors moved through the gallery, the story unfolded, aided by the caption cards that noted the artifacts' approximate years and provided descriptions.

Tears stung Alessandra's eyes as she took in the magic in front of her. She felt the spirits of her ancestors surround her, welcome her, thank her. Zach moved next to her and slid his arm around her waist.

"You did it," he whispered, before kissing her cheek. "Congratulations."

"Not without your help."

"Girl," Traci said breathless, "this is…incredible." Her widened eyes scanned the space before settling back on Alessandra. "Girl," she said, pride ringing in her voice.

Alessandra sniffed, then drew in a breath. "Well…let's not stand around like tourists," she said, her voice choked. "Folks are waiting."

Stephanie led them to a small room where they deposited their coats and were offered flutes of champagne.

Alessandra had decided to splurge on her "opening night" outfit. The white crepe sleeveless top crisscrossed and tied at the waist above coordinating wide-legged pants that flowed when she walked. Her long locs were twisted into an intricate swirl atop her head. Heavy silver earrings shaped like arrowheads hung from her ears, and a matching chain surrounded her neck.

"You look and smell edible," Zach whispered in her ear as he helped her out of her coat.

"I like the sound of that," she said over her shoulder.

The small entourage nibbled on grapes and sipped champagne until Stephanie returned to let them know the gallery was open to the waiting public.

"Ready?" Stephanie asked. She opened the door of the small lounge and led them back into the main gallery.

The evening was pure magic. Alessandra floated among the throng, catching snippets of conversation: "Can you imagine...incredible...I never knew...Paul, did you see this...right in our own backyard...this is so amazing...all the way back to the 1800s..."

Alessandra smiled for group pictures, answered countless questions, nodded, and explained some of the items, all while Laura Martin from *The Times* took notes and asked her own questions and her photographer documented every moment.

Halfway through the evening, the gallery owner introduced Alessandra to the gathering and escorted her to the front of the space.

Public speaking was not in her DNA. She'd always let her photographs speak for her. But she had a duty of sorts to weave the tale of how she had come upon the chest and how, with the assistance of anthropologist Zach Renard, she began to reconstruct the arrival of her ancestor Ayah and all of her descendants that followed. She drew in a long breath, focused on the encouraging smiles of her newfound family and friends and not her racing heart and wobbly knees. She linked her shaky fingers together in front of her and began.

"Learning the history of my family, traveling with them through their letters and notes, touching items that were once part of their lives, has irrevocably changed me. I was a firm believer that we each make our way—on our own. The past was the past."

She slowly shook her head. "Not true. We are the sum of all the parts that came before us. Our stories must never go untold. We must speak their names. Honor their legacies.

"*I* am Ayah," she said proudly. "Because of her perseverance, I exist."

CHAPTER THIRTY-EIGHT

The following morning, Alessandra was still flying high on the overwhelming success of the opening. Her veins strummed with electricity. The evening replayed over and over in her head, and she was filled with pure joy. Deep in her spirit, she felt the strength, pride, and love of her ancestors all looking down on her, and they were glad. "Rest," she whispered. "I got this now."

She was putting on a pot of coffee when Zach walked into the kitchen with a stack of newspapers tucked under his arm and a big grin on his handsome face.

"What?" she asked, sharing his smile.

He flipped open the *Sag Harbor Gazette*, where her face graced the cover. She giggled with embarrassment. Then he opened *The Times* and turned to the Arts and Entertainment section. There was a full-page spread, complete with photos and the headline "New York Photographer Brings Untold History to Life."

"I think you might be the New York photographer they're talking about," he teased.

She playfully shoved him and took the paper from his hand. She tugged on her bottom lip with her teeth as her eyes swept across the page. "They mention your name a few times, too, buddy," she said. Her heart thumped at the accolades noting that her collection might be one of the most important in decades. "The astonishing work of photographer Alessandra Fleming is only eclipsed by what she has captured with her lens."

This time, Zach nudged her. She heaved a satisfied sigh and sat down. To think that only a couple of months ago, she was willfully ignorant of her own history, her family. She'd been trapped in the trappings of trying to "get somewhere," never believing that the "somewhere" was the very place she'd run from.

So much had changed. The loss of her dad had led to finding him, finding her mother, discovering herself, and finding the man who was meant for her. She wasn't the same woman who had arrived uncertain, directionless, and regretful. The missing pieces of her, the broken pieces, were filling, healing, and she'd found the love she was certain would hold it all together.

Zach pulled up a chair and sat beside her. "Pretty amazing," he said.

Alessandra dragged in a breath and nodded.

"So, have you thought about what you want to do with the house?" He drew circles on the table with his index finger.

She blinked and looked at him. "Not exactly," she said slowly. "Clearly, it's paid for." She swallowed. "I still have my apartment in Manhattan—"

He took her hand, cutting her off. "Never in a million years would I believe what has happened between us would have ever happened." He shook his head. His brow creased. "But it did. Took every theory I've learned in science and tossed it out the window."

He paused, looking like he was trying to organize his thoughts. "Look, my work takes me around the world for weeks and months at a time. I'm not the home-by-six kinda guy." He swallowed. "I never really cared much about what I came back to or to whom other than Gram—until you came into my life." He held her hand a bit tighter, looked into her eyes. "I want to be able to come back to you, Ali, to a place to call home—with you."

She leaned in and cupped his face in her palms. "Whatever it is you're asking me, Mr. Renard, the answer is yes. For sure." She smiled at the look of relief that softened the line between his brows. She pressed her lips to his. "Yes. For sure."

Zach pulled her into his arms, kissing her long and deep, and the swirl of time and space that intimately surrounded them swept them together and apart and back again.

Distance and time didn't matter, only destiny.

* * *

The two weeks that the gallery had given her to mount her show had ended. The work of organizing and packaging much of the fragile material in moisture-proof containers had taken her and Zach three days. The living room looked like a museum under construction.

"I still can't believe that the Smithsonian wants my work," Alessandra said from the depths of her closet. "Or that they'd even heard about it." She pulled out two shirts and a sweater and tossed them on the bed.

"The contents of your family chest are what we in the biz call an 'anthropological find.'" He chuckled.

She gave him a withering look from over her shoulder.

"That and the fact that a Mr. Zach Renard, a fellow at the Smithsonian, is part of the 'anthropological find.'" She lifted a teasing brow.

He gave a shrug. "Ha, there's that, too. The big spread in *The Times* turned on the lightbulbs of research centers all over. The Smithsonian is only the beginning."

Mere days after the opening at the Grenning Gallery, Zach had received the call from Horace Mann at the Smithsonian, who wanted first dibs on exhibiting the work in the fall. The next day, Horace, along with several Smithsonian curators, had come to Sag Harbor to see the exhibit themselves and, upon viewing the collection, had enthusiastically renewed their request. When it was revealed to them that what was in the gallery was not the entire collection, their excitement rose even further.

"Of course, it's up to you what you want to do," Zach said.

"Hmm, the Smithsonian is a dream come true," she said thoughtfully. "And it will give my work and the story of my family untold recognition." She sat down on the side of the bed. "I think it'll be a good platform. But ultimately, I want to tour the collection to smaller galleries."

"Well, now that you're 'independently wealthy,'" he winked, "you'll be able to research the galleries and map out schedules."

She rested her palms behind her and smiled broadly. "Yeah, you're right, I am independently wealthy. So I can loll about and do what I please at my leisure," she said in a really bad British accent.

Zach screwed up his face.

"Too soon?" she asked.

"Yeah. Very," he droned. "Listen, I need to run some errands in town before we head into Manhattan in the morning. Need anything while I'm out?"

"Hmm." She sat up straighter and crossed her legs. "Since this is our last night together in this house for a little while, how about a great bottle of wine?"

"Not a problem." He slipped on his coat.

"Oh, wait. As a matter of fact…" She reached toward the nightstand, picked up a slip of paper, stood, and handed it to him. "Got a call yesterday from Dunleavy Cleaners on Main. He left a message on the machine, and I haven't had a chance to call back. He said he was contacting all his customers who had merchandise in his shop. He's liquidating the business, apparently, and has to empty the store. He came across the name 'Fleming' and called." She shrugged. "Probably something of my dad's. Would you mind?"

"Sure." He crossed the room and kissed her lightly. "Ya know, I can really get used to this whole *wake up next to you, kiss you goodbye, and find you here when I get back* thing. Hey. Who knew?" he said with a grin.

"In that case," she said, coming to stand in front of him, "hurry back."

Zach tapped the bridge of her nose with the tip of his finger. "Will do."

. . .

"Miss me?" Zach asked, walking into the living room to find Alessandra reclining on the love seat with her laptop propped on her thighs. The sight of her continued to take his breath away, and it probably always would.

"Hey," she greeted.

He deposited a rectangular brown box that had seen better days on the wood table. "This is whatever Dunleavy had of your dad's."

She angled her head and frowned. "Hmm. A box? What happened to clear plastic?"

"He said it was among about a dozen boxes that had been placed in cold storage. His wife kept the records, precomputer, and there was only a handwritten ledger with names and phone and item numbers."

"What?" She sat up and set the laptop aside. She swung her feet to the floor and stood.

Zach strolled over to the wall unit that contained the stereo and albums and began to flip through them. He picked Nancy Wilson's Greatest Hits. Her unmatched phrasing of "I Wish You Love" wafted in the air.

"Oh my God!" Alessandra cried.

Zach jerked, turned toward her, crossed the space in two long strides to the now-open box. "What? What is it?"

"It's the dress," she whispered. "The dress! The wedding dress." She peeled back the yellowing tissue paper to view the dress enclosed in its clear plastic.

"Are you sure?"

She nodded, reached into the box, and lifted out the zippered bag with its delicate contents. The plastic crackled as she unfolded it. She stretched her arm upward, and the dress that they'd only read about was in her hands. Her mother's wedding dress. Her ancestors' wedding dress. The dress that he knew he'd ask her to don for him someday.

She turned to Zach as she pressed the dress to her body. Her lids drifted closed for a moment, and Zach knew that she was seeing all the women who had come before her.

He saw them, too.

Mom, I miss you. Every day, I miss you. I miss what we could have shared. I'm not afraid of the dreams and the visions anymore. I understand them now. I understand that they were trying to speak to me and lead me to Zach.

I got to see Dad again. Talked to him. Made peace. It was Dad who told me that everything I needed to know was right here in the house. He provided for me, Mom. The house, a settlement... Dad was always the organized one.

No more secrets. No more hiding from who we are or our journey to get here. I'll make sure of it. Promise.

I've decided to keep my apartment in Manhattan, Mom, and even keep working at Steven's gallery part-time. It means Zach and I will have a second place to call home whenever we want a night out in the Big Apple. But the house in Sag Harbor will be where we set down roots. That's the most important thing.

Well, that and the here and now, standing on the sandy shores of what was once Mendeland with the vast blue ocean in front of me, the one that carried off millions of my people to foreign lands, dispersing them across the globe.

But behind me firmly stands my past—Sadie, Ella, Mae Ella, Olivia, and you, Mom. Plus Kwaku, Winston, Carter, Stanley, and Dad. As surely and firmly as my present—Traci, Edith, Grandma O, Morgan, and even Steven—to be my anchors should I ever falter.

Next to me, always at my side, is the man the ancestors ensured would find me—to have and to hold on every journey from this day forward, and not even death will us part.

When I look into the dark eyes that sought mine through the ages, and which mesmerized me from the moment they met—again—my heart swells with love and promise.

Sheathed in the delicate antique wedding gown of her

mother and of her ancestors, Alessandra places her hands and her trust in Zach's.

That slow, sensual smile moves his full lips. He speaks so that only she can hear it. "Say her name," Zach whispers lovingly.

"I am Ayah. I'm home."

ACKNOWLEDGMENTS

This project was a compilation of storytelling and research. Much of my research was a result of Andrea Meyer of the East Hampton Library. I cannot thank her enough for providing access to the digital catalog of the library that provided so much of the historic information of Sag Harbor and its storied history.

I must thank my amazing editor Stacy Abrams for her guidance and patience and the team of editors who combed through every line and hung in there with me in finding just the right handwriting samples for each of the letters in the novel.

This book would be a lot of words on my computer without the hard work of Curtis Svehlak, who puts it all together. And, of course, the design team who crafted my amazing cover!

Thank you one and all.
Donna

Essence bestselling author Donna Hill brings us an emotional love story set against the powerful backdrop of the civil rights movement that gripped a nation—a story as timely as it is timeless...

Available now wherever books are sold.

Media Praise

"This is a knockout."
–Starred Review, Publishers Weekly

"A captivating and skillfully constructed
weaving of history and romantic drama."
–Kirkus Reviews

"11 New Romances That Will Keep
You Warm This November"
–PopSugar

"Most Anticipated November Romances"
–Goodreads

I Am Ayah: The Way Home is an emotional, poignant read about family, history, and love; however, this story includes elements that may not be suitable for all readers, including slavery, rape, miscarriage, violence, and death of a parent. If these elements could be considered triggering to you, please take note.

SIDEWAYS